ENDLESS LOVE

A PSYCHOLOGICAL ROMANCE

ENDLESS
BOOK 2

M. JAMES

1

CHARLOTTE

When I wake up, for a moment, I have no idea where I am.

My head aches. I don't usually drink enough to get a hangover, but once or twice, I've ended up with one, and this feels worse than that ever did. As soon as I open my eyes, a bright sliver of light stinging them and adding to the sharp pain, I close them just as quickly.

But that can't change the fact that I know I'm somewhere other than where I should be. I should be in my apartment, at home, in my own bed. Wherever I am, it's not there—this place smells wrong, clean in an antiseptic way, almost hospital-like, but not quite. Empty, like too-filtered air. Nothing like the soft lavender scent of the room spray I use at home, usually underlaid with the scents of lemon and basil from my cleaning products. The sheets and blanket feel stiff, nothing like the soft, cozy bedding I have at home.

I'm afraid to open my eyes and find out, because then I'm going to have to accept that something has happened. That the man in my apartment, the sudden pressure on my throat, everything swirling dark—that wasn't all some awful dream.

That text from Nate's brother must not have been a dream either, then.

I squeeze my eyes tighter, trying to get that picture out of my head. But I can't. Nate, bloody and stripped naked, a message carved into his chest. I can't imagine who would do such a thing, and why. Nate is an asshole, a pretentious dick with an overinflated sense of self, who thinks he can justify having cheated on me with excuses about *respecting* me too much to ask for what he wanted in bed.

But I can't imagine what would have warranted *that*. A level of violence I've never really imagined existing outside of fiction.

Was it him? Venom? I feel a stab of guilt, thinking that my online fantasies might have led to this. I'm furious with Nate, and I don't want him back in my life, but that doesn't mean that I wanted—*that* to happen to him.

I'm not sure I want that to happen to anyone.

Oh god, is that going to happen to me?

A flare of panic jolts through my chest. I have to open my eyes. I have to be brave, and find out what's happened.

For a moment, just before I open them, I have a brief flicker of hope that maybe I really *did* imagine it. That maybe I'm imagining all the sensory cues that tell me that I'm not in my bedroom, at home.

I blink, letting the light flood in, and all that hope is dashed.

I'm in a hotel room. That much is immediately obvious. A fairly mid-grade one, too, from the looks of it. The bed is covered with a stiff floral-pattern duvet that could have been put in here anytime in the last two decades, and the floor is covered in a beige shag carpet. The walls are cream, the furniture is dark-pressed wood. There are two small lamps hooked on either side of the bed, their push-button switches underneath the only nod to modernity.

There's no phone. I notice that almost immediately, and I push myself upright, that flare of panic worsening. There are always phones in hotel rooms. *Always*. Someone has removed this one.

I press a hand to my chest as my heart starts to beat faster. The memories of last night come flooding in again, pushing me closer to the edge of what I think *might* be an oncoming panic attack. I don't know. I've never had one before. The closest I think I might have come was the night I found out Nate cheated on me. I've never lived the kind of life that *causes* panic attacks.

I didn't realize just how lucky I was until this moment.

I've been so stupid. I thought there was no way Venom could find me in real life. No way my fantasies could track me down. I thought I was safe, because I knew enough about the internet to cover my tracks. I *work in tech*, for fuck's sake.

But he must have been better. Good enough to find me. Obsessed enough to come after me.

I shouldn't have gone home after getting that text about Nate. I should have gone to Jaz's house. Gone to a hotel. Anything other than walking into my apartment alone, where a man in a mask was waiting to grab me.

Gingerly, I reach up and touch the spot on my neck that's still sore. He must have known where to find a pressure point. *At least he didn't drug me.* The thought makes me let out a choked, near-hysterical laugh—because I can't believe that's legitimately something that just went through my head. That something has happened to make that a reasonable thing for me to think.

My clothes are still on, too. Another good thing. I push the duvet back, frowning as it occurs to me that not only did he not strip me, he —tucked me in?

I was stalked, knocked out, kidnapped, taken to a hotel in god knows where—and then respectfully tucked in with all of my clothes still on until I woke up.

Something feels off about all of this.

Gingerly, I swing my legs out of bed, remembering that I had my phone and purse when I walked into the apartment. I might have dropped them when I was grabbed, but that doesn't stop me from starting to look for them anyway—in the drawer next to the bed, around the desk, the chair, and even in the drawers of the dresser. But there's nothing. Just my shoes, which he *did* take off and set next to the bed.

It's then that I realize the shower is running.

I glance at the digital clock next to the bed—it's seven in the morning. Assuming I'm still in the same time zone, no one from work, or Jaz, will have noticed I'm gone yet. The only clue that Jaz might have that something is wrong would be that I didn't text her last night that I made it home.

Carefully, I get up, trying not to make any sound as my feet hit the carpet. My mouth feels dry, and my head still hurts, a dull ache at the base of my neck that makes me reach back and press my fingers against it, wishing for some kind of painkiller.

But I need to try to get out of here. As far as I know, there's no way to lock a hotel room door from the inside to prevent someone getting out—

I try the door handle, and it doesn't budge. I stare at it for a long moment, trying to figure out how that's possible. There's something next to the door, a small black box—

Close to frantic now, I dig at the side of it with my nails, trying to pry it off. It won't come loose, and I feel my pulse racing faster, my eyes starting to burn with frustrated tears as I yank at the door handle again. Short of pounding on the door with my fists and screaming, I don't know what else to do.

Pivoting, I look towards the window. *How high up are we?* I cross the room as quickly as I can, the carpet muffling my footsteps, and lean up against the window, looking down.

We're on at least the second floor, maybe higher. There's nothing beneath the window but asphalt. If I could get the window open, I wouldn't make it out of that fall unscathed. I'd probably hurt myself badly enough that I wouldn't be able to get help before he got to me again—or even if someone saw me, I might hurt myself badly enough that it wouldn't be worth it.

I want to get out of here. I don't want to end up paralyzed or permanently damaged doing it.

What do people do in situations like this? I don't know. I don't watch true crime or read the kind of books that would tell me the answer to that. I'm trapped, and the sense of panic builds until my thoughts feel foggy, that pounding, dull pain at the back of my head only getting worse—

The sound of the shower switches off.

Fuck. I swallow hard, spinning to face the bathroom door, my hands gripping the windowsill behind me as I look frantically around for something to use as a weapon. I don't want to be defenseless. I don't want—

The door opens, and I brace myself, ready to scream.

My mouth drops open, but no sound comes out as I see him standing in the doorway, wearing nothing but a towel wrapped around his hips.

Ivan.

2

CHARLOTTE

"Wha—what's going on?" I stammer as I stare at Ivan, confusion blocking out every other thought. I know what I saw right before I was knocked out—a man in black clothing, wearing the same mask that Venom was wearing when he sent me those pictures online. I'd expected to see a stranger come out of the bathroom, but instead, Ivan's all-too-familiar frame is filling the doorway, distracting me for more reasons than one. He looks like a chiseled statue, all smooth pale skin overlaid with those swirls of dark ink, all the way down to where the towel is hanging indecently off of his hip bones, showing the deep lines on either side, and the strip of dark blond hair in the center just below his navel.

It's worse because I know what's under the towel. And I know just how good it feels.

"What are you doing here?" I demand, trying not to think about how close to naked he is or how there's a perfectly good bed right in between him and me. "I was—you weren't—"

Ivan swallows hard. I see his throat move, see the sudden uncertainty in his face, and a cold feeling slithers down my spine.

"Ivan." My voice drops, harder than I've ever heard it before, more serious. There's a faint tremor of fear, still, but I see his eyes widen slightly at the sudden demand in it. "Tell me what's going on."

There's hesitation in his face. I don't know him completely—we've only been on a few dates and slept together once. But I can read it there. He's holding something back, and I need to know what it is. My hands tighten on the windowsill, my heart beating hard enough that I feel sure he must be able to see my pulse.

"Ivan."

He clears his throat. "There was a man in your apartment."

"No shit." I feel my nails scrape against the paint on the windowsill. "He knocked me out. Why are *you* here?"

"I brought you here." He lets out a sharp breath. "To keep you safe."

"Safe? From what? Who? From Venom? The—the man in my apartment?" My cheeks flush suddenly, heating at the idea that I might have to explain to Ivan who that man was and how I knew him. Or why I called him *Venom*, from his username on the chat site, the only way I can think of to refer to him. I wasn't doing anything wrong, Ivan and I have never been exclusive, but still—

It was foolish behavior. It got me here. And the thought of trying to explain all of it to Ivan makes me feel beyond embarrassed.

He presses his lips together, letting out another sharp breath between them. "From him. I got there just in time, Charlotte. I—I got you out of there. But it's not just him. It's—"

"It's *what*?" I shove myself off of the windowsill, some of my fear receding, quickly replaced by frustration that borders on anger. "It's *what*, Ivan? Stop talking in circles. Why am I in a hotel room? Why didn't you just take me back to your place and call the police, if you got me away from him? And what—" I frown, my thoughts in such a scramble that they're catching up to what's going on a little at a time. "What were you doing at my apartment?"

"I—" Ivan rubs his hand across the back of his neck again. "I needed to see you. I understand how that must sound right now, especially after what's happened. I needed to talk to you, and your door was unlocked. I heard a noise—"

Everything he says seems to come out haltingly, as if he doesn't really want to say any of it. As if he's struggling to tell me. I walk around the bed, slowly, sinking down on the edge of it as I look at him. There's less space between us now, and I can't help but wonder, as I sit down, if that was a good idea. Being closer means I have an even better view of his near-nudity, and it's distracting. This close, I can see that there are beads of water on his skin still, trickling down his tattoos, making me itch to trace their path with my fingers. Or my tongue—

Fuck. Charlotte, concentrate.

"You needed to see me," I repeat slowly. "What does that mean, Ivan? What could have possibly been so important that it couldn't have waited until the next day? Or that you couldn't have texted, or called, or—" I trail off, seeing his jaw tighten. He looks away, his dark blue eyes fixed off in the distance for a moment, and then he looks back at me.

"My family is Bratva, Charlotte."

I stare at him for a moment, not quite comprehending. "Bratva? I—what does that mean, Ivan? I don't understand."

"It's—" He swallows, looking away and back again. "Like— Russian mafia. An underground criminal organization."

"Like—in *John Wick,* or something?" I blink at him. "You can't be serious."

"Yes, if that gives you a better frame of reference." He reaches up, running his fingers through his still-damp hair. His muscles flex, rippling over his chest and stomach distractingly, and I glare at him.

"Could you put on a shirt?"

That all-too-familiar smirk quirks the corners of his mouth. "Why? Am I distracting you?"

"Maybe if you hadn't just told me you were part of some Russian crime syndicate. Or your family is—"

"I am." The words come out flat, clipped, his jaw tightening again as if forcing them out. "That's why I needed to talk to you, Charlotte. I needed to get you out of there. But then—" He takes a deep breath, and I stare at him, trying to comprehend what he's saying.

"You're telling me that you showed up to my apartment to tell me about your family—you—being part of this...Bratva. Only for you to find me being attacked by a masked man, who you what—beat up? Got me away from him somehow? And then, instead of literally anything else, you took me to some hotel, and waited for me to wake up, so you could tell me all of this?" I rub my hands over my face, burying it in them for a moment.

This is a dream. A nightmare. Someone roofied me at the bar. Any second now, I'm going to wake up in my apartment or at Jaz's place, and I'm going to realize that none of this is real. It's going to all be okay.

I count to five, and drop my hands. When I do, Ivan is still standing there.

Frustratingly, he's also still in nothing but the towel.

"*Please*, put some clothes on." I look at him helplessly, and he smirks, shrugging as he pushes away from the doorframe and turns, dropping the towel as he does so.

"Ivan."

He ignores me. I stare at him, helpless to *not* look at the muscled curve of his ass, where the tattoo on his back ends just at the top of the muscle, trailing down slightly over the sides, or at his thick cock, hanging between his equally muscled thighs, slightly swollen as if this conversation is turning him on.

He glances over at me as he takes his boxer briefs off of the pile of clothes, and his cock twitches, stiffening a little. My cheeks flush as I look away sharply, my pulse suddenly beating harder in my throat, a tingle running over my skin all the way down between my thighs, tightening my nipples as it goes.

I know how good his cock feels. I know how good *all* of him feels. But I refuse to be distracted—any more than I already am, anyway.

"There." Ivan clears his throat, and I look back to see him dressed in a pair of tight black jeans, frayed at the cuffs and pockets, with a short-sleeved, cream-colored henley. He shoves his hands in his pockets, leaning against the doorframe again. "Can we talk about this now, Charlotte?"

I swallow hard, still blushing as I nod. "This is crazy, Ivan," I whisper, and he drops his gaze for a moment before looking back up at me.

"I know. But I needed to tell you. And once I saw what was happening—well, I had to get you out of there. This was a snap decision. Charlotte—my family knows about you. They know I've been seeing you. And I—I'm not on the best of terms with them. They're threatening you, and—"

"*What?*" I feel my eyes widen as I stare at him. "They're—*threatening* me? For what, why—" I shake my head. "I don't even want to know. Just take me home. Leave me alone, and they'll leave me alone, too, right? I want to go home."

When I tell him to *leave me alone,* I see him flinch, as if I've slapped him. As if the idea is unthinkable. But his face smooths just as quickly, and he shakes his head.

"I can't do that, Charlotte. They're almost certainly watching your apartment. As soon as I leave you there, they'll grab you."

It feels like everything he says clicks a moment after he says it. Like there's a lag between his words and my mind comprehending them. I blink at him, shaking my head.

"I want to talk to Jaz," I demand, pushing myself up off of the bed. "You have my phone, don't you? I want to talk to her. Give me back my phone." I'm pacing at the foot of the bed, firing off rapid demands as an increasingly helpless look crosses Ivan's face.

"I don't have your phone—"

"You're lying!" I whirl to face him, emotions bubbling up fast and thick in the face of something that seems so incredibly impossible. "You're lying about all of this. I don't know why, but—"

"I'm not lying." Ivan's voice is infuriatingly calm, the kind of measured calm that only seems to throw my panic into overdrive.

"You *are* lying!" I fling myself at him, shoving him hard as my palms connect with his chest. He barely budges; he's a wall of muscle, and I'm not all that strong. "Give me my phone! I want to call Jaz! I want to go home!"

Dimly, I can hear myself. I'm aware that I'm crossing into tantrum territory, that I'm losing it, but in a strange sort of way, it feels *good.*

I've never lost it. I don't think that, other than that night when I found out Nate was cheating on me, I've even ever yelled at anyone. It's not just this that's bubbling up out of me, it's years of shoving things down, not speaking up, keeping the peace, keeping *quiet*. And god, it almost feels *good*.

"Charlotte—" Ivan tries to catch my hands in his, but I slam them against his chest again, and again. "Charlotte, *please*. Listen to me. I'm doing this for your own good—"

"Oh, shut the *fuck* up!" I screech, that last sentence tipping me entirely over the edge. Rearing back, I swing, slapping him across the face hard.

The crack of my palm against his flesh startles even me, the hot sting of it burning into my hand, too, as if I've hurt us both. Ivan's eyes are wide, and he freezes, as if he can't believe I did that.

To be fair, I can't believe it, either.

This time, when I go to hit him again, he succeeds in grabbing both of my wrists. "Charlotte!" My name is a whip-crack this time, as sharp as the impact of my hand against his face. "Charlotte, if you go home, they will take you. And what my father will do to you, my brothers—Lev..." he trails off, an expression wrenching his face that's something between misery and hate. "I can't let that happen, Charlotte. Not when it's because of me."

I stare at Ivan, still not completely comprehending what he's trying to say. "What does he want with me? I don't know anything that could help him with...anything. I barely even know anything about *you*." I fling that last word at Ivan, and he flinches again.

"This isn't a joke, Charlotte," he warns me, his hands still gripping my wrists. They feel delicate in his broad, rough palms, his fingers wrapped around them. "My father isn't someone to trifle with. He *sells* women, Charlotte. Do you understand me?"

I freeze, blinking at him. "He—"

"He trafficks women. Do you get it now? Why I don't want him to get his hands on you? What he could do to you?"

I can feel my blood running cold, my mind trying to catch up to what Ivan is saying. Sex trafficking is one of those things that I know, theoretically, happens. But it happens to *other* women, women who go on vacation alone to places they shouldn't, women who trust the wrong men—

Oh god. I did that. I trusted the wrong man. I think of the site I was on, on the corners of the internet where a man can get away with things like that, a place I *knew* better than to go, and my stomach turns over.

"Is that what that man was doing in my apartment? He works for your father? He was going to take me to—" I can't even finish the sentence; the idea is so horrifying.

Ivan blanches. "I don't know about that. But I've been trying to stop him. I've—" He sucks in a breath. "I've been working with the feds. Trying to get information, enough that they can put a stop to what he's doing. It's incredibly dangerous, working with the law against a man like my father. And I think he and my oldest brother have started to catch on to what I'm doing. So, they want you, so that they can use you against me. To hurt me."

I shake my head, yanking back against Ivan's hold on my wrists, but he doesn't let go. His grip feels like iron bands. "I don't get it," I seethe, glaring up at him. "How could *I* possibly be used to hurt *you*?"

Ivan goes still, his hands still holding me tight. With one quick jerk, he pulls me up against him, his hands holding mine against his chest, and when he looks down at me, there's an expression on his face that makes me go still, too. It makes the entire room go quiet for a moment.

An expression that I can't quite put a name to—or maybe I just don't want to, because right now, I couldn't possibly accept what that means.

"You should know by now," Ivan murmurs, his voice soft suddenly, like a caress. "After that first night we spent together, you should know."

His hands on me, his touch, the way he's looking at me—it's enough to bring it back, even in this moment. Enough to bring back the way he looked at and touched me that night in my bedroom, the hungry look in his eyes, the way it felt like he was devouring me.

Whatever else is happening here, that was real. That was something that couldn't be faked.

And I know, when he lets go of one of my wrists and buries his hand in my hair, dragging my mouth to his for a vicious, almost painful kiss, that's real, too.

3

IVAN

I know better than to kiss her. I know better than to give in to the desire raging through me right now, the feeling that I *need* to have her, no matter the consequences.

That feeling has gotten us here. To this moment, right now, with my cheek still stinging from her slap and her eyes sparking angrily at me in the moment before my lips slam against hers. But I can't stop.

I can't fucking stop.

I've lied to her again. I've only told her half the truth. I couldn't keep what my family is from her, not and have any logical reason why she's here with me, in a shitty Illinois motel instead of at her apartment or mine in Chicago. I couldn't keep what I was from her, either.

But the rest—

I should tell her the whole truth. That *I'm* Venom. That I was the man at Masquerade, too. That I've been stalking her this entire time, that I broke into her apartment masked to kidnap her—yes, to keep her safe from my family, but also because I needed to buy time. Time to figure out what to do next.

Instead, she thinks I saved her from him. That he was working with my father to kidnap her, that 'Venom' is some cover for a man who uses the dark web to lure women in as victims for my father's trafficking ring. And it makes sense. It's a story that fits everything that's happened so far.

And I'm willing to let her believe it, because if I told her the rest of the truth, she wouldn't be in my arms right now.

I won't be able to keep her much longer. I have a solution for keeping her safe from my father, but it's not one that keeps us together. And the truth is—I don't think she wants that, anyway. I don't think she'd stay no matter what I said.

Take me home, and leave me alone.

Those words felt like a dagger, one that's still in my heart, twisting as I kiss her. As I lick into her mouth, my tongue tangling with hers, one hand fisted in her hair tightly to keep her from getting away. As I know, even as her mouth softens and she starts to kiss me back, that this is almost certainly the last time I'll ever touch her like this.

Which is just another reason why I can't stop.

I let go of her other wrist, and I wait for her to shove me away. To break the kiss and scream at me again. It's not as if I don't deserve it. I deserve every slap, every curse. Every awful thing she could say to me.

I'm the reason her life is falling apart. Why, even though she doesn't know it yet, it will never be the same again.

And I can't stop myself from taking this one last thing that I don't deserve.

Instead of pushing me away, her hand curls into my shirt. I feel her gasp as my arm slides around her waist, pulling her into me, letting her feel how hard I am for her. How desperately I want her.

I can't stop kissing her for even a moment. If I do, she might remember why she shouldn't want this. It might give her a moment to think. So instead, I kiss her harder. I nip at her lower lip, suck it into my mouth. I slide my tongue against hers, memorizing the taste of her. I kiss her like I'm starving, like I'm a drowning man, and she's air.

She moans, a small, tiny sound of desire, and it snaps something in me. My fingers press against the back of her head as I back her up towards the bed, my hand on her waist, grabbing at her shirt, yanking it up. I need to feel her skin—I need to feel *her*, to have this one last taste of her before she's gone forever.

I can feel her trying to make the shape of my name against my mouth, but I don't stop kissing her long enough to let her speak. I yank at the buttons of her shirt, ripping them open, hearing the *pop* of them against the fabric as I tear the shirt away from her. I feel her gasp, hear a small cry of what might be protest, but I'm already spilling her back onto the bed, dragging my own shirt up over my head as I push her down onto the mattress and spread her legs open with my knee.

She lets out another mewling cry against my mouth as I yank open the button of her jeans, grabbing a handful of the denim and the cotton underneath and dragging them both down her thighs. The moment she's even partially bared to me, I drop to my knees in front of the bed, one hand gripping her hip as I lean in and press my mouth between her legs.

"Ivan!" Charlotte cries out my name, her hips bucking against me as I drag a hot line from her entrance to her clit with my tongue, sucking the already-wet flesh into my mouth as her hands grip the duvet. There's nothing slow or gentle about the way I eat her out—I devour her, licking and sucking, nipping at her folds as I feel her hot arousal coat my mouth and chin, and I slide one hand down, roughly shoving two fingers into her as I feel her thighs start to tremble.

"I—I'm going to—" One of her hands catches in my hair, yanking at it as her back arches, as I drive her into an orgasm faster than I ever have before. I feel her clench around my fingers, and my cock throbs against the fly of my jeans, rock-hard and aching to be what she's tightening around instead.

I keep fingering her, yanking her jeans down off of her legs and tossing them aside as I spread her wider. I slide my other hand under the curve of her ass, sliding one finger against the tight hole there, teasing the entrance of it as I keep sucking her clit and lapping at it with my tongue.

"*Ivan*—Ivan!" She cries out my name, the sound of it making me harder with every moan. The need to possess every part of her feels obsessive, primal, and I push my finger against her asshole, the tip slipping inside as her hips buck, and she lets out a startled cry.

I've been inside of her mouth, in her tight, perfect pussy, and even if I never get to fuck her in the ass, I want to know what it feels like for her to come while some part of me is buried there.

She doesn't tell me to stop. She writhes against me instead, her head falling back against the bed, her legs spread wide for me as I roll my tongue over her clit again and again, sliding my finger deeper into her tight asshole as I add a third inside of her pussy, scissoring them back and forth. The sounds she's making turn to helpless gasps and moans that sound like they want to be words, but can't quite make it there. She's dripping wet, every movement of my fingers inside of her, impaling both of her holes, driving her arousal higher and closer to a second climax.

I want to make her come again before I fuck her. I want her so dripping wet that I don't even have to struggle to get my cock inside her. And then I want to feel her come all over it, too.

She's so close. I can feel her trembling underneath me, her thigh muscles tightening, and I curl my fingers inside of her, holding her pinned between my tongue, my fingers in her pussy, and my finger filling her ass. She's going to come for me like this, and I can feel from the way she's shaking how much it turns her on, how filthy this makes her feel, and how much she loves it.

This is what she was chasing, all those nights when she logged on to that website to talk to Venom. That night she came to Masquerade. This feeling is what she wanted, and I'm going to give it to her, even if it's the only chance I get to do it. *Especially* if it's going to be the only chance.

I feel her thighs tighten around my head, feel her buck against my tongue, and then she comes hard.

The sound she makes is a scream that turns to a shriek, building as she rides my tongue and my fingers, writhing against me. I hold her there, her arousal flooding my mouth, her entire body shaking as she moans something that sounds like my name, clenching around me as she keeps coming, wave after wave of pleasure that leaves her limp and gasping against the bed by the end of it, her eyes tightly closed as she tries to catch her breath.

I don't give her a chance. The moment I feel her orgasm start to ebb, I push myself up with one hand, the other frantically undoing the button and zipper of my jeans as I free my throbbing cock, line it up with her dripping entrance, and thrust hard.

I don't have a condom, and at this moment, I don't care. The feeling of her bare is what I want, wet and tight and hot, gripping my cock in a way that I've never felt before. I've never fucked a woman raw before, not even when I was an idiot teenager, and I shouldn't be doing it now—but if I never do this with her again, I want to know what Charlotte feels like without that thin barrier of latex between us.

And *god*, it feels so fucking good.

"Ivan!" She cries out as I thrust into her to the hilt, her nails sinking into my shoulders as I thrust so hard that I push her a little further up on the bed. I slide one arm under her, lifting her a little so that there's enough room for me to kneel on the mattress between her legs, holding her up on my cock for a moment before I lay her back down, thrusting hard again. I don't want to slip out of her for even a second. I don't want to lose the feeling of her wrapped around me. It's better than anything I've ever felt in my life, so good that I have to cling to what little bit of self-control I have to keep from coming in her too soon.

"Tell me you're on birth control," I growl as I thrust again, hard, moaning as I draw out to the very tip and then push myself back inside, reveling in the hot, velvet feeling of her wet pussy clenching around my bare cock. I don't know how I'm ever going to stop. I don't know how I'm going to do what I promised myself I'd do to keep her safe. I don't know how I'm going to fucking give her up.

"Wh—what?" she gasps, her nails still digging into my shoulders, her hips arching with every thrust to meet mine. There's no question about her eagerness; as wrung out as she was after those first two orgasms, her body is still responding to mine, meeting me with every rock of my hips against hers. Whether she'd admit it out loud or not, she wants this every bit as much as I do. Including the fact that I'm fucking her without a condom.

"I'm going to come inside of you." I thrust again, moaning as my hands flex against the bed, my cock throbbing dangerously close to the edge. I want it to last, to keep going, but she feels too good. Too perfect, as if she were made just for me. I don't know how much longer I'm going to be able to hold on. "Tell me you're on birth control, before I fill you up with my cum, Charlotte."

Her mouth drops open, her eyes so wide that for a moment, I think she's going to tell me she's not. *I'd stop if she said that. I would.* I tell myself that, that I'd pull out, that I wouldn't come inside of her with no safety net, leave her with another potential problem that I caused. But even as I think it, I don't know if I could. Only the tortuous pleasure of feeling her rubbing along the length of my cock has me thrusting at all, when part of me just wants to bury myself as deeply inside of her heat as I can, and stay there.

"Yes," she manages, her voice a hushed whisper. "I am."

Her legs wrap around mine, pulling me deeper, an unspoken permission to let me come inside of her, to fill her up. I want to tell her that I've never done this with anyone else, that she's the first woman I'll ever come inside of like this, the first one to ever have my cum dripping down her thighs after we're done, but I can't speak. I'm too close to the edge, her acquiescence pushing me there even faster, the thought of her swollen, pink pussy dripping my cum making my head spin with the need to do just that.

Just a little longer. God, I don't want it to stop. I rock my hips against hers as I sink into her again, reducing the friction, grinding against her in an effort to get her there a third time. I want to feel her come, to feel her rippling along my length, and then—

"Oh god, Ivan, I—" Her nails bite into my skin, her voice trailing off into a gasp, a high-pitched sound following it as her hips buck upwards and her mouth opens on a cry. "Keep doing that, please, I'm going to come, oh god, please—"

I feel her clench around me, hear her moan that turns to a shriek as the orgasm shatters her, and I lose all semblance of control. I've felt plenty of women come on my cock, but never like *this*, never when there's nothing between us but skin, and *god*, it's indescribable. I feel my hips jerk, my cock throb, my body take over, and I have a split second to be grateful that she told me it *is* safe to come inside of her, because there's no fucking way I could have pulled out.

Not when it feels like this.

Charlotte's nails rake down my back, stinging hotly as she screams my name, and I feel my cock go stiffer than I ever have in my life, throbbing as I manage one more thrust before the first hot spurts of my cum start to spurt, my balls tight and aching, my entire body rigid as pleasure like nothing I've ever known jolts through me.

I said I was going to ruin her for any other man. But she's ruined *me*. Nothing else will compare after this. There's nothing in the world that could feel as good as this does, and I bury my face in her throat, breathing her in as my cock throbs and jerks inside of her, twitching as the last of my cum spurts into her. "You're *mine*," I breathe into her skin, so quietly that I don't think she hears me, but it's the truth. She is mine. And even though I can't keep her, nothing will ever change that.

For a long moment, neither of us moves. I can feel my cock softening inside of her, but I'm still large enough that even soft, I don't slip out. I want to stay inside of her as long as I can, sweat-slicked and breathing each other's air, and I don't want to let her go.

We have a little time before we have to leave, before it is too dangerous to stay here any longer. I ditched my phone, anything that might allow my brothers to easily track us, and made a few purchases on my credit card to confuse them. Airline tickets to the wrong places, a trip on a Greyhound bus going to New York, things like that. It will take them a little while to realize that all of those are dead ends, and by the time they do, we will have already left here. I paid for the room in cash, and there are burner phones in the car for any calls I need to make. I intend to make both Charlotte and I as difficult for them to track as possible.

But they'll manage, eventually. My father is intelligent and resourceful, and he won't let me go so easily, especially now that it's clear I haven't been dealing truthfully with him all this time. All that matters, though, is that I get Charlotte to safety before they catch up. I'll lead them on a merry chase after me for the rest of my life if I have to, but I need to be sure that Charlotte is out of their reach.

And I know how to do that.

I feel Charlotte shift underneath me, and I reluctantly move away from her, letting myself slip out of her soft warmth as I roll to one side. A shiver of pleasure runs through me at that last bit of contact between us, and I can't help but hope that maybe we'll get to do that at least once more before we get on the road again. That maybe she won't come to her senses so quickly.

One look at her face tells me that she already is. She looks away from me, biting her lip, and she closes her legs just as I get one glimpse of my cum dripping out of her, pearling white in the slick folds of her pussy. It's enough to make my cock twitch again, swelling until I'm half-hard, and I have to stop myself from reaching for her and spilling her back onto the bed.

Her gaze flicks down to my cock, and her eyes widen. "Already?" she whispers, and I have to bite back a laugh.

"Charlotte, I could fuck you for the rest of the afternoon, take a nap, and then fuck you all night if that's what you wanted me to do." I roll towards her, unable to stop myself from pinning her wrists to the bed as I lean over her, and I feel myself hardening, as if I didn't just come. "There's so many fucking things I want to do with you."

"Like what?" she whispers, her voice small, and I groan, clenching my teeth against the urge to thrust into her right now while I tell her.

"I want to pin you down and tell you to lick my cock clean, so I can slide into you and fuck you until I'm covered in your cum and mine again. I want to fill you up a second time, so that you're dripping down your thighs while I'm still inside of you." I shift, pushing her legs apart with my knee as I hover over her, my cock angled between us. I tighten my grip on her wrists, and she moans, making me throb as I lean down.

My shaft is pinned against her clit, wet with both her arousal and mine. I rock my hips, grinding against that oversensitive spot, and Charlotte lets out a gasping moan.

"Tell me to stop." I rock my hips again. "Tell me to stop, and I won't make you come a fourth time. Tell me you weren't thinking when you let me fuck you before. Tell me you didn't realize until it was too late that I was fucking you raw." With every sentence, I slide my hips against her, rubbing her clit with the shaft of my cock. "Tell me, and I won't fuck you and fill you up again after you come on my cock."

The only sound she makes is another breathless, helpless moan. I pull her hands up, pinning her wrists above her head, and start to grind against her in earnest, rubbing my slick length over her as I feel her hips move and her breathing turn to eager pants. "That's right, Charlotte," I growl. "Come for me again. Let me see what a dirty little slut you are. Begging for more of my cum. You want this cock so badly you can't even tell me to stop after I've fucked you once. You want to come again. Greedy girl."

She's so close. I can feel her trembling, and I can see the guilt on her face, the *knowledge* that she's doing something she shouldn't, and it's turning her on. With every thrust, every wash of pleasure, every orgasm, she knows she should tell me no. That she should tell me to stop.

She knows half the truth now. She knows she's fucking a criminal. A son of a Bratva patriarch. She might not understand exactly what that means, but she gets enough to know that she shouldn't let me inside of her. And she's doing it anyway, so lost to pleasure that she can't make herself stop.

Just the thought has me dripping pre-cum, slick and hot against her, so turned on that I know it won't take me long to come inside her a second time.

"Ivan." She half-sobs my name, writhing under me as her hips arch up greedily. "I—I'm—"

"Come for me, *milaya*," I croon, snapping my hips against her, every thrust pushing me dangerously close to the edge, too. "Let me feel you come."

Her mouth opens on a cry, her hips driving up against me as I *feel* her clit pulse against my bare cock, her body bucking as she comes for the fourth time. I hold her pinned as she moans and gasps, and just as I feel her start to come down, I pull my hips back and thrust into her still-clenching pussy, hard.

She's wetter than before, full of my cum now too, and I feel it around my cock, feel it dripping out around us, sticky on her thighs. Once, twice, a third hard thrust, and I can't hold back. It's too much, the most erotic thing I've ever done, the best sensation I've ever felt, multiplied with every moment that passes, every filthy way she's let me have her, and my cock explodes for the second time, filling her up as I feel myself spill out of her, wet and hot as I come hard enough that I see stars.

I can hardly breathe as I roll off of her, exhausted and wrung dry. My cock is limp and spent against my thigh, and Charlotte is still next to me, one hand going to her chest as I let go of her wrists.

"I'm going to go take a shower," she says after a long moment. She pushes herself up, her dark hair falling into her face, and she doesn't look at me. "Shit," she breathes a second later. "My shirt is ruined."

"I have an extra one." I push myself up on one elbow, resisting the urge to reach out and nudge her hair away from her face, so that I can see it. Some instinct tells me not to touch her right now, that I've already pushed her further than I should have. "In the top drawer."

She nods, and a shiver runs through her. For a split second, I think she's crying, and I feel a sharp jolt of alarm, but when she starts to get up, and her hair falls back, I can see that her face is clear, if pale.

But she doesn't look at me. Not when she collects her clothes, or takes a shirt out of the top drawer of the dresser where I stashed my things last night, or walks to the bathroom. And as she goes, I can feel the divide between us, the moment when she remembers what she *should* feel, and not what she does.

And I know I'm going to spend the rest of my life aching to relive the last hour, again and again.

4

CHARLOTTE
WHAT DID I DO?

Reality, cold and unwanted, comes rushing in, in the moments after Ivan rolls off of me for the second time. Everything feels like a blur as I grab my clothes and retreat to the safety of the bathroom, closing the door behind me and locking it as I twist on the taps of the shower and wait for it to run hot.

What was I thinking?

I can't pretend that I didn't want it. That from the moment he kissed me, savage and hungry, I didn't want everything he was offering. That I didn't want to be horribly, inescapably *bad* for a little while.

I wanted him, and I let him have me. *Twice.* I can feel the evidence of it, sticky on my thighs, and my face blushes red as I drop the stack of clothes on the small, chipped sink counter. I let him fuck me without a condom, something I've never done with anyone before. Even though I've been on birth control since I first started having sex, I've always insisted on being extra careful. Something I was grateful for when I found out that Nate was cheating on me—I would have been a lot more worried at my first gyno appointment after that if I hadn't always made him use condoms. But I was all clear, and I'm sure it had something to do with that.

I'd always thought it would mean something, if I let a man fuck me without using protection. If I let him actually come inside of me. I'd always thought it would be more than—

More than what? I bite my lip, thinking of what he said just before he kissed me. That I should have known, after that first night, why it is that his father believes I can be used against Ivan. That hurting me would hurt him.

I told myself what happened between Ivan and me that first night was just sex. Just a hookup. But it felt wrong, even then. The way he touched me felt like *more* than anything I've ever felt with anyone before. And what just happened between us—

I swallow hard, walking quickly into the small, cramped shower and yanking the shower curtain shut over the lip of it. The water is almost too hot, but I step under it anyway, wishing for it to wash away the feeling of intimacy. The feeling that Ivan and I shared something that won't be easily forgotten when this nightmare is all over.

You fucked a criminal. I rake my hands through my hair as the water soaks it, unable to believe how quickly I let myself fall into his hands. *After you already knew, you still fucked him.* And I can't pretend that I didn't want it. I can't pretend he forced me. I know what he is, at least to some extent, and I still fell into bed with him because I wanted to experience how good he makes me feel one more time before I figure out how I'm going to get out of all of this.

Twice more, apparently.

My face is burning red, and it has nothing to do with the hot water. I'm utterly ashamed of myself, but that's not enough to stop the shivers of pleasure that run through me every time I think of what Ivan did to me. The way he touched me.

Letting him fuck me without a condom wasn't the only thing he did that I'd never done with anyone else.

I grab one of the washcloths off of the rack at the end of the shower, and the bar of citrus-scented soap that's on the small dish attached to the wall. I scrub the washcloth with it until it lathers, hard, as if I need to focus on that and nothing else, and then scrub myself clean. Over and over, until there's no trace of Ivan on my skin anywhere that I can feel, and I can't smell him on me any longer, that delicious combination of his cologne and warm skin.

I won't let it happen again. That was the last time. I tell myself that, firmly, as I wash my hair and get out of the shower, toweling off and slipping my underwear and jeans back on. Ivan's dark grey t-shirt is a size too big for me, and I gather it up at the hem, tying it in a knot just above the waist of my jeans. A sliver of pale skin peeks out between the shirt and my jeans, and I realize that far from looking like a disheveled mess that's just been kidnapped, I look—*sexy*. In my jeans, Ivan's knotted-up shirt, and my wet hair, I look wild. Unkempt. Like a woman on an adventure that could end anywhere.

A small, unwanted thrill of excitement churns through me. I let myself imagine, just for a second, that I'm going along with whatever happens next. That I'll stay with Ivan, wherever it is that he thinks we need to go to get away from his family. That I'd leave everything behind to let myself just *live* for once in my life.

But that's going too far, isn't it? I look at myself in the mirror, pressing my lips together tightly, reaching up to brush my fingers against the spot where Ivan left a small red mark at the base of my throat. I wouldn't have ever even given him my number, if I'd known the truth from the start. If he'd told me, that day that he sat down at the cafe, that his *confidential* job was confidential because it involved working for a criminal organization.

One that his father is apparently very influential in.

That's why he was at the gala, I realize suddenly, some of the pieces are starting to click together, although there are still huge, gaping holes in what I actually know for certain. Sarah had mentioned to me that sometimes members of various criminal organizations in the city show up, trying to seem like more above-board members of the community. That must have been why he was there, why he had a date with him, the woman that he'd said he was there with because it was easier to tell his father 'yes' instead of 'no.'

That makes sense now, too.

I grip the edges of the sink, feeling more and more like a fool with each realization. I don't know how I could have ever come to the conclusion that he was a part of some Russian crime syndicate, and yet—

Now that I know, I need to get away. It doesn't matter that he makes me see stars when he touches me or that I feel more alive than I ever have before when we're together. It doesn't matter that I'm going to think about the way it feels when he touches me for the rest of my life, or that that life feels horribly dull and mediocre now compared to the thrill I feel right now, looking at myself unkempt and flushed in the mirror.

Ivan is a drug. An addiction that he's gotten me hooked on, and with every hit, I'll sink deeper into the mire of this world that he's already started to drag me down into. I need to get out, while I still can.

Swallowing hard, I unlock the bathroom door, looking out into the bedroom. Ivan is lying atop the duvet, head pillowed on his arm, still naked and fast asleep. I can't help but think that, like that, he looks younger, even with all his carved muscles on display, swirled with black ink. He looks more innocent, and it's hard to believe that this man is a criminal. That he's done things I can't begin to let myself imagine. Things I won't ever really know the truth of, because I need to leave.

And I need to leave *now*.

If I can get out of the room while he's still asleep, I can run somewhere. I don't know if whoever is at the front desk of this hotel will help me, but someone will. I can get to a restaurant or a gas station, and beg to use the phone. I can call 911, or maybe I can find a police station—

And do what? The thought of turning Ivan in, makes my chest ache. But he said he was working for the FBI. If that's true, then maybe they'll go easy on him. Maybe he won't get in trouble, if I tell them that he was trying to protect me from the same people he's working with them against. That I just need to get home.

Ivan doesn't stir as I carefully pad out of the bathroom, stepping lightly across the carpet. I crouch down where he shoved his jeans off just before we had sex the second time, reaching into the pocket. It takes three tries before I find the one that has the keycard to the hotel room in it, and I slip it out, hoping that it will unlock the door from the inside, overriding whatever that little black box does.

Barely breathing, I tiptoe to the door, not bothering to get my shoes. They're on the other side of the bed, close to Ivan, and I'm afraid I'll wake him if I try to get them. I'll just have to make a run for it barefoot.

I can barely breathe as I turn my back on him. I hold up the keycard to the door, waiting for the click—and just as I hear that small grinding sound that tells me the door is unlocked, I feel an iron grip around my other wrist.

On instinct, I yank away, dropping the keycard as I slam my free hand down against the door handle and shove the door open. It opens, but just a crack as I feel Ivan's hard, naked body cage mine in as he grabs the handle and slams it shut again.

I flail, trying to open it once more, but he wheels me away from it, pushing me face-forward against the other wall in a hilarious parody of someone being patted down by a cop. Or at least, later, it will be hilarious.

Right now, I'm torn between impotent fury that I was so close to escaping, and frustrated distraction by the fact that I can feel every inch of his body pressed against mine...naked. I can almost feel him searing hot through my clothes.

"Charlotte." His voice is calm, hard, brooking no argument—which just makes me want to fight him all the more. "We talked about this."

"No." I buck against him, and he chuckles, grinding his hips closer to my ass. I can feel him getting hard again, and a flush of heat washes over me. *Ignore it, Charlotte. Don't end up in bed with him again.* "*You* talked about this. I told you I wanted to go home. And—"

"And, what?" His mouth is close to my ear, his breath warm against the shell of it, and I can feel desire pooling warmly in my blood. "And, wait for my brothers to come, and kidnap you all over again? But this time, with much less pleasant results." There's a thread of anger in his voice, and I realize, with a shiver that runs down my spine, that it's because of me. He's frustrated with *me*, maybe even on the verge of getting angry with me, and somehow, that adds to that warm feeling spreading through my veins.

It makes me wonder what it would feel like for him to fuck me when he's angry. To take it all out on me. What I would do if *I* fucked *him* angry. I've never had angry sex before. I've never been that angry with someone, or them with me, and still wanted them.

I wonder what that says about the relationships I've been in. And I know the answer almost immediately, even though I don't want to admit it.

They've all been bland. Boring. Relationships that check off boxes and look good on paper, but lack desire. *Passion*. Things that I didn't understand until Ivan showed them to me.

But that doesn't mean that what we're doing is good, or right.

"Or maybe you were going to go to the cops," he continues. "And find out what they could do for you. I promise you, Charlotte, that there are two options. Either they're already in my father's pockets, or they won't be able to protect you from him."

"So, what?" I buck against him, still trying to get free, and immediately regret it. I can feel how hard he is, pressing against me, and I think with another shiver of his finger sliding inside of me earlier, somewhere that I've never let anyone touch me before. I shove it away, hard. "Am I just supposed to go on the run with you?"

"No," he says shortly, the word clipped. It sounds angry, almost as if he doesn't want that, and I wonder why. *Is it because he does, and can't? But why not? He's taken everything else he wants, so far.* "I have a plan. But we need to get moving. I'm going to make a call."

He lets go of me, shoving himself away from both me and the wall, and for a brief moment, I feel my stomach drop, regretting the loss of the feeling of him against me. I want him there, more than I should.

Before I can try to grab the keycard again, Ivan bends down, scooping it off of the carpet. "Nice try," he tells me, a little of that humor back in his voice. "You almost made it. But it wouldn't have done you any good."

That cold certainty in his voice makes my stomach swoop. I turn to face him, staring as I wrap my arms around myself, and for the first time since I woke up, his nudity doesn't distract me. I'm too focused on those last words and what they mean.

"What's your plan?" I manage, and Ivan ignores me for a moment, pulling his clothes back on.

"I'll tell you in the car," he says finally, shoving the keycard in his pocket. "I've got burners in there; I'm going to go use one of those to make the call. I'll come get you in a few minutes. Don't bother trying to get out again," he adds. "You won't have any luck, and you'll just hurt yourself going out the window."

He already thought of everything, then. It makes me feel embarrassed, remembering the minutes I spent frantically looking for an escape after I woke up. It was *never* going to do me any good.

"I'll be right back," he says, and holds the keycard up to the door, opening it before slipping out and letting it slam shut behind him.

I flinch at the sound, sinking down onto the foot of the bed, trying not to think about what we did there less than a half hour ago. It's useless, and I get up instead, pacing to the armchair in the corner of the room and trying not to look at the bed at all.

It won't happen again. No matter how many hotel rooms we stay in. It won't happen again.

By now, Jaz will know I didn't show up for work. She will have tried to call me, texted me, and gotten no answer. She might even have left work early, used her spare key, and gone to my apartment to find out that I'm not there. My boss will know that I didn't show up and didn't call in, something that I never do. They will have alerted authorities. The cops. *Someone* will be looking for me.

Ivan said the apartment will be watched. My stomach clenches, thinking of his brothers watching my place and seeing Jaz go in there. Of what they might do to her instead. My stomach drops again, nausea flooding me, and I blurt it out as soon as Ivan walks back into the room, shutting the door heavily behind him. His face looks grave, as if every bit of humor has leached out of him, but I can't bring myself to care why. I'm too worried about Jaz.

"You have to call Jaz and tell her not to go to my place. If you don't want me to call her, that's fine, but you—"

"Why?" he interrupts me, and I stare at him for a moment.

"You just told me that your brothers would be staking out my place. Waiting for me to come back. She has a key—once she realizes I didn't come to work, and she can't get ahold of me, she'll try to come check on me. And you said they traffick women—" I trail off, the reality of what might happen to her too horrible for me to even say out loud. But Ivan is already shaking his head.

"They won't take her."

I stare at him, uncomprehending. "Why not?"

"Because she means nothing to me." He says it so bluntly that my mouth drops open, and he lets out a heavy sigh. "I don't mean that I wouldn't care if they did take her. Of course, I would. I care about any of the women that my father is trying to sell. That's why I've been risking my life working with the FBI." He gives me a long-suffering look. "But I wouldn't put you in danger to save her. And they know me well enough to know that. So they won't take her, because it wouldn't serve their purpose of getting to me."

My mouth clicks shut abruptly. "I would want you to risk me in order to save her."

"All the same." Ivan takes a deep breath, shoving his hands into his pockets. "I wouldn't. And while she's beautiful, I doubt she's a virgin, and she doesn't have an influential family, as far as I know. So they wouldn't be able to get a high enough price to make it worth it, not with the other concerns they have right now. Namely, dealing with me."

The way he says it is so flat, so matter-of-fact, that anything else I might have said flies straight out of my head. It feels like a shock, like cold water thrown in my face, and I think Ivan sees that, because he holds out a hand. "We need to go," he says gently, and just like that, I can feel the intimacy, the hunger from earlier fading away. I can't remember how we got there, how I let this man touch me like that.

He doesn't seem like the same Ivan, passionate, heated and vulnerable. This version of him seems cold and closed-off, and I stand up without taking his hand, resigning myself that I'm going to have to go along with his way, for now.

"Fine," I tell him, every bit as flatly. "I'll follow you."

He leads me out to a car that isn't the black Mustang I expected. "My brothers would have known to look for the Mustang," he says, seeing the surprised expression on my face, and I hear the hint of regret in his voice. "I couldn't risk taking it. It's a rare car."

The car that's waiting outside for us is a burnt orange Acura RSX. Ivan opens the door for me, and I hesitantly slide in, wondering if I should make a break for it while he's going over to his side. But he'd catch me before I could get far; I feel fairly certain of that. By now, I feel sure that he's already thought five steps ahead of any escape I might try to make.

"Is this one yours, too?" I ask as I click my seatbelt, looking over at Ivan. "Or did you steal it?"

He pauses, taking in a slow, deep breath. "Whatever you're thinking of me right now, Charlotte," he says slowly, with that same hint of regret and a tinge of bitterness in his voice, "I promise, you don't know the half of it."

And then he puts the car into drive, as we pull away from the hotel.

5

CHARLOTTE

"Where are we going?" I ask him, as he pulls out onto the highway. "What's this plan of yours?"

Ivan is silent for a long moment. "If I don't answer, is the next question going to be, *are we there yet?*" he asks finally, that same hint of bitterness still in his voice, and I flash him an angry look.

"I'm not a child."

"You listen like one." His hands tighten on the steering wheel, all of his earlier desire and humor gone. He feels remote now, cold, and I wonder if I could reach him now at all, if I wanted to. I wonder who usually sees this side of him, and I have a feeling that I don't want to know.

That what he said was true—that I don't know the half of it. I doubt I ever will.

The small flicker of disappointment, of *sadness* that I feel at that thought, startles me. I shouldn't feel that way. I shouldn't want to know anything more about him. All that I already do know should be enough—he's a criminal, a man willing to kidnap a woman under the guise of rescuing her, a man who will fuck a woman even though he knows it's wrong.

You knew it was wrong too, I chide myself as I stare out through the windshield, at the rapidly rolling empty fields and highway ahead of us. *You can't pretend he was running the whole show.*

"I'm listening now." I knot my hands together in my lap. "The uncertainty is killing me, Ivan."

Saying his name seems to get through to him. He lets out a heavy sigh, glancing over at me before returning his attention to the road. "I told you that I've been working for the FBI as an informant. Helping them try to catch my father. I'm going to ask them for help keeping you safe. I already have, as a matter of fact—that was the call I made. They've already helped another woman my father targeted—a daughter of his rival. The woman you saw me with at the gala," he adds, and I blink, startled.

"Your father wanted to—"

"Kidnap and sell her? Yes. He and her father are longtime rivals, fellow *pakhans* who have tried to bring each other down for years. My father decided revenge was best served through punishing his daughter for her father's sins."

I can't even speak for a moment, as I process that. "That—that's horrible," I manage finally, and Ivan nods.

"It is. And it's far from the worst of the things my father has done."

"And you?" I ask the question before I can think better of it, and I see Ivan's hands tighten on the wheel again, hard enough that his knuckles whiten slightly.

"They helped her," he says finally, ignoring my question. That, in and of itself, feels like an answer, and I feel that cold sensation slither down my spine again. "They'll help you."

The way he says it almost sounds as if he's trying to convince himself, and that cold, shivery feeling intensifies. I wrap my arms around myself, afraid to ask the next question, but I want to know. I *need* to know.

"What does that mean?"

Ivan lets out another heavy breath. He doesn't answer at first, and

I squeeze my arms around my waist tighter, a feeling of dread starting to build in the pit of my stomach. "Ivan."

"They'll talk to you once we get there."

"You know something," I insist, chewing on my lip. "You wanted me to listen. Fine, I'm listening. Just tell me the truth. What does 'helping me' mean?"

Something tells me that it doesn't just mean taking me home. Ivan's hesitation and the look on his face is enough for me to know that.

"They put Sabrina in witness protection," he says finally. "Or at least that's what I was told that they would do. I imagine they will likely do the same for you."

For a moment, I feel like the wind has been knocked out of me. "I'm not—witness to anything," I manage, that protest feeling like my best chance of explaining why this solution can't possibly work.

"I don't know what else to call it." There's a tinge of exasperation in Ivan's voice now, his hands still gripping the steering wheel hard. "What they do to keep people adjacent to criminals who need protection safe. It's the same thing, I think. Basically."

"Criminals like you."

His mouth forms a thin line, and I can tell that I've hurt him. But he doesn't deny it. I almost feel bad for saying it, but I can't. Not entirely, because if what he's saying is true—

"No." I shake my head. "No, that can't happen. That means—my entire life would be erased, Ivan. A new name, a new place to live…I can't do that. I'd lose everything. Not just my job and my apartment, but my friends. Jaz, Sarah, Zoe—they'd never know what happened to me. I—"

"I know what it means, Charlotte." Ivan's voice has never sounded heavier. "This is why I didn't want to tell you. It will be easier hearing all of this from them—"

"Do you really believe that?" My voice is rising, angry and loud in the small interior of the car, and I see Ivan wince, but he says nothing in response. "Do you really think that hearing this at *any* time would be easier?"

He still says nothing, and somehow, that makes me even angrier. "Last night, everything was fine!" I shout, twisting around to look at him. "I went out to dinner, and I hung out with Jaz, and I was looking forward to another date with you, and you were just a normal guy, and—"

Ivan's hands twist back and forth on the steering wheel. "I was never a normal guy, Charlotte," he says quietly. "I just hadn't told you yet."

I slump back into the seat, tears pricking hotly at the corners of my eyes. "Were you ever going to?"

His silence tells me all I need to know. And deep in my chest, I can feel the first cracks starting to make their way across my heart.

―

We drive like that for what feels like a long time, in silence. Ivan doesn't look at me, and his hands never unclench from the steering wheel, not until he turns into the parking lot of a small motel. I'm not even sure it's still operating—the parking lot looks empty, except for a black car with tinted windows parked on the far side. I glance over at Ivan, fear suddenly curdling my stomach as a new, horrifying thought occurs to me.

He said he was taking me to the FBI so that they could help me, but what if that, too, was a lie? What if he's handing me over to someone to take me away for something even worse? What if all of this, all along, was a ruse?

"That's going to be Agent Bradley," Ivan says, gesturing towards the other car. There's a grim look on his face, tinged with what looks like hurt, as if he knows what I was thinking. "Let's go."

I open my car door myself, not waiting for Ivan to come around and do it for me. I stand up, feeling a little unsteady, and watch as Ivan comes around the car to stand in front of me. The way he's standing partially blocks out the sun, making it so that I can see his expression clearly, and I can't quite read what he's thinking on his face.

"I want to tell you I'm sorry," he says quietly. "I wish I could say that. I *should* say that, because you're right. Your life is never going to be the same after this, and that wouldn't have happened if I'd just left you alone. But—"

Something about the look on his face, the hurt that I see there, softens something inside of me. I'm terrified, angry, and confused, but there's still the part of me that cares about him, that thought that there was something between us that could have become so much more. The memories of laughing with him and picking apples and baking a pie, of sitting in a movie theater, of his mouth and hands on me, all of those things are still there, and even if it's all tangled up in so many lies, I know at least some of it was real.

And it's all about to be over.

"What about you?" I ask hurriedly, as I see one of the doors to the black car on the other side of the parking lot open. "What happens to you now? You said you weren't on good terms with your family, and if I've gotten away—"

"Don't worry about that," Ivan says tersely. "All that matters is that you're safe, Charlotte. Everything else is secondary."

The utter sincerity with which he says it makes me go very still, staring up at him. There's no trace of anything else in his voice, nothing to make me think he isn't telling the truth. And the way he dodged my question suddenly makes me afraid for him. "Ivan—"

"Mr. Kariyev. Ms. Williams." A sharp, businesslike voice cuts through the air, interrupting, and both Ivan and I turn at the same time.

A man is walking towards us, one that I can only imagine is Agent Bradley. He's wearing ordinary clothes, jeans and a polo shirt, and yet he screams *cop*. Or, I guess, in this case, *FBI agent*. There's a smirk on his face, but it lacks the charm of Ivan's. There's no humor in it—he just looks satisfied, like a cat who's caught a particularly irritating mouse. And the way he's looking at Ivan—as if Ivan is the mouse—instantly makes me feel uncomfortable.

"I don't want to go anywhere with him," I say quietly, under my breath. Staying with Ivan isn't—*can't*—be an option, either, but right now, all I know is that I don't trust this man. I don't want to get in that car with him. And I don't want to entrust him with wiping away my entire identity and giving me a new one.

"He'll help you," Ivan insists. "No matter what, you'll be safe, Charlotte. And that's all that—"

He breaks off as the back door to the black car opens. And my heart feels as if it falls out of my chest as I see the man who slides out, straightening in the afternoon sun stiffly and looking across the parking lot at me with that same self-satisfied smirk that's on Agent Bradley's face.

"Nate?" His name spills out of my mouth before I can even fully register what I'm seeing. "What are you doing here? What—"

Bradley's smirk deepens. "Well, that's the thing, Ms. Williams. It seems that your little boyfriend's criminal activities haven't been limited to the vast and varied world of the Bratva's jobs for him."

"He's not my—" I start to say, but Bradley keeps talking over me.

"He apparently has plenty of time for extracurriculars, too. For instance—" He motions for Nate to hurry up and get to his side. The moment Nate is standing next to him, Bradley turns and hooks a finger in the v of Nate's t-shirt, yanking it down so sharply that Nate winces.

There, across his chest, is a bandage. And because of the text that Nate's brother sent me, I know what's under it.

Keep your mouth shut.

It seems that Nate didn't do that.

"Ivan?" I whisper, looking over at him. Ivan doesn't glance at me, doesn't take his eyes off of Bradley for a moment, and that's when I know with that still-sinking pit in my stomach that Ivan did, in fact, have something to do with it.

And he doesn't look guilty. He doesn't even look upset. He looks *angry*.

"I need you to get her out of here," Ivan says, ignoring Nate as he speaks directly to Agent Bradley. "Just like you did for Sabrina. We talked about this, just a little while ago—"

"Of course we did. I'll deal with Ms. Williams shortly. I'll need to know everything that she knows about you, of course, although I imagine you kept most of those secrets close to your chest." Bradley smirks, and Nate winces. I can't stop looking between the two of them, feeling dizzy and shell-shocked, unsure of what's going on. Between everything I found out after waking up this morning, and now this, I'm not sure how much more I can take.

I want to drop to the ground, cover my face with my hands, and not get up for a long time. I want to sleep for a day, or more, maybe. And more than anything, I want everyone around me right now to disappear. Even Ivan.

Maybe, after everything I've learned today, *especially* Ivan.

"Mr. Taylor here," Bradley looks over at Nate, "was wise enough to go to the police after his assault. Or, at the very least, his brother was, just before Mr. Taylor was taken to the hospital. The local police were quite unable to determine who the assailant might have been, but they contacted the FBI, since there was a possibility of linking it to one of the criminal organizations in the city. We, of course, are well aware of Mr. Kariyev's connection to you, Ms. Williams, and your former connection to Mr. Taylor. All put together, and with some simple tapping into your phone, we were able to put together that Mr. Taylor had recently sent you some unsavory messages. We were also aware that Mr. Kariyev had been tracking your phone and laptop activity. He must have been aware of Mr. Taylor's—shall we say, threats to you, and engaged in some good, old-fashioned vigilante justice. Which, of course, we disapprove of, being the law."

"You were *what*?" I pivot, looking at Ivan, my mouth dropping open. But he still won't look at me. He's staring directly at Bradley, never flinching, and the expression on his face is near-murderous. For the first time, I can see the man that Ivan says he is, clearly, in his face. I see a man who could work for an organization like the one he says he's a part of. I see a man who could do what he seemingly did to Nate. And it terrifies me.

It also makes me wonder, in some small, wicked part of my mind, what it would be like to have a man like that in love with me. Protecting me. Keeping me safe, forever, from men like Nate. From men like Bradley, who I still don't trust. Who I maybe trust even less now, after everything he's said. Some deep, instinctual part of me says that I shouldn't go with him. But I'm trapped, and I don't think I'm going to be given a choice.

Bradley's smile broadens as he finishes, but it still never meets his eyes. "Now, Mr. Kariyev, we have you on assault. Your information has been useful, but not useful enough. So you'll also be brought up on kidnapping and trafficking charges, for the abduction and attempted trafficking of Ms. Williams—"

"That's not what happened!" I burst out, but once again, Bradley continues talking over me.

"If you don't want to die within a few days of being sent to a supermax facility, Mr. Kariyev, you'll give us more information than you have thus far. Of course, that information won't buy you your freedom any longer. It will, at most, buy you your life. In solitary, of course. But that's life, at least."

"And you're coming home with me," Nate interrupts, looking at me. "Charlotte, I've had enough of all of this. I get that you were pissed about the cheating, but I've explained myself already. There's no reason to throw away five years of a relationship over it. You've gotten me back with this trash—" he looks disparagingly at Ivan, then back at me. "It'll be hard for me to get over the fact that he's touched you, but I'm sure in time—"

Before Nate can finish his sentence, Ivan shoves himself forward, putting his body in between me and Nate. "*You'll* touch her again over my dead body," he spits, and this time, Bradley's smile *does* reach his eyes.

"That can be arranged, Mr. Kariyev," he says smoothly, and I feel Ivan tense.

"Charlotte, get in the car," Ivan says, his voice low, and Nate almost immediately interrupts him.

"Charlotte, come *here*. What you saw in that piece of trash, anyway, I'll never understand, but we can talk about your little rebellion later—"

"I'm not a child!" I snap, lurching around from behind Ivan to glare at Nate. "I'm not going to let you talk to me like that. And I'm not a dog, for you to whistle at—"

"Enough," Bradley snaps. "You're coming with *me*, Ms. Williams, for questioning. And then—"

"She's not going anywhere." Ivan's hand comes up, and I feel all the blood drain from my face as I see a gun in his hand, one that I have no idea where it came from. "Except with me."

6

IVAN

Putting a gun in Agent Bradley's face is far from the smartest thing I could have done. But I've long since established that when it comes to Charlotte, all of my better sense goes out of the window.

This is just another symptom of that.

I knew that Agent Bradley had it out for me. I still knew that this morning, when I called him on the burner phone and told him what had happened, and that I needed his help getting Charlotte out of trouble. And I'd believed him when he'd said that he would help.

I'd believed him because he'd helped Sabrina. I don't know for sure where she is, or if the promises that the FBI made her panned out, but I know that my father didn't get to her. If he had, I'd know *that*. Which makes me think that Bradley kept his promise to help her.

It made me think he'd keep his promise about Charlotte.

Right up until I saw Nate get out of the car.

I was still willing to play along, if it meant Charlotte getting to safety. I would have let Bradley throw me into the deepest, darkest hole in the most maximum security of prisons if it meant that Lev and my father couldn't get to her. There's nothing I fear more than prison—not torture or death—but I'll take it if it means she's safe. I'll do anything to make sure she's safe.

Especially because all of this is my fault.

But I knew when Nate started talking that Charlotte wouldn't be. That he'd find a way to end up taking her home. That Bradley doesn't give a shit what happens to her—that maybe he resents me enough to let her be a scapegoat, because it would be one more knife to dig in.

I can't let that happen. So I slip the gun free, fast enough that Bradley doesn't see it coming, and level it at his face.

"We're leaving," I say flatly, coldly, but the smile never leaves his face.

"You really think I came here alone?" He doesn't flinch, and just behind him, I can see the other doors to the black car opening. Two more agents. "They'll bring you down, Kariyev, and take her. Who knows what happens then? She probably doesn't have enough answers for us. Not enough to make protecting her worthwhile. I wonder if your father will still want her, with you dead or locked away? Probably, even just as—"

"I'll drop you before they get to me," I growl. "Call them off, and let us go."

Behind me, I can feel Charlotte flinch. I know what this must be doing to her. This is already more than she could have ever imagined dealing with in reality, a gritty level of violence before a shot ever goes off that she should never have had to confront. And now that Bradley has drawn his line in the sand, there will be more.

I should never have gone near her. But I did, and now it's too late. And I can't even say I'm sorry.

Not and have it not be a lie.

Bradley drops in the instant before I pull the trigger, with an instinct born of years of training. He's a piece of shit, but he's good enough at his job to know when a bullet is coming. My shot goes wide, just missing one of the other agents, and I react in the split second before they fire, pushing Charlotte down to the asphalt as their bullets hit close to us, spraying bits of it in both our faces.

They're not going to stop shooting until they've killed us, or fucked up my car so badly I can't drive. Bradley is already starting to push himself up, and I fire again from where I'm lying on the ground, clipping his arm. He grabs it, rolling onto his back with a groan as blood spills out onto the asphalt, and Charlotte lets out a high-pitched scream.

Winging Bradley might have distracted the other agents just long enough. "Get in the fucking car!" I growl at Charlotte, shoving myself up and firing twice more at the other agents' feet, spraying gravel at them as I bolt for the driver's door. I want to fling her into the car myself, but I don't have time. All I can do is hope like fuck that she follows instructions as I yank the door open, jumping inside, and shoving the key into the ignition.

To my relief, she slides in next to me, just as the agents fire again. I slam my foot down on the gas, the car peeling away, and for a second, I wish I'd angled it so I could have run over Nate's fucking face.

Or at least his hand.

Gunshots are still peppering the asphalt behind us as the car swerves, and Charlotte screams, clinging to the side of the door as we jolt out onto the road, accelerating as I drive with only one thing in mind—getting us as far away from that fucking motel as I can.

When I finally look over at Charlotte, I can see that her face is paper-white. She's still gripping the side of the door, frozen still, her lips pressed tightly together. She hasn't cried, not through any of this, and I don't know whether to be impressed or worried. I can't think of many other people who wouldn't have. At least a little.

"I'm sorry," I tell her finally, when we're back on the highway and it's clear that we're away from any pursuit. I intend to stay on the highway for a little while, and then get off on surface roads, to make it harder for them to follow us. "I had no idea that he would pull that shit. I definitely didn't know that Nate would be there—"

"Because you thought you killed him?" Charlotte swings sharply towards me, her face bloodless, and I'm so shocked that it takes me a second to answer.

"What? No, of course I didn't fucking think I—"

"So you did do it." She faces forward again, ramrod straight in the seat. "You beat him to a pulp and then...carved that awful message in his chest." The last part sounds forced out from between her lips, as if she can barely bring herself to say it. "Holy shit, Ivan."

Fuck. I let out a slow breath, trying to think of what I can possibly say to her. I was right about one thing—she doesn't belong in this world. What I did to Nate was child's play compared to what I've done to other men, and not nearly as bad as what I thought he deserved, and yet, Charlotte is clearly horrified. And I can't blame her. That kind of violence isn't normal for her—and I don't want it to be. I never did.

"He threatened you," I say quietly, staring straight ahead at the highway in front of us. I check my GPS and take the next exit off, and Charlotte tenses immediately.

"Where are we going?"

"Surface roads. Make it harder for us to be tracked. What, do you think *I'm* going to hurt you? That I'm going to take you somewhere and...what? Leave you in a ditch?" I try to hide the hurt in my voice, but I can't. I'm willing to do anything to make sure this woman is safe, and it's pretty fucking clear that she's afraid of me now, too.

On one hand, I can't exactly blame her, after what she's just seen. But on the other—surely she's also seen what I'm willing to do to keep her safe.

"Maybe." Her jaw is clenched now, too. "Clearly, I don't know you at all, Ivan."

That dagger she shoved in me when she told me to take her home and leave her alone twists, and before I can stop myself, I slam my foot against the brake, wrenching the car over to the side of the road and skidding to a stop in the grass. We're out in the middle of fucking nowhere, Illinois, and there's no one to be seen for miles. Charlotte seems to realize this, but for all the wrong reasons, because her already bloodless face seems to go even paler.

"You know some things," I say quietly, my voice hard and sharp. "You know I'd rather eat a burger out at a pub than drop five hundred dollars on a Michelin-starred meal. You know I'll go apple picking with you on a fall afternoon, when all your other boyfriends would rather stay in and watch the game. You know I'm shit at baking, but I can at least peel an apple, so you make up for the rest of it. You know I make you laugh." I reach out, my finger tracing down the line of her jaw, because I can't stop myself from touching her. Even like this, angry and frightened, she's beautiful. Even like this, I can't make myself stop wanting her.

"You know what it feels like when I kiss you. You know the way I look at you when you're all spread out for me naked, sweet as that apple pie we baked. And you know how hard I can make you come." My fingers close around her chin, and I turn her face to look at me, but she jerks it away just as quickly.

"And how much of that was real?" She looks out of the window, twisting as far away from me as she can get. "How much of that was just you trying to get me to fall for you, so you could have what you wanted from me?"

All of it was real. But I can see that she's not going to believe that. Not right now. Maybe not ever, with the way things are going.

"Fuck, Charlotte." I shake my head, putting the car back into gear and pulling back out onto the road. We don't have time to sit here and argue, not with what we have on our tail. "We can finish this conversation later," I mutter, gritting my teeth as I start to drive again.

"Let's finish the one where I found out that you beat the shit out of Nate," she spits. "And—"

"Put a reminder on him, since he's too stupid, or too much of an asshole to know when to quit?" I look over her, feeling a jolt of anger that she won't let this go. "I didn't think you gave a shit about him. He cheated on you, remember? Made you feel like shit, even though you didn't deserve it. Wasted five years of your life. Why the fuck do you care what I did to him?"

"I—" Charlotte stammers, looking down at her hands. "I don't know if anyone deserves anything like—that. Even if they—"

"Plenty of people do." I feel my jaw clench as I twist my hands on the steering wheel. "And some people don't. I've hurt both, Charlotte, doing what I do for my father. And that's what's really bothering you, isn't it? Not that Nate got the shit beat out of him, but that it was me that did it. *Me*, who you've eaten dinner with and baked pie with and watched movies side by side with, like a normal girl with a normal boy. *Me*, who you've let inside you, who you've let—"

"Stop!" Charlotte shouts the word, throwing up her hands. "I get it! I let you fuck me, but I didn't know, and—"

"You knew this morning." The hurt is in my voice again, icing over every word, and I can't hide it. I know I've done more wrong in this than I can probably ever make up for, but Charlotte seems intent on pretending that she has no hand in it. That she was fooled in every little thing, and while I've lied to her about plenty that she doesn't even know about yet, there are some things she did know. And this morning is one of those things I'll hold on to, even though I know I didn't deserve that, either.

Her mouth sets in a thin line. "You stalked me." She swallows hard, the delicate line of her throat moving, and the sight of it makes me twitch in my jeans, aroused despite the argument. Hell, maybe partially because of it. Sweet, innocent Charlotte is beautiful and desirable in every way, but angry Charlotte is a spitfire, and it makes me want to pin her down and fuck her while she spits those angry words at me, until I find out if I can turn those curses into moans.

"You *tracked* me," she continues, and the anger is back in her voice. "*Spied* on me. I heard what Bradley said. That's how you knew what Nate was saying to me. I never told you about it. That's how you knew where I ate lunch. You finding me at Cafe L'Rose wasn't an accident—" she trails off, and I feel myself tensing, knowing how close she is to putting together the rest. To figuring it all out, and then god knows she'll never forgive me.

I should just tell her. I shouldn't keep dragging it out. But once I do, any chance of there being anything more between us will be gone. And I'm not ready to let her go just yet.

"You're right," I tell her quietly. "And I shouldn't have. All of that was wrong, but—"

"What do we do now?" She cuts me off, clearly uninterested in my apologies. Which is probably for the best, because I still don't know how to tell her that I'm sorry in a way that feels sincere. In the end, what I want is still what I shouldn't have—a way to keep her. "Your plan with Bradley clearly isn't going to work out. He wants to throw you into the deepest pit available. And I'm almost inclined to agree with him," she adds acidly, bitterness coating every word. "I just trust you *slightly* more than I trust him."

"I suppose I should be glad for that," I mutter, and she looks over at me, her face still bloodless and mouth set in a hard line.

"He's a snake," she says flatly. "He felt—wrong. And he betrayed you, so clearly, he's not someone to be trusted."

"I'm a criminal, and he's a fed." I chuckle darkly. "Isn't that just what he's supposed to do?"

Charlotte seems to consider this for a moment. "Not if you had an agreement," she says finally, folding her hands together in her lap. "He should have kept his word."

It's a naive view of the world, but I don't tell her that. "He's going to be after us, too," I tell her quietly. "We'll have the FBI and the Bratva on our asses now. We're going to have to be careful, and you're going to have to listen to me, Charlotte."

"Then maybe you should tell me what we need to do." Her voice is icy, and it hurts to hear her like that. I want to hear her soft again, breathy, her voice pleading for more. I want to hear her laugh. I want her happy, and the hardest thing to accept by far is that it's almost certainly never going to be me that gives that to her.

All I can do now is focus on getting her *safe*.

"I'll tell you when we stop for the night," I say finally, unwilling to have this argument right now, in the car. "We can talk about it then."

We drive in silence on the surface roads for a long time, until the sun starts to set. I see Charlotte lean against the door, looking out at the bright oranges and yellows streaking across the sky, and the expression on her face makes my chest ache. Her face has softened, her eyes almost dreamy as she watches it, and it's as if she's managed to forget for a moment what's happening. As if she's her old self, just for these few seconds as the sun sinks beyond the horizon.

I can't help but wonder if that's what she wants to be—her old self. When Charlotte and I went out on our first date, she told me that she thought she was boring. That she'd lived a predictable, unexciting life. It seemed as if she wanted to break free from it. That's what she was doing, after all, playing in the dark corners of the internet with Venom. That's what she was doing that night at Masquerade. But now that reality has hit her, I can't help but think that she likely wants to retreat back into the safety of that boring, ordinary life.

A life that I've taken away from her.

Guilt churns in my stomach as the sky starts to darken, and I pull off of the road into the drive-through of a fast food place. Charlotte looks over at it, and her nose wrinkles.

"I'm not hungry," she says flatly, and I let out a slow breath, trying to keep my patience. She seems determined to try it, and I deserve that. But I'm exhausted, too, and I wish she wouldn't fight me on every little thing.

"You haven't eaten all day, because we couldn't spend the time to stop. Not until we put a good distance between us and them. But you have to eat something."

Charlotte sets her jaw stubbornly, and I sigh, rolling down my window. I order a burger for myself and chicken tenders for her, figuring that she'll pick at them when she gets hungry enough. Fries, too. I set the greasy bag of takeout on the floor next to her feet, and look at my map on my phone for a nearby cheap motel.

I could afford nicer, of course. But those places usually look sideways at anyone trying to pay with cash, and without using real names. The shadier the motel, the more likely that I can keep our stay as anonymous as possible.

Charlotte doesn't touch the bag, moving her feet away from it as if it might burn her. I chuckle darkly, pulling back out onto the road. "I thought you liked simpler things." I can't resist the urge to rib her, just a little. She's behaving like a diva all of a sudden, and I know that's not her. She's trying to get under my skin.

"I like casual places," she says stiffly. "I don't usually poison myself with that garbage."

"Well, unfortunately, restaurants are a little too visible. And they put others in danger. My brothers or the feds get wind of someone fitting our description having been seen—and the feds will put out pictures of us, soon enough—and they'll start questioning other guests. Waitresses. Hotel clerks. Anyone who might have seen us. So we need to lay low, and keep out of sight as much as possible. That means drive-throughs and cheap motels, and getting back on the road as early as we can."

"Sounds like you've done this before. Gone on the run." She still won't look at me, and I sigh heavily as I pull into the motel parking lot.

"No. But I've always been prepared. Comes with the territory." I turn the car off, looking over at her. "Are you going to try to run again? Or are you going to accept that we're going to have to stick together for the time being."

Charlotte's mouth tightens. "I barely even know where we are right now," she says, her voice still stiff and cold. "I don't think I *can* try to run. There doesn't seem to be a police station for miles."

"And if you called them, you'd end up with Bradley," I tell her flatly. "And Nate, right by him, waiting to pay you back for what happened to him."

Her head whips around at that. "He wouldn't hurt me," she says sharply, clearly startled by that insinuation. "He's a cheating piece of shit, but he'd never—"

"He would." I look at her, fighting the urge to reach out and touch her, as if by holding her in my hands, I can drive my point home somehow. "Look, Charlotte, I get that all of this is strange to you. That you're seeing sides of human nature you've never had to see before, and never thought about outside of television and maybe some books. But what I need you to understand is that you have no idea what some men are capable of."

She looks at me evenly, unflinching. "Men like you?"

I choose to ignore that, and the jab of pain in my chest. "Nate might've never laid a hand on you before this. I'll agree with that. But now he's been hurt in ways he couldn't have imagined either, before.

Hurt by a man you slept with. Humiliated by him, too. If he gets half a chance, he'll take that out on you. I promise you that."

For once, Charlotte doesn't look away. "Then that'll be your fault, too," she says coolly. And before I can respond, she shoves her door open, stepping out into the chilly night.

I want to offer her my jacket, but I already know she'll refuse. I can see the prickling of her skin as she wraps her arms around herself, but I just grab my duffel bag out of the back of the car, locking it as I lead the way to the clerk's window.

Fifteen minutes later, I have a key and a room. Charlotte follows me in silence, and I grab the bag of our food out of the car, unlocking the room and letting us in. We're on the upper floor, which I'm glad about—we'll be able to get some warning, most likely, if anyone is coming after us. I plan on keeping an eye out as much as I can.

I let Charlotte go into the room first, and I can see her taking it in—the old carpet, the pressed-wood furniture, the stiff duvet on the one bed. She looks at me, and I let out a sigh.

"I'll sleep in the chair. Or on the floor."

She doesn't argue, or tell me that I've been driving all day, so I should take it, or even give me a chance to try to convince her that she should have the bed. She just nods, sitting heavily down on the end of it, and I can see what looks like defeat cross her face as she unrolls the bag of food and takes out a single chicken tender.

I know I'm about to make that feeling even worse.

We eat in silence. I scarf down my burger without really tasting it, and Charlotte shreds the chicken more than she actually eats it. When the trash is thrown away, I wash my hands and come back out, noticing that she hasn't moved at all. She's just a statue, sitting at the end of the bed.

"We're going to go to Vegas," I tell her, and she looks up at me.

"Vegas?" There's clear confusion on her face, and I nod.

"I have a contact there who can make fake identification for us. Licenses, social security, the works. Good enough that we can go anywhere, with no trouble."

Charlotte swallows hard. "And we need that because—"

"We're going to have to scrub our old identities, Charlotte. Leave the country, probably, to be safe. Together, separately, whatever—the old Charlotte and Ivan, those are going to have to go, if we want to survive. This guy can do that for us."

The look of horror on her face is frozen there for a moment, and I realize that she believed, somewhere deep down, that I was going to find some other way out of this for us. That she was going to get to go home, eventually. I don't think it's settled in yet that that's impossible.

Unless I could pull off a miracle somehow, she's not going home. And the feeling that I've failed her settles on me, a weight that I can't shrug off. Leaving, starting over—that's what I've always wanted, but she has a life that she didn't want to shed. Maybe she wanted to lose pieces of it, but not all of it—not her friends, her job, or her home.

I've cost her all of that. And all I can think, as I look at the dawning grief and shock on her face, is that I have to find some way to get it back for her.

Keeping her safe isn't enough. I need something more. Something that can undo what I've done.

"No." Charlotte shakes her head frantically, breaking my train of thought. "No, I'm not doing that. I'm not going to just—become someone else. I won't do it. We'll have to figure something else out, Ivan. My life, everything—I can't just walk away from that!"

I let out a sharp breath between my teeth. "You can't escape the Bratva, Charlotte. My father is relentless and merciless. My oldest brother, Lev, is cruel. My other two, Niki and Ani, will do what he says. They're my father's spares, there to do as they're told, and to follow Lev. That's their purpose, beyond reminding Lev that he can always be replaced, if he puts a foot wrong."

"That he can—" Charlotte's eyes narrow, her forehead wrinkling as she shakes her head, running her hands through her hair. "This is awful, Ivan. Everything you tell me about your family is awful. This is—"

"I know." I breathe out heavily. "Believe me, I know. I've lived all my life with them, and I've spent a good bit of it plotting how I'll escape, eventually."

"And that's what this is. Your escape." Bitterness laces every word. "You're just taking me down with you."

"This isn't how I planned it. And I never wanted to drag you down with me." That, more than anything, I want her to believe. I want her to understand that I never, *never* would have sacrificed her safety, for anything. I would never have put her in this much danger, if I'd believed my family would come after her.

"So I'll go to Bradley." She spreads her hands out in front of her. "Maybe he'll protect me from Nate. He wants the Bratva to go down. He—"

"That's not an option any longer." I cut her off, before she can keep traveling down that path. "He's not going to help you, Charlotte. He's going to want information from you that you don't have—he made that clear earlier today, when we met up with him. He'll probably hand you back over to Nate. It's clear they have some sort of agreement. He might threaten you with all sorts of things, to try to get you to tell him what he thinks you know. He might not care enough to even put you in witness protection. And if he does—"

"Isn't that what you wanted?" she demands, her voice cracking slightly, and I run my hand through my hair.

"*None* of this is what I wanted, Charlotte. But yes, I thought Bradley was the best option. I thought he would help you, get you safe. But it's clear he doesn't give a shit. So even if they do put you in witness protection, I'm no longer convinced that's enough to keep my brothers from getting to you. From finding you and using you. Charlotte, you don't want to know what Lev will do to you—"

"I have some idea." She cuts me off, shoving herself up from the bed and starting to pace. "So—what? Now I'm dependent on you. I'm going to road trip with you to Vegas, where some man you say we can trust but I don't know is going to get us new, fake identities, and then —" She spreads her hands out. "We ride off into the sunset? 'The beginning of a beautiful friendship?'" The sarcasm in her voice, dripping off of every word, bites into me like acid on my skin. "I don't believe this, Ivan. I don't believe you wanted Bradley to help me. I don't believe that all of this has been some massive fuck-up on your part, that you didn't want this from the start! That this isn't what you always intended to happen—"

I jolt up from my chair, my anger rising to meet hers. I've been shoving it down all day, throughout one of the longest days I can remember having in recent memory, telling myself that I deserve every cutting word, every angry remark, every cold shoulder. And fuck, I know I do. But at the same time, she's accusing me of things that *aren't* true. And that pisses me off, because god knows I've done enough wrong that she can be furious at me for. She doesn't need to be angry at me for what I haven't done, too.

"I never wanted this," I growl, pacing towards her. She holds her ground, eyes sparking angrily up at me, and I shake my head, my anger sparking to meet it. "This is exactly what I *didn't* want to happen. I knew I should have stayed away from you. I knew I was bad for you, that everything about me was *wrong* for someone like you, but I couldn't. I fucking couldn't! From the moment I saw you at Masquerade, I knew—"

Her mouth drops open, her eyes so wide that her eyebrows shoot up almost to her hairline, and I realize what I've said a moment too late. That it's all coming out, and Charlotte is going to realize the extent of what I've done.

That because I let my mouth run away with me, because I let myself get angry for a second, I might have doomed her even more.

She'll never stay with me after this. Not even long enough for me to make sure she's safe.

7

CHARLOTTE

From the moment I saw you at Masquerade, I knew—

The words slam into me with the weight of a punch. It takes me a moment to fully grasp what he's saying, the awful truth of what he's let slip. And with everything else that's happened since I first woke up this morning, the force of it nearly sends me to my knees.

"You were the man at Masquerade." The words sound broken as I whisper them, the full extent of how deeply Ivan has lied to me sinking in. "You—god, you didn't even use your real voice?"

"That's the point of that place, isn't it?" Ivan runs a hand through his hair. "Anonymity. I always wore gloves there, so no one could pick me out by the tattoos on my hands. The mask. A fake accent, so no one knew I was Russian. All of it to keep my identity secret, the way that place is meant to—"

"Which just means you're a fucking hypocrite!" I spit out, an inch from slapping him again. The only reason that I don't is the memory of this morning, the fear that if I touch him, somehow all this anger will transmute into desire, and we'll end up in bed again. There are sparks flying between us, hot and angry, but I learned this morning how quickly those sparks can turn into a different kind, when there's what there is between Ivan and me. "That *is* the point of that place! *Fucking secrecy!* I was promised that my identity would be safe, and you—what? Got it somehow?"

Ivan lets out a heavy sigh, and just as he looked younger this morning, when I saw him sleeping as I came out of the shower, he looks older in this moment. As if the weight of all his lies crashing down is aging him. "I'm a hacker, Charlotte," he says tiredly. "An exceptionally good one. I've used those skills for my father for years, but I also use them for myself."

"To stalk women?" I spit out angrily, and he shakes his head wearily.

"No. To bolster my finances, so I could work on setting aside money that had no ties to my father. Money I could use to get away, eventually, that was hidden from him. I have plenty of things I've hidden over the years. A house, for one." He chuckles grimly. "And I also, in more recent months, have used those skills for the FBI to try to help bring down my father's trafficking business."

"And to stalk me, then. Just me?" I look at him disbelievingly. "Your stories are all over the place, Ivan. You're a criminal, but I guess sex trafficking is too far, so you're double-crossing your father on that. But stalking a woman you ate out at a secret sex club one night *isn't* too far, so that was fine—"

"It's not!" Ivan interrupts me, his voice cracking in the space between us, raw and angry. "No, it's not, Charlotte. It's not fine, and I knew it wasn't fine. Is that what you want to hear? I knew I was wrong, from the moment I hacked into those records and looked you up. *All* of it was wrong. Finding you, tracking your phone—"

"You're Venom, too, aren't you?" I stare at him, the rest of the puzzle pieces clicking into place, and I feel those cracks in my heart spreading. "You said you were tracking me. Bradley said you were tracking me. You found me on that site. You got me to tell you all those things—" My face burns red at that thought, and I press my hands over my face, feeling tears sting the corners of my eyes. I don't want to cry in front of him, but the weight of this betrayal, added to the rest, feels like too much.

I feel so ashamed of myself, of everything I told him, of everything I've let him do to me. Ivan sees it, I think, when I drop my hands away from my face, because he crosses the space between us in one quick step, cupping my face in his hands as he tilts it up.

"Nothing about what you told me, or anything we did together, has anything to do with this," he whispers. "You don't need to be ashamed of it, Charlotte—just because you wanted those things, maybe *still* want them—"

"Not with you!" I wrench away from him, tears hot on my lashes. "You lied to me about *everything*!"

"Not everything—"

"You didn't save me from Venom. You *were*—*are*—him!" I shake my head, backing up, away from Ivan. "You stalked me, and tricked me, and trapped me. *You* were in my apartment that night. *You* knocked me out. You lied to me again this morning, when you said that you showed up—"

"I did show up to talk to you. To get you out of there, because I knew my brothers were coming for you. But I knew if I showed up as myself, there would be too much explanation. You would have questions—understandably—and you would argue, and they might have gotten to you, to us, before—"

"So you grabbed me and knocked me out?" My voice rises to a shriek, but I don't care. I don't care that I sound hysterical, or like I'm losing my mind. I think I might be. This is all too much to take in, too fast.

"I needed to get you safe, Charlotte. And then I could explain—"

"Would you have ever told me the truth? *All* of it?" I stare at him, fighting back tears. "If Bradley hadn't spilled that you were tracking me, would you have ever told me about that? Or Masquerade? Or Venom?"

Ivan goes silent, and I know he doesn't have an answer for that. Not one that either of us will be satisfied with.

"You lied about everything to get into my life." Every word sounds cracked, broken, as I feel my heart shattering. I'd insisted that we weren't exclusive, insisted that I needed time—but I'd felt myself falling for Ivan, or at least, the version of him that he showed me before all of this. I'd thought that we might have a future, that I might have been lucky enough to find a man who wanted me exactly as I was, who would love all the parts of me that others found boring, and at the same time encourage me to try to find adventure. But all of it was a lie.

"Charlotte, it wasn't everything—"

"If I'd known all of it," I whisper, "we never would have gotten past that first night. I never would have seen you again."

Ivan's shoulders slump, and the expression on his face is as hurt as if I'd hit him. He sinks back into the chair he was sitting in, rubbing his hands over his face and through his hair.

"I know," he says finally, miserably. "I always knew that. And I always knew it would end up like this, eventually. I knew I couldn't keep it from you forever. I couldn't lie to you forever. You're too smart, and I—" He breaks off, his teeth sinking into his lip as he looks away from me. Whatever he was about to say, he forces it back, his elbows on his knees as he drops his head into his hands for a moment before looking up at me again.

"I thought I'd get over you, after a while," he says softly. "I thought there couldn't be a woman in the world who could hold onto me like you have. I never knew there could be anyone like you, Charlotte. I thought I'd show you the things you wanted to experience, and I'd get to enjoy you for a little while, and I told myself it wasn't selfish because there were things you wanted that you'd get out of it too, even if I knew you'd never have done it if you knew the truth about me. But I don't think I'll ever get over you. I was going to ruin you for other men, make you mine and then leave, like an asshole, but—" he shakes his head, swallowing hard. "You ruined *me*, Charlotte. I'm never going to find another woman like you. And I want to tell you I'm sorry, but I can't even do that. Because the best moments of my life so far have been the ones I've spent with you. Even right now, with you pissed at me, ready to claw my face off if I say another word wrong, I'd rather be here with you than anywhere else. And *that's* the truth, Charlotte."

I stare at him as he speaks, every word battering my already broken and bruised heart. I can feel tears of disbelief and shock welling up in my eyes, and I try not to listen, but he's making sure that I have to at least hear this. And what he's saying—

No one has ever said anything like that to me before. No one has even come close. Nothing any boyfriend has ever said to me, any declaration of love—nothing has ever been like that. What Ivan is saying is the kind of thing that I'd always shrugged off as fiction. As the kind of emotion that no real person ever really has.

I want to believe him. But all the lies that came before that are too much, and too many. And what's facing me now, because of those lies, is too overwhelming.

"Even if I wanted to believe you," I say softly, "how would I even begin to know you're telling me the truth?"

And then, as he looks at me with that same wrecked, miserable expression on his face, I turn and walk out of the door of the hotel room, into the cold night outside.

8

CHARLOTTE

The cold air is bracing, and it brings me back to my senses, a little bit. I close the door behind me, not caring that I don't have the key—sooner or later, Ivan is going to come out here after me, anyway. But I need a moment alone, away from him. I need a wall between me and him, some kind of space to think about everything I've learned and what's happened.

This one day feels like it's lasted a week. It's hard for me to reconcile that twenty-four hours ago, I was in a bar with Jaz, having a drink. I still believed Ivan was who I thought he was. I didn't know Nate had been attacked. I didn't know that the Bratva was a real thing. I was going to go home, sleep off the too many drinks I had on a work night, and wake up probably a little hungover in the morning. I was going to go to work, text Ivan, and set up another date.

I never realized how quickly an entire life can shatter. Even Nate's cheating couldn't have prepared me for this. That took away a five-year relationship and forced me to reframe my plans for my romantic future, but it didn't take away my job, my home, or my friends. A sharp, bitter laugh spills out of my lips as I remember how thoroughly broken I'd felt right after that. How it had been the biggest betrayal I'd known. How it had felt like the most impactful, hurtful thing to ever happen to me.

The worst sundering of something in my life that had ever occurred. I couldn't imagine it getting worse than that.

I had no fucking idea how bad it could get.

And somehow, Ivan's lies hurt so much more. On the surface, it doesn't make sense. I had five years of memories and plans with Nate that were stripped away in an instant, but somehow, the last few weeks with Ivan being ripped away and reframed feels like a knife that's digging so much deeper. Maybe it's because nothing with Nate ever felt that profound, or meaningful—not like those few dates with Ivan did. With Nate, he always checked off my boxes, made me feel like I could cross things off the to-do list of *find a boyfriend.*

Handsome. *Check.* Polite. *Check.* Decent job. *Check.* Gets along with my friends. *Check.* Isn't controlling. *Check.*

But he didn't like going on dates with me that weren't his thing. He'd tell me to take my girlfriends instead. He didn't go out of his way to make time for me, or try new things. He didn't encourage me to be more adventurous. And he definitely didn't ever make me feel the things in bed that Ivan did.

He never said anything like what Ivan just said to me, either.

The best moments of my life so far have been the ones I've spent with you.

I squeeze my eyes shut, feeling tears drip onto my cheeks. Everything Ivan just said to me is the kind of thing that twenty-four hours ago, I'd have been thrilled to hear from him. Maybe a little shocked, because it would have felt so soon, but still—I would have believed him. I would have believed that I'd somehow been swept up in an intense, passionate, whirlwind relationship, the kind that Jaz always told me existed and that I never believed in.

Now, I don't know what to believe.

Think about your future, I tell myself firmly, scrubbing my hands over my face to wipe away the tears. How I feel about Ivan, or how he feels about me, isn't what matters any longer. Not right now, because he isn't my future. Not anymore.

The idea of wiping my old life away and starting a completely new one, with a new identity, leaving everything behind and never speaking to my friends again or going back home, makes me feel a grief so intense that it makes me feel as if I can't breathe. Like a death—and I suppose, in a way, that's exactly what it is. A death of myself, my life, my dreams, my relationships.

I can see how someone like Ivan—if he's telling me the truth *now* about his life and what it entails—would see that as a good thing. As a chance for a clean slate, a fresh start. But I can't fathom it being anything but a nightmare. A lonely, lost existence, where I have no direction and no plan.

It's the complete antithesis of how I've lived my whole life. And when I said I wanted adventure, to try to be less uptight, to try to branch out—I meant traveling to a new country as *myself*, or maybe just...going to a new restaurant without looking the menu up first. I didn't mean burning every bridge and starting completely fresh, reborn as a new person.

That feels impossible.

But what other choice do I have? I lean my elbows on the rusted railing of the balcony, burying my face in my hands. My skin feels dry and rough—without my skin care products and after the hard water of the shower this morning. I don't feel like myself. And I don't know how I'm meant to make decisions right now. I feel completely unmoored, cut loose from everything familiar.

If Ivan is telling the truth, this is the only way to escape his father. His brothers. The *Bratva*. And while a part of me thinks that he's lying, that he wants me to depend on him and him alone so that he can keep me here with him, another part of me isn't so sure.

He's said, over and over, that that wasn't his intent. That it's not what he wanted. And he's the only source of information I have on just how dangerous the Bratva are. On his claim that they're inescapable, unavoidable, unless we start fresh. That they want to do the terrible things that he's hinted at.

My only other option seems to be Agent Bradley. And while on the surface, he *should* be the person I trust, the person I should go to —I can't shake the instinctive feeling that I had from the moment I met him. That feeling had nothing to do with Ivan. It was before I even saw Nate get out of the car. Everything in me screamed that Bradley was someone I shouldn't trust. Shouldn't get in a car with, or go anywhere with.

And then there was Nate. I press my face harder in my hands, resisting the urge to scream into them. His getting involved in all of this has only convoluted it more. I think of what Ivan warned me of earlier, that if I go to Bradley, I'll also be going back to Nate, and that he'll take the humiliation Ivan inflicted on him out on me—

That feels even more unthinkable. Nate has never been violent. I never feared him, not even during that last argument, when I found out about his cheating. Even when he sent me those texts, I just ignored them, assuming it was the tantrum of a man who wasn't getting his way. I didn't fear him *hurting* me.

But I think of the satisfied look on his face when he saw me. That flicker of anger in his eyes when he looked at Ivan, and said that we'd talk about how I let Ivan touch me. I think of how I thought I knew Ivan, and how wrong I've turned out to be. Of all the horror stories women always hear of domestic violence, of women who never believed their partner would hurt them until it was too late, of boyfriends who no one saw it coming from until it happened.

I can't deny that there's a chance Ivan is right. That Nate, *after* all of this, isn't the same Nate as before. That by going to Bradley for help, I'd be putting myself in danger in more ways than one.

There's what Bradley threatened Ivan with, too. I shouldn't care, but the thought of Ivan being killed in prison or locked away in a solitary cell, makes my stomach churn. I don't know what Ivan deserves, but *that*—

Yesterday, I would have said threats like those were bluffing. That that sort of thing doesn't really happen. But now I'm no longer entirely sure. The world is a much more terrible place than I ever imagined, and I'm only just now realizing how narrowly I saw it before. How much better I thought people were than they actually are.

I can't believe that my only options are to go home, and risk being taken captive by the Bratva, to go to a man who I should be able to trust and don't think I can and throw myself on his mercy, turning Ivan in in the process, or go to Vegas with a man who has lied to me, and erase my entire life and start over. Those *can't* be my only options, and yet, they are.

I don't know what to do, and I have no one I can ask.

In the parking lot below, I think I hear the sound of a car door closing. I lean over the railing slightly before I can think better of it, and in the shadows at the far end of the parking lot, I see three figures, dressed in black clothing. They look bulky, masculine, and I shrink back, my heart suddenly racing.

They could be anyone, I tell myself, closing my eyes tightly shut for a minute. *They could just be other guys on the road, stopping for the night.* But Ivan said he had three brothers. He said they would come after us. And I know, in the part of my mind that's thinking logically through all of this even as I fight it, that three men in black clothing, moving stealthily through the parking lot, is too much of a coincidence to be that.

I bite my lip, feeling my heart start to beat faster, panic rising up thickly in my throat. I push myself away from the railing, rattling the knob on the door. I'm afraid if I knock, it will be too loud, and lead the men right to our room. I peer into the window, through the crack of the curtain, and rattle the knob again, harder this time.

The door opens a second later. Ivan's gun is in his hand, his body tense and eyes narrow, but he relaxes when he sees that it's just me. "Charlotte—"

"I think your brothers are here," I blurt out, and his eyes widen in the instant before we hear a scream downstairs, and a gunshot.

"*Shit.*" Ivan grabs my arm, yanking me into the room, slamming and locking the door behind us. "They'll be up here in a minute. *Fuck.* I thought I gave them enough false leads to buy us more time—"

"What was that?" All my anger has fled, replaced by cold fear, as I look up at him. "Ivan—"

"They must have given the hotel clerk our description. Probably got it out of him. People like that aren't built to withstand questioning from men like my brothers."

I thought I'd already run cold, but the matter-of-fact way Ivan says it makes me feel as if my blood has turned to ice. "That shot—"

"Either wounded him to get information, or killed him." Ivan is leaning around me, looking through the small gap in the curtains. He turns abruptly to face me, his hands on my upper arms as he shakes me, lightly. "Charlotte, listen. I need you to do as I say. *Everything* I say, without arguing or questioning it. Do you understand?"

I want to argue, but my self-preservation has kicked in, and I nod instead. I don't know how far I can trust Ivan any longer, and I'm beyond angry and heartbroken by his betrayals, but I'm not so foolish as to think that he's not my best shot at getting out of here alive. And right now, if those men down there really are his brothers, that tells me that at least one thing he said was true.

His brothers are after us. And what they'll do if they catch us won't be pretty.

The thought of Ivan hurt or killed, makes my chest wrench, nausea flooding me. However angry I am at him, it hasn't gone so far that I want him dead, at least. I can't imagine wanting *anyone* dead.

"There are stairs to the left and right of the balcony," Ivan says calmly. I don't know how he can be so calm, not when my insides feel like churned butter, panic rising up and on the verge of choking me. But he keeps talking, as normally as if he's giving me a grocery list. "The ones to the right are closer to our car. If my brothers are smart, and Lev can be wily, they'll block off both. We're going to go for whichever side Lev *isn't* on. He's slower than us both, and Ani and Niki will be more likely to hesitate. I feel confident I can get us both through them. Not as much as him. Okay?"

"Which one is Lev?" I manage, and Ivan winces.

"The oldest one. And the biggest. Built like a bodybuilder. You'll know. Now stay with me, Charlotte, and follow what I say."

He checks his gun, and looks at me as he lowers it to his side. Something hot and dark flickers through his gaze, and for one wild second, I think he's going to kiss me.

Either he changes his mind, or we don't have time. He goes for the door, and I stay close behind him, my heart pounding so hard that I think I'm going to be sick. I look at the bed that I didn't get a chance to sleep in, exhaustion hitting me like a wave, and I want to slide under the covers and not come out. I want to hide from all of this, and I can't.

Ivan opens the door, and steps out onto the balcony.

I follow right behind him, so close that I'm almost pressing up against him. He looks left and right, and pivots left, his gun raised.

"Ivan!" A rough, Russian-accented voice, thicker than Ivan's, calls from behind us. "Hand over the girl, and *otets* will go easier on you. She'll fetch a pretty price, even once I'm done with her."

A shudder crawls down my spine, and I fight the urge to look behind us. I see two other men coming up the stairs in the direction we're heading, the left side, and I feel certain that the voice behind us is Lev.

The other two men are built more like Ivan, lean and rangy. They both have lighter blond hair than Ivan, one nearly buzzed to his scalp and the other long, hanging in his face. They're wearing all black, guns in hand, and they pause on the stairs, blocking our way.

"Give up, Ivan," one of them says. "You got away last night, but you're not going to keep getting away. *Otets* wants you to pay for your betrayal, and what he wants, he gets. He wants the girl, too. You'll make it less painful for everyone if you come along now."

"That's right. Come along." The voice from behind us, Lev's voice, is closer now. I have a feeling they could have closed in on us by now if they wanted to, but Ivan hasn't made a move, and I think they're toying with us. Or Lev is, at least, and the other two are following orders. Lev is playing with his food.

That nausea rises up again, threatening to choke me, because I can't imagine the kind of person that does this. That revels in pain and fear. But I can *feel* it, the pleasure radiating off of him, the thrill of the hunt.

Lev whistles, like someone would for a dog. "Come on, girl. Come to me, and I'll make sure you enjoy at least some of what I do to you. Drag this out, and I'll take every one of my brother's sins out on you."

Fear spikes through me, cold and sharp, and I want to run. I want to break away from Ivan, and flee back into the room, or *anywhere*, but both exits are blocked, and Ivan made me promise to stay close. I don't know what his plan is, but he's the best chance I have.

Right now, he's the *only* chance.

It all happens so fast that I barely have time to register it at all. One minute, Lev is whistling, taunting from behind us, and then Ivan pulls the trigger, shooting as the sound explodes in my ears, and I fight against the urge to drop to the ground.

Bullets spray at his other two brothers' feet. I hear one scream as a bullet strikes him in the calf, the other shrieks as one hits his shoulder. They go toppling backward, flailing on the stairs as blood spatters, and Ivan keeps shooting as he walks, firing twice more towards them as he grabs my wrist with his other hand and hauls me forward, breaking into a run.

"*Ivan!*" Lev roars from behind us, but Ivan keeps going, dragging me along, and I don't know how I manage to stay upright as we tear down the stairs. My feet slip in the blood, and I almost go down, but some combination of Ivan holding onto me and my own determination keeps me upright.

"Don't stop," Ivan says harshly, as we bolt across the parking lot. "Get in the car, and get down."

Behind me, I hear shots. I flinch, a high-pitched sound of fear escaping from my lips before I realize I've even made it, but I keep running. For once, I don't argue. I just fling myself into the car as Ivan yanks open the door, huddling down in the seat as he leaps in next to me and hits the gas the moment the engine roars to life.

Tears are running down my face. I don't know when I started crying, or shaking all over, but I roll into a ball as tightly as I can in the seat as Ivan careens out of the parking lot, driving like a bat out of hell as he flees the motel.

I don't ask if they're following us. I don't ask if they're behind us or what happens next. I wrap my arms around my head, burying my face in the side of the seat as the movement of the car wrenches me back and forth.

For the first time since I woke up this morning, I don't fight it. I just let myself cry.

9

IVAN

The sound of Charlotte crying feels like it tears something out of my chest, but I can't think about it right now. I have to get us away. Lev will be chasing us, with Ani and Niki, and he'll run me off the road if he can catch up. He's not going to stop. I have to get us far enough away, off the beaten path, that he won't follow.

I had planned to cut a straight line across to Nevada. Four states lay between us and a new identity, and I was going to go there as fast as I could manage it. But I see now that the only chance we have is by zigzagging in a way that won't make sense, and will hopefully throw Lev off long enough for us to get to Vegas well before he does.

I also have to hope he hasn't figured out my contact yet. This man is *my* contact, not one that I've gotten through my father's connections, and that gives me hope. But only a small amount.

Using the map on my phone was a rookie mistake, one that I only did because I thought I'd thrown them off enough with fake leads that I could get a good distance away, and then stop using it. I turn the phone off, using one hand and my teeth to pry open the side that has the SIM card. I yank it out, dropping it on the floorboard and grinding it under my heel. The phone is next, and I slam my foot against it as I drive, cracking the case until the phone is in pieces.

The shattered SIM card goes out the window. The phone is next, a piece at a time. All the while, Charlotte is still in a ball next to me, shaking in the passenger's seat.

"You need to put your seatbelt on." It's far from the first thing I want to say to her—far from the *only* thing I want to say to her, but right now, it feels like the most important one. If Lev catches up to me and tries to run the car off the road, I need her to be protected.

"What?" Her voice is cracked, and I reach over, grabbing the seat belt and yanking it over her.

"Your seatbelt. Lev is coming after us. He might try to get us into a wreck."

"This is insane," she whispers. "This is all insane."

"I know." I let out a heavy sigh, pinching the bridge of my nose between my fingers.

"Why didn't they shoot us?" Her voice is tiny, small, muffled from where she's still curled in the seat, and I hate hearing her like this. I hate that it's because of me.

"He doesn't want us dead. And he wants us hurt, but not like that." I let out another heavy breath. "My brother is cocky. Arrogant. He doesn't think I can get away from him. He's just as happy to keep chasing because, in his mind, the more of a pain in the ass I make this, the more I justify every terrible thing he wants to do. And the more freedom my father will give him to do those things, if I keep making this harder."

Charlotte nods slowly. I see it out of the corner of my eye as she slowly pushes herself up, swallowing hard as she tugs on the seatbelt, adjusting it. "He's not going to stop, is he?" she says softly, and I shake my head. "You were telling the truth about that."

"And some other things." I glance in the rearview mirror, speeding up. Right now, getting pulled over is the least of my worries. "As soon as I think it's safe enough to stop for even a minute, or when we need gas next—whichever comes first—I'm going to get a road map. We're going to go up, through Wisconsin and go north, the longer way around. It'll be longer before we get to Vegas, so more dangerous in terms of time. But if we take a straight shot, and don't try to confuse Lev at all, he's just going to come after us. Same for Bradley and the feds. And we have to stop sometime. We'll need food and sleep. We can't run on empty, or we'll start making mistakes."

Charlotte is silent. It's a heavier silence than her angry one before, because I think she's coming to terms with some of this, like it or not.

I grit my teeth as I focus on the road. I didn't want to be this person for her. I didn't want to be the one to rip her rudely into the truth of a world where no one is kind and death waits around every corner. I told myself I could have her, and keep her separate from it all, and it was the stupidest thing I've ever done.

I was selfish, and now she's going to pay the price for it. The well of self-hatred in my gut is bitter, bleeding through my veins and burning in my chest. I grip the steering wheel hard as I drive, unable to look at her again.

Her silence is worse than anything she could scream at me.

I realize with a start, twenty or so minutes into the drive, that her silence is also because she's fallen asleep. The fear and adrenaline must have wrung every last bit of energy she had out of her, and I can hardly blame her. I'm exhausted, too, staying awake on sheer willpower at this point. Even the floor of that shitty hotel room is something I'm starting to look back on with a feeling of longing.

I slow to a more reasonable pace, now that there's been no headlights behind me for some time. Getting pulled over isn't the greatest of my concerns, but it *is* one of them, and it's something I'd rather not have to deal with. Being on the run from the feds is bad enough, and if they pick up our trail, they'll start alerting the local police. The last thing I want is to be on the run from the regular cops, too. That will make any kind of stops even more difficult, if they're trailing us as well.

Ironically, the only way for me to keep Charlotte from becoming an accessory to all of this, if we're caught, is to admit to kidnapping her—one of the sins I'm only *technically* guilty of, and only at first. She said so herself, to Bradley, that she doesn't feel that I did. But if the police catch us, it'll be the only way to keep her from going down with me.

Just another reason to try to keep them from ending up on our tail, too.

As the lights of another small town start to break through the night, I slow down, pulling into the first gas station I see that looks decent enough to have a road atlas. In the seat next to me, Charlotte stirs, and I hear the soft growl of her stomach. She's barely eaten today—she has to be starving, and even if she's too stressed or stubborn to admit it, her body recognizes that she needs to eat.

I'm hesitant to leave her in the car alone. Not because I think she'll run—I feel confident that, at this point, she realizes that running is fruitless. She needs me, whether she likes it or not. Whether *I* like it or not—because the truth is that if Charlotte was ever going to need me, I didn't want it to be like this.

I didn't want it to be forced on her. But that's exactly what ended up happening.

I'm honestly afraid that if I leave her out here, someone will snatch her while I'm gone, even though there hasn't been any sign of a possible tail for miles. It's irrational, but once again, I'm having a hard time being rational when it comes to Charlotte.

I don't want to wake her up, though. I watch her for a moment, before I shake myself and open the car door carefully, stepping out into the chilly night and locking it behind me. I parked right in front of the store, so I'll at least be able to keep one eye on the car while I grab what we need.

A road atlas is the first thing. I pick up one of those, glancing out towards the car every other second as I pick up some snacks and an energy drink for myself, one of those caffeine bombs that will have me buzzing all the way into tomorrow. I'll feel like shit, but it'll be worth it to put some distance between us and anyone chasing.

Beef jerky and chips for me, a couple of candy bars, and I grab a bag of air-popped crispy green beans tossed in some kind of spice for Charlotte. After her comment about the fast food, I want to give her something that she might actually want to eat. Or at least make sure she knows that I do give a shit. I add a couple of bottles of water, still obsessively checking to make sure that no one has approached the car as the cashier rings it all up.

She's still asleep when I walk back out. The sound of me setting the bag in the backseat is what finally makes her stir, and she blinks, slowly waking up for a brief second before she jolts, pushing herself up as she shoves her hair out of her face like she's just come back online and remembered what happened earlier.

"Are we—" Charlotte looks around frantically for a second, as if she's still a little bit asleep and trying to get her bearings. I know the feeling. There's a sort of liminal sensation about waking up after sleeping on the road, a feeling of being half out of reality before you come back into it. Especially out here, where there's not much civilization.

"We're fine for now," I tell her calmly. "If Lev was tailing us, he's lost us and dropped off. Not to say we won't run into trouble again, but for the moment, anyway, things are alright."

Charlotte looks at me with a slightly disbelieving expression on her face, as if she can't quite comprehend that I just said that. "Nothing is alright," she says slowly. "I'm on the run. I can't even call Jaz and let her know I'm alive. My best friend is definitely worried sick about me, and there's nothing I can do about it. My entire life has been upended, and I've been told that I'm never going to get it back, on a day that just ended with me being threatened and chased *twice*, and it isn't even over yet."

"Okay." I hold up my hands, letting out a sharp breath. "I get it. I'm sorry. I just meant—we're not in immediate danger of that happening again." I reach over the back of the seat, rummaging around in the plastic bag sitting back there. "I got snacks. Some bottled water. We're going to need to drive through the night, so—"

"Are you going to be okay doing that?" she interrupts me, then stops, seemingly as shocked as I am that she might care about my well-being. "I mean—if you run us off of the road because you fell asleep, that's not good for either of us."

I let out a dry laugh at that. I can't help it. "You're right. But I'll keep driving for as long as I can, at least."

She nods, reaching into the plastic bag. "Alright. Do we need to get gas?" She glances at the speedometer, which thankfully is off, since I haven't started the car back up yet. We don't need to get fuel, but I don't want to tell her why. I don't want to break what feels like a momentary truce between us. And I know she's not going to be happy with the answer.

"No. But we do need to get on the road." I start the car, watching out of the corner of my eye as she grabs a bottle of water and the bag of green beans. Her mouth parts slightly as she looks at them, and then at me.

"This was...thoughtful." She sounds startled, which hurts a little. "Thank you."

"Contrary to what Agent Bradley wants the FBI to believe, and contrary to what you might feel right now, I'm not *actually* abducting you." I glance sideways at her as I pull back out onto the road. "You can leave if you want. I *tried* to leave you with Bradley, for fuck's sake, before he showed his true colors. I've just told you what the consequences will likely be if you do. I'm not tying you up in the backseat and shoving fast-food cheeseburgers down your throat."

Charlotte grimaces, opening the bag. "That's not what I said."

"The point still stands." I can hear the edge in my tone, but I'm having a hard time softening it just now. I'm exhausted, vigilant to the point of feeling like my nerves are rubbed raw, and Charlotte's startlement that I bought her a healthy snack makes me feel like that knife is being twisted one time too many.

She goes quiet, except for the crunching as she slowly eats her food. I'm just glad that she's eating at all. I drive the speed limit through the small town, slowing down as I see what I am looking for.

On my left is one of those shitty buy-here-pay-here car lots. The kind that doesn't keep good records and probably has enough shady dealings of their own to not want the cops poking around too closely in their business. I pull into the dark lot, and Charlotte sits up a little straighter, dropping the bag of green beans into her lap as she looks over at me suspiciously.

"What are we doing here?"

I think she already knows the answer to that, but she wants to hear me say it out loud. "Lev's seen this car. So has Bradley. And it's fucking orange, which makes it a lot easier to pick out than, say, your run-of-the-mill silver car. So we're going to swap it out for something else."

"We're going to steal a car." Her tone is so disbelieving that it makes me laugh, because stealing a car is very far down the list of the worst things I've ever done.

"I wasn't going to use those words." I turn off our car, killing the headlights immediately. "Mostly because I knew how you'd feel about them. But yes."

Charlotte goes very still. The only sound is the crinkling of the bag between her hands as she freezes, and I let out a slow breath, searching for patience.

"We don't have a lot of time, Charlotte. I need to get this done before anyone driving around out here sees us parked here and decides to call it in, or notices and says something tomorrow when the owners open up and find a car that wasn't here before, and one gone. The idea is for it to take as long as possible for them to catch on. I can't sit here and argue with you about this. This is what we have to do.'"

Her tongue darts out, wetting her lips nervously, and I feel a jolt of unwanted arousal. This isn't the time or the place for distractions, but my body doesn't seem to be on the same page, because just that swipe of her tongue over her lower lip has me throbbing.

"Just—sit here," I tell her, forcing back my frustration with a heavy hand. "I'll handle everything. Just get in the car I tell you to when I'm done, okay?"

The space between her eyes wrinkles, an irritated line that tells me that she doesn't like me telling her what to do. Not in this context, anyway.

"Fine." She crumples the bag between her hands. "Just tell me how high to jump, Ivan."

The sarcasm in her voice is thick, but I don't have time to deal with it or evaluate it. I don't have time to make her feel better, which is what I desperately want to do.

But I also need to keep her safe. And even if that means driving a deeper wedge between us, that's what I have to do. Losing what there might have been between us is my penance for what I've done, and I'm just going to have to live with it.

I pulled into the back of the lot, as far from the office building near the front as possible. I look for the most nondescript vehicle I can—a Toyota, Honda, or Nissan in a bland color, something that there could be hundreds of on the road. When I find one—a late nineties Corolla in a beige green that makes me cringe, I quickly go about swapping out the plates. This will get us to the Dakotas, probably, at which point I'll steal something better suited to snow, in case we get a mid-autumn snowfall. And then, closer to Vegas, I'll swap back to something like this.

To her credit, Charlotte doesn't get out and try to argue with me, or run, or do anything at all. She sits stock still in the passenger's seat, statue-silent, as if by checking out of the situation entirely, she can simply not be complicit in it. She's in denial, I know that, but I'd rather deal with denial than her spitfire fury in this particular moment when time is of the essence.

The spitfire fury will come later, I'm sure, and I can't say that I hate it. The memory of her fighting with me earlier today is a strange mix of hurt, regret, and arousal that makes me feel sick and turned on all at once, a jumble of emotions that I've never experienced before. It's unique to her, and I have a feeling that it's because I feel things for her that I've never felt for any woman I've ever fucked before.

Of all the women in the world, I had to fall in love with this one. But just looking at her is enough to tell me that if I haven't fallen all the way, I'm close to the edge. My heart does a strange twist in my chest when I look at her stony face, and I have to look away quickly, refocusing on the process of hotwiring the car we're going to steal.

Once I get it to start, I back it out of the spot, getting back into our current car and pulling it into where the Corolla was parked. I grab the keys, our bag of road snacks, and do a quick sweep to make sure that there's nothing identifying left in the car—this one was mine. I hate leaving it behind, but it's yet another reason I'm glad I didn't bring the Mustang.

"I need you to follow me in this," I tell Charlotte calmly. "We're going to dump it somewhere where there's plenty of trees and it will take a while for anyone to find. By the time one of the idiots on the town police force figures out how to add, and puts this car and the stolen one together and gets us, we'll be long gone."

She looks at me like I'm the idiot. "What?" I try not to snap, but a little of the tired exasperation I'm feeling slides into my tone.

"I can't drive a stick, Ivan."

"Shit. Of course not." I run one hand through my hair. "Okay, fine. Drive the Corolla and follow me. Just drive it like normal, I'll have to detach the battery wires to turn it off."

Charlotte stares at me for another long second, and I realize what I've just asked her to do—drive a stolen vehicle, as if I were asking her to pick up milk from the grocery store. "Charlotte, I—"

"Don't say you're sorry." She holds up a hand, shaking her head. "Fine."

She slides out of the car, grabbing her bottle of water as she goes, and stomps over to the Corolla. She seems intent on letting me see just how displeased she is, but I can't exactly blame her. I'm just relieved that she's doing it.

Guilt slithers through me. The only way she's getting out of this without catching a charge herself if we get caught is by me admitting to all kinds of things I haven't actually done—like threatening her if she didn't go along with it.

That's a problem for the future, if it happens, I tell myself, starting up the Acura and putting it in gear. I see Charlotte getting into the driver's seat of the Corolla, a grim expression on her face, and I let out another sigh.

Another wedge. Another thing for her to not forgive me for. The tally is adding up, and every day that goes by is probably going to only make it worse.

There's nothing I can do about it except focus on what I *can* change.

And that's whether or not she gets out of this safely.

10

CHARLOTTE

I feel like I'm in some kind of alternate reality as I follow Ivan out of the small town that we drove through. I don't even know what it's called—I've been too distracted to look for any identifying signs. It's not as if it matters. I'm not going to run for a police station or commit any of this to memory to give someone as evidence later.

Now I'm an accessory to car theft.

The sentence keeps tumbling over and over in my head like a load of clothes in a dryer, the word *theft* the annoying buckle that keeps hitting the side. I didn't do any of the actual stealing, but I'm driving it, and I didn't do anything to stop it. If we get caught, the only thing that will get me out of this is more lies. Lies about Ivan, specifically, that even though I'm angry with him, I don't want to tell. I don't want to make up stories about him threatening me, or violently abducting me, or making me do this.

I also don't want to go to prison for stealing possibly one of the ugliest cars I've ever sat in.

I feel numb as I follow Ivan out of the town, down a street that's so dark I almost can't see the lines, until we get to a long stretch of wooded road that he pulls off of, following a trail that I don't see until the headlights are shining directly on it. Every bump jolts the car, and I wince as I follow him, rattling around until he finally comes to a stop.

He gets out, illuminated in the lights, and I hate that even now, every time I see him again, my heart jolts a little in my chest. He's unfairly gorgeous, the kind of man that I've sworn all my life didn't interest me, only to find out now that I was apparently lying to myself the whole time.

Women like bad boys, and I guess I wasn't an exception to that after all. My breath catches as he walks over to my door, tapping on the window so I can roll it down.

"Wait here," Ivan says. "I'm going to take my car a little further in, make it harder to find. I'll come right back. Turn the lights off."

I obey without a word, even though I want to argue. There's no point in arguing, other than that it would feel good, and right now, I'm not even sure that that's true. Right now, I think it might feel the way that squeezing something like a hangnail feels good—it would hurt, and make things worse in the end, for a momentary relief of pressure.

Instead, I sit there with the headlights off, the darkness all around me feeling as if it's closing in, sipping at my water bottle as if there's nothing wrong. As if it's actually *alright*, the way Ivan said earlier, which was absolutely laughable.

Nothing is alright. It might not ever be again.

I've never been afraid of the dark, and I'm grateful for that as I sit there in a strange car, waiting for Ivan to come back. I have the momentary, insane thought that maybe he's left me, that maybe he decided to abandon me here and go off on his own, but the idea feels oddly ridiculous.

Whatever lies Ivan has told, whatever awful things he's gotten me caught up in, I believe one thing. And that's that he wants to keep me close, because he believes it can keep me safe.

It's the only thing I have to hang onto right now, and that thought makes my eyes burn again, so close to tears that I lean my head back against the seat, closing them to try to stave off another wave of crying. I don't think I can take anymore. Not even on late college nights studying for exams do I remember ever having been so exhausted.

When I open my eyes again, I see Ivan walking towards me. Or at least I think it's Ivan—a dark shape moving through the trees towards my car, just a silhouette in the thin moonlight. My heart thumps in my chest for a different reason—ironic, since I was just thinking that I wasn't afraid of the dark. But there's a number of men looking for me now that could be that shape walking towards me right now.

The urge to turn on the headlights and see who it is, is strong, but I brace myself instead, ready to throw it into reverse and hit the gas if anyone other than Ivan appears out of the shadows. My hand clenches around the gearshift, my other white-knuckling the steering wheel, and I don't realize that I'm holding my breath until the shape gets close enough for me to see features—and I see that it is Ivan, after all.

He taps the window, and I open the car door, almost falling out in my hurry to get outside. The chilly evening air hits me like a slap, and as I look up at the sky briefly, I wonder what time it is. The sky has that strange light that it sometimes gets after midnight, and there's that feeling in the air when the world is still around you, and it feels like you're the only one awake in all of it.

"Charlotte." Ivan's hand touches my arm, and I almost jump out of my skin. "We need to get going."

"I—yeah." I run my hands through my hair. "I'm just tired. It's making me delusional, I think."

"I'm pretty tired, too." Ivan lets out a heavy breath. "We need to keep going for a little while. Next town we get to, we'll stop for the night. Or what's left of it, anyway."

I nod, walking around to slide into the passenger's seat. Ivan is silent as he pulls back out onto the road, turning on the headlights a moment later. The roads are empty, and he drives the speed limit, wordless, as he stares out at the road ahead of us.

I think I doze off for a little while, because before I know it, Ivan is pulling into another darkened parking lot, this time in front of an Lshaped, two-story motel that's very much like the last one we left behind. I've never stayed at a place like this in my entire life, and now I've been to two in one day.

I can't help but wonder how many more of these I'm going to see before this is all over.

I can see in the way Ivan moves that he's exhausted, that he's pushed himself harder than he should have, and I know I shouldn't care. I should be glad that he's suffering in some way, too, after what he's put me through, but I'm not.

It feels like I can't quite match up all the versions of this man, I think as I follow him to the small window where he pays cash for a room and gives the clerk fake names for us both. There's the man at Masquerade, and Venom, and the Ivan I went on dates with in Chicago, and then there's *this* Ivan, the one who I have a feeling is probably the closest version of his real self. And that's what scares me, because *this* Ivan, the one who seems to be neither bad nor good but some combination of the two, a bad boy with not quite a heart of gold, but maybe of very-tarnished silver, is a man that I sometimes like and sometimes hate—and one that I don't know if I really want to leave behind.

A man that I also want, despite everything he's done. It hasn't changed my attraction to him, which I proved in spades this morning. I want to blame him for that, but as he threw back at me earlier, I knew at least part of what I was doing when I fucked him this morning. I didn't know *all* of it, but I knew enough that I shouldn't have let it happen again.

But I won't let it happen again now, I tell myself as we walk into the small room. Ivan yanks the drapes fully shut as soon as we walk in, flicking on the light in the tiny bathroom and next to the bed on the far side, but leaving the main light off. He drops his duffel bag on the floor, moving purposefully and quickly around me as if I'm not even there, as he latches the door with the chain on the side and then drags the worn armchair next to the window in front of it, shoving it firmly up against the door.

"It won't do much if anyone finds us here and gets the room

number," he says heavily, his words slow and almost slurred with exhaustion. "But it will slow them down. Buy me a few seconds to wake up and get my gun."

The word *gun* jolts me. I watched Ivan shoot it at his own brothers earlier, but it still hasn't fully sunk in. I'd never even seen a gun in person before today, other than glimpses of them on police officers' hips. Now, the one that Ivan sets on the nightstand next to the bed is real and violent, like a snake coiled up next to where I'm going to sleep.

"Get some rest," he says quietly, walking past me again to the closet, where he folds back a door to take out an extra pillow and thin blanket. "We need to be back on the road early."

I wrap my arms around myself as I sit down on the edge of the bed, feeling cold even though the room is actually too warm, even for the autumn night. *Should I leave my clothes on to sleep?* I think as I numbly tug the blankets back, and almost laugh out loud at how ridiculous the thought is. Ivan knows parts of me more intimately than some of my actual boyfriends have gotten to know them. I've let him do things with me that I've never done with anyone else. The idea that I should sleep in my jeans because I'm mad at him is ludicrous.

Still, I can feel his eyes on me as I turn around and start to unbutton them, and the warmth that slides over my skin, banishing the chill I felt a moment ago, makes me wonder if I should have anyway. I start to tell him to look away, but that seems like it would make it worse, by acknowledging the fact that I can feel him watching me.

A tingle runs down my spine as I push my jeans over my hips, and a different feeling replaces the discomfort, a petty feeling that I let myself relish for just a second. I bend over a little as I slide my jeans off, letting his t-shirt that I'm still wearing ride up my waist, so he can see the curves of my hips and ass in my cotton panties as I kick off the jeans and bend down, reaching to pick them up off of the floor.

Behind me, Ivan is silent and unmoving, until I think I can hear him audibly swallow. I straighten, his shirt falling back down around my thighs, and I can imagine what he's thinking. How badly he wants to cross the room right now and grab me, bending me over the bed with a hand on the back of my neck as he pulls my panties to one side. As he—

I hear the sound of him shuffling, shaking out the blanket, and the fantasy breaks. Not a moment too soon, because I can feel the hot throb of arousal between my thighs, the dampness there as I yank back the covers the rest of the way and slide quickly into bed. The sheets are cold, chilling my heated skin, and I drag them all the way up to my chin, looking away from Ivan as I roll onto my side towards the window.

My face feels hot. I'm embarrassed that I let myself think about it. That I wanted that petty moment of power over him, and instead ended up just as turned on. Just as painfully aware of the fact that he's going to be sleeping inches away from me on the floor.

I feel a different kind of throb at that thought, one of guilt. Ivan is the one who is going to be driving us across several states, and he's sleeping on the floor. He shouldn't be, but I don't want to sleep on the floor either, and after this morning, there's no way we're sleeping in the same bed.

I know exactly what would happen, if we did.

11

CHARLOTTE

The thin morning light filtering between the drapes, still pale enough to let me know that it's barely late enough to actually *be* morning, comes so quickly that I wonder if I actually fell asleep. I can hear Ivan moving quietly around the room, folding up the blanket, and I wish to the depths of my soul that I could just fall back to sleep.

Better yet, that I could do that in my own bed, in my own apartment, at home where I'm safe. Where in another few hours, I'll wake up again and get dressed for work and meet Jaz before going about the same, boring day that I lamented not all that long ago.

"Charlotte." Ivan's voice is soft, but it scratches over my skin. "We have to go."

I squeeze my eyes tightly shut for a minute. The bed is uncomfortable, the duvet is stiff, and the room got cold at some point during the night, but I still don't want to get up. Somewhere behind me, though, Ivan is waiting patiently, and I force myself to roll over and sit up.

"I left out another shirt for you." Ivan points to a black t-shirt at the end of the bed. "We can stop and get different clothes soon. Once we cross over into Minnesota, anyway."

"Great. I can't wait to stop at the first TJ Maxx we come across." I know I sound like a diva, which I've never been, but apparently, not getting enough sleep isn't good for my mood. Along with the sort of abduction, being on the run from the law, threats, and car theft that I've experienced over the last twenty-four hours. "Can I at least take a shower?"

Ivan glances at the window, letting out a heavy breath. "Ten minutes."

I want to argue, but I decide to take what I can get. I head into the bathroom, locking the thin door behind me—as if Ivan couldn't come right through it if he wanted to—and turn on the hot water. The steam that the small, closet-sized bathroom quickly fills with is soothing, at least, and I strip down, eager to wash off the last day.

A little over ten minutes later, with my hair wet and all of me smelling like cheap motel soap, I put my old jeans back on and slide Ivan's t-shirt over my head. I don't bother trying to tie it up at the waist or do anything cute with it this time. I can already feel my urge to care slipping away. It's not as if anyone is going to see me except for Ivan, and he—

I swallow hard, biting my lip as I grab the small tube of travel toothpaste next to the sink and squirt some onto my finger. I don't think it matters what I wear, when it comes to Ivan. He's going to want me no matter what.

Unfortunately for me, the feeling is far too mutual.

Ivan's arms are crossed over his broad chest as I walk out of the bathroom. "That was—"

"More than ten minutes. I know." I push past him, going to shove the armchair away from the door, just for something to do. "It was fifteen, tops. I needed to do some semblance of brushing my teeth."

"We'll get some toiletries and stuff when we stop in Minnesota, too." Ivan is right behind me as I walk out into the crisp, grey morning, following me down the rusty steps out to where the Corolla is waiting. In the daylight, the color looks even worse. But it looks like a hundred other sedans being driven around to errands and school drop-offs by moms and students and other people who *aren't* in the Bratva or on the run, and I'm sure that's why Ivan picked it.

Ivan doesn't say anything as he starts the car. He's been quiet since we had to run from the hotel last night, and I can imagine why. The part I can't imagine is how it must feel to have a family that hates you so much that they try to hurt you. A family that wants to hurt Ivan in ways worse than shooting him. That want to use *me* to hurt him.

It doesn't seem like it's something new or surprising to him. He seems to be taking it in stride, but I can't help feeling that there's got to be some deeper hurt underneath it. I don't see my family all that often, and there are certainly some old wounds from things my parents did wrong as I was growing up—but I can't imagine them ever wanting to hurt me. The idea of it is unthinkable.

Ivan pulls into a fast-food place that serves breakfast, and after looking at the options, I decide a chicken biscuit seems like the least terrible of the greasy options. I ask for some strawberry jam to put on it, and I see Ivan looking at me with interest as I spread it on the inside of the biscuit, while we sit in the car in the parking lot. He's parked at the back, facing forward so we can see the entire lot, a level of paranoia that I would never have even considered until now. Now, it seems like the smart thing to do.

"What?" I ask him, a little bit crossly, as I take a bite of the biscuit. It's better than it has any right to be, and I hate that a little, after a lifetime of avoiding fast food. The coffee, on the other hand, is terrible, and I feel a wave of longing for the little coffee shop near my work that I used to stop by as a treat once or twice a week. I'll probably never go there again, if everything Ivan has told me is true, and that longing turns into that feeling that's very much like grief.

It's followed by guilt, because so many other people in the world have worse things to grieve than the loss of their favorite coffee place, and there are hundreds of coffee shops all over the world I could visit even after my life is wiped and rebooted. But that was a part of my life, my little corner of the world, and it's been ripped away from me.

Some of my anger at Ivan comes back with that thought.

He shrugs at my question. "I've just never thought of putting that on that particular food before."

"Do you eat like this often?" I can't believe that he does, given that he has plenty of money.

"No." Ivan takes a bite of his breakfast, a sausage and cheese biscuit that makes me feel faintly queasy looking at it. It's probably the stress and not the food itself, but I don't like the smell. "But I like diners. The same way I like a nice pub. Simple, unassuming, good."

I can't help but think of the Michelin restaurant we went to on our first date. "Our first date wasn't either of our preferences, was it?" I ask quietly, wiping a little bit of jam off of the corner of my mouth with my thumb, and reaching for a napkin. "It wasn't real, either."

"I wanted to impress you." Ivan sets his sandwich down, as if he's lost a little of his appetite with that question. "That was real."

"Why?"

He lets out a long, slow breath, and I can tell he doesn't have an answer. Maybe because whatever the answer would have been then, it isn't true now. Or maybe he never really knew. Maybe it was a compulsion, an obsession, just like the rest of it.

A wave of tiredness that has nothing to do with the lack of sleep washes over me, and I lose what little remains of my appetite, too. Ivan starts the car, and I crumple up the remainder of the biscuit and the wrapper, dropping them into the bag as he pulls back out onto the highway.

Halfway through the day, we stop for another fast-food lunch and fuel. I can feel the difference in how I'm eating; I feel sleepy and lethargic, and I drift off in the car after a while, the monotony of the road lulling me into sleep despite the fact that we could be being chased by the Bratva, or the FBI, or both, right now. They're not here right now, and that's enough for me to fall asleep, exhausted.

I wake up a little while later when Ivan pulls into another gas station, the slowing of the car waking me. I go in with him this time, and I feel him watching me as the clerk standing behind the counter tries to make small talk. I glance over at Ivan, wondering if he's jealous. There's nothing between us now—and there is, all at the same time. Whatever there was has been irreparably broken, not least of which because I have no idea if there was ever anything real at all, but there's still something there. For me, it's desire and anger all twisted up together, and for Ivan—

It's not jealousy that I think I see in his face, though. It looks like concern. And I don't understand it until later that evening, when we stop well after nightfall at another crappy motel, and we're behind a closed and barricaded door with another bag of greasy food.

"We're going to have to get something to dye your hair," Ivan says bluntly, without any preamble, and I'm so startled that a french fry falls out of my hand onto the carpet.

"What?"

"We need to dye your hair. I don't know what color." He frowns. "It's hard to dye hair so dark anything from a box. But we'll have to try something—"

"Are you going to dye yours?" I retort, still shocked just by the suggestion.

"My brothers know very clearly what I look like," Ivan says, crumpling up his food wrappers and dropping them in the trash. There's a heaviness to his gait as he gets up that tells me he's still exhausted, but I'm too upset to care right now. "They don't need to bother with descriptions. It's bad enough that they can get information on where we've been just by asking about me, if we're seen together. But they only know what you look like from pictures, and having briefly seen you. If we change how you look, they'll be giving people a description of a woman with me that doesn't match up. It may help throw them off."

He sighs, sitting back down. "You're beautiful, Charlotte. Men look at you. Men like that clerk today. If Lev walked into that gas station and described you, he would remember you."

"I thought you were jealous." A laugh bubbles up behind my lips, and Ivan pauses, his gaze fixed on mine in a way that sends a shiver down my spine.

"If I thought a man who could take you from me was looking at you, I'd be jealous." There's a rough edge to his voice that makes my skin tingle. "But it wasn't going to be him."

"No one can take me from you." I wrap my arms around myself, looking away. "I'm not yours."

The silence that follows tells me that Ivan doesn't entirely agree with that sentiment. How he can think I *am* his, I have no idea. Not after what's happened. But when I look up at him again, there's that same intense expression on his face, his gaze resting on me as if he's memorizing me for a day when I'll no longer be sitting here in front of him.

It should make me uncomfortable. Uneasy. But instead, it makes me feel something else—a deeper, more primal feeling that I'm afraid to look at too closely. It reminds me of that moment, just a couple of days ago, when I wondered what it would be like to have a man like Ivan love me.

The way he's looking at me now makes me wonder what it would feel like to have him *possess* me, too.

Ivan stands up. "I know you don't like it, Charlotte. Truthfully, I don't, either. But we just need to get to Vegas." He says that last as if he's repeated it many times over in his head. "After that—"

I bite my lip, still looking away. "I can't believe this," I say softly. "Every day, it's something else. Some new thing I'm just supposed to be okay with. Some other huge change that makes me feel like I'm losing my grip on what few parts of myself I have left."

Ivan looks around sharply at that, meeting my eyes again. "Charlotte." There's something like a plea in his voice, but I don't have any room to care about it right now. Not when he's the reason all of those parts are gone.

I never knew it was possible to desire someone, hate them, and care about them all at the same time. And now I wish I'd never learned.

"I need space." It sounds ridiculous, in a hotel room this small, with one bed and another closet-sized bathroom. There's nowhere for Ivan to go, and I can't imagine that he'll leave me in here alone. But to my surprise, he nods, sliding a pack of cigarettes that I've never seen him smoke before out of his pocket. It's a small indication that he's feeling as badly as I am, even though he's doing a better job of hiding it.

"Alright." He swallows hard, his throat moving. "I'll be right outside."

I blink back tears as I watch him walk out. I want to cry, but I'm worried that if I start again, I won't stop.

Instead, I go into the bathroom, and splash cold water on my face, wishing for my face soap at home that smells like watermelon, and the velvety cream on my sink. And then I toss my jeans onto the floor and slide into bed, as the faintest whiff of cigarette smoke slides into the room from outside.

—

IN THE MORNING, Ivan wakes me up a little bit later than yesterday. "So far, so good," he says tiredly, and I can't help but notice that the dark circles under his eyes look deeper today. "No sign of anyone closing in on us. Or, alternatively," he adds, as if he can't let me get too relaxed, "they're just waiting for the right time."

"So, what?" I sit up, rubbing my hands over my face. "Getting back on the road?"

"We'll stop at a store first. And somewhere for clothes. We'll get the things we need, toiletries and maybe some decent food, and—" he pauses, pressing his lips together. "Dye."

My stomach tightens at that, and I want to argue, but I don't. I know it's a stupid thing to be upset about. It's hair—it will grow out, and grow back, and whatever I put in it now will be gone eventually. But like most women, I've always been picky about my hair, and I've gone to the same stylist in Chicago since I was a freshman at Northwestern. She's always done the same thing for me, perfectly—lowlights painted on by hand, perfectly scattered throughout to make my hair look dimensional, the same cut—

The same boring thing, every ten weeks. The thought crosses my mind as I splash water on my face in the bathroom again and rub toothpaste over my teeth. The same cut and color, just like most other things in my life. A routine that I've never shaken up.

Everything around it is awful, and difficult to reconcile, but this—
Maybe box-dyeing my hair a new color isn't the worst thing.

I try to keep that sliver of positivity as Ivan and I go to the first store we find that has clothes—a Ross—and then to a Walmart to get toiletries and some food that isn't deep-fried or pre-frozen. Some cut-up fruit, some sandwiches with cold cuts, a half gallon of milk, and some cereal cups. Ivan buys one of those insulated bags to put all of it in, enough to last us a couple of days. The fruit looks so good after two days of fast food that I want to eat it in the middle of the store.

The last aisle we stop in, after getting toothbrushes and floss, some drugstore skincare products for me, and whatever else we can think of, is the one with the hair dye. I look at the rows of boxes for a long time, as Ivan picks up one that promises to turn me ash blonde.

"That's going to make my hair orange." I swallow hard, picking up a box labeled 'Cherry Cola.' "What about this."

"I don't think it's different enough." Ivan lets out a sharp breath. "Adding a little purplish-red tint isn't going to make you look like someone else."

"I could dye it blue." I laugh, picking up another box. "Semi-permanent." I have a feeling it will wash right out, but the suggestion is more to lighten the mood than anything else.

Ivan picks up a box of medium red. "This?"

"It's going to look awful. Like Ariel." I wince, turning it over to see what it says brown hair will change to. "I'm not suited to be a Disney princess."

Ivan sets the box down. "No, you're not very princess-like."

I think it's a compliment. The way he says it makes it sound like one. And I suppose this could have been so much worse, if I were the kind of woman to throw tantrums and complain. Since I yelled at him that first night, before his brothers showed up, I haven't shouted again. I will, at some point, I have a feeling—I can feel it pressing behind my ribs, all of the anger that I haven't let out because I keep thinking that it won't do any good. It won't change anything.

But it will burst out, eventually. Something will make me snap. But until then, I don't know what else to do besides keep bottling it up.

I'm definitely not a princess. I don't think I've been inside of a Walmart since I was a college freshman and it was the only place we could get snacks after one in the morning when Jaz and Zoe snuck weed outside of the dorm. I didn't smoke, of course, because it could have gotten me into trouble, so I was the one who drove us to get the snacks.

Now I wish I had. I wish I'd just done it, so I could have laughed and been silly along with them, walking up and down the aisles buying ice cream sandwiches and popcorn and taking it all back to the dorms while giggling the whole way, instead of being borderline annoyed because they were high and I was sober, and I wanted to go to bed.

I might never see either of them again, and I wish I'd taken more risks, when I had the chance.

Before I can think twice about it, I reach out and grab two boxes of the ash blonde, dumping them into the basket.

"Let's go," I tell Ivan, striding past him to the checkout line.

12

CHARLOTTE

By the time we get to the shitty motel we're spending the night at, basically a cut-out copy of the ones we've stayed in before, the bravado I had at the store has deserted me. I walk into the small bathroom with the two boxes of hair dye, look in the mirror at my thick, dark brown hair that I've so carefully taken care of all of my life, and promptly burst into tears.

A few minutes later, I hear a soft knock at the door. "Charlotte?" Ivan's voice carries through, and I wipe my hands across my face, not wanting him to know how upset I am.

"I'm fine." My voice comes out a little cracked, which makes it pretty clear that I'm *not* fine, but I don't take it back. Even if he can tell that I'm crying, I don't want to admit it.

I should say something else. I can feel Ivan on the other side of the door, waiting for something else. But I can't think of anything to say, and after a long moment, I hear him walking away.

I wipe my face again and start going through the motions. I wish I had my cell phone to put music on to distract me, or that I didn't mind Ivan watching me do this so that I could open the door and listen to whatever is on TV, but instead, I just clench my teeth and bulldoze my way through it, feeling a little dizzy from the bleach fumes halfway through. By the time it's done and I turn on the hot water to wash the first round out, I start to wonder if the combination of steam and bleach is going to fry more than just the ends of my hair. By the end of the second, I'm coughing a little bit, and my eyes are watering.

My hair feels sticky, like straw. I pour all of the conditioner that came with it into my palms, slicking my wet hair back against my scalp and running it all through, for once ignoring the 'from the ears down' advice that I've followed with conditioner my whole life. I wait ten minutes, resisting the urge to sit down on the shower floor—the tile is yellowed, and the idea of sitting naked on it makes my stomach turn a little bit—and then wash it all out.

I wrap a bathrobe around myself, get out the cheap-feeling hair dryer that's under the sink, and start to dry my hair.

There's something that feels final about this. According to Ivan, my life as I knew it is destroyed. I won't be able to go back home for a long time, if ever. Every time I remember that, I feel like a yawning pit has opened up in my chest, a feeling so dark and sad that I have to constantly yank myself away from it and not think about it for too long, or else I won't be able to keep going.

But there's something undeniably thrilling about all of it, too. If I ignore how *real* it all is, I feel that shifting adrenaline in the pit of my stomach, the hint of excitement at how *different* things suddenly are. The slumming it in motels, the cheap food, the new hair color, even the stolen car—all of it is something out of a movie, something that I'm just playing a part in, is exciting. The kind of thing I never, ever, imagined happening to me.

It's a coping mechanism, I'm well aware of that. It *is* real. It *is* happening. But I have to cope with it somehow, and if letting myself pretend that it's all temporary and feeling that thrill helps, I'm going to just have to go with it for a little while.

The reality hits again when the steam clears from the glass as I finish blow drying my hair, and I see it in the mirror for the first time.

I'm blonde. Not salon-blonde—that's impossible for a brunette to get from a box dye, but the toner I bought helps. It's not as orange as I feared. But it doesn't exactly suit my skin tone, and the bad motel lighting doesn't help. I sink my teeth into my lower lip, fighting back tears again. My hair doesn't look too damaged—I still have an expensive cut, and dried, it still looks thick and fairly shiny. But I don't look like *me*.

I feel ugly. My eyes burn again, and I hear Ivan's footsteps, just before he knocks on the door again.

"Charlotte? Did you pass out in there from the fumes? I can smell the dye out here."

I swallow hard, searching for the courage to open up the door. I can tell myself all I like that I don't care if Ivan wants me, that there should be nothing between us any longer, that it would be easier if he *didn't* want me anymore. The thought of opening the bathroom door and seeing alarm, or worse, disgust in his eyes, makes my stomach turn over, and my chest tighten.

"Charlotte. I heard the blow dryer, but I'm still worried. Can you say something?" He sounds anxious, like he genuinely cares, and I force myself to ignore it. The worst thing I could let myself believe is that Ivan actually cares about me. That he wishes he'd gone about this all differently, because he has real, genuine feelings for me.

I grab the handle of the door and shove it open, almost hitting him in the process. I cross my arms over the front of the thin bathrobe, glaring at him in a way that dares him to tell me it looks bad. But the way he's looking at me tells me in an instant that he thinks anything but.

He takes a step forward, one hand on the doorjamb as if he's afraid that I'm going to slam the door closed on him. His gaze sweeps over my face, over my hair, and I see his throat move as he swallows.

"You've always been gorgeous," he murmurs, and his hand tightens on the doorframe as if he's trying to stop himself from reaching out and touching me. "Nothing about that has changed."

"You don't have to lie." The retort comes out sharp and bitter. It would be so much easier if he was lying. If there wasn't this thick, raw feeling in the air that springs up every time one of us comes close to the other, that tells me without question that he *isn't* lying. The way he's looking at me, his blue eyes darkened, the way his muscles tense as he holds himself there in the doorway—it all tells me that he wants me as much now as he did two days ago. As much as he did last night. As much as he always has—to my ruin.

And, arguably, his as well.

"Charlotte." His voice drops, rough at the edges, sending heat washing over me. I take a step back, and he steps forward, on the verge of following me into the bathroom. Alarm flares sharply in my chest, because I know what will happen if he does. I can feel the spreading desire washing over me, and I'm painfully aware of just how little clothing I have on. The thin bathrobe is nothing. He could push me against the wall, and then—

I glance down, and I can see how hard he is, straining against the front of his jeans. He pushes away from the doorframe, reaching out to touch me, to slide his hand into my hair and pull me in—and on reflex, almost desperately, I slap his hand away, hard enough that he recoils.

In that split second, I duck under his arm, darting away from him and out of the bathroom. I shove the door as I go, and I see Ivan turn, his mouth opening, in the instant before I slam the door shut hard behind me, cutting him off.

I stand there on the other side of it, breathing hard, my arms wrapped tightly around myself. I wait for it to open, for him to burst out, to grab me, to back me up to the bed and start all over again what happened between us two days ago, when I woke up in that first hotel room.

But the door doesn't open. There's silence for a long moment, and then I hear the sound of the shower turning on, and the curtain being opened and closed. And I feel almost—disappointed.

That's ridiculous. I can't be disappointed that Ivan didn't burst out and ravish me, because that's not what I want. What I want is for him to leave me alone, for me to find a way out of this as soon as possible, and I'm getting the first part of that. I didn't tell him no, but my actions spoke pretty loudly, and he respected that.

I should be happy about it.

The other question, the one of why a man who stalked me and lied to me would suddenly start respecting my unspoken refusal, I ignore. I stand there for another few beats, listening to the sound of the shower, and then I go over to where the bags with my new-to-me clothes are sitting on the bed, pulling out a pair of jeans and a loose t-shirt that ties in the front, with a dinosaur skeleton etched on it. Not my usual style, but I get dressed, biting my lip as I look out to the balcony just outside our room.

I know Ivan wouldn't want me to go outside. But I need fresh air. Not just from breathing in bleach and dye fumes for the better part of the last hour, but because of—everything. I remember what happened the last time I left the room while Ivan was inside, and right now, he wouldn't be able to help me, while he's in the shower. But that thought isn't enough to stop me from grabbing the room key and stalking towards the door.

On the desk near it, Ivan's pack of cigarettes is sitting next to his now-useless car keys. I pause, and, on impulse, reach for the pack and his lighter, slipping one of the cigarettes free before I step out onto the balcony.

The nights are getting colder now, closing in on the end of October. I shiver a little as I lean up against the wall, looking at the slim cigarette in my fingers. I've never smoked before, and I think of my regrets earlier, about not having as much fun with my friends as I could have when I had the chance.

I flick the lighter, raise the cigarette to my lips, and take a deep breath.

The acrid scent and burning sensation instantly hit my lungs, making my chest feel tight and making me cough. Stubbornly, I take another drag, just as I hear the door open behind me.

"What the fuck are you doing?" Quick as a snake striking, Ivan snatches the cigarette out of my fingers, tossing it to the concrete and stubbing it out. "That's a shitty habit to start—"

"Don't tell me what to fucking do!" Some of that anger I've been repressing bubbles up, as acrid as the smoke still in my lungs. I go to push past him and go back into the hotel room, but Ivan shifts, blocking me in as he presses both of his hands to the wall on either side of my head, his large body looming over me.

My heart thumps, my skin prickling as Ivan looks down at me, his dark blue eyes catching mine with a promise. A promise of finishing what he started just a few minutes ago, in the bathroom.

His gaze holds mine, and I feel myself freeze, like a deer caught in headlights. And then, before I can think or move, he darts in as quickly as he knocked the cigarette from my hand, his lips covering mine.

The kiss is rough, demanding, *hard*. His mouth presses against mine, his tongue sweeping over my lower lip, pushing into my mouth as he groans. He breaks it for the briefest moment, stopping almost as quickly as he started, a ravenous hunger in his dark eyes as he looks down at me.

"You taste like me," he growls, and then he's kissing me again.

Every part of my body wants to give in. He surges against me, hot and hungry, and I feel myself arch into him for a moment, wanting it. I know how good he can make me feel, the things he can do to me, and I feel particularly susceptible to it tonight. The stress, the upheaval of my life, the changes that keep hitting me hard and fast, all of it makes me feel like I'm hovering on the edge of a precipice, and the feeling of Ivan's hot, hard body against mine makes me want to fling myself off of it, even if I know I'll have to crawl back up afterward.

"Charlotte—" He groans my name against my lips through the kiss, and I feel it vibrate against my skin. His hips press against mine, his hard length grinding into my thigh, and I'm suddenly viscerally aware of where we are—on a walkway outside of a motel room, in full view of anyone who might walk up. We're also an inch from the door that goes into our room, and the temptation to tell him to take me inside is strong. To spill me back onto that bed and let me sink for a little while into the fantasy that all of this is something I *want*. That it's just an adventure I'll wake up from eventually.

His tongue slides along my lower lip again, teasing. One of his hands is still braced against the wall next to my head, but the other drops to my hip, pushing under the fabric of my shirt to run his thumb over the strip of bare skin just above the waist of my jeans. His pace has slowed, almost savoring me now, but it still feels just as hungry. Just as desperate.

And if I give in, it will be harder to say no next time, and the time after that, and after that—all the way to Vegas, where I have to decide what my new life will look like.

How can I do that if Ivan is confusing me, distracting me, fogging me up like this?

Is that what he *wants*, to drag me under with pleasure and lust until I can't make a clear decision to leave him at the end of all of this?

The thought shoves my rising arousal aside just long enough for anger to flood in and take its place. I plant my hands against his chest, shoving him back away from me. He's bigger than me, but he's so lost in the kiss that I catch him off guard, and he stumbles back.

"Charlotte—" His eyes are dark, his mouth reddened and slightly swollen from kissing me, a look of such *need* on his face that I feel that lust threatening to sweep in again, and I almost give in. No one has ever looked at me like that. Like if he doesn't kiss me again, he'll die.

He's manipulating me. Trying to make me forget what he's done.

I shove myself away from the wall, grabbing for the key in my pocket and opening the door. "I might have to rely on you for my safety right now," I spit out, wedging myself into the room as I look at him standing there. "But you are never, *ever* going to touch me again."

I slam the door, leaving him standing out in the cold. And I feel hot, damp tears, sliding down my cheeks as I hear it shut behind me.

13

IVAN

I have the other key, so I can get back in the room. But I don't, not for several long minutes after Charlotte bolts back inside and slams the door.

For one thing, it's clear she needs space. I'd rather her be inside and me outside while she calms down, instead of the other way around. It's more dangerous to be out here, if anyone is watching. Or if anyone finds us here.

For another—I need a minute alone, too. I can still feel the need for her, throbbing through me like a demand, and it's hard to shove it down. I want her with a ferocity that feels painful.

The change in hair color didn't make her any less beautiful to me. She still looks just as gorgeous as a blonde as she did when she was a brunette. And I don't give a shit that it's not some salon-fancy job. It's not just Charlotte's looks that make me want her. It's everything about her.

And it's something intangible, too. A chemistry, a connection that I've never felt with anyone before. Even when she's angry with me, even when we're fighting, I want her more than I've ever wanted anyone in my entire life. When she slapped me in the bathroom, I swear it got me fucking hard. I had to take that shower just to cool off, so that when I came back out, I'd be able to think straight. And then I came out to see her smoking, and the thought of tasting the smoke on her lips that I've tasted in my mouth before made me so turned on I couldn't think straight.

Her yelling at me after I told her to stop didn't help, either. And I know she doesn't want me telling her what to do. But I'm not about to be the reason she picks up a bad habit like that. I've screwed up her life enough already.

I run my hands through my wet hair, feeling it snag on my fingers as I lean back against the wall, looking out to the empty parking lot. This isn't the life for someone like her. She's no princess, I meant it when I told her that earlier, and she's holding up remarkably well. But Charlotte deserves better than back road motels and fast food dinners. Better than a life spent looking over her shoulder, waiting for the hot slice of a bullet to end all of it when the shit finally catches up.

I was born into this. She wasn't. And I shouldn't keep trying to drag her down with me.

I glance back into the room, where I see the shape of her underneath the duvet, facing away from where I'm standing. She's turned off all the lights except the one small one on the other side of the bed, and my chest tightens as I wonder if it's for my benefit, or hers. If it's a small, subconscious kindness to leave a light on for me, or if it's because everything that's happened has made her afraid of the dark.

I want to crawl into that bed with her, wrap my arms around her, and let her fall asleep feeling safe. I want to be the one to make her feel that way.

But I've all but ensured I'll never be the one to make her feel that way again.

I glance down regretfully at the stubbed-out cigarette on the concrete, and I consider going in and getting one of my own. The nicotine would feel good right now. Something stronger would feel even better, but I don't have the time for that. I have to be on my guard, to keep her safe.

To make sure no one else hurts her.

With a heavy sigh, I reach for the key and walk quietly into the room, doing my best not to wake her. As I reach out to turn off the light, I take one long, lingering look at her face, soft and beautiful as she sleeps.

Even with the badly dyed blonde hair.

—

CHARLOTTE IS BACK to giving me the silent treatment when we leave the motel in the morning. Her hair is in a messy bun atop her head, and I have to fight the urge to reach out and run my fingers down the back of her neck, where I know her skin feels like silk. Even harder is resisting the urge to wrap my fingers around the nape of it, pull her towards me, and kiss her like I did last night.

She's a constant temptation. A penance for everything I've done. And as we head down the highway in silence, I try to think about Vegas. About my contact. About what I'll do after this.

Anything other than how much I want to touch her.

The routine is the same. Gas station stops and long stretches of silent highway. We have better food today, thanks to our grocery store run, and I can tell Charlotte is happy to have some fruit and something not cooked in grease. Seeing the smile on her face when she eats a handful of strawberries makes me feel like I'd rob an entire grocery store blind, if that's what I needed to do to keep her smiling like that. It's the first time I've seen her smile since I took her from her apartment.

It makes me feel like I'd give anything to be the one who makes her happy.

That feeling persists as we drive through Minnesota, every time I glance over at her. She watches as the landscape changes as we drive into South Dakota, and I see her sit up a little, her eyes widening at the spray of color across the trees.

"I love fall," she says softly, and then she laughs, a sound that's as ironic as it is bitter.

"What?" I look at her curiously, and she laughs again.

"Every year, for as long as I can remember, I told myself I'd get out of the city this time of year and go on a road trip. Somewhere remote, where I could look at the leaves and nature and just have some quiet for a little while. I thought about conning Jaz and Zoe and Sarah into going with me, or sometimes I thought about just going alone." That laugh again, the irony thicker now. "I never once thought about asking Nate along. And now look at me. On a fall road trip with a man who conned *me* into it."

There's that stab of pain in my chest, harsher this time. It hurts more and more when she says things like that, with every passing day, and I know why. It's because, with every one of those days, I'm falling more and more for her—and also losing her, all at the same time.

But I think I have an idea of how to make her smile again. Just for a minute.

I don't say anything about it. I just wait until we're well into our drive for the day, and then spread out the atlas on my lap again, looking for the roads I'll need to take. Charlotte says nothing as I take an exit, probably assuming we're stopping for gas or food or headed for some out-of-the-way motel that will help shield us from my brothers and the FBI—provided they haven't figured out that we're going to Vegas and just headed straight there to ambush us. Which, ordinarily, would be correct.

But this time, I keep driving. Further out, towards one of the national parks I've been to before. The landscape changes, wilder, but still full of color, emblazoned with the reds and yellows, and oranges of fall. I turn onto a small side road and park in a tiny, barely-graveled lot, getting out to unhook the wires so the car will shut off.

Charlotte is watching me warily from inside the car. Her gaze keeps flicking from me to her surroundings and back again, and I can't help but wonder what she's thinking. I don't think it's anything good, and I feel that jab of pain in my chest again.

I open up her door. Her hands are clenched in her lap, and I hold out one of mine. "Come take a walk with me?"

One of Charlotte's eyebrows rise, slowly, but she gets out of the car without taking my hand. She walks past me, towards the thin trail that's just barely visible, and then pauses, looking back at me. "Are there bears out here?" She sounds uncertain, glancing at the path and the brightly-colored woods.

"Actually, not really. Not many of them out here any longer."

"But there's got to be some predators, right?" She looks at me for a moment too long, and I have an uncomfortable feeling that it's a jab at me. "Is this safe?"

"There's some snakes and mountain lions. But I've got a gun." I pat my hip. "I won't let anything happen to you."

"Mountain lions?" Charlotte pales slightly, and I walk towards her, resisting the urge to touch her. I want to, badly, but I have a feeling it would upset her, and I don't want that. I want this moment that I've arranged with her as badly as I want to give it to her.

"You kept saying, every time we were out together, how you wanted to be more spontaneous. Less worried about the danger of things. Less of someone who needed to plan and think about every outcome."

I wait for her to say *and look where that got me*. But instead, she bites her lip, and nods.

"Alright."

I haven't forgotten when we went walking together before, when she still didn't know any of the truths about who I am. When she hinted that she wanted me to push her up against a tree and have her there, and I told her that wasn't going to be our first time. But I don't make any allusions to that now, even though the thought hangs in my head—all of the things that I still so badly want to do to her. I don't want her thinking about all of that right now. If she's going to think about anything at all, I want her to think about what could be, not what was.

It's a beautiful walk. The air is crisp and cool, and not far into it, Charlotte shrugs on the denim jacket that she bought on our little shopping trip. I see her hand twitch once, as if she's on the verge of reaching for mine and stops herself, and I try not to think about what it would feel like if she actually had reached out to hold my hand. What that would mean.

"Is it really a good idea for us to be out just walking like this?" A chilly wind whips past us, and Charlotte pushes a lock of hair behind her ear. "We're on the run, right? Shouldn't we be, you know —*running* until we absolutely have to stop for the night?"

"We're pretty far out. And I don't think they'd expect me to take this route. As far as my family knows, I prefer the city to being out in the woods like this, but they don't know me that well. But then again, Lev can be crafty, when he takes the time to rub all of his brain cells together. So maybe he would think for me to take this route, because he'd think that maybe I'd do the opposite of what he'd expect. But either way—" I run a hand through my hair, sucking in a deep lungful of the crisp, clear air. "There's been no signs of anyone tailing us for a good bit. So I thought it'd be alright for us to take a little break."

Charlotte nods, shoving her hands into her pockets as we walk. "Did you just pick a random spot?" she asks, and I shake my head.

"I've been up here before. Maybe five-ish years ago, a little more now, even. When my family's shit started to get to be too much for me the first time, I realized that I didn't want to be a part of them for the rest of my life. Doing the things they asked of me for the rest of it. I took off on my own for a week or so, drove the Mustang up here in the summer, and spent some time just thinking. I did actually see a mountain lion," I add with a chuckle. "Scared it off."

Charlotte snorts at that, and I realize she doesn't believe me. "You *scared* off a mountain lion?"

I shrug. "I shot at it."

"You didn't just shoot it?"

"Why kill it if I didn't have to?" I shrug again, looking away so that she doesn't see the expression on my face, and I hope she doesn't try to dig much deeper. She knows enough about the worst parts of me, and not enough about the best. I don't want her to know that the reason I didn't want to shoot that mountain lion, no matter how deadly, was because I do enough killing in my day-to-day life. I didn't want to kill something that didn't need to die. Especially not when I was the one invading its space.

Charlotte looks pensive at that, as we keep walking. "So you've been here before. Where are we going?"

"Patience." I give her a crooked smile. "Just wait. We'll be there in a minute."

She looks at me sideways, but keeps walking. A few minutes later, we round a copse of trees, and come out to the view of a huge, glassy lake, fringed by more vibrant trees, reflected in the shimmering lake. I stop, shoving my hands into my jacket pockets as I look out at it, feeling the same way I did five years ago when I came up here. A feeling that, ever so briefly, a weight has been lifted off of my shoulders.

"This is beautiful," Charlotte says softly.

"Isn't it?" There's barely half an arm's length between us, but it feels like a gulf. I want so badly to reach out and put my arm around her waist, to pull her to me. "Sometimes I think I could stay out here forever."

"Why haven't you?" She glances over at me, and I see a hint of curiosity in her eyes.

"It's not far enough." I clench my hands in my pockets, wondering how much of this I really want to tell her. "They'd come after me. Three states away? Might as well just walk up to my father and tell him to his face that I'm walking out on the family business. It'd do me as much good when it comes to what he'd do to me." I shake my head. "I'll have to run a lot farther than South Dakota to get away from my father."

Charlotte lets out a slow breath. "That's awful," she says quietly, and the hint of sympathy in her voice is something I want to grab onto and hold, this small glimpse of her feeling something softer for me. "I'm sorry your family is—what they are."

"I was born into it." I shrug. "I've made some bad choices of my own, Charlotte, there's no doubt about that. But I didn't choose that part of it. And I want to get out. And I—"

The words stick in my throat. I should tell her that I'm sorry I dragged her down with me. But I don't want to lie to her. I wish that it hadn't turned out like this—but I can't feel sorry for the time I've gotten with her.

"We should probably head back." Charlotte shifts next to me. "Unless you actually brought me out here to get rid of me and leave my body in the woods."

She's joking, but I feel cold wash through my veins at the thought of anything happening to her. "I would never hurt you." I turn to look at her, my expression serious. "I would never hurt you, and as long as I have anything to do with it, I'll do everything in my power to make sure no one else does, either."

Charlotte laughs softly. "I was joking. But you did want to *pretend* to hurt me, at least. Remember what you told me as Venom? About chasing me through the apple orchard in a mask, and pinning me down in the dirt?"

My entire body tightens. I *do* remember, and it's a memory that's half pleasurable, half one that I hate, because it's a reminder that my relationship with Charlotte started with lies. "This isn't exactly an apple orchard."

"No, but you *could* chase me through the woods." She smirks at me, and I can't tell if she's being serious, or teasing. Either way, it isn't funny. Not to me. Not when I feel like this is some way of her testing me, using the fantasies we shared with each other at one point as a way to dig that knife in deeper.

"I don't want to talk about that." I turn away from her, glancing back up the path. I might not want to talk about those fantasies, but my body is aching at the thought, my cock stiff in my jeans just from the memory of that conversation with Charlotte.

She's quiet behind me. I start to walk, and I hear the rustling as she follows me, catching up on the path. I can feel my nails biting into my palms, where my hands are still shoved in my jacket, as I fight the urge to touch her. Sometimes I think I can still taste her on my lips from kissing her at the motel, right after she stole my cigarette.

Sweet and acrid all at once, just like this thing between us. Something I want so desperately, something that has felt like, every moment, that it's the only good thing I've ever really had.

And I can feel her using it as a weapon. Turning it back on me, to remind me that it was all strung together on a web of lies, one that she wants to punish me for.

I deserve it. That thought rattles around in my head, the entire walk back to the car, the autumn color somehow dulled by the fact that we're leaving this place. I wish I could stay here forever. I wish I could stay here with *her*.

But I've hurt her, and now she wants to hurt me in return.

14

IVAN

Not wanting to talk about those old fantasies, not wanting to remind her of the fact that I lied to her and pretended to be someone else, doesn't mean I'm not turned on by the memory. The tension between us is thick as we drive back to the motel, and the churning emotion in my gut is difficult to grapple with.

I'm upset that she shattered what was a tender moment between us because she's afraid to let herself give a shit about me. Because she's scared of what will happen if she lets herself admit that she still feels something for me, even if she's rightfully angry as hell with me, too. I'm frustrated that we can't try to figure out what this is, because of all the ways I've fucked up in the past. And I'm so painfully, achingly turned on that I can't begin to sort all of that out.

The minute we're back at the motel, and in our room, I stride to the small bathroom, closing the door and feverishly yanking open the front of my jeans. I let out a sharp hiss of breath through my teeth as my hand wraps around my cock, the feeling of my palm against the straining flesh, not the pleasure I want, but still pleasure nonetheless.

I grip the side of the sink with one hand as I stroke my other down my length, not bothering with anything to lube it. I need to come more than I need anything else right now. I need to be able to think straight.

If it were anyone else, I'd be able to think. To focus on what needs to be done, rather than how badly I want to just take Charlotte and run as far as possible, across state and country lines, to another continent, another fucking *world* if I could, just to keep her safe.

And, if I'm really being honest—just to *keep* her.

What I'm doing right now isn't about pleasure. It's about clearing my head, salving a need, like eating or drinking, because Charlotte drives me to the point of distraction. I just need to come, and I grit my teeth, so focused on getting there that I don't hear the door open until it's too late.

"Oh." The soft, startled sound of Charlotte's voice almost tips me over the edge, just hearing it. The only thing that stops me is the shock of hearing her there, enough to pull me back from the precipice. I half turn away from her, my hand still gripping my cock as if I can't pull it free, heat rushing up my neck.

"I—" I don't know what to say. *I'll be done in a minute? Knock next time? God, let me fuck you, please, because it's all I can think about?*

But I don't just want to fuck her. What I want is so much more than that. And what I want, she won't give me.

To my utter shock, she doesn't leave. She steps into the bathroom instead, closing the door behind her as she looks at me, her eyes wide and full of something I can't quite read.

"That first time I chatted with you online." Her tongue darts out, trailing over her lower lip, and my cock throbs in my fist. I should let go, tuck myself away, and put an end to this before it goes somewhere that isn't good for either of us. But my fist stays clenched, like I touched an electric wire and froze there, and I stare at her, my heart slamming against my ribs. I thought she would leave it alone, after I didn't buy into her efforts to bring this up by the lake, but it seems she's bound and determined to reopen it all. And right now, my willpower to resist is failing.

"You told me about a fantasy. About sneaking into my apartment and waiting for me. Telling me to get on my knees for you, because I'd made you wait all day." Her gaze flicks down to my stiff cock, still clenched in my fingers. "That's because of me, isn't it?"

I swallow hard, a strange feeling that I'm going to laugh, tightening my throat. "No one's made me hard other than you since the night I met you, Charlotte." The words come out taut, rough, scraping past my lips. "Every time this happens, it's because of you."

Her tongue darts out again, and I feel the dampness of my precum against my fingertips as my cock throbs again at the sight, begging me to start stroking again. To finish what I started. But I can't move. I'm too transfixed by what's happening in front of me, knowing that I should put a stop to this and desperately wanting it all at the same time.

"Tell me to get on my knees," she says softly. "Tell me to take care of it for you. Tell me to—"

"To suck my cock?" My voice is hoarse, rasping, thick with desire, and a touch of anger that burns up through the lust. "Why, Charlotte? So you can hate me more, for telling you to do something that you said we wouldn't do again? So you can put more distance between us? So you can remind me that this all started with a lie, and reduce it down to just a cold, sexual relationship that doesn't mean anything else?"

She flinches with every word, standing there against the door, and every fiber of my body feels like it's trembling with a mixture of lust and frustration bordering on anger. "You don't want me?" she whispers, and I grit my teeth, staring at her like she's lost her mind.

"Charlotte, I want you so badly I can barely fucking breathe. I'm in here right now because I want you so much I can't think, and I *need* to think, so I can keep us safe." I let out another sharp, frustrated breath, a corner of my mind marveling at the same time that I'm still so fucking turned on. It's as if my body isn't getting the message that Charlotte and I are arguing right now. That she's—I don't even know. Hates me so much, maybe, that she's found a different way to hurt me by turning what I want against me.

And I'm so fucking close to just saying *fuck it*, and giving in.

"Do you know how many times I've imagined that?" I growl, staring at her. "You on your knees, your pretty lips wrapped around my cock. I've gotten to feel it *once*, and I'm going to dream about it for the rest of my fucking life."

"So tell me to do it." She tips her chin up, returning my stare. "Tell me to get on my knees for you, and I'll let you come in my mouth. I'll even swallow." A small, taunting smile curves the corners of her lips, and I stare at her, trying to understand what she's doing here. This is some kind of punishment; I feel sure of it. Some way for her to get me back. And I also feel almost certain that she's trying to throw up walls between us by doing this. By reminding me of how this started. Just lies and sex.

"This is what you wanted, isn't it?" She pushes herself away from the door, stepping closer to me. I can smell her skin, clean and soft and warm, without any of the lotions or perfume she used to wear. Just her, and it's enough to make me feel half-insane with desire. "You lied for this. Made up an entire other persona for this. Tricked me and got close to me for this." She inches closer with every word, honey laced with acid, and all the while, my cock is throbbing against my palm as if there's anything about this that should turn me on.

I can't stop wanting her, even when I'm angry with her. Even when she's angry with me. It's an obsession, an addiction, and no matter how much this conversation should do the opposite of make me want her more, taking the lash of her tongue just seems to make me ache for her even more.

"So make it worth it," she whispers, so close now that she's almost brushing against me. "Tell me to get on my knees, Ivan. After all of this, shouldn't you at least get what you wanted out of it?"

Her hand wraps around mine, her fingers brushing my cock, and I'm lost. The sensation of her fingertips between mine, pressing against the hot, straining flesh, is enough to snap whatever self-control I have left. I should tell her that this isn't what I want, that this isn't what I did it for, that even if it started out that way, what I want from her has become so much more. That just having her mouth around my cock is so far from being enough that it's laughable.

But her fingers stroke against me, her lips dripping the kind of temptation that I've become so, so weak to with her, and I feel my other hand reaching up to slide into her hair, tugging her head back so that she's looking up at me.

"Fine. You want my cock in your mouth so badly that you have to taunt me for it, Charlotte? Get on your knees and suck it."

She drops like a shot, down on her knees on the tile, and I know I've given *her* what she wants instead of the other way around. Another reason to believe I'm nothing but the deviant who lied to her, who wants her body and nothing else, who would ruin her life just for a chance to ruin *her*. And while that might once have been true, I'm not giving her a reason right now to think that it no longer is.

But I also *can't* think right now. Not when she's yanking a hair tie off her wrist, piling her now-blonde hair up on her head and wrapping that black elastic around it, baring her neck for me to wrap my fingers around the back of it. Not when her full lips part, and she pushes my hand away, wrapping hers around the base of my cock as she leans in to brush her lips over the head of it.

A shudder runs down my spine at that light touch. *God*, it feels so fucking good. Just that—the softness of her lips pressed against the tip, her warm breath against my sensitive skin, the promise of her tongue touching me. My hips arch forward, pushing myself between her lips, and she slides them over the head of my cock, sucking hard enough to make my eyes roll back in my head before she slides back and releases me with a sharp *pop*.

"Tell me what you want," she breathes, her fingers rubbing along the thick, throbbing veins in my shaft. "Tell me how you want me to suck it, Ivan."

Stop this. You should stop her. The thought rattles around in the back of my head, but I can't think clearly enough, not past the sensation of her fingers around me and her lips sliding over my cockhead again, her tongue flicking out to tease the underside.

"Like that," I gasp hoarsely. "God, you're already so fucking good at it. Like you know what I want. Just like that, baby. *Fuck*—"

Her lips slide over me again, hot and tight, taking me in over her wet, warm tongue. I feel her wrap it around me, sliding over my length, her lips tightening as she moves down and my tip pushes into the back of her throat.

She looks up at me, eyes wide, and I swallow hard, one hand reaching out to grab the edge of the sink. My knees feel weak, my entire world narrowed down to the eight stiff inches between her lips, and how fucking good her mouth feels on me.

"Don't stop. Don't fucking stop." I press my fingers tighter around the back of her neck, and I feel her shudder. I feel her *moan* around my cock, and that's what sends me over the edge.

I don't have time to warn her. I feel myself go stiff, that heat unfurling at the base of my spine as my balls tighten, and my knees nearly buckle as the pleasure bursts through me with the force of an explosion. I feel my cum spurt out over her tongue, feel her take me deeper as her throat tightens around me, my cock throbbing in her mouth with every jolt of white-hot sensation. She sucks, hard, and I moan helplessly as she swallows it all down, trembling as I feel myself spill into her mouth.

She looks up at me, eyes wide and damp as she swallows every drop of my cum, and then she pulls back, her tongue sliding over the too-sensitive flesh and making me shudder as she lets go of me.

I feel almost dizzy as the pleasure ebbs, the desire to sink down and collapse, washing over me. It feels like relief, like I could sleep for a week now, but I see Charlotte wipe her mouth with the back of her hand, an action that's so blatantly filthy that it's arousing in and of itself, and as she starts to get up I know exactly what she's about to do.

She thinks she can back me into a corner, tempt me into telling her to suck me off so she can put more distance between us, so she can tell herself that I'm nothing but the man who lied to her to get her to fuck him and then leave. But I'm not going to let her do that.

If she's going to make me face the darkest parts of myself, I'm going to do the same thing to her.

As she gets up and turns to leave, my hand shoots out, and I grab her wrist, yanking her back.

"Where do you think you're going?"

15

CHARLOTTE

I can still taste him on my lips, thick and salty, as Ivan yanks me back from the door and into his arms, holding me against his chest with one arm as his other hand slides around the back of my neck. His eyes bore into mine, hard and lustful and angry, and his fingers tighten around my nape as his mouth comes crashing down onto mine.

The feeling of him gripping my neck jolts through me, heat blossoming through every inch of my body as he turns me sharply, pressing me back against the sink. His tongue pushes between my lips, forcing itself into my mouth roughly, as if he doesn't care that I just swallowed his cum. As if all he wants is to taste me, even if it means tasting himself, too.

I can feel myself starting to tremble as he kisses me, his tongue sweeping through my mouth, his body pinning me to the sink. He knew what I was doing from the moment I told him to tell me to get on my knees. He knows me too well, better than he should, and *maybe*, I think as Ivan devours my mouth, making me moan as he nips at my bottom lip, *maybe it's because whatever dark part of him sought me out is in me, too. Maybe that's why I went looking for what I found, in the first place.*

He was right in saying that I was trying to put distance between us. I was doing the same thing earlier, too, when I broke up what could have been a sweet moment by reminding him of Venom. I don't want to care for this man. I don't want to feel more for him, when he's stripped so much away from me. When he's so fucking confusing that I don't know if I hate him or if I'm falling in love with him, because the man who ruined my life also seems like a man who wants to be *good*.

I wanted to reduce him back to that. Someone who just wanted me for sex. Who didn't care if he ruined my life in the process. But by doing that, by pushing him over that edge, I just reminded myself of how much I want him, too.

His thick, rasping voice telling me to get on my knees turned me on. His hand on my neck made me ache, made me wet while I knelt there, and gave him every bit of pleasure I could imagine how to give. And when I made him moan, when I felt him come in my mouth, that momentary feeling of power, of *lust* was so good that I wanted to keep going. To beg him to give me what I just gave him.

So I tried to run, and like every other time I've tried to run from him, he wouldn't let me.

And now, he's going to make me admit what I want, just like I did to him.

Ivan runs his tongue over my lip again, teeth grazing over it before he pulls back. "You made me tell you what I wanted," he growls, his hand holding me firmly in place. "So you're going to do the same thing, Charlotte. Don't think you're going to get away with reminding me of the things I fantasized about, and then not have to do the same."

He spins me around so that I'm facing the mirror, and the look on his face sends a shiver down my spine. The hand not on my neck slides down my back, over my shirt, down to the edge of my hip. "You wanted to make me come and then walk away. To pretend that you could reduce me down to my basest desires and pretend that you have none of your own. But when I pull your jeans down, Charlotte, I know what I'm going to find." His hand slides around to the button in front, thumbing it loose as his fingers rest against the zipper. "Are you wet, *milaya*? Are you going to try to tell me that you're not dripping for me?"

I sink my teeth into my lower lip, refusing to answer. Wanting to find out what he'll do. This is one of the games we played, too, when he was Venom, and I was his dove. A game of asking what he'd do if I fought him. How he'd punish me. And that dark, secret part of myself wants to find out.

What if I stopped being ashamed of it? What if I admitted that I want Ivan, the bad and the good, the liar and the romantic, the devil and the angel? What if—

He slides down the zipper, slowly, teasing me. His gaze holds mine in the mirror the entire time, taunting me the way I taunted him.

"You're going to watch me while I make you come, Charlotte. And you're going to tell me how much you want it while I do it. Now answer me. Are you wet for me?"

I shake my head stubbornly, silently, and I hear Ivan's dark, rasping chuckle behind me as he yanks my zipper down.

His hands slide over my hips, broad palms gripping me for a moment before he grabs the waist of my jeans and panties together and yanks them down, all the way to my knees. One hand rests against the back of my neck again, fingers rubbing almost soothingly before he wraps them around my nape.

"Hold onto the sides of the sink, Charlotte," he murmurs, his voice silky, full of a promise and a threat all at once. "Don't let go, or this will be so much worse for you."

A shudder runs down my spine as I obey, my teeth still sunk into my lower lip, my fingers curling around the cool edges of the counter as Ivan slides my shirt up, so that the lower part of my back, all the way down to my bare ass, is visible. I can feel the cool air of the room on my legs, between them, and I let out a whimper as his fingers trail down my spine.

I want this. I can pretend that I don't; I can tell him not to touch me, but I can't help but think that some small part of me knew this would happen when I walked out of the room. That Ivan isn't the kind of man who would let me go down on him and then not return the favor. That he would let me walk out without admitting that I have desires of my own.

"I've been thinking about this wet pussy since that first morning in the hotel," Ivan murmurs, his fingers drifting down further, his palm resting against the curve of my ass briefly. "But you're insisting you're not wet for me, *milaya*. So let's find out."

It takes everything in me not to moan when he dips two fingers between my legs, sliding them deftly between my folds and up to my clit, through the sopping mess of my arousal. I'm drenched, so wet that I can feel it, and Ivan groans as he rubs his two fingers back and forth over my swollen clit, a dark chuckle following.

"You're drenched for me. Just like I knew you would be. My pretty little slut, getting so wet from my cock in her mouth. Such a good girl." He rubs his fingers back and forth again, the pleasure nearly making my knees buckle, and I clench my teeth against a moan.

"But you're a bad girl too, aren't you, Charlotte?" He scissors his fingers around my clit, still rubbing, but now it's not nearly enough. Now I can feel the swollen flesh aching, wanting more direct contact, and I grip the sink so hard it bites into my palms, trying not to buck into his touch. Not to let him know how much I want it.

"You lied to me. Lied about how wet you are. And now you're depriving me of hearing those pretty moans of yours. Holding yourself still so you can pretend you aren't dying for me to finger you until you come, lick your pussy until you drench my mouth, and then fuck you with my cock until you scream."

His hand drops away from my pussy, and *that* makes me want to scream. I squeeze my thighs together, desperate for friction, and let out a sudden, startled yelp when I feel the hot sting of Ivan's palm against the back of my thigh.

"You want to revisit fantasies we talked about, *dove?*" He slaps my thigh again, not hard enough to hurt, but hard enough to sting. "I remember the one about punishment. What I'd do if you lied to me about how much you wanted me, dove. So now, I think it's time we talk about that one."

A shudder ripples through me as his hand slides up, palming the side of my ass again. "I can feel you trembling. And maybe it's fear, maybe a little—but it's desire, too. You want this. You wanted it when we talked about it, late at night, when you thought I was a faceless man you'd never have to see. But that wasn't a lie, was it, Charlotte? That you wanted me to spank you until you were dripping down your thighs, until you'd be a good girl for me again? And it wasn't a lie that I wanted to do it."

I barely have a moment to brace myself before his hand comes down on my ass, hard enough to burn. "Spread your legs for me, dove. As wide as you can." His hand comes down again, on the other side, with a sharp *crack* as I hesitate. "I want to see your pussy getting wetter for me while I spank you. I want to see how much you like your punishment." Another slap, this one harder, and a helpless whimper slips from my lips, through my clenched teeth. "*Charlotte.*"

I can't help it. The burn spreads through me, melting into a heated need that has me moving my legs apart, spreading open for him so that he can see the most intimate parts of me, swollen and dripping and aching for him. His hand comes down again, two sharp spanks, and I moan, my head dropping forward as I feel his fingers tighten around my neck.

"*Fuck*, little dove—" Ivan groans as he brings his hand down again, and then slides it between my thighs, finding that I'm even more drenched than I was before. "*God*, you get me so fucking hard."

His fingers dip into me, two fingers pressing deeply inside as I clench around him, moaning helplessly. "Look at me," he growls, his fingers wrapping in my hair and tugging. "Watch me while I make you come, Charlotte."

I look up, his eyes are wide and glazed with desire, and the ferocity of the lust on his face makes me clench around his fingers, my entire body trembling as I arch into his hand. I need to come, and everything else fades into the background as I rock backward onto his hand, watching him as he lets go of my neck and slides his other hand beneath me to play with my clit as he keeps fingering me.

"Come for me, little dove," he growls. "I can feel how much you need it. Let yourself come for me."

I couldn't stop myself even if I still wanted to. Yelling heatedly at him that he'd never touch me again feels like it happened in some other lifetime, some other *universe*. My world has narrowed down to the feeling of his fingers thrusting inside of me, curling, the roll of his rough fingertips over my clit, the way his dark blue eyes hold mine in the mirror the entire time, watching me as he pushes me over the edge.

"Don't look away," he growls, as he feels me tense. "Eyes on me, dove. Watch me while you come. Or I'll spank that pretty ass until you're too sore to sit down for the rest of the trip."

The orgasm hits me, pleasure tightening every muscle in my body, sparking through my veins, made a thousand times more intense by the fact that I'm looking into his eyes the entire time, watching him in the mirror as I shake and moan, rocked with sensation as I cling to the countertop for dear life.

Ivan groans, and I feel both of his hands on my hips as he drops to his knees behind me, and I feel the sudden hot slide of his tongue between my legs before I've even fully come down from my first orgasm. I gasp, my knees nearly buckling, and he pushes me forward against the counter, holding me there as his tongue lashes mercilessly over my sensitive flesh.

It's the hottest thing I've ever experienced. No one has ever gone down on me like this before, almost as if it's wholly for *his* pleasure and not mine, as if he's so desperate for the taste of me that he can't stop himself from devouring me. His tongue curls against my clit, rubbing, licking, and I let out a cry that's something between a moan and a shriek as I feel a second orgasm building, crashing over me like a wave that drags me under, gasping and nearly collapsing even with Ivan's hands holding me up.

He pushes himself up, and when I look up in the mirror, his gaze is dark and hungry, his mouth still wet from me. I feel the hot, heavy press of his rock-hard cock against my lower back, and then I feel him angle it down, sliding the swollen head through my dripping folds.

"I'm so fucking hard," he growls. "Like I didn't just come in your mouth ten minutes ago. Like I haven't come in fucking months. That's how much you turn me on, Charlotte. How much I fucking want you."

He rubs his cockhead against my pussy, down between my folds, over my clit, and up again, and I moan, arching backward. I've forgotten I hate him, forgotten he lied, forgotten everything about how badly I want that thick, hard length filling me up, how much I want him to fuck me with it, to come all over it—

Ivan laughs, that dark, rasping sound again. "You want my cock so badly, don't you, dove?" He pushes against my entrance, not enough to slip inside, and when I arch back to take him in, he pulls back.

"Oh no, little dove." He rubs himself against me again, teeth gritted as if it's taking everything in him not to thrust into me. "I just wanted to give you a taste. To remind you what my cock feels like. But the next time I fuck you, Charlotte, it's going to be because you want *me* to fuck you. Not this fantasy that you want to hide behind."

He steps back abruptly, shoving his erection—still glistening with my arousal—back into his jeans. And then without another word, his jaw clenched, he stalks out of the bathroom and slams the door.

—

WE BARELY SAY a word to each other for the rest of the night. In the wake of those two violent orgasms, I feel drained and embarrassed at how he left me. Angry, hurt, and other emotions that I can't even begin to put a name to.

I shower and get dressed again. Ivan is out on the walkway, and I ignore him, getting the last of the food we bought out of the insulated bag. I don't bother to ask him if he wants any, and I don't see him eat. He stays outside for a long time, until I turn off the lights and crawl into bed.

I don't fall asleep easily. I pretend, listening to the sounds of him making up the bed on the floor, and I feel a flicker of guilt again that he's sleeping down there when he's the one who drives all day. I think of him taking me out to the lake, how it clearly meant something to him.

I can't care about him. I can't. He lied to me. He destroyed my life. I bite my lip, closing my eyes as I focus on those last two things. Not the man who, in so many quieter moments, seems like someone I could love. Not the man who gives me pleasure that I never imagined existed before this.

The man who lied. The man who kills. The man who is responsible for all the terrible things I'm facing now.

That's Ivan. That's the *real* Ivan.

But I'm having a harder and harder time believing that, with every day that passes.

I wake up feeling sore and out of sorts, my ass bruised from the spanking Ivan gave me. With the pleasure long gone, it makes me irritable, and I'm tense, keeping my distance from him. He doesn't say anything, and I can't help but wonder what he's thinking as we load up the car and make another grocery stop, getting back onto the highway. His jaw is clenched as he looks out at the road, and I look at the sharp, handsome lines of his profile, my skin tingling as I remember what happened yesterday.

After a few hours, I can't take his tense silence any longer. Even the hum of the old rock station that he put on in the background can't ease the heavy feeling between us.

"Why did you take me out to that lake?" I ask abruptly, shifting uncomfortably in the seat.

Ivan doesn't answer for a long moment. "Why did you sign up to that site where you met Venom?"

I grit my teeth. I can feel him spoiling for a fight, still upset at me from yesterday. "I told you why."

"Because Nate cheated on you, and you wanted to get back at him. Because you wanted a safe place to explore your fantasies. Is that it? Because I don't really believe that, Charlotte. I don't think you actually believed it was a safe place. I think you're smarter than that."

I swallow hard. "I thought it was safe."

"No, you didn't." His hands tighten on the wheel. "If you want to be angry at me for lying, Charlotte, then stop lying to yourself. Stop lying to me."

"I'm not—"

"You did it *because* of the danger. Because danger was what you wanted. You didn't really think going on the dark web and talking about primal fantasies with a man who called himself Venom was *safe*, or *smart*. You wanted a thrill. You wanted to be bad. And you just didn't believe that the worst of those consequences would ever come back on you."

I whip around, staring at him angrily. "Don't you dare say *you* lying was my fault! That any of this was my fault—"

"I'm not." Ivan lets out a heavy breath. "I lied. I fucking get it. Every possible facet of how I went about getting to know you was wrong, Charlotte, and I know it, even if I can't say I'd take it back, not unless I want to lie to you again. And I've been doing my fucking damnedest *not* to lie to you now. But you can't sit there and tell me that you did all of that thinking it was safe. That you didn't want the danger." His jaw works, a muscle twitching there. "I should spank you again, for lying to *me*."

"Fucking try it." I sit back, looking out the window, anger churning in my stomach. I'm pissed that he's daring to say a single thing about anything I've done, when everything *he's* done is so much worse—but I'm also pissed because he's right, and I don't want to admit it to myself anymore than I want to admit it to him.

I *did* want the danger. The thrill, without any consequences. It doesn't make Ivan lying to me any better—but I'm not entirely without blame, either.

What if it had been someone other than Ivan? My stomach tightens, and I bite my lip. I never intended to meet Venom, before I knew who he was, but Ivan can't be the only person in the world talented enough to track me down. The odds that someone else could have gotten around my safeguards and found me are slim—but it could have happened. Someone with far worse intentions.

It doesn't make it right. I cross my arms, looking out of the window, refusing to look back at Ivan. I don't want to give him another inch. Because the more I let myself believe that there's more to him than I want to admit, the closer I come to admitting a truth that shouldn't exist.

I'm still falling for him, despite all of his lies.

Despite everything.

16

IVAN

This woman is slowly killing me.

As the afternoon turns into evening, we find another motel, stop, and sleep. We're close to Montana, the longest of the stretches before Idaho, and then Vegas. And I find myself dreading when we finally get close to the city.

After we get those fake papers, there's nothing keeping her with me any longer. For all I know, she's going to give me the middle finger and walk off into the sunset, and she'd be well within her rights to do so. I'm pretty sure that's what she intends to do. But the thought makes my stomach twist, an ache like nothing I've ever felt filling me.

Running from the Bratva and the FBI is anything but normal, but these last few days have filled me with a desire to be just that. *Normal.* It's not a possibility that ever existed for me, but with each passing day, it's harder and harder to push away the fantasies of what it would be like to be with Charlotte as the kind of man she would want.

Down the long stretches of road, as she sits in silence or naps, the radio a hum of white noise—I imagine different trips with her. Trips we take on *purpose*. Nicer hotels, locations we've chosen. Adventures with a woman who I'm finding out is tougher than either she or I knew she was capable of being. A home to go back to, one that she and I chose together.

I think of what she said when I took her out to the lake, that for years she'd told herself she'd take off on a trip, get out of the city, and never did. I can only imagine how many other adventures she might have thought of taking, and pushed them to another month, another year, until they would eventually become another lifetime.

I have plenty of money. I could take her all over the world twice, and still have enough for us to live for the rest of our days. I could show her everything she could ever dream of, fulfill her every desire, and spoil her beyond her wildest dreams. And God knows I want to.

But that's not what Charlotte needs. And that's what I'm realizing, with an ache that sinks down to my bones, what I began to understand from our very first date, when I took her out to a Michelin-starred restaurant in an Aston Martin in an effort to impress her.

Charlotte doesn't need to be spoiled, or impressed, or wined and dined. She needs a man who is honest. Trustworthy. Genuine. Someone who will lean into the simple, small moments with her, who will build a life with her that feels like a home.

I want to be that for her. I wish I'd done it all differently. I wish I'd told her from the start, taken her to my little house in the Chicago suburbs, and told her *yes, I'm a criminal, and yes, I'm part of an organization that might hunt me until I die, but this is all I really want. Something simple—and you.*

I wonder if that would have really changed anything, or if she would have just run before she'd ever gotten a chance to know me.

That train of thought could drive a man mad. It feels like it *is* driving me mad, throughout the long day of driving, to the hotel that night, to my hard bed on the floor as Charlotte sleeps on the other side of the room.

I want to be in that bed with her. Not even for sex—just to hold her in my arms. Just to feel her, warm and soft, against me. I can't remember the last time I spent the night next to a woman. And now, the only woman I want to do that with is Charlotte.

The one who is going to leave me, in just a few short days.

"Let's get something different for breakfast," I suggest as we pack up the car to leave. "Stop somewhere and eat."

Charlotte raises an eyebrow. "I thought you said it was too dangerous to go out. I thought you said if someone saw us—"

"I know what I said." It comes out sharper than I mean for it to, and I instantly soften my voice when I see the way her eyes narrow at me. "I just—"

It sounds foolish to say it out loud, when we're in so much danger. That I want to sit and eat a meal with her, in a public place, like everything is okay. It's *not* okay, as she's reminded me so many times, and it *is* a risk. It's a stupid risk to take for something so small.

But it doesn't feel so small to me. And the ticking clock of how much time I have left with her is so loud that I feel almost desperate to claw out what small moments I can get. Even if the rational part of me knows it's the wrong call.

I'm supposed to protect her. This isn't safe.

It's just breakfast.

Charlotte sighs, running a hand through her hair. In the daylight, I can see the tint of orange to the blonde, but I don't hate it. It's obviously a bathroom dye job, but with the backdrop of the vibrant leaves on the trees to the far side of the motel parking lot, there's something charming about it. Something free.

She looks at me narrowly for a moment, as if she's trying to figure out what it is that I'm doing this for. I can't tell if she figures it out, or what exactly she sees in my face, but she finally nods, sighing again heavily. "Fine," she says, stalking towards the car. "I'd like a hot breakfast that wasn't dipped in grease first."

The car is another problem, I think, as I get in and start it up. We'll have to swap it out soon, not least of which because it could snow as far north as we're getting, and the Corolla might not hack it the whole way. I can already feel some tremors and hear some odd noises from how far we've driven it—this car definitely was heading towards the end of its life before I stole it. But I'm not looking forward to Charlotte's reaction when she hears that we're going to commit grand theft auto for a second time.

"Where are we going to go?" she asks as we drive away from the motel. "For breakfast, I mean," she adds, and I shrug.

"There's bound to be a diner on the way out of town. Those kinds of places are always the best. The few times I've taken off on a road trip, they've never disappointed."

Charlotte lets out a small hum of amusement a few minutes later when I pull up in front of exactly that, a homestyle diner with big windows that look in on vinyl booths and a long counter towards the back of the space. "I promise it'll be good," I tell her, and a hint of a smile quirks the corners of her mouth.

"You're not what I would envision a man in the mafia to be," she says, her mouth flattening as if she's trying to hold back a smile. I want to tease it out of her, to see it spread across her face. Her smile feels like it lights me up from the inside out.

"What do you mean?" I think I already know, but I want to hear her say it. I want her explanation.

Charlotte shrugs, still fighting a smile. "I don't know. Our first date, I would have absolutely believed you if you'd told me. The expensive car, the fancy dinner out, all of that fits what I would imagine. But this?" She gestures at the diner. "You'd rather drive your Mustang than the Aston Martin. You'd rather go here than eat that chef-curated dinner. You'd rather wear what you're wearing right now than that suit you had on. It's not what I'd expect."

"I think you're picturing the Italian mafia." I grin at her. "Although my father likes his elegance. But that's never been me, Charlotte."

She breathes in, studying me, and I can see her thinking. I wish I could hear her thoughts at this moment. I wish I knew if she was thinking that she'd like to know me better. To understand who I really am.

"Let's go eat, Charlotte," I tell her gently, and she nods, seeming to break out of her reverie. "I'm hungry, and I'm sure you are, too."

She reaches for the door, opening it, and slips out into the chilly air. I suck in a deep breath as we step out, filling my lungs with the freshness of it. It feels clean and crisp, and I want to linger instead of continuing on to Vegas.

There's a different appeal to Vegas, one that I've very much enjoyed in the past. It's a city of lights and excess and sin, a whirlwind of debauchery and overindulgence, and there's any number of pleasures to be had there. It feels like a place out of time, in its own liminal space, and I would be excited to take Charlotte there if it wasn't also the place where I'm going to lose her.

Here, she's still with me. Here, it still feels like there's a chance that we might still be together somehow, even if I know that's just a fantasy. Here, it feels like there's a possibility we could hide away forever.

Every state line brings me closer to the fact that none of that is going to be our reality.

The warm scent of fresh-cooked food, wood, vinyl and coffee hits my nose as we walk into the diner, the small bell above the door chiming as I hold it open for Charlotte. There's a handwritten sign by the hostess desk telling us to *seat ourselves*, and I notice with some relief that the diner is mostly empty. I'm well aware that this wasn't the wisest choice, and the fewer people here to see us, the better. I've yet to see my face or Charlotte's on the news when I've turned on the TV at night in our motel rooms, which means Bradley is still keeping this particular chase quiet for now—probably for reasons of his own. But I don't want too many people to be able to describe us to anyone.

Especially my brothers.

I feel fairly certain at this point, however, that they're waiting for us in Vegas. The fact that we haven't seen a hint of them since they tracked us to that first motel makes me think that Lev found out about my contact, and opted to lay in wait. It doesn't follow what I know of my brother—he likes the hunt, the chase, likes to taunt and torment and play with his food. But it's possible those directions came from my father, who Lev won't disobey, even if he disagrees.

Charlotte is looking around, tense, as we walk to one of the booths. But I see her relax a fraction a moment later when we sit down, and a woman comes over to bring us menus, a pot of coffee already in her hand.

"Coffee for you both?" she asks, and I nod at the same time that Charlotte does. "Creamer?"

"Please," we both say in unison, and I see Charlotte's teeth sink into her lower lip in an effort to not laugh.

That smile is still quivering at the edges of her lips as the waitress walks away, and Charlotte looks down at the menu. She's trying to be upset that we're doing this, because she knows as well as I do that it's a bad idea, but she's faltering.

I take a chance, and reach out to touch her hand. "We needed this," I say softly. "*I* needed this."

Charlotte looks up abruptly, but she doesn't move her hand away. "Why?" she asks simply. "Why the trip out to the lake? Why this? Why do you need anything other than to get to Vegas and get what you need to scrape our identities clean so you can start over? This is what you've always wanted, right? Or at least, what you've wanted for a long time."

I hear the trace of bitterness in her voice. She's still upset with me, and I can't blame her. But *fuck*, what I wouldn't give to hear her speak to me the way she did before all of this, when she still didn't know who I was.

"This isn't how I wanted to do it. It's not what I planned." I tap the fingers of my other hand against the laminated menu, my stomach growling as I look down at the list of food on offer. As much as I haven't minded the quick meals on the road, something hot that we have to sit down to eat sounds incredible.

Charlotte pauses for a moment, pulling her lower lip between her teeth as she looks out of the window, as if she's making up her mind about something. "Okay," she finally says slowly. "Tell me how you planned it, then."

17

IVAN

This is a chance, and I know it. An opportunity to tell her what I really wanted, to emphasize that it was never my plan to steal her away to go with me. That she was a wrench in what I'd imagined for myself for a long time.

I think about what I want to say as the waitress comes back and takes our orders—a Belgian waffle with fruit and a side of scrambled eggs for Charlotte, and corned beef hash with fried eggs and toast for me. Charlotte asks for orange juice as well, amusement in her eyes as the waitress brings it.

"I suppose I need to keep myself healthy if we're going to be on the run." She takes a sip from it, looking at me with a hint of curiosity that gives me hope. "Well? Tell me what you want to say."

I hesitate for a moment. "You know I have three brothers," I say finally. "You've met them."

"Met." She makes air quotes with her fingers, rolling her eyes. "It wasn't exactly the introduction to my new boyfriend's family that I would expect. Although I guess by then we were broken up, weren't we?" The humor in her voice is tinged with sarcasm.

She's not going to give me an inch. It impresses me, in the same way that it strangely turns me on. I've never sought out especially combative women before—although I swear when Charlotte yells at me, it makes me hard—but I do like strong women. Women who know their own minds. And while Charlotte might have started out being uncertain of her own desires, all of this has brought out a strength in her that's making me fall even faster down the slippery slope to being in love with her.

The sound of her calling me her boyfriend, even with sarcasm, even when following it up by saying we're not together any longer, does something strange to my insides. It makes me want to reach for her, pull her across the table to me, tangle my fingers in her hair, and tell her to say it again, even if it's not true any longer.

Even if it never really was.

The waitress comes back, setting our plates down in front of us, and I clear my throat. "I'm the youngest," I say slowly, as the woman walks away, glancing up at Charlotte as she unrolls her silverware. "And my brothers are my half-brothers. I'm my father's fourth son, and a bastard."

She presses her lips together. "That's an archaic word."

"Crime families can be archaic. Arranged marriages, hierarchies, inheritances. We live by codes and traditions and sets of rules that the rest of the world has left behind. And while the Bratva may be more blatant about their brutality, we're far from the only organization like this."

Charlotte swallows hard, but she nods slowly. "That seems so strange," she says finally. "So you were never going to inherit anything from your father, then."

I shrug. "Some money, probably. He's a hard man, and a cruel one, and if he feels any love for me, it's wrapped up in expectations and pride that smother love. But I think he would probably leave me some remnant of his legacy—not that I want it. As far as the wealth and businesses he's built and most of what belongs to him, as well as his position, that would go to Lev when my father—Dima—is gone."

Charlotte winces. "From the little I saw of Lev, I can't imagine he would be good at running anything."

"He wouldn't." I can say that confidently. "He's cruel, and not particularly smart, vengeful and someone who takes pleasure in hurting others."

"You don't?" She looks at me, that same curiosity in her gaze. "Isn't that what men like you do?"

"I can't say I've never taken pleasure in it." It's the closest I can get to telling her the truth about the kind of man I've been without horrifying her so deeply that she won't even want to ride in the same car as me. "But I don't look forward to it. Sometimes—there are some people who deserve it, Charlotte. I don't think you can understand that, and I don't really want you to."

Her jaw tightens. "I'm not a child, Ivan."

"I know." I press my hands against the edge of the table, wondering how I can explain these things to her and coming up empty. It's not that I think she's stupid, or a child, it's that I don't know how to begin to explain to her the difference between looking forward to hurting someone and being good at it. The reasons why a man might deserve the kind of pain I've meted out.

"I'm not so sheltered that—"

"No, but you've lived a very different life. And I've already made you have to acknowledge more of the world I live in than I ever wanted to." I let out a heavy breath. "You mentioned who would inherit from my father."

What I want is to change the subject. Charlotte nods, jabbing her fork into her waffle. "Does that have something to do with—all of this?"

"In a way." I'm not about to be rushed, not when I finally have a chance to explain some of myself to her, with her listening. I've wondered if I should try at all, if it would only make things worse. But that ticking clock makes me feel like I *have* to try. If only to hope that when she leaves, it will be with a clear picture of who I am. Or as clear of one as I can paint, anyway, without her running from me before we even get to Vegas.

"Lev is my father's heir," I explain slowly, as we work our way through our food. "The other three of us are tools. Niki and Ani especially, because they are legitimate products of my father's union with his wife, Katya. Niki and Ani do as they're told, out of a slim hope that one day Lev will anger my father enough that one of them will be put in his place, instead. If one of them was, they'd quickly turn on the other, just as Lev easily turns on them if they don't obey."

Charlotte draws in a slow breath, her lips pressed together as she nods. "And that leaves you—where, exactly?"

"If Lev is my father's right hand, I've been his left. The one he uses for vengeance, to keep others in line, to enforce his rules, because while Lev is brutal and a bit stupid, and Niki and Ani are weak, I'm none of those things. And I think, deep down, he wishes that I were legitimate enough to inherit from him. He—" I pause, thinking of how much, exactly, I should say. "He often reminds Lev of it. Niki and Ani, too. That if they're not careful, he'll give it all to me, and a bastard will inherit instead of them."

Charlotte's eyes widen. "Could that really happen?"

"It's complicated. Technically, my father can do as he pleases. But he's not a monolith. There are other *pakhans*—patriarchs of other crime families, who would see it as a reason to move in and try to take what he's built. I'd inherit a war, that's for certain, if he made that choice. But it doesn't matter, because I don't want it. I never have."

"Then why stay? Why did you ever do anything to help him?" Charlotte's brows draw together. The expression on her face could be read as judgment, but I choose to interpret it as curiosity. Mostly, I imagine, because the thought of her judging me for the life I've led feels painful.

"There's no leaving the Bratva, Charlotte," I tell her quietly. "There's no leaving *any* crime family easily. Long before I was old enough to understand, or make these choices for myself, I was being implicated in my father's crimes. It's difficult to leave, without coming up against the law—or other members of the organization. They're more dangerous than any police officer or FBI agent. And fleeing requires connections and money that take years to build up." I let out a breath, holding Charlotte's gaze for a moment. "There's no easy way out. I've planned my exit for years. It wasn't until my father started doing things that I deemed unconscionable that I decided to try to take him out on the way. The drugs, the warmongering, I could handle that. Those are sins that plenty of men, all over the world, participate in every day, and I can't stop them all. My own freedom was more important to me—take that as you will. But selling women was a step too far. So I stepped in."

"Which is why you were working with Bradley." Charlotte sets her fork down halfway through her waffle, as if her appetite has failed. "But he doesn't think you've given him enough. He said so himself."

"He resents that I could get out of this scot-free, if I provided enough information to them. So he keeps moving the goalposts for that." I run a hand through my hair. "He wants to see me go down with my father. And I have no intention of letting that happen."

Charlotte chews on her lower lip, and the ache to kiss her sweeps through me again. I imagine her mouth tastes like syrup right now, like fruit, and just the thought makes my cock twitch in my jeans. I want her so badly that it hurts all of the time. I want her to be mine. That obsession, that feeling that she's the only thing that can ease my need, that sensation of needing a hit that only she can provide—none of that has gone away. I've just been keeping a tighter grip on it, and like any addiction, the withdrawal hurts.

"You're not a good man," she says quietly, and I feel that raw stab in my chest, that pain that only she seems to be able to deliver.

"No," I agree. "I'm not. But I never wanted to hurt you. I never meant for you to get caught up in all of this. I've lied to you, Charlotte, and I'll admit it—but that's always been the truth."

"So you were going to make me fall for you and then leave me behind. Use me and break my heart." She twists her napkin in her fingertips. "That's not any better."

"No, it's not." My heart feels heavy, listening to her, because she's right. And I have no idea what I can do to redeem myself in her eyes. What would make her feel that what I've done is forgivable?

I glance up, about to tell her that we should ask for the check and get moving—as much as I don't want to—and stop. The words die on my tongue as I see a black car at the far end of the parking lot—and a too-familiar figure getting out of it.

"Shit." I dig in my pocket for enough cash to cover the meal and then some, tossing it on the table. "We have to go."

Charlotte freezes with her glass of orange juice still touching her lips. She swallows hard, dropping it with a *thud* on the table, and follows my gaze out of the window.

"Shit," she echoes, and I stand up, reaching for her elbow.

She shakes me off before I can tug her out of the booth, standing up on her own as she quickly turns her back to the large window. I'm impressed by her quick response, but there's no time to tell her that. Bradley is striding towards the diner, and I have no idea if he actually thinks we're here, or if it's just bad timing that he decided to stop and eat at the same place that we did. A hell of an unfortunate coincidence, if so, but not impossible.

Charlotte moves quickly towards the back entrance, not bothering to wait for me. I catch up to her in two strides, my hand brushing against the small of her back, but she once again shakes me off. It makes me grit my teeth, because there's nothing more I want than to protect this woman. I want to keep her safe, to make sure that men like Bradley never get to lay a hand on her.

I'd hoped that what I just told her would have softened her towards me a little. But it only seems to have made her more determined to push me away.

"We'll loop around the diner once he's gone in," I murmur, as we burst out of the side door of the diner, the door closing behind us just as I hear the chime of the front door opening. I can't be sure that was Bradley, and I pause, wrinkling my nose against the smell of the dumpster next to us. There's a stand of trees just ahead, the dumpster to my left, concrete under my feet littered with cigarette butts from the staff. It's hardly pleasant, but I hesitate, moving slowly toward the corner to look and see if Bradley is still in the parking lot.

He's not. I turn to Charlotte, about to tell her to take a stealthy peek around the back to see if he's slipped back there to lie in wait for us, but she's already pressed to the corner, glancing ever so slightly around it.

Once again, I'm thoroughly impressed. That feeling tangles up with every other complicated emotion that she makes me feel, and I curl my fingers into my palms, suppressing the urge to cross the space between us, pin her to the diner wall, and kiss her until she forgets her name and only remembers mine.

The setting is less than romantic, but right now, I couldn't fucking care less.

Charlotte glances back at me. I mouth *do you see him*, and she shakes her head, chewing on her lower lip. I glance towards the parking lot once more, and when she looks again, she still raises her hands as if to say she doesn't know where he's gone.

He's inside. And our car is parked out front.

Stupid. But I wasn't thinking about Bradley being right on our heels when I made that mistake. I was thinking about an hour with the woman who seems to be the only one in the world who addles my better sense, and makes me do things solely because I want a few more seconds with her.

She could very easily be the death of me. But I can't seem to bring myself to care.

Not enough, anyway.

I move towards her carefully, poised for the side door to open and for Bradley to come bursting out. "When I tell you," I murmur quietly, "go around the far side to the car. I'll go around this side, and get it running. Run as fast as you can, and jump in. Bradley is going to see us, and we have to get a head start. Just run. Don't stop."

Charlotte nods, and I can see her pale slightly. Her lips are pressed together in a thin line, but she says nothing, looking around the corner again. I move slowly back to the other side, and when I see the parking lot still empty of people, I glance back at her.

"*Go,*" I mouth, and she darts off without arguing, jogging behind the building as I take off for the car.

There was no other side door, so I feel confident she won't be surprised on that side. I bolt for the car from my side, and I see a glimpse of Bradley sitting in one of the vinyl booths. He hasn't looked up yet, and my breath catches in my throat as I yank the door open.

I've had to hotwire cars in a hurry before, but never under this kind of pressure. I fling myself into the driver's seat just as Charlotte comes running from the other side of the diner, allowing myself one more look to see if Bradley is still staring at his menu before I duck down and reach for the wires to start the car.

Charlotte flings herself into the passenger's side just as the engine turns over. I sit up, and the moment I do, I see Bradley's eyes lock with mine through two sets of glass.

The sound of the engine alerted him. "Lock your door!" I snap, throwing the car into gear just as I see Bradley rising from his booth, already reaching for his keys. My heart is hammering, adrenaline flushing my entire body, and I can hear Charlotte panting next to me. Out of the corner of my eye, as I swing the car hard to the left, I see her gripping the side of her seat with one hand, the car door with the other. She's frozen straight, and I think I hear her shuddering gasp as Bradley's voice shouts across the parking lot.

I can't hear what he says, and I don't fucking care. All I care about is getting us out of here.

Charlotte is trembling in her seat next to me. I can hear her trying to breathe, in through her nose, out through her mouth, and I want to stop and comfort her. But right now, all I can focus on is getting us as far away from him as possible.

I've been taking surface roads and back roads, making our route as far off the beaten track as possible to throw off any scent. But it hasn't been good enough, apparently, and I take the highway instead this time, if only to put as much distance as I can between us and the chase that's started.

"He's going to catch us, isn't he?" Charlotte asks, her voice trembling, and I shake my head sharply in a quick jerk.

"Not if I have anything to do with it," I tell her grimly, flooring it as we merge into traffic on the highway.

Charlotte lets out a high-pitched squeak as the car jolts forward, and I grit my teeth with frustration. I'm pushing the little sedan we're driving to its limits, and I'd give anything right now for my Mustang, or the Aston Martin, or that RSX I had to leave abandoned in the trees. This car isn't any better than Bradley's, maybe worse, and the only benefit we have is that I got a head start.

I keep looking in the rear-view mirror, watching for Bradley's black car to come up on us. I think I see one that could be his, but it's too far back to tell. Instead, I veer in and out of traffic, trying to get as far ahead of any possible pursuit as I can. Charlotte is white-lipped next to me, both of her hands clutching the seat now, but I can't think about that.

At the next exit, I get off of the highway, my pulse in my throat as I wait for a black car to do the same. But as I turn right, driving onto a side road, nothing appears in my rear-view. After another ten or fifteen minutes, I feel my shoulders start to come down from around my ears, my pulse slowing down. We're not safe by any means, but we're out of the woods for a little while.

When I look over, Charlotte is chewing on her lower lip, agitated. "Are you alright?" I ask quietly, and she's quiet for a long moment before she finally nods.

"That was terrifying," she says softly. She looks out of the window, her nails scratching at the edge of the seat, like a nervous tic. "And thrilling."

The last is said softly, so softly that I almost don't hear it, so softly that I think I'm meant not to. I see a faint flush on her pale skin, and I realize it's something she's grappling with. She feels that she should be horrified by all of this. But there's a part of her—a small part, that found it all exciting. That *didn't* hate it. And I know her well enough by now to see the guilt written on her face because of that.

She licks her lips, staring out of the window, but she doesn't say anything else. "What about your brothers?" she says after a little while. "We haven't seen them since the first attack."

"I think Lev's figured out where we're going." I grip the steering wheel a little tighter, rotating my hands back and forth. "I imagine they're waiting for us in Vegas. And that's something I'll have to deal with when I get there." I glance over at her. "I won't let them hurt you, Charlotte. No matter what."

"You keep saying that." She still isn't looking at me. "But you're one man, Ivan. They're three."

She goes silent again after that, and I don't know what to say in response. I want to convince her that I'm better than the man she thinks I am, I want to protect her, and yet every effort to do that feels as if it's pushed to the side. As if none of it is good enough, convincing enough, to make her believe me.

Is it obsession, to want to keep trying? There's never been a woman in my life before that I would go to such lengths to make her want me. To make her trust me. But with Charlotte, I can't let go. I can't accept that she'll always think of me as the villain in her story, as someone who destroyed her life, as a *mistake*.

There's a way to fix it, and I just have to figure out what it might be.

We drive until it's well after dark, and I find another small, shady motel for us to spend the evening at. Charlotte remains quiet as I pay for our room, and my pulse beats a quick staccato in my throat, the need to touch her after the day we've had so strong that it feels painful.

It's not just a sexual need, either. I want more than that from her. And I want her to feel it. I want her to know that it's more than just how much I want to fuck her.

I fight that urge all the way up to our room. But the moment we step inside, and I feel her brush against me as she goes to close the door, her warm scent filling my nose—I can't stop myself from reaching out for her.

My arm slides around her waist, pulling her in against me. I don't push her up against the door; I don't move fast or rough at all. I just hold her, one arm wrapped around her, and I slide the other into her hair before she can do more than let out a small gasp of surprise, lowering my mouth to hers.

It's not a rough kiss or a passionate one, although the need and desire churning through me wants to demand both. Instead, I kiss her in a way that I'm not sure I ever have before.

I brush my lips against hers, softly, running my tongue over her lower lip as I draw it between mine, my hand splayed over her hip as I hold her close. The kiss is tender, sweet, and I pour every bit of emotion that I feel into it, my fingers tangled gently in her hair, my chest rising and falling against hers. I'm falling in love with her, and if I said it out loud, she'd turn away from me and call it another lie. But this isn't something I can fake—and so I want her to feel it instead.

I expect her to pull away, to fight, to slap me. But instead, I feel her tense, her lips parting under mine, and my tongue sweeps into her mouth. She tastes as sweet as always, like ginger soda and candy, and I deepen the kiss, tangling my tongue with hers as I breathe her in.

I'm so fucking hard, just from kissing her. I know she can feel it pressed against her belly, but I don't push it further. I just want to kiss her right now, and I know she's going to stop me in a minute, when she regains her senses. There's no way she's going to fuck me tonight, and I don't think I would, even if she begged. I want to believe that I wouldn't, at least, that I'd stick to what I told her the last time I had her wet and coming on my fingers.

The next time I fuck you, it's going to be because you want me to fuck you. Not this fantasy that you want to hide behind.

I meant it then, and I still do, even if every cell in my body is screaming that I need to be inside of her. If that's ever going to happen between us again, I want it to be because it's real. Because she wants me, exactly as I am, exactly as the man she now knows me to be.

For the briefest moment, I feel her tongue drag against mine, feel her fingers dig into my biceps as she kisses me back. I feel her arch against me, the press of her hips to mine, the way my hard cock rubs between us as a small moan spills from her mouth into mine.

And then she jerks back, as I knew she would, panting as she drags her hand over the back of her mouth. The unintentional lewdness of the gesture makes my cock jump, and I grit my teeth against the wave of desire that threatens to drag me under, as Charlotte shakes her head violently.

"*No*," she says sharply, just the one word, bit off as if it tastes bad in her mouth. And then she pivots on her heel, stalking towards the bathroom, slamming the door behind her.

I sink against the cracked desk on one side of the room, reaching down to adjust myself in my jeans. I groan under my breath as I feel myself shift against the fabric, just that sensation enough to make me throb, pre-cum dripping down my shaft. I hear the shower turn on, and for a brief second, I consider slipping my cock free and giving myself the relief I so desperately need.

But the last thing I *need* is for Charlotte to come out and catch me doing that. So instead, I give myself a reluctant squeeze, sinking down into the nearby chair with a sigh.

One thing is for sure, though.

I'm definitely going to be taking a shower after she's done.

18

CHARLOTTE

I can still feel Ivan's kiss, stinging my lips as I turn on the taps for the shower forcefully, listening to the water gurgling through the pipes before the spray finally comes on.

He's never kissed me like that before. I expected him to push me against the door, sit me on the edge of the desk, back me up to the bed, and tumble me back onto it. I expected passion, force, for him to take what he so obviously wants from me.

But he didn't. He just kissed me, and it was almost—sweet?

It confuses the hell out of me. Ivan is a forceful man, a man of violence and brutality. I know that now. But he's different with me. He's careful, considerate, and when I said *no*, he stopped immediately, even though I could see how badly he wanted it to be *yes*. I could *feel* it, when he was kissing me.

I've never slept with any man who gets as hard for me as Ivan does. Who wants me so desperately. And it's harder and harder with every passing day to ignore how much that turns me on, too.

He's the most confusing man I've ever known. I should hate him. I *do* hate the things he's done. I hate that he's lied to me. That he's blown up my life.

But I don't hate the man who took me out to the lake and told me things about himself. Who is risking everything to get me to some semblance of safety, when he could have just cut loose and left me with Bradley—or even before that, when his brothers were coming for me at my apartment. He could have run then, but he didn't. He came to get me, and even if—in my opinion—he went about it all the wrong way, he *did* save me.

What the fuck, Charlotte? I cover my face with my hands, groaning into my palms. My mind is clearly getting scrambled by days on days spent with this man, and the mind-blowing pleasure that comes with every time I give in to what he offers me physically. I'm making excuses for him now, looking for the best in this, and I can't believe I'm actually doing that.

But what if there is some good to find? I think of what I said to him in the diner this morning, that he isn't a good man, and the way he didn't argue with me. I saw a shadow on his face when I said it, but he accepted my judgment. And wouldn't a truly bad man have tried to argue with me, to justify himself?

I'm not exactly the good girl that I used to be anymore, either. A good girl, a practical, rational, *safe* girl, the kind I used to be, doesn't talk about fantasies of being chased and captured and spanked on the dark web with a faceless stranger. She doesn't fuck the man who conveniently happened to be at her apartment the same night she was kidnapped, not once but *twice* in the same morning. She doesn't let that man finger her bent over a bathroom sink after finding out he's been lying all along.

And she definitely doesn't get soaking wet when he kisses her like he's falling in love with her, in yet another seedy motel.

He can't be. That's not possible. The old me would believe that a man like Ivan is incapable of real love. But I'm learning that the world isn't as black and white as I once thought.

I want things I shouldn't. Getting a thrill from being on the run from the law. The adrenaline of us running from the diner left me more aroused than I wanted to admit, fantasies of Ivan pulling over on the side of the road and yanking me onto his lap, filling my mind as we raced down the highway. I imagined leaning over and unzipping him, making him come with my mouth while he drove. I pictured him fucking me before we even got out of the car when we pulled into the parking lot tonight.

I was wet before he even kissed me. And now—

I reach down, dragging my fingers between my legs. I'm slick, hot, my clit throbbing under my fingertips. I want to turn off the water and go out to Ivan naked and dripping, sit on the end of the bed, and pull his mouth between my thighs. I want him to bend me over like he did after I went down on him, except this time, I want his cock, and not his fingers. I want—

I want things I shouldn't have. Things I have no business thinking about, that make me a hypocrite for even imagining them.

Bracing my hand against the wall, I slide my fingers down, slipping two inside of myself. I feel myself clench instantly around them, hips arching into my palm, desperate for release. But it's not my own hand I want rubbing between my legs, not even when I press those two fingers between my folds, grinding them over my clit.

Ivan was rock-hard when he kissed me. I wonder if he's out there now, frantically stroking himself to a quick, messy orgasm before I come out of the shower. Before I come—

I bite my lip hard, my breath catching in my throat. I could come like this. I'm so close. But at the last second, as I roll my fingers over my swollen clit, I yank them away.

I have to fight this. I can't give in. I'm so close to letting Ivan off the hook. Making excuses for him that I shouldn't. And every time I make myself come thinking of him, I'm edging closer to a line that I shouldn't cross. One that will send me into his arms, and make it all but impossible to drag myself out again.

Forcing my thoughts away from the throbbing between my thighs and the possibility of what Ivan is doing outside, I finish my shower, drying off with the thin, rough towel on the hook outside. I drag on a pair of sweatpants and a loose T-shirt that I got when we went shopping, hoping that the less-than-sexy outfit will be enough to deter Ivan from kissing me again. From wanting me. But the minute I walk out of the bathroom, he looks up at me, and I see his gaze darken.

When he stands up, I see the outline of his erection, still pressing stiffly against the fly of his jeans. I see the muscle in his jaw twitch as he walks past me, my breath caught in my throat at how unfairly gorgeous he is.

He's going to jerk off in the shower. I know it. There's no way he's going to deny himself that relief. The door closes hard behind him, and I sink down on the edge of the bed, gripping the sides of it as if it takes physical effort to keep from following him into the shower.

I could have him inside of me right now. I feel that throb between my legs, my chest constricting, the thought making me breathless.

I can't pretend that I don't want him. But I can fight it.

I flop back on the bed, turning out all the lights except for the one right next to me as I skim through a book, not really focusing on anything on the pages. Twenty or so minutes later, I hear the shower turn off, and Ivan walks out, still toweling off his wet hair. He's put on a pair of sweatpants and nothing else yet, his t-shirt tossed over the arm of the chair, and my stomach tightens at the view of him shirtless, his chiseled torso covered in swirls of black ink.

My fingers itch to trace over those lines. To slide over them until he's hard and begging for me to touch lower. I want to repaint those designs with my fingers while I slide my lips over him, feeling every muscle twitch as I run my lips and tongue over his cock. I want—

Fuck. Fuck, fuck, fuck.

I roll over on my side, trying not to look at him, trying to push that image out of my mind. I don't know why tonight it's harder than ever to ignore my attraction to him, but it feels like my body is screaming for him to touch me. For me to touch him. For us both to forget all of the reasons why we're not supposed to do this any longer and just *feel*.

I hear the familiar sound of him getting out blankets and pillows to sleep on the floor, and guilt once again washes over me. It's not fair, and I know it's not.

"Come sleep in the bed." I roll over to face him, feeling a small burst of relief when I see that he's put a shirt on. "There's enough room for us both. You shouldn't keep sleeping on the floor."

In the low light, I see Ivan's jaw tighten as he spreads a blanket out. "It's fine," he says tersely, his voice so tight that I wonder if he didn't get himself off in the shower after all. If he's still just as frustrated as I am.

Or maybe it's not enough for him, either.

That thought makes the muscles in my stomach tighten, desire pooling lower, that tingling shiver washing over my skin. I force it away, focusing on the conversation at hand.

"You're driving constantly," I argue back. "You should get to sleep in the bed, too. I can put pillows between us, if the idea of accidentally touching me in the night bothers you so much." The last comes out more acidly than I mean for it to, and I see Ivan's hands go still in the process of smoothing out the blanket.

"That's not the problem, and you know it." His voice is a taut, husky growl, and I feel that warmth blooming through me again at the sound of it.

"Then I'll sleep on the floor." I push myself up. "You should get a full night's rest, Ivan. I sit in the passenger's side all day. I can nap if I want. You're the one who shouldn't be pushing yourself so hard."

His hands are moving rhythmically over the blanket now, smoothing out the same spot again and again. "Almost sounds like you give a shit about me."

Irritation, a different kind of heat, mixes with the warmth of my desire. "Sounds like you just get off on being difficult," I snipe back, and Ivan looks up sharply, his dark gaze catching mine.

"Oh, that's not what I get off on, Charlotte," he murmurs, and the rasp of his voice makes my breath catch.

I should drop it. I should *not* let this man share a bed with me. If he agrees to take the bed, I should sleep on the floor. But there's something more to this too, something I'd never admit to him—and can barely admit to myself.

I'm lonely. Night after night of him sleeping on the floor, so close and still so far away, day after day spent with him oscillating between arguments and tense silence and the occasional truce, has left me aching for a gentler human connection. It's left me aching for exactly what he gave me earlier, when he kissed me like he cares for me. Like he's falling for me. And that kiss made me want more. Not just sex, but closeness. Comfort.

I want him next to me in bed, because it would make me feel less alone. Just for a little while.

I let out a heavy breath. "Just get in the bed. I'll sleep on the floor if you want. But you need—"

"Fine." Ivan pushes himself up from the floor, his muscled frame even more threatening in the near-darkness. "I need to sleep, most of all. So I can't spend the whole night arguing with you."

I start to get up, but he shakes his head. "No," he says firmly. "If I'm sleeping in the bed, then we both are. Don't worry, I won't touch you."

The bed is a queen, so theoretically, there is enough space for us both. But it feels like so much less as I slide back down under the blankets, and feel the dip in the mattress as Ivan slides in next to me.

There's an arm's length between us, still. But I can *feel* his presence next to me, as if he's touching me. My pulse feels lodged in my throat, the air between us thick with the knowledge that if he reached out, I'd feel him brush against my skin.

Maybe this wasn't the best idea, I think as I lie there, listening to him breathe, feeling the heat of his body fill the space between us. *I don't think either of us is going to get any sleep like this.*

—

SOMEHOW, though, we do. I wake to thin sunlight filtering through the curtains and over the bed, and the warmth of Ivan's body pressed against mine, his arm over my waist. His chest is rising and falling slowly against my back, his breath ruffling the small hairs on the nape of my neck, and I feel desire jolt through me like lightning when I register the stiff, hard shape of his cock pressed against my spine through his sweatpants.

I go very still, not wanting to move. I don't want to wake him yet. I want to stay in this moment a little longer, this feeling of being held, this liminal moment where I can pretend that it's alright that Ivan is holding me. Where I can pretend that I haven't fully woken up yet, and I'm still unaware that the last man who I should be allowing to touch me is curled around me as if I'm his.

It feels so good. The hard, muscled press of him against me, the warmth of his skin, the masculine scent of him filling my senses. Without meaning to, I squirm back against him a little, and in a flash of movement, Ivan rolls onto me, pinning me onto my back as he nuzzles into my neck.

I freeze, my heart pounding as he breathes in, his stubble grazing the sensitive skin of my throat and making my entire body tighten. His hips are pressed to mine, his cock hard against my belly, and I can feel the pounding of his heart against mine.

I'm not entirely sure that he's awake. He's braced on his elbows on either side of me, breathing shallowly, his hips rocking gently as he grinds into me. That throbbing desire that keeps flooding through me at his every touch answers his, and I realize with a flush of heat that crawls up my neck that if I could spread my legs wider for him, I would.

"Charlotte—" My name is a sleepy murmur, breathed into my neck, and I can feel my resistance to him fading. I'm wet, aching for him, and with the last bit of my self-control, I reach up, shoving my hands against his chest in an effort to both wake him up fully and get him off of me.

"Get *off*," I snap, and Ivan lifts his head, the sleep vanishing from his expression as he blinks down at me.

He takes in our position, him wedged tightly against me, my legs trapped between his and his cock pressed against me. A slow, amused smirk twitches the corners of his mouth, and I glare up at him as he smiles down at me. "Why?" he asks lazily, and I start to tell him it's none of his business. But the dark amusement in his expression tells me that he won't be satisfied with that. That he wants to hear me tell him the truth.

After being so angry at him for all of his lies, I guess it's the least I can do.

"If you don't stop touching me—" The words come out whispered, choked and tight. "I'm going to ask you to fuck me again."

Ivan draws in a sharp breath, his hips rocking into me as if what I just said struck him physically. I feel him throb against me, feel his body grinding against mine for a moment, his eyes dark with the same desperate need that I've felt ever since last night. It feels like torment, and there's an odd satisfaction in knowing he feels the same.

I want to use it against him. To wield it like a weapon, brace it between us like a shield, the way I tried to do when I went down on him. To reduce this thing between us to a base, filthy need. But he won't let me do that. I know it already, from that last time. And I can feel that what this is could too easily spin out of control.

It's more than that, and we both know it, even if neither of us will say it out loud.

Ivan swallows hard, his throat moving as he looks down at me, his body suddenly very still against mine. "Would you believe that it was real, if I did?"

The question comes out as a hoarse rasp, but there's a softness, a sincerity in it that cuts me to the quick. And once again, I can't give him anything other than the truth, even when he's lied to me so many times.

Even if it would feel good, for a moment, to punish him by telling him yes, when I know the answer is no. It would hurt me later, after. When he realizes that I've lied. That I've taken something from him as revenge for what he's taken from me.

I should want that more than I do. I should *do* it. But I can't bring myself to, and that's how I know this has gone so much further than it should.

My hesitation is all the answer Ivan needs. But he doesn't move, his gaze hardening. "Answer me," he says roughly, and his fingers touch my chin, forcing me to look at him. "Would it be real?"

I bite my lip as I shake my head, one quick, brief movement. And just as fast, Ivan pulls away from me, rolling off of the bed. I can see the evidence of his arousal tenting the front of his pants, but he ignores it, striding to where his clothes are tossed over the chair. He grabs them up in his hand, heading to the bathroom, and he slams the door behind him, hard.

I feel tears sting my eyes, watching him go. And I can't figure out why I'm about to cry over a man, who I never should have gotten feelings for at all.

19

IVAN

I slept better than I can remember having slept in a long time. I wasn't entirely sure why that was, until I woke up on top of Charlotte, and realized what must have happened.

I spent the night curled around her. The first time I've slept next to a woman all night that I can recall—and it meant nothing. Nothing to her, anyway.

That shake of her head when I asked if it would be real felt like that knife slicing through me all over again, so hot and sharp that I half expected to see my blood on her hands. A physical cut might have hurt less.

The tension between us is as thick as ever as we leave. I'm short with her, my frustration making me wound tight, and there's no solution for it. None that I'm willing to give into, anyway. I got myself off in the shower last night, and again this morning before I dressed after I left her in bed, but it's like patting an itch you want to scratch. It barely takes the edge off.

All that will satisfy me is her. And I refuse to fuck her again until she's willing to admit that it's me she wants. Just like this, just as I am.

Those thoughts dig at me all day, only agitating my already bitter mood. But all of it flies out of my head when we pull into the

Starview Motel for the night, the only one in the one-red-light town that we just drove through, and I see two familiar figures leaning against a silver Acura.

I know that car. And I know my brothers, even from the distance we're at, as I slow down.

I slam the car into park, and Charlotte gasps.

"Shouldn't we be running?" she whispers, and I shake my head sharply, drawing my gun.

"I'm going to make sure they don't chase us again," I growl, that frustrated need that's been chewing at me all day morphing into a thirst for violence. I want either sex or blood right now, and where one isn't possible, the other is a decent enough substitute.

"They're your brothers—"

"Stay here." The words come out sharp, clipped, and I leave the car running as I open the door and step out onto the pavement, the gun visible next to my side as I stride towards the two of them.

Both Niki and Ani push off the side of the car, taking a step towards me. I narrow my eyes when I see that neither of them appears to have a weapon in their hands.

"Ivan," Niki calls out first, raising his hands slightly to show that they're empty. "Talk to us."

"The only thing I want coming out of your mouth is your own blood," I snarl, my finger brushing against the trigger of my gun as I stride closer. "I'm done with this bullshit, Niki. I'm done being chased by you two *and* the fucking FBI."

Niki blanches slightly. "Why—"

"None of your fucking business." I raise the gun, aiming it at him. "I said, I'm done with this."

"Ivan—"

I'm on him in another stride, backing him towards the car. I shove my gun into the hollow of his throat just as I see Ani slip his hand out of his pocket, a switch knife in his fingers. In one swift movement, I reach out with my left hand, grabbing the handle and Ani's fingers at the same time, and twisting hard enough that I hear them pop.

Ani lets out a high shriek, stumbling back, and I shove the gun harder against Niki's throat.

"I've been running a wild goose chase ever since we left Illinois," I snarl. "How are you finding us? How did you even catch up to us so fast?" I see Ani moving towards me again, and I hold up a finger, glaring at him sideways. "Keep moving, and I'll blow his throat open."

I honestly don't know if the threat will work. If it was Lev, he'd tell me to go ahead and fucking kill him. But Ani and Niki have always had the common thread of being my father's bonus children, the ones he ignores until he needs to use them for something, and I have a feeling that's created a bond between them. It's what I'm banking on, and as I see Ani hesitate, I know it was the right call.

Ani slowly puts his hands up, backing down. "Fine," he says shortly. "Lev managed to get the security footage of Charlotte's apartment building. He saw you leaving with her in the car you were driving before. He sent some guys to follow up on your decoys, and when none of them led him to you, he figured you'd just taken Charlotte out of town and were making a run for it. And he was right, obviously."

"And he followed us how?" I jolt the barrel against Niki's throat again, and he coughs.

"It's hard to disappear now. The whole fucking world is on camera all the time, man." Ani shakes his head. "Traffic cameras, gas station security—and Lev won't falter at getting what he wants. He's fucking violent, and he'll hurt anyone, threaten anything to get results. You know that."

I do know that. Lev's brutality makes him an inefficient torturer, but it yields results in almost every other aspect of the Bratva world. If he needs or wants something, there is no moral code standing in his way. He'll stop at nothing.

"Well, he's not with you two idiots now." I lower the gun slowly, keeping it poised in case either of them gets any ideas. "So where is he? And how did you find us?"

"I'm not a complete idiot," Niki chokes out, rubbing the base of his throat. "And I'm not fucking telling you where Lev is. It's not worth my life to do that. But it wasn't fucking hard to figure out where the two of you would be. Every time we've run across you or almost caught up, you've been staying at the shittiest motels in existence. There was only one of those in this town, and based on how much time you've been making, you were probably gonna stop here. We gambled, and it worked out." He shrugs.

"Except it didn't," I snap. "Because I'm not going to let you two assholes just walk out of here."

Niki looks at me levelly. "Why not?" He keeps talking before I can answer, his gaze narrowed in on me. "Give us the girl. You've got to be bored with her by now, anyway. We'll take her straight back to Dima, as we're supposed to. Lev wants to get his hands on her first, but we'll make sure he doesn't. We'll say we're following *otets* orders, and get her right back to Chicago. And then it won't be the worst thing. You know what kind of clients *otets* sells to. And she's gorgeous. She'll end up some billionaire's toy or in a prince's harem. She'll live a life of luxury, and you get to go on your way, writing yourself a new future. That's what you wanted, isn't it?" Niki narrows his eyes. "To get out? To leave? Do that, while we're all distracted getting the girl back to *otets*. Get the fuck out."

"Dima will be angry with you for not bringing me back, too. So will Lev."

"We'll deal with that. The girl is what he really wants. He'll believe she'll lure you back. And when she doesn't, he'll sell her and try to find you some other way. But by then, you'll be long gone."

Not all that long ago, with anyone else, I would have been tempted to take the deal, even as abhorrent as I find my father's flesh peddling to be. My efforts to stop my father's trafficking are an attempt at some small measure of redemption, after all, and redemption never comes without temptation. But in the end, I know I'd still say no. I haven't come this far and put myself in this much danger to let my father get away with it in the end.

And with Charlotte at the crux of it all, there's not a chance in hell.

"Ivan?" I hear her voice a second later, far too close for her to still be in the car, and I have a feeling she's heard more of the conversation than I'd like. My chest tightens at the thought that she might have thought even for a second that I'd turn her over to them, and I move fast as a striking snake, the gun wedged against Niki's throat again.

"Is this what you really want?" I hiss, grinding the barrel into his skin. "You and Ani both? To be Lev's lackeys, my father's spares, used and discarded and only cared about for what small, petty services you can provide for the family? You should be running, too, if only because it's the only chance either of you have at not being ground up in the disposal of Lev's whims when Dima dies, and you're no longer needed."

I feel Niki's throat move against the gun, but his gaze is full of disdain as he stares at me. "I'm not stupid enough to think that the brief time we'd be free is worth the death Lev would mete out when we're caught."

"I'm running. And you just tried to get me to hand over Charlotte by saying that by the time Dima came after me again, I'd be long gone. So do you think it's possible to get out, or not?"

Niki flinches, and his gaze flicks sideways. It's the only thing that keeps me from being taken completely down by Ani rushing me, Charlotte's cry of warning coming a second too late.

As it is, I'm knocked to one side, my finger bumping the trigger of my gun and sending a bullet into the pavement. Charlotte screams, and I hear the patter of her feet as she starts to run for the car. Ani veers towards her, going straight to grab her, and without a thought, I pivot and put a bullet in his knee.

He drops to the ground, screaming, grabbing at his leg with both hands, even the one I just injured. I see Niki coming for me out of the corner of my eye, a switchblade in one hand and the other pulling a gun out of his waistband, and I swing my arm out towards him, shooting without looking.

I don't want to kill him. I truly don't. But in that moment, getting to Charlotte is all that matters. I hear Niki's cry of pain, mingling with Ani's, and hear him stagger back and hit the pavement, and I look to see Charlotte almost to the car, flinging herself inside.

I look back, just once. Niki is holding his stomach, blood flowing out from between his fingertips. It could kill him, I know that—and I also know that I could kill him right now.

I could kill them both. I could end one-third of the threat to Charlotte, and to myself. Lev would still be wherever he is—probably already in Vegas—and Bradley would still be after me, but Niki and Ani would be dead.

My finger brushes the trigger. I should do it. But I feel my gut twist at the thought of ending their miserable lives that have been spent as nothing more than pawns, as my father's knives in the dark, and not even particularly sharp ones.

I could say it would be mercy, but it doesn't particularly feel like that. And more than anything else, I selfishly don't want Charlotte to see me kill them.

I don't know if she would look at me the same, after that. I doubt that she would. Whatever flicker of desire and caring that led her to kiss me back last night, to offer me the bed instead of leaving me to sleep on the floor, would be extinguished by seeing me do something so brutal.

So instead, I turn and jog towards the waiting car.

Charlotte is dead silent as I veer out of the parking lot, leaving the two men as I speed out onto the open road. The truth is that Niki will probably be dead by tomorrow, anyway. But at least she didn't see me put the final bullet in him.

"We're going to have to keep going." I press my lips tightly together, looking ahead at the darkened road. My adrenaline is high, so I don't feel tired right now, but before we pulled into that parking lot, I was exhausted. It will catch up with me again before long, and I don't really know what to do about that. "I didn't want to have to ask you to drive, especially since there's always a chance that someone will be on our tail, but it might be unavoidable. Niki and Ani will be out of commission for a bit, but Lev might still be out there, and they've figured out what kind of motels we're staying at."

"So—do we stay at nicer hotels? With like—key cards and security?"

I shake my head. "For one thing, we're going to be hard-pressed to find anything like that out here. For another, that opens up a whole other can of worms—people who can be questioned about us, cameras, all that shit that can be used to track us."

"We can't just keep driving straight through." Charlotte runs a hand through her hair. "Even switching off, we'll be exhausted."

"It's possible. It won't be pleasant, but we can do it." I shrug, as if every fiber of my body weren't clambering to lie down right now. I'd even take the floor happily. The days on the run are catching up with me, and I'm fucking exhausted.

"Why don't we camp?" Charlotte asks suddenly, the suggestion coming entirely out of the blue. "Somewhere off the beaten path. We're in Montana, there's got to be places for that, right?"

The suggestion startles me, and I glance sideways at her. "Not afraid of bears any longer?"

Charlotte grimaces. "They're hibernating by now, aren't they? It's almost Halloween."

I shrug. "Most of them, probably. But are you actually serious? You want to go camping?"

She drops her gaze to her lap, and I instantly regret making light of it. "I never have," she says finally. "Another one of those things I always wanted to do, and didn't. Like—*actual* camping. I could have probably talked Jaz, Sarah, and Zoe into glamping, but pitching a tent and gathering firewood and all of that? They'd all have broken out in hives."

My chest tightens, hearing the way she talks about them. I can hear the sadness in her voice, the yearning knowing that she'll never see her friends again. *And it's my fault.* The thought feels like a cudgel, beating me until I feel a steady ache in my bones.

"One of those bucket list things, I guess," Charlotte says, shrugging. "And I have no idea what my life looks like after leaving Vegas a new woman, so—"

She trails off, and I can hear the forced casualness in her voice as she says that, too. She's afraid of what her life will be afterward, I can tell. And I can hardly blame her.

"Let's do it," I tell her, and I see her look sharply over at me, clearly surprised by my acquiescence. "Why not? It's a little cold, but not too cold yet." *And we can cuddle for warmth.* I almost say it, but stop myself at the last moment. I don't want to ruin the way she's suddenly starting to smile, a flicker of excitement in her expression.

"Really?" she asks, and I nod.

"We'll have to stop for some supplies. I don't think this car came outfitted for camping." I grin at her, and she raises an eyebrow.

"Are we going to steal those, too?" she asks archly, and I chuckle, shaking my head.

"No, I think those we can just buy."

We stop at the next decent-sized town we drive through, going to a 24-hour Walmart that should sell tents, a lantern, and anything else we might need. I gather all of it up, along with some food and a bottle of wine that I snuck into the supplies, and we take it back out to the car, loading it into the back before I get it started again.

There's a definite chill in the air. It's not exactly ideal camping weather, but I'm not about to discourage Charlotte. I look at the road atlas for the nearest campground, one that doesn't come with a lodge, amenities, and cameras, but is just an out-of-the-way spot where a traveler can stop. I hope that no one else will be there—if there are other campers, we're going to have to keep moving. I can't risk others seeing us, or putting others in danger by being nearby in case we are found. But when I drive down the path leading through the trees to the open space, it's entirely empty.

Entirely ours, just for tonight.

It's a beautiful view. The flat, open space is fringed with trees, a lake visible just beyond, shimmering black under the night sky with just a flicker of moonlight glinting across it. Charlotte shivers a little when we step out of the car, and when I look at her, she shakes her head quickly.

"I'm not too cold," she says, fast enough that her words almost trip over each other. "Don't worry about it."

Her eagerness not to leave tells me just how happy she is that we made this decision. And I wouldn't ruin it for the world.

"We'll be warmed up once we get everything ready," I tell her with a grin.

"I don't actually know how to do any of it." Her mouth twists as she looks at the bag with the tent and stakes. "I don't think I'll be very much help."

"I don't mind you watching." I raise my eyebrow, a clear innuendo in my words, and Charlotte looks away with a blush.

She gets the rest of the supplies out of the car as I start to put the tent up, the two of us working in relative silence at first. There's the sound of the wind rustling the trees and the lap of the lake further off, and it's so peaceful that I almost jump when Charlotte speaks a moment later.

"Are you okay?" she asks softly, and I freeze, startled by both the words themselves and the genuine concern that I can hear in her voice.

"I'm fine." It comes out more curt than I mean for it to, a defense against how badly I *want* her caring. "Why?"

"I just—" She pauses for a second. "I just wanted to know. After—"

"I'm fine," I repeat, more gently this time. "I'm not unused to that kind of violence, Charlotte."

She chews on her lip, setting down the firewood starters that I bought. "Would you really have killed your brothers?" she asks a moment later, looking up at me.

"They would have killed us, if I hadn't stopped them," I say quietly. I bring the mallet down, driving a stake in harder than I strictly need to. "But I didn't kill them."

"No, but you—" She pauses again, clearly struggling for what to say. "You hurt them."

"Didn't you hear what they offered me?" I drive another stake in, hard. "What they would have done to you? I had no other choice."

"They're your brothers." Charlotte sits down heavily as I finish setting up the tent, looking at the spot where I'll build a fire in a moment. "I just—"

"I know you can't imagine it." I move next to her, where the campsite's firepit is, and start to stack wood and take out the kindling. "But, Charlotte—"

This is it, I realize. We'll be in Vegas before too much longer, and we're going to have to make fast time over the next few days. I relented tonight, because Charlotte wanted so badly to go camping, and I wanted to give her that experience. If I'm being honest, I wanted to *share* it with her. I wanted to be here, with her, out in the woods all alone together, grasping for the glimmers of romance in this moment.

But what this really is, is a chance to tell her the rest of the truth. What I am, what I've done. The kind of man I've been. Because, after all, I've been asking her if it would be real if we were together again, without actually letting her see all of what that would look like.

Even if she said yes, it couldn't be the truth unless she knows *all* of the truth. And so, I drag in a deep breath, looking over at her as the wood starts to catch fire.

"There's more that I should tell you," I say quietly. "If you're willing to listen."

20

CHARLOTTE

If you're willing to listen.

There's a part of me that wants to say no. That wants to push him away. I don't know if I want to hear this, if I want more of my worldview to be challenged, if I want to hear the rest of the terrible skeletons in Ivan's closet.

But I can also see this for what it is. I know we're not far from our destination, not far from the place where my identity will be scoured clean, and I'll be cut loose to do as I please, a new woman with a new identity, and a terrifyingly blank slate for a life. This is Ivan, baring himself to me, stripping himself not only naked but raw, and asking me to listen. To hear him tell me who he really is, at last.

For better or for worse.

I nod slowly, wrapping my fingers together as if they're cold. The fire is surprisingly adequate against the chill, actually, but I need to do something with my hands. "Okay," I say softly. "Tell me."

"I told you that I was my father's enforcer," he says, his voice low and rough. "But I'm not sure you know what that means, really."

"You said you enforced his rules. I assume with violence." I twist my fingers tighter together, feeling the quick beat of my pulse form a ball of dread in my stomach. "I assume—a lot of violence."

"I gathered information for him." Ivan swallows hard, the movement of his throat visible in the firelight. "Lev is cruel and vicious, but he lets that brutality run away with him. I'm capable of controlling my emotions, precise and detached. I don't take pleasure in pain the way he does. And that's what—" He swallows again, his fingers digging into his jeans at the knee as he looks straight ahead at the flames. "That's what a man who tortures other men for the Bratva needs to be able to do."

A chill that has nothing to do with the temperature runs down my spine. I can't even repeat what I just heard aloud. "Oh," I whisper softly, my throat so tight that I'm half afraid I won't even be able to speak. "That's—"

"Horrible. Beyond what you imagined, I'm sure. And it wore on me. You remember that I told you I didn't kill that mountain lion, when I went on that trip?" He waits for me to nod, and then continues. "I'd gotten so tired of death, Charlotte. So exhausted with violence."

"But you did it. For a long time." I try to keep the judgment out of my voice, but it's difficult. I can't imagine being willing to do that. I can't imagine what it would take for someone to be faced with that task, and not run in horror. What kind of person it takes to do it.

"I was horrified at first. But there was no way out. I was seventeen then, and there was no running from my father. No money that belonged to me, no path to freedom." Ivan's jaw tightens, and I feel a sudden pang of guilt at my own judgment.

"Seventeen? That's—that's awful." I sink my teeth into my lip. I can't comprehend the kind of father who would tell his teenage son to do that. The type of world Ivan has been immersed in. We're from two such different lives—we might as well be from different planets.

And yet we're both sitting here, in the cold October night, the world silent except for the two of us, as if we're the only ones that exist at this moment.

"It's normal, for Bratva." Ivan blows out a sharp breath. "In time, I became numb to it. And then the fact that I was numb became horrifying, in its own way. I started to think of a way out. I started to make plans, seek out my own contacts, lay a foundation to escape. It took years. Enough blood that I can't ever stop seeing it. But eventually, I was close. And then I found out that my father had started trafficking women." He turns his hands over, palms up, lifting them and dropping them again. "I couldn't leave that alone. I couldn't run, knowing that new horror was something my family was a part of. So, I set out to stop him. I made a deal with the FBI. Information, for my own record wiped clean, and a new identity. All of my money was transferred over to accounts I could still use afterward. A clean slate for me, and my father's operation brought down."

"But you hadn't managed it yet." I think of Bradley, saying that Ivan hadn't brought him enough.

Ivan shakes his head. "I was close," he says quietly. "But I also got distracted."

The emphasis on the last word leaves no doubt as to what he means. "With me."

He nods. Slowly, he angles himself towards me, his chiseled silhouette glinting in the firelight as he looks at me. "You were the one thing I didn't account for, Charlotte," he says quietly. "The thing I didn't plan. I went to Masquerade that night because it was a place I went with my friends. Somewhere, I could blow off steam without anyone knowing who I was. There, I wasn't a bastard son of the Bratva, or Dima Kariyev's torturer, or an FBI informant. I was just a man, seeking pleasure, like everyone else there. I planned to go there, enjoy myself, and leave, like every other night."

He draws in a slow breath, looking down at his hands. "I've never tried to find the identity of anyone I met there before. I've never tracked down *any* woman, the way I tracked you." He swallows hard, and I can tell that he can't quite meet my eyes. "You caught me off guard. I can't even entirely explain why. The reasons you were there, the way you reacted to me, the sounds—"

Ivan breaks off, his hands tightening on his knees, and I see the shudder that goes through him. He looks up at me, his eyes finally meeting mine, the blue as dark as the night around us. "Just thinking about that night still turns me on, Charlotte. I could get off just remembering the way you moaned. The way you tasted. I could spend the rest of my life using that as my only fantasy, and never get tired of it. You are—"

He shakes his head abruptly. "I wanted you to understand," he says finally. "That's all. I never planned to ruin your life. I never planned for *you* at all. I just—lost control. I saw you, and all that precision, all that patience—I lost it. And it's my fault, not yours."

"This world you're describing to me—it doesn't seem real," I whisper, looking at the fire. It sounds like something from another place, foreign and unimaginable. A world of such violence, such brutality, full of traditions and hierarchies that don't make sense in the world I live in—none of it feels real. But Ivan lived it. And now he's out here, with me.

Because of one night. One night that dominoed into so much more.

"I should be afraid of you," I say quietly, still staring into the flames. "You know I should."

His hand flexes as if he wants to reach out for me, but he doesn't. "I would never hurt you," Ivan murmurs. "I wanted out of that life, not to compound it. I don't want to hurt *anyone* any longer, not if I don't have to. And I would never, *ever* hurt you. Not in any way that you didn't want."

A flicker of heat runs up my spine at that last, that reminder of his hand against the curve of my ass, that burn warming my skin that had turned into a different kind of heat. I bite my lip, shoving back the unwanted desire.

"You keep asking me to believe you," I whisper. "And I want to. But—"

"I know."

As we sit there, the fire flickering next to us, I feel something cold on the back of my hand. And then, a moment later, another, and another, until I look up and realize that it's started to softly snow.

"Oh my god." I laugh, covering my mouth with my hand. "I would decide to go camping, and it would snow."

"It's not ideal," Ivan agrees with a chuckle. "But it's not the worst thing. And the fire is warm."

"It's—beautiful, actually." I move closer to him without thinking, leaning into his body heat, as he leans forward to put a little more wood on the fire. It flickers up, sending a few sparks onto the ground, illuminating the slow, drifting snowflakes that shimmer through the air.

It probably won't even stick, I know. In the morning, all evidence of it will be gone. But somehow, that makes the moment feel even more magical. The transience of it, the fact that it's only here right now, for us, makes me feel something so dangerously close to an emotion that I shouldn't name that I try to push it away abruptly.

But I can't. The night is beautiful, and the moment is romantic, and I've never experienced anything like it with anyone else before. I can't stop myself from reaching out, sliding my fingers over the back of Ivan's hand and slipping them between his, and I feel him tense next to me, hesitating before his fingers curl around mine.

My heart is beating hard in my chest, and I feel a little breathless, just from that small touch. We're going to be sleeping next to each other, out here in this peaceful silence, so isolated that it feels as if nothing that happens here is real.

And that's a dangerous, dangerous feeling.

"I know I'm going to be glad when I get back to a city," I say quietly, thinking of all of the things Vegas will have that I've missed. "But for now—this is really nice."

"It is." Ivan's fingers are still wrapped around mine. "And I still have to impress you with my outdoor cooking skills."

"That *is* impressive." I let him take his hand away from mine as he reaches for the insulated bag of food, complete with a grill pan meant to be used over a campfire. "Wait—are you *actually* going to make me a steak? That doesn't seem like a skill that a man with an Aston Martin should have at all. Aren't you supposed to have a cook who does all of that for you?"

"Actually, no," Ivan says with a smirk. "Truthfully, I've lived off of takeout most of the time. But occasionally, when I've decided I want a meal that doesn't come in a Styrofoam container, I've learned to make it myself."

"I'm already impressed." I can't keep the smile off of my face. I've been trying *not* to smile at him this entire trip, trying not to let him see that I take any pleasure in his company, but right now, in this setting, I can't help it. I know that he's doing this all for me. That all of this is to make *me* happy, when Ivan would have just pushed through to the next town, and the next, for as long as he could manage it before exhaustion overtook him.

"I only grabbed a couple of spices. It can't compare to what I could make for you at home. But it'll be something better than what we've had on the road so far." Ivan reaches for a small container of some sort of steak spice, dusting it over the meat, and the smell of the crackling oil and the chopped garlic that he put into it makes my mouth water.

"I'm sure your penthouse in Chicago is full of every spice and condiment and cooking utensil known to man," I tease.

Ivan's hand goes still on the pan, and I see his jaw tense suddenly. It's not the reaction I would have expected, and I look at him curiously.

"Did I say something wrong?"

Ivan shakes his head. "I just—there's somewhere I wish I could have taken you, Charlotte. From the very start." He stares at the pan as he drops the meat into it, not looking at me. "I wish I'd told you who I was, let you make up your mind for yourself—and then, at the same time, I'm glad I didn't, because you would have run the moment you heard the first few words. I would have never gotten to share any of what I did with you. It's something I've never experienced before." His jaw tightens further, the muscle there twitching. "Regret, and at the same time, not regretting it a bit, even if I should."

"What are you talking about?" I rub my palms on my jeans, feeling as if my hands are sweaty despite the chill of the evening. "The Bratva?" I hate to admit that he's right. If he'd told me the truth about who he was from the start, I would never have given him a chance. I would have bolted, and written him off as a dodged bullet. And I would have missed out on—

On him, awakening feelings in me that I never knew were possible that night at Masquerade. I would have missed out on laughing in my kitchen while he peeled apples. On walking through the orchard while we picked them. On him, kissing me on my couch with *Beetlejuice* playing in the background. On, for once, feeling like being myself was enough. Like I wasn't boring, or just being tolerated, or too basic for someone interesting to want.

Ivan made me feel, for that brief time, like I was *everything* he could possibly want in a woman. And he keeps insisting that it was real. That out of all of the lies and deceptions, how he felt about me was the one truth. The reason for all of the lies in the first place.

I don't know how to let myself wrap my head around that. Because if it's true—

How do I just walk away from a man who feels that way for me? Who is exactly what *I* wanted—except for the part where he couldn't tell me who he really was.

But if he had, I would never have found out.

It makes my head ache. Ivan has gone silent, seemingly aware of the struggle that I'm enduring in my own head. He flips the meat, then glances over at me.

"Not the Bratva," he says quietly. "I told you about all that. But—" He swallows hard, taking the pan off the flames and setting it aside to let the steaks rest for a moment. "You joke about a penthouse, but I do have one. On the Gold Coast, all fancy and looks probably exactly the way you would expect. But I don't really spend any time there. Not unless I think my father or brothers are watching me, or my father's driver needs a place to pick me up or drop me off. It's where I like him to think I live, but it's really not."

I frown at him, thoroughly confused. "What do you mean? Where do you live, then?"

Ivan sits back, dusting his hands off on his jeans. "A place I wish I could show you pictures of, if I still had my phone. I wish I could've taken you there. I *should* have, and maybe you would have given me a chance after all, if only because it's not what you would have expected."

I'm still lost, and Ivan can see it on my face. He sighs. "A house, Charlotte. Out in the suburbs. Just a normal place. Two stories and a basement, typical Midwestern ranch, the whole thing." He heaves a deep sigh, lifting one shoulder as he turns back to the food. "I imagine I'll never see it again, now."

I stare at him for a long moment, trying to wrap my head around what he's saying. A normal house. His *home*, from the longing in his voice, the same way I know I sound when I talk about my friends, or my apartment, all lost to me now. But once again, it doesn't fit with my image of who Ivan should be.

"Why would you have a house like that? When you also have—" I can feel myself frowning so hard it's almost giving me a headache. Everyone wants the kind of luxury Ivan is claiming that he has, and doesn't use. *Everyone.* Jaz would do filthy things for a man who had a penthouse.

Or almost everyone, I suppose—I don't particularly want that. And Ivan is making it sound as if he doesn't, either.

"Was it because you were hoping to have a family? To raise them more—normal?" It's the only explanation I can think of. But Ivan shakes his head.

"No. To be honest, when I said I didn't expect you, Charlotte—I didn't expect what I feel for you with *anyone*. I've never wanted more than a few nights with any woman. Even the ones I've spent more than that with, it's always been a casual thing. I never saw a long-term relationship fitting into my life, and definitely not a family. Before I decided to make plans to leave, I couldn't imagine how that would happen. No woman associated with the Bratva would want to marry Dima Kariyev's bastard son, not when so many better men would be on offer. And I didn't want to drag a woman outside of it into that hell." His jaw tightens. "And once I left, I didn't imagine I could ever rationalize putting anyone I cared about in the kind of danger that would always follow me."

That stings. "Except for me." I move away from him, the harsh reality settling in, all of the warmth I'd felt dissipating and leaving me painfully vulnerable to the cold inside and out. "Or you don't actually care about me, then."

"No. That's not—" Ivan scrubs a hand through his hair, looking at me as if he's desperate for some way to make me understand. "You were inevitable, Charlotte. I couldn't resist you. I *knew* it was wrong, I *knew* I shouldn't do what I was doing, and I couldn't stop myself. It's no excuse, but—" he shakes his head violently, looking up at me with those dark eyes. "I have that house because it's my haven, Charlotte. It's something of mine that my father doesn't know about. That *no one* knows about, other than you, now. You're the first person I've ever told about it. And you're also the only person who's ever made me feel the way that place does."

The admission shocks me into momentary silence. I stare at him, the crackling of the fire and the distant sound of the wind fading into an echo, and I swallow hard.

"I think the food is done."

Ivan's jaw tightens, and for a second, I think he's going to snap at me. I can feel the weight of what he's just told me, and I pushed it aside. But I don't know what to do with it.

I don't know how to hear a man that I'm supposed to hate tell me that I feel like his home.

Especially not when he's made me feel that way, too.

Ivan turns, putting the pan between us. "I got some plasticware," he said. "Forgot to grab plates. And we don't really have sides, except this." He pulls out a bag of chips sheepishly. "Not exactly a five-star dinner."

"The steak is delicious." I'm startled by how good it is, actually, the meat is tender and flavorful. It tastes different from anything I've had before, as if something about it being cooked outside like this, in the open air over a campfire, has made it better in some way. I tear through mine hungrily, not bothering to worry about looking ladylike as I eat. I don't think Ivan cares, and I want the distraction of the food. It's also the best thing I've eaten in days.

"I'm glad you like it." Ivan eats his more slowly, and I can feel the tension in him. I can't pretend that I don't know where it's coming from, that it's not because of what he said, and my lack of response. "We should probably get some sleep soon. It's going to get colder, and we need to be up early tomorrow, before anyone else shows up here."

I nod. A part of me wants to say something, anything, to make this better. But I have no idea what I could possibly say in response. The knowledge of what Ivan feels for me is terrifying. My reaction to it, how it makes *me* feel, is terrifying.

Inside the tent, Ivan has spread out a soft memory foam mat, covered in a sheet. There are two pillows and a couple of heavy blankets, and I swallow hard, realizing how closely we're going to be sleeping. It's not really any different from last night—but it *feels* different, all the same. It's something about how far out we are, how isolated, that feels romantic and terrifying all at once.

Ivan follows me into the tent a few minutes later, and I realize he was giving me privacy to change clothes while he cleaned up outside. I slip into my sweatpants and t-shirt as quickly as I can, given the chill inside the tent, and I feel an uncomfortable tightness in my chest as I see him unzip his duffel bag.

Turning away, I slide under the blankets, but I feel painfully aware of every movement he makes behind me. The sound of his zipper, the shift of clothing over skin, the knowledge that an arm's length away, he's half-naked. I want to roll over, slide my hands under his shirt, feel all that hard, muscled flesh against my palms. But I stay firmly rolled away, thinking of what he said, and how impossible that is for me to even begin to face.

He can't really feel that way about me. And I definitely can't feel that way about him.

But my breath catches when I feel the blankets shift, Ivan sliding into our makeshift bed on the other side of me. My pulse lodges in my throat, beating hard in the hollow of it, and I curl my hands into fists, fighting the urge to roll over and look at him with everything in me.

He's tense, too. I can hear it in his breathing, feel it in every line of his body. I can feel him fighting off the same desire, and suddenly, I can't remember why we're both fighting it at all.

I want him. Emotions aside, my anger with him aside, I can't grasp onto the certainty that I had before that we shouldn't enjoy each other's bodies at least once more before we get to Vegas and split off forever. Ivan has made me feel things that I never thought I would, that no other man has ever accomplished. And right now, the craving feels so intense that I can't remember why it's a bad idea to do it *just one more time*.

Is this what it feels like to be addicted to something? I wouldn't know, but I can imagine that it must be. It feels like a hunger, and it feels like one that I can't fight.

This must be what addiction feels like, what Ivan means when he says I became an obsession for him. Because right now, I can't recall why this is a bad idea.

Before I can stop myself, I roll over to face him. Ivan is on his back, staring up at the ceiling, his arms crossed over his chest. I can see him breathing, see the tense set to his jaw, and a hot jolt of desire crackles through me at the thought that he's fighting the same urges I am.

With more success, apparently.

"Ivan," I whisper his name, but it sounds loud in the silence of the tent. He shifts, his jaw tightening further, and it's not until I whisper it again that he turns to look at me.

There's a warning in his eyes when he does. "Charlotte—"

I shift closer, across the soft flannel sheet that he put on the mat, towards the hard warmth of his body as if drawn by a magnet. "I'm cold," I say softly, and I think it's the first time *I've* ever lied to *him*.

I'm not really cold. The rampant arousal running through me wouldn't *let* me get cold, even if Ivan's body heat hadn't already radiated beneath the blankets enough to warm us both. But I want to be closer to him, and I want him to give in.

That muscle in the hollow of his cheek leaps. I see his throat move as he swallows, shifting slightly closer to me, his arms still wrapped over his chest. He doesn't look at me, and I reach out, resting my hand against his chest as I move closer, my breasts brushing against his arm.

Ivan turns so quickly, I suck in a startled breath, his hand sliding into my hair. One hand braces against the mat as he rolls me onto my back, his knee pushing my legs apart as he leans over me.

He looks down at me, something fierce and hot in his eyes, and his mouth crushes against mine.

Yes. This is what I want. Not the complicated emotions or long conversations about what happened before. *This.* Ivan's kiss drives every thought out of my head, every feeling out of my chest other than that tight, desperate need for *more*. I wrap my legs around him, pulling him closer, moaning into the kiss as I feel him press against me, hard and as eager as I am.

His teeth nip at my lower lip, sucking it into his mouth, the hand that was in my hair dropping to cup my breast through my t-shirt. He groans when he feels that I'm not wearing a bra, molding the soft flesh through the fabric, his hips grinding against me as if he can't wait to get inside me.

I'm panting against his mouth, all thoughts of being embarrassed about any of it fleeing under the onslaught of his lips and hands, his body against mine. He feels so fucking good, hard and virile and masculine, and I tighten my legs around him, arching my hips into his as I rub myself along the clothed length of his cock.

"Fuck me," I gasp against his lips, too desperate to feel ashamed any longer. This need has been steadily coiling inside of me since that afternoon at the hotel, when I went down on him in an effort to throw up a wall of *sex and nothing else* between us, and he forced me to confront how much I wanted him. That memory has been haunting me, the need to feel that kind of pleasure, that kind of release again, building until there's no longer any reason for my begging other than sheer desperation. I'm not toying with him any longer, not trying to use his lust against him, not attempting to reduce us down to our basest, filthiest desire for one another.

I just need him inside of me.

"Ivan, please." I run my hands under his shirt, over the ridges of his abs, nails scratching up his back as he groans against my lips, breathing raggedly. He feels so fucking hard, wedged between my thighs, and I want to wish away the layers of clothing between us. Even like this, I can feel the pressure of his thick length against my clit, rubbing the fabric of my panties against me in a way that could make me come if he just doesn't stop. "Please. Fuck me."

I buck against him again, digging my nails against his shoulders as I squirm in an effort to get more of that delicious friction, and Ivan lets out another helpless moan, bucking into me as his forehead presses against mine and his tongue slides into my mouth.

And then, just as his hand slides down my waist, fingers hovering at my waistband, just as I think he's going to yank down my sweatpants and slide his fingers inside of me—or better yet, yank down his too and make it his cock instead—he pulls away, panting so hard that I can see his breath misting in the cold air.

"Tell me you believe me," he growls. He looks down at me with that dark blue gaze, his eyes so intense that it makes me shudder. "Tell me it's real, Charlotte. Tell me you believe that what I feel for you is real. Tell me you feel the same way."

I stare up at him, trying to process what he's saying through the fog of lust clouding my mind. I'm dripping wet, my panties clinging to me, soaked through. My entire body is throbbing with unfulfilled need, and I'm on the verge of saying *anything* if it would make him get me off. If he would give me his tongue, or his fingers, or—God, *please* —his cock. I can see it straining against the front of his pants, rockhard, and I sit up halfway, reaching for the waist of them. My fingers graze against his skin, between his shirt and the pants, and Ivan jerks back as if I've burned him.

"I told you," he breathes out raggedly. "The next time I fuck you, it will be real, Charlotte. It'll be because you want *me*. Just as I am. Because you believe that even though I lied, what I felt for you has always been the truth."

I swallow hard. "And if I say yes?"

His expression darkens, and he surges forward, pinning me back against the mat again, his fingers running through my hair. "If you say yes," he breathes, "I don't know how I'd ever let you go again."

His mouth presses against mine, and the kiss is different this time. It feels more like that kiss just after we ran from Bradley, the one that felt like he was saying he loved me without ever saying the words, a kiss so intense and tender all at once that it made me wonder if I'd gotten him all wrong. His mouth slides over mine, nipping, licking, *savoring* me, and I feel the hard length of his cock trapped against me, his body pinning mine down.

"Please," I whimper against his mouth. "I need you in me, Ivan. Please."

His hands slide down my arms, and I feel him heave another breath. "Say it," he whispers against my lips, his eyes opening. "Say it."

A beat passes. Another. I open my eyes, and look into his. And I can't make the words slide past my lips.

I'm too afraid to say yes. I don't know for sure what I believe.

I can't lie to him.

"I'm scared," I whisper, and the look on Ivan's face is like I just slapped him.

He pulls back, staring down at me with a look of abject hurt, of desperation, like he's starving and I've just told him he can't eat. His jaw clenches, and he lets out a long, shuddering breath before he wrenches around, yanking the tent flap open and stepping out into the night.

I hear it close behind him. I can see his silhouette, walking back towards the banked fire. I hear the sound of him groaning and see him turn his back—I know what he's doing.

Something like jealousy rips through me. *I want his pleasure. I want him to make those sounds with me, to come because of me.* But sex isn't enough for him. One more night of giving and taking the unimaginable pleasure we seem to find with each other isn't enough. He wants something I can't give.

Something I'm afraid to give.

And why? I know the answer before I'm even done thinking the question. All my life, I've been the one who does the safe, rational, measured thing. I've checked off boxes and made lists, and always, always done what I was supposed to.

Letting a criminal love me, running away with him, *loving him back* isn't what I'm supposed to do. It's not on any checklist, not on anyone's five-year plan. Fucking one is bad enough, but hearing him say that he's obsessed with you, that you're his home, that he can't let you go, and *believe* it? *Wanting* it?

That's so far removed from how I've always been that I don't know how to let myself admit that it might be exactly how I feel. And if I can't admit it to myself, I definitely can't say it out loud to him.

My body is begging for release. I'm wound tight, still breathless, and it wouldn't take much to tip myself over the edge. To give myself exactly what Ivan is doing right now, out in the cold.

But it isn't my fingers that I want making me come. It won't be good enough. And the emotions in my chest, knotted up and hurting, make me roll over instead, curling in on myself under the blankets as I close my eyes and wish for him to come back.

It feels cold without him.

And I have a feeling that it always will.

21

IVAN

I've rarely been angry with Charlotte. Even now, I don't know if it's her that I'm angry with, or myself. But when she whispers that she's scared, that emotion rips through me, tightening my chest and making me want to scream.

I don't know if she means that she's scared of me, or of what she feels. Logically, I know it's probably the latter. That by telling me that at all, she's letting me know she feels what I want her to say.

But I need to hear it out loud. And until I do, I refuse to give her what we both so desperately need.

The only thing I can do is get away from her. If I don't, I'll give in, and I'll hate myself afterward. I rip open the tent, stumbling out into the cold darkness, with only enough presence of mind to close the tent against the cold for her before I sink down next to the banked fire.

It doesn't give off much heat, but it doesn't really matter. The desire raging through me is hot enough to ward off the cold. My head is pounding, muscles wound tight as I yank down the front of my sweatpants, fisting my cock before it's barely even out, before I even register the chill against the hot, straining flesh.

I moan when my palm connects with it, my fingers wrapping

around my length. I'm slick with pre-cum, so wet from it dripping down my shaft that I wouldn't even need lube if I had it. I run my hand down to the base and up over the head, gasping as the sensation curls my toes, the need to come, shoving every other thought out of my head.

There's nothing slow or purposeful about how I get myself off. Just a frantic, desperate need to come before I give in, go back into that tent, and give Charlotte what she begged me for. My hips thrust into my fist, desperate for something softer, wetter, hotter. My cock throbs, desperate for *her*. No other woman will ever do, after this. I'll never want anyone else like I want her. I feel certain of it, as I fuck my fist like I'm going mad, slamming my hand down my length again and again as I feel my balls tighten and that hot burst of pleasure unleash at the base of my spine.

I'm going to spend the rest of my fucking life thinking about her when I come. How she smells, how she tastes, how she feels around my fingers and around my cock, the sweet, whimpering sound she makes when she comes—

"*Fuck!*" I snarl the curse as my cock erupts, throbbing in my fingers as my cum spills out onto the dirt, spurting from the tip as I thrust into my hand. I grab onto the log next to me to keep from tipping forward, squeezing my cock as I fist it roughly, spurt after spurt shooting out as I moan Charlotte's name under my breath and pant wildly, the pleasure and the need prolonging my orgasm. I'm still throbbing when I let go, cum dripping from my cockhead as I gasp for breath, the cold air softening me as I reach down and tuck myself back in.

I wait for the desperation to recede. For the need to not feel as frantic. To remember that there will be other women, and other beds, that I'm going to Vegas, where there are more gorgeous women than I could run through in a year if I wanted to take one to bed every night. For the relief of the orgasm to clear my head, and for me to remember that Charlotte isn't the only woman in the world I could want.

It doesn't happen. I don't care about what's waiting for me in

Vegas. I don't care about taking anyone else to my bed. I don't want anyone other than her, and that knowledge, coupled with what I said to her earlier tonight, slams into my chest like a fist.

I told her that she felt like home. Like *my* home.

I love her.

Sitting there on the log, my breath misting in front of me, I can't pretend that isn't the truth any longer. Out here, in the dark silence of the night, it's unavoidable. I love her, and I want her to believe that the way we started isn't the way things have to continue to be. That even if I can't be sorry that I found a way to make her mine for a little while, I can't regret the time we spent together—I do regret the way it turned out. I regret that I didn't find some other way.

Even if there wasn't one. Even if this is just regret for getting caught instead of regret for actually lying. I don't know how to reconcile that—but I do know I'd spend the rest of my fucking life trying to make it better if she'd let me. Trying to show her that I'll never lie to her again.

Frustration wells up in my chest, hot and thick. She wants me. She was trying to get me to fuck her, trying to get pleasure from me without admitting how she feels. Without making herself face how *I* feel. And I can't help the agitation that wells up in me, knowing that she's pushing me away because she can't accept wanting me as I am.

She can't accept that she wants a criminal. That a criminal loves her. That she loves me, too.

I'd bet money that she does. Ironic, considering where we're going. But she's planning to leave me there, just as soon as she can.

I brace my hands on either side, curling my fingers against the rough wood of the log. I almost gave in. Almost gave her what we both want. But if I do, that's all it'll ever be.

Glancing over at the tent, I feel a flood of guilt. I should be in there, helping keep her warm. Now that the worst of the storm of lust has passed, I have no real excuse to be out here, leaving her alone.

I slip back into the tent, under the blanket next to her, leaving an arm's length between us. I can't tell if she's sleeping or just pretending to, facing away from me on her side, the rhythmic movement of her breathing visible under the blanket.

There's very little chance that I'm going to sleep at all. I lie on my back, staring up at the ceiling of the tent, my chest aching. I *want* to fall asleep, to get some rest for the days ahead, but all I seem to be able to do is run through the litany of memories that I have with Charlotte, thinking back to every moment when I might have been able to do something different. Where I might have been able to change how things went between us.

In the morning, I wake before she does, as if the silent chill of our out-of-the-way campsite has lulled her into a deeper sleep than she's managed in days. There's a certain safety to where we are, a feeling that we won't be found, and whether that's actually true or not, I can see how it might have earned her a better night's sleep.

I wish I could say the same.

I wake curled against her, my body having sought hers out during the night despite everything, my arm draped over her waist. I lie there for a few moments, still, wanting to soak up the feeling of having her so close to me.

After what happened last night, I have every intention of not sleeping in the same bed with her again. Regardless of her protests, I don't think I can take another night of being so close to her, another morning waking pressed up against her like this. *Every* part of me aches to be closer to her, to the point that even my hard cock feels like an afterthought. And this morning, I'm filled with something very close to regret.

I've never opened up to anyone the way I did with her last night. And now, in the cold daylight, I'm not sure that I should have. I let her see more of me than anyone else ever has, and it didn't make a difference. I feel raw this morning, like an open wound, and there's nothing to salve it. Even her closeness, at this point, only makes it feel worse—a reminder of what I can almost touch, but never actually have.

I should have known better than to ever start anything with her. I want to shove the thought away as soon as it enters my mind, but it lingers, an unwanted heaviness on my mind and my heart.

She feels so good, pressed up against me. Warm and soft, a promise of something I can never have. A dream that I want to keep going back to, again and again.

I feel her start to stir, and I pull back, clenching my teeth against the wave of need that washes over me. I don't want to pack up and get back on the road. I don't want to keep driving, all the way to where Charlotte Williams will be erased and replaced with a woman who will walk away from me and do her best to forget that any of this ever happened.

I want to stay here with her. Right here, pretending that the world can pass us by while I lose myself in her, over and over again.

Pushing myself up from the mat, I stifle a groan as I reach for my bag. I'm far from old, but so many nights of sleeping on the floor—and now a mat on the ground—not to mention days and days of driving, is doing a real number on my back. I reach for my bag, quietly unzipping it to get my clothes out, and I hear her shift behind me.

"Ivan?" Her voice is sweet, sleepy, and something tugs hard in my chest at the sound of it. But I shove it down, refusing to let myself soften for her again. It's not getting me any closer to her forgiveness, and it feels like it's tearing me apart.

"We should get on the road." Even I wince at how curt my voice sounds, but I tell myself it's for the best. If all she wants from me is temporary pleasure until we part ways, that's not what I can offer her. Continuing to pretend anything else will only keep hurting us both.

I hear her shift behind me, silence falling heavily in the tent. Out of the corner of my eye, I see her wrap her arms around herself, looking away as if my comment cut her deeply.

Grabbing my clothes out of the bag, I lean forward and unzip the tent, slipping out. I'd rather dress in the cold morning outside than keep suffocating in the tense hurt between us.

I have the car packed up by the time Charlotte slips out of the tent, wearing slim jeans that make it hard for me to drag my gaze away from her legs, a soft-looking grey pullover hoodie, and her denim jacket over top of it. Her outfit is plainer than anything I ever saw her wearing in Chicago, but she looks so utterly beautiful all the same that I have to clench my hands into fists to keep from going to her, the bite of my nails against my palms bringing me back into the present.

Charlotte was made to torment me. It's the only thing I can think as I pack up the tent in quick, jerky motions, trying not to think about last night—or waking up next to her this morning, or how much, in a few days, I'm going to miss her.

It feels unthinkable that she's going to walk out of my life. But I can't make her stay.

She's already sitting in the passenger's seat of the car when I toss the last bag in the back, and come around to slide in on my side. She doesn't look at me, and I grit my teeth as I start the car, biting back everything I want to say.

This is over, Ivan. Just fucking accept it.

I can do what I set out to, and get her to Vegas safely. I can get her new identification, get her what she needs to start a new life. Maybe she won't ever be able to put everything that she's lost because of me behind her, but that's not my problem. It's *not*.

"I'm sorry about last night," she says a little while later, her voice so soft that I almost don't hear it under the growl of Guns & Roses from the radio. I swallow hard, wondering if I should just pretend that I didn't.

"Me too," I say finally, and Charlotte doesn't say another word.

Halfway through the day, I pull into a gas station to refuel and get something to drink. I glance over at Charlotte as I pull up in front, but she doesn't move, or give me any inclination that she wants to get out. So I just go in myself, keeping an eye on her every few seconds to make sure that she's still safe.

And it's fine, until I look away for a second too long and glance back to see a black car pulled up next to the Corolla, and Bradley sliding out of the driver's side.

I freeze, a bag of potato chips falling out of my hand and hitting the tile floor. Bradley's hand shoots out, grabbing Charlotte's door, but it's locked. I see his jaw tighten, see him press his fist up against the glass as he leans forward.

Charlotte's face is white. I can see that even from where I'm standing. And I see his mouth open, saying something to her as she frowns, twisting in the seat.

My pulse jumps into my throat; every nerve in my body is suddenly wired. I'm cursing myself for not making her come into the store with me, my mind racing with how I could have possibly prevented this. Between this and the run-in with my brothers, who no doubt won't stop so long as they're still alive, I feel like I can't keep her safe. Like I'm failing at the only thing left that matters to me.

But in a world where there are cameras at gas stations and traffic lights, where even with our cell phones destroyed, it's impossible to avoid tech altogether, I can't stay ahead of everything all of the time— but it still feels as if I've failed, seeing Bradley leaning over her window.

I feel my hand twitch involuntarily towards where I know my gun is hidden, waiting for him to make the wrong move. To try to break the window. To scare her into getting out.

Shooting an FBI agent would be by far the worst decision I've made so far.

But no one, not even him, is taking Charlotte away. If she's going to leave me, it'll be her decision.

No one else's.

22

CHARLOTTE

It's not until a shadow falls over my passenger's side door that I realize Bradley is standing there. I look up when I see it, thinking that Ivan has come back to ask me if I want something, when I see the tall, dark-haired FBI agent, and my stomach plummets to my feet.

Shit.

My first reaction is to look and see if the doors are locked. My second is to flinch back as I hear the sound of him trying to yank my door open.

Thank fuck. Ivan always locks the doors when he leaves me alone in the car for even a few seconds. I didn't think anything of it before, but now I'm so grateful that I could almost cry. Bradley can't get to me now, and by the time Ivan sees what's happening—

Bradley's fist hits the window with a hard sound, and his face leans close to the glass, so menacing that he's almost more frightening to me than Ivan's brothers were.

This is all wrong. My stomach tightens, my thoughts grappling with the confusion over how Bradley instinctively makes me feel, and how I know I should feel. He's an FBI agent. He's supposed to be one of the good guys. He's supposed to help me. But as I look at the expression on his face—the clenched jaw, the fury that he's directing at me, I'm terrified.

"Open the door!" he growls, his voice muffled but still audible. "Now!"

I shake my head, my hands trembling as I knot them in my lap, swallowing hard as I think desperately of what to do. My heart is pounding so hard I can barely hear anything else. I glance towards the store entrance, silently willing Ivan to hurry back. How long has it been? Surely, he'll be out any second now. *But what is he going to do? He can't shoot an FBI agent. That would be suicide.*

But is it? I think of what Ivan told me last night, the things he's done for his family. *A Bratva torturer.* It still doesn't seem real—if it did, I don't know how I would have gotten in the car with him this morning. But after that, shooting someone like Bradley seems small in comparison. I can't imagine Ivan has that much respect for the law. And there's no love lost between them, I'm sure of that. Besides, when we get to Las Vegas, his contact is going to scrub his identity clean, if what he told me is correct.

So does it matter what he really does to Bradley, then?

Ivan, hurry up.

Bradley's fist connects with the window again, harder this time. I jump, a small yelp escaping my lips. For a horrifying moment, I think the glass might actually shatter.

"I said open the door!" he snarls, and I flinch back again, my heart still hammering painfully in my chest.

I don't know if Ivan has seen him yet. I don't know what he could possibly be waiting on. But despite everything, in this, I trust him. I trust him with my safety—that as soon as he sees what's happening, he'll put a stop to it. I just have to be brave until then.

I tilt my chin up, glaring back at Bradley. "I don't want to go with you," I tell him flatly. "I've made up my mind about that."

Bradley raises an eyebrow, that barely controlled anger still on his face, but it's clear he's trying to soften it. Trying honey instead of vinegar. "Look, Charlotte, whatever you've been told—whatever you're thinking—"

"What I'm *thinking*," I snap, "is that you brought my ex with you to the handover. A man who cheated on me, who—"

"That's hardly a crime," Bradley snickers, and I feel my throat tighten, my own anger threatening to overtake my better sense.

Ivan might be a fucking criminal, but he hasn't talked over me. He hasn't told me that he knows better. He hasn't treated me like I'm a child that needs coddling, something breakable to be tucked away until it's needed. And between Nate and Bradley, I'm sick to fucking death of it.

"—who sent me text messages that verged on stalking," I continue, as if he hadn't spoken. "Who made me feel uncomfortable and unsafe. Who *you* made it clear I'd be going back with, since he was working with you. You're an FBI agent. You know the statistics for domestic violence. This entire setup makes me think that I'd be ripe for that if I went back to Nate. If he was allowed anywhere near me. And I don't think you'd protect me from that. I don't think I'd trust a single goddamn fucker with a badge to protect me at this point. So—"

Bradley's eyes narrow, his face contorting with rage. He slams his palm against the window, making me jump again.

"You don't know what you're doing," he hisses. "You have no idea who you're dealing with. That man is a killer, Charlotte. A monster. You think he gives a shit about you? You think he won't do worse to you than you can imagine when he finally gets bored of whatever game the two of you are playing?"

The cold certainty in his voice sends a chill down my spine, but I force myself to stare right back at him, my jaw set, too. I don't want him to see how afraid I am of him, how confused I am about Ivan, about this situation, about *everything*. "I know exactly who I'm dealing with," I lie, my voice steadier than I feel. "And I'd rather take my chances with Ivan than with you."

Bradley's laugh is cold, humorless. "You stupid girl. You have no idea what you're doing. When he's done with you, you'll wish you'd come with me." He stares at me through the glass, his muffled voice every bit as menacing as if it were clear and unfiltered. "You'll wish you had the kind of protection I can offer you. Because if it isn't him that makes you realize what a stupid fucking choice you've made, it'll be his family."

That shiver spreads over my skin, making me feel cold down to the bone, and from the way that humorless tone spreads into the smirk on Bradley's face, he can see it. I might not be scared of Ivan, but I'm fucking terrified of his family. His brothers didn't seem like the most capable apples on the family tree, but I've seen enough of Lev to know that I should be terrified of him. And I know what Ivan's father, Dima, wants to do to me if they manage to get ahold of me.

I'd rather die than let Ivan's family sell me to some billionaire. I'd rather take Ivan's offer of the clean identification and a fresh start in Vegas. At least that's a real chance. Because if the Bratva catch me and sell me off, who is going to save me?

Agent fucking Bradley? Unlikely.

I open my mouth to respond, my throat tightening until I'm not sure I can get the words out. My instinct is to defend Ivan, and that feels insane. Because from everything he's told me—he *is* a killer. He *is* a monster, or at least, he's one by the standards of the life I've always lived.

But a part of me, the part I keep running from because it terrifies me more than anything that's happened so far to admit, can't stop the thought that runs through my head.

He's my *monster.*

And in a way, it's absolutely true. I created him, unwittingly, as thoroughly as Victor Frankenstein ever created his, if what Ivan has said to me is to be believed. According to him, he never even thought of stalking a woman the way he stalked me before we met. Whatever this *thing* is between us, this chemistry, this magnetic pull that keeps dragging us to each other again and again—it created everything Ivan has done. And now I feel so thoroughly tangled up in it that when I look back and imagine never having met Ivan, never having felt any of the things that I have with him, even if it meant getting my life back—

I don't know what choice I would make any longer. I should know, but I don't.

And that's why I can't tell Ivan that I believe him. I can't say *yes* to any of his questions. Because saying that out loud would make it real.

"Charlotte." Bradley's voice is coaxing now, and I see him glance up at the gas station window, as if he's wondering why Ivan hasn't come out yet, either. He leans in, propping his forearm against the edge of the window as if we're friends, just catching up. "Look, just come with me. Nate isn't here. I'll explain more to you about Ivan and the Bratva, and why you're in danger here. Why I've kept pursuing you. It's for your own good. And you can tell me more about Nate. Maybe you're right, and I should give him a second look—"

He's cut off mid-sentence as Ivan comes into sudden view, his hand going around Bradley's throat and flinging him back against the unmarked FBI vehicle, his body weight leaning into the arm that keeps Bradley pinned. My heart leaps into my throat at the one glimpse of Ivan's face that I get as he lunges forward and rips Bradley away from my window, his expression a mask of cold fury.

"What the fuck do you think you're doing?" Ivan growls, his voice low and dangerous.

Bradley struggles against Ivan's grip, his hand fumbling for his gun. Ivan knocks Bradley's hand away, sharply, the edge of his hand connecting with Bradley's wrist. The agent yelps in pain, and his face reddens with embarrassment, that furious hate filling his gaze again. I'm frozen in my seat, my breath caught in my lungs, my hands gripping my thighs hard enough that I can feel the press of my nails through the denim.

"Let go of me, you Russian piece of shit!" Bradley snaps, spit bubbling from his lips. Ivan leans in, his forearm sliding over Bradley's windpipe as he holds him against the car. "Someone—will—see you—"

His words come out choked, even more muffled now, and I feel a sense of satisfaction that startles me. I shouldn't be happy to see Ivan pinning an FBI agent to a car, hurling threats at him. This is, as far as I've been taught my whole life, *not* what I should want. Ivan is a criminal, and Bradley is the one I should run to for help.

But Ivan is the only one who has ever made me feel safe.

Ivan leans in closer, his back ramrod straight. I can barely hear what he hisses at Bradley; the words are faint, but I can still make them out.

"Stay away from her. She made her choice."

Choice? What choice is he talking about? A little bit of that unresolved anger I still have for the situation Ivan has put me in flares up, because the truth is, my choice was gone when I became Ivan's obsession. When that obsession made me a target for his family. My choice was gone when he attacked Nate, and made him even more a part of all of this.

It was gone when scrubbing my life clean and starting over became my only option.

Or does he mean himself? Because I haven't chosen him. I *haven't*.

I'm going to leave, as soon as I have what I need.

Last night didn't change that. Nothing will change that. But the voice that whispers it feels more fragile than ever.

Bradley snorts. "She doesn't know what she's choosing, if that's true," he spits out. "But she's as stupid as I thought, if it really is."

I watch in horror as Ivan switches his grip so quickly that I almost don't see the movement, his other hand gripping Bradley's throat so tightly that his knuckles start to turn white. He reaches with his other hand for Bradley's gun, yanking it out of its holster and throwing it onto the pavement, kicking it away as Bradley's face starts to turn an alarming shade of purple. His eyes bulge, and he reaches up, clawing at Ivan's arm as he struggles. It's never been so clear to me how strong Ivan is, until this moment. His arm is flexed, muscles taut under his shirt, and it would be arousing if this moment wasn't so fucking terrifying.

Why the fuck did I just think that? What is wrong with me?

"Ivan!" I shout, my voice muffled through the glass. "Stop!" I can see him on the verge of strangling Bradley, about to make a choice that he can't take back. I know rationally that he's made dozens of those before, hundreds—that he's been walking down a road that's been disappearing behind him as he goes for a long time. But this is the first time I'm seeing it personally. The first time I'm witness to something that he can't undo.

It might be hypocrisy, but I'm genuinely afraid for him.

For a moment, I think he hasn't heard me. He doesn't move, and I catch a glimpse of his face in the side mirror of Bradley's car. His eyes are locked onto Bradley's, a cold fury in them that sends a fresh wave of chills down my spine. He looks entirely capable of killing a man, of killing *this* man, and I can see the side of him that he told me about last night. The brutal enforcer capable of torture and murder.

I open my mouth to shout at him again, terrified of what happens if Ivan steps over the line of killing a cop, an *FBI agent*—when Ivan's grip loosens slightly, and Bradley sucks in a ragged breath, gasping as he lets out a flurry of violent coughs.

"You listen to me very carefully," I hear Ivan hiss, his face inches from Bradley's. "You come near her again, you so much as look in her direction, and I will kill you next time. If you try to convince her of your bullshit, I will shoot you dead. I will *end* you and your miserable existence, and my only fucking regret will be that I didn't have time to do it more slowly. Do we understand each other?"

I doubt Bradley would agree. But I don't find out. Ivan kicks the gun again, sending it spinning out across the parking lot pavement far enough that it would take Bradley several strides to catch up to it. He grabs the front of Bradley's jacket, yanking him forward and slamming him back against the car hard enough that Bradley's head bounces back against the glass, and then he gives me one quick look over his shoulder before he darts to the front of the car.

It's still running. I'm hoping with everything in me that I'm reading his signals correctly as I lunge over and hit the lock for Ivan's side, unlocking the door just as he grabs for it, flinging himself into the driver's side.

He doesn't even finish closing his door before his hand is on the gearshift, flinging it into first as he hits the gas, the tires spinning as we burn rubber across the parking lot with a high-pitched squeal. The smell is acrid, making me cough, and I don't dare look back as

Ivan drags his door shut, accelerating across the parking lot as he heads for the road.

"Does this ever get old?" I try for a joke, feeling myself starting to shake as Ivan lurches out onto the road, speeding for the exit. "These constant car chases? We've had what—three in as many days? Or am I miscounting? Is this a new record for you, or—"

Ivan's eyes flick to me for a split second before returning to the road. His jaw is clenched tight, his knuckles white on the steering wheel. "This isn't a joke, Charlotte," he says, his voice low and tense. "That was too fucking close." His voice has the same hard edge that it had this morning, when I tried to talk to him when we first woke up. Like what happened last night threw up a wall between us.

A wall that, ironically, a few days ago, I was trying desperately *to* put up. Last night, I tried to take it down. To have a moment of connection with him, to meet what he told me with what I could give him. But it wasn't enough.

I swallow hard, my attempt at humor dying on my lips. He's right, of course. My heart is still racing, the adrenaline coursing through my veins making me feel jittery and on edge. I've felt this way for days, and no amount of nights spent in the quiet, cold Montana wilds can drain it out of me, I'm starting to fear. I'm wondering just how long it will take after my 'new life' begins for me to feel safe again. To feel normal.

Maybe never.

"I'm sorry," I whisper. "I just—I don't know how to process all of this."

Ivan takes a sharp turn, the tires squealing against the pavement. I grab onto the door handle to steady myself, my stomach lurching. "You need to understand something," he says, his voice tight with barely controlled anger. "These people, they're not playing games. Bradley, my family, they'll hurt you, Charlotte. They'll—"

I stare at him for a moment, uncomprehending. "I know that," I whisper. "Of course, I know that, or I wouldn't be—"

His jaw tightens, his gaze fixated on the road ahead as he swings towards the next exit, and I realize he's not saying it to me. Not really. And he's not angry with me, either.

He's angry with himself. He's angry that he left me alone. That Bradley had a chance to get to me at all. I see the muscle in his jaw working, the hurt in his face, and a part of me that I haven't managed to quell cuts through all the anger and all the hurt, wanting to comfort him.

I reach out, my hand touching his forearm. "Ivan, I—"

The words are ripped from my mouth as a hard weight slams into our car, knocking me sideways, stealing all the breath from my lungs. And then we're flying, rolling, *falling*—and I'm certain it's all over.

That I won't ever know what I was going to say next.

23

CHARLOTTE

The world is spinning around me. It *hurts*. Everything hurts, the slamming of my body against the door and the seat and the dashboard, the shattering sound of glass, the crunching of metal as the car flips over and over, rolling down the hill to one side of the exit. I didn't see what was beyond it, and I close my eyes, feeling hot tears on my cheeks as I think about the awful possibilities. Trees. A ravine. Another road, one where traffic will pummel us until we're nothing but paste—

My head slams against something hard, and pain explodes behind my eyes. I'm dimly aware of the sound of Ivan's voice, shouting my name, but his voice sounds far away and muffled, like he's yelling through that glass window he was on the other side of with Bradley. Every word is muffled by the ringing in my ears.

When the car stops rolling, it takes me a minute to register it. I'm hanging upside down, held in place by my seatbelt, digging painfully into my hips and chest. But *god*, I'm so fucking thankful that I had it on, that I never took it off while I was sitting in the parking lot. I'm pretty sure that's the only reason I'm still alive right now.

I keep forgetting to practice safe sex with a criminal, but points for me for remembering to put my seatbelt on. I have the urge to laugh, but when I try, it hurts too much.

Blood rushes to my head, making me dizzy, my vision swimming in front of me. I blink, trying to focus on something, anything, through the haze of pain and confusion. I can hear Ivan, but I can't make him out yet.

"Charlotte!" Ivan sounds more panicked than I've ever heard him. "Charlotte, say something, *please!*" The urgency in his voice, the bald fear, cuts me to the bone. I've never heard anyone say my name like that. Never heard the frantic pleading that's in it now.

I try to tell him that yes, I'm okay—or at least that I'm alive, *okay* is still undetermined—but all that comes out is a weak groan. I can't take a full breath, and I can feel something warm trickling down my face.

Probably my own blood.

Ivan curses in Russian, fumbling with the catch of his own seatbelt. My vision clears enough for me to realize that he's next to me, scrambling out of his own seat. "I'm going to get you out of here, Charlotte," he promises. "I'm—"

"*Ivan!*"

A loud, Russian-accented voice fills the air from Ivan's side of the car, and a new fear fills the hollow space in my chest. I'd wondered, for one insane second, if it had been Bradley who had run us off the road. If he'd really been crazy enough to do that.

But now I know it's not. It was Ivan's brothers. One or more of them. *Lev?* My chest squeezes tightly at the possibility that it might be. Out of the three of them, I'm most terrified of him.

Ivan twists next to me, abandoning his efforts to get me out as he starts to crawl out of the shattered window on his side. I don't even realize that he's pulled his gun until I hear the shot, close enough that I know it's him, the sound only adding to the ringing in my ears as I scream helplessly.

It makes me feel weak, but I can't hold it back. This is too much. It's all been too much for too long, and this feels like a tipping point, a moment past which I can't pretend that I'm okay any longer.

None of this is okay, just like I've told Ivan from the very beginning.

The gunshot echoes outside the car as Ivan wrenches himself free, my ears hurting with the noise, and I vaguely hear a muffled cry of pain. My heart is pounding wildly, my chest hurting with a stabbing sensation that's frightening, and I don't know if it's the adrenaline or an actual injury. I struggle against the seatbelt, desperate to see what's happening, but I'm trapped upside down, helpless.

"Ivan!" I manage to croak out his name, my voice, hoarse and barely audible. "Ivan!"

There's no response, just the sound of scuffling and grunts outside the car. I strain my ears, trying to make sense of the chaos. Another shot rings out, then another. My ears are ringing, and I can't tell who's firing or if anyone's been hit.

Suddenly, a face appears at the cracked window on the other side of me, in my periphery. A broad hand reaches in to grab me, and I wrench away, screaming again. I hadn't thought I could be any more afraid than I already was, but now I know I was wrong. This fear, the fear of whichever brother is trying to drag me free of the wreckage, is new and sharp and compounds all the rest of it a hundredfold.

"No!" I scream, thrashing wildly against my seatbelt, trying to wrench further away from him. The movement sends jolts of bright, white-hot pain through my body, but I can't stop fighting. I'm more afraid of being taken by them than anything else. There's no coming back from that.

The hand withdraws for a moment, then returns with something glinting in the dim light. A knife. My heart leaps into my throat, fear of the knife jolting through me, but I quickly realize that he doesn't plan to hurt *me* with it. He's going to cut me loose.

I renew my struggles, ignoring the agony it causes, desperate to stay where I am. At least in here, Ivan can still come for me. I'm still free of *them*. His family. The future awaiting us in Vegas isn't the one I wanted, but it's a better future than I'd find in the hands of Ivan's family.

"Stop moving," a gruff voice orders in heavily accented English. "It will hurt more if I nick you with this. And *otets* will be displeased if you're damaged."

"I don't know who that is," I snap, still wriggling like a fish on a hook. "But I don't fucking care."

The man chuckles, reaching in anyway and starting to saw at my seatbelt, the other hand grasping the back of my neck with an intimacy that makes me shudder.

"Stop touching me!"

"Stop squirming," he retorts, still sawing away. "Better if you—"

He never finishes his sentence. The knife jerks backward, narrowly missing my stomach as the man is hauled back, away from the car, and I catch a glimpse of Ivan, bloodied and holding a gun in his other hand—a gun now pressed to his brother's temple. The same brother that he had pinned to the car outside of our motel with that same gun.

I gasp, my heart pounding as hard as my head is as I watch Ivan drag his brother further back in the grass, blood smearing it as he does. There's no sign of the other one, and I realize with a sinking feeling that means that Ivan's either knocked him unconscious, or killed him.

I don't know what it says about my own naïveté that I hope it's the former. I should know by now, from everything Ivan's told me, that their deaths were coming when they wouldn't give up on chasing us. That Ivan gave them both their one chance, when he didn't kill them last time.

Ivan's face now is that same mask of cold fury that I saw with Bradley. There's no mercy, no quarter that he's going to grant. Cold wracks my body, and I wonder if I'm going into shock, or if this is just the natural response to watching a man who I've slept with, who I've spent days upon days with, who I could have fallen for, holding a gun to his own brother's head.

Blood trickles down the side of Ivan's face, staining his shirt collar, only adding to the savagery of the scene in front of me. But he seems oblivious to it, all of his focus on the man he has grappled in front of him.

"I told you the price you would pay if you came after us again," Ivan growls, his voice low and dangerous. He's never been more a predator than he is in this moment, violent and savage, a brutal creature on the verge of killing. "I won't enjoy killing my own family. But it ends here. I won't take this chance again."

Niki, I think I remember. The bigger of the two. I think I remember Ivan saying his name. Niki laughs, as if there wasn't a gun pressed to his head, the sound cold and hollow. "Or what, little brother? You'll shoot me? You don't have the fucking balls. You would have done it by now, if you did. And *otets* will never forgive you, if you kill me."

"As if I give a fuck," Ivan spits. "My forgiveness was gone the moment I ran with her, and you know it. And I don't want to go back. I don't want any part of this, not any longer. Besides," he adds, his voice cracking with a bitter laugh. "*Otets* won't actually give a shit if you're dead. He never would have, and he still won't."

I think, through my bleary vision, I see Niki blanch at that cruelty. And it *is* cruel, enough that I feel almost momentarily sorry for him —before I remember that he and his other brother ran us off the fucking road.

I see, too, that Ivan might be more hurt than he's letting on. That trickle of blood is coming from a gash on his forehead, and his shoulder looks slightly odd, as if he wrenched it in the crash. But he's holding the gun steady against Niki's temple, and I see the other man go white as it seems to settle in that Ivan isn't bluffing. Not any longer.

"You did this to yourself," Ivan snarls. "You and Ani both. Lev, too, when you brought her into this. When you made it about anything other than our family issues—"

"And what would you know about family?"

The third, rougher voice sends my heart clamoring into my throat. It's rougher, harsher, with the heavier Russian accent that I remember from the one time I heard Lev speak, that first night.

I twist in the seatbelt again, ignoring the hot jolts of pain, and I see Lev standing behind Ivan, his gun leveled at the back of Ivan's head.

"I told you I wouldn't let you hurt her," Ivan spits, not turning to look behind him. "I told you to leave her the fuck alone."

Lev chuckles, the sound low and menacing. "*Brat*, when have I ever listened? To you, especially. *Otets* has, at times. But now, after all of this, I think he's learned his lesson. You are finished, Ivan. And I will do with her what I please."

"This has nothing to do with her," Ivan spits, and for the first time, I think I hear a thread of fear in his voice. "We'll talk this out like brothers. Let her go. Let me get her out, and she can go."

Lev laughs again. "You made it about her when you chose her, *brat*."

"Ivan—" I croak out his name again, unsure if he can even hear me. My voice is a cracked whisper, the world trembling again, blurring at the edges. I have no idea if I'm that badly hurt, or if it's just that the stress and exhaustion coupled with the accident has caught up to me, but I feel as if I'm about to pass out. "Ivan—"

I can see the tension running through every line of Ivan's body, the slight tremble in his hand now, as if he's growing exhausted, too. And for the first time, I think I see him wavering, as if he's no longer entirely sure of what to do.

That, more than anything, makes me feel like breaking. I didn't realize how much I've relied on Ivan's certainty until this moment, when I see it fading. And I want to reach out to him, to tell him—

I don't know what I would tell him. Not to kill his brother. But I don't want to go with them, either. And I don't want to see them hurt Ivan.

That feels unbearable.

Lev's gaze flicks to me, a cruel smile teasing the corners of his mouth. "Ah, she's awake. Watching this entire petty drama play out. Tell me, *devochka*," he growls, his cold blue gaze meeting mine. "Was he worth all this trouble? Was he worth throwing away the life you had? And it was a good life, too, wasn't it? A good job, a beautiful apartment. Friends who cared for you. The kind of life all women like you want. Was it worth it to have a few nights with my bastard brother?"

I want to spit something back at him, to tell him to go to hell, that every moment was worth it. That I wouldn't change a thing. I want to wipe that fucking smirk off his face, to defiantly defend Ivan in the face of this much-crueler man.

But anything I could say dies on my lips. Because, after all—that exact question is what I've been asking myself this entire time. *Was it worth it?* Was the time I spent with Ivan, the things he awakened in me, the things I felt with him—was it worth everything I lost?

When I walk away from him and start a blank slate of life, will it *still* feel worth it, even if it feels like it now?

"I'll give you one last chance," Ivan growls. "Let her go. Let her go *now*, or—"

"Fuck you, brother." Lev cuts him off, and for one horrifying split second, I think I'm about to watch Ivan die in front of me.

But instead, he pulls the trigger.

I scream, the sound swallowed up by the gunshot as Niki's head explodes in a wash of red, his last words lost too in the echoing sound and the ringing in my ears. Ivan ducks forward as he pulls the trigger, flinging himself to one side as Lev fires, too.

I watch in horror as the bullet strikes Niki's dead body instead, the corpse moving in a way that seems all wrong as Ivan launches himself forward, kicking out with one foot and hooking Lev's ankle with his. Lev wrenches around as he falls, shooting at Ivan again, but Ivan rolls away, shoving himself to his feet and firing twice into Lev.

I don't see where the bullets land. I don't see if Lev is dead. All I see is Ivan, scrambling up through the bloody grass as he grabs the knife out of Niki's hand and runs to my side of the car.

"Charlotte." He gasps my name, sawing at the seatbelt in an effort to finish what Niki started. This time, I don't struggle. I don't think I could move if I wanted to, as in shock as I am.

I just saw a man die. Two men, maybe. I saw Ivan kill him—*them*. I saw—

I close my eyes tight, and I feel Ivan's hand against my cheek.

"I'm sorry," he whispers, and I feel the seatbelt give, his arm wrapping around me as he tries to cushion my fall down to the roof of the car. "I'm sorry for all of it. I'm sorry you had to see that. I don't know how badly you're hurt, Charlotte, but right now—" He looks up, over the car, as if searching for something. "Right now, we need to run."

I can barely process anything Ivan is saying through the fog of pain. It's turned from a jolting, white-hot stabbing to a sort of heavy, thick sensation that's settled over me, chilling me deeply and giving me that sensation that I might pass out again.

"*Charlotte.*"

The way he hisses my name cuts through the daze. I nod weakly, trying to gather myself. *I must be going into shock. This must be what that feels like.*

"Can you move?" Ivan asks, his voice tight with worry. "Can I move you? Do you need help?"

It occurs to me that if Lev isn't dead, we need to get out of here sooner rather than later. Not to mention the fact that Bradley wasn't far behind us, and he saw our car. This accident might attract his attention shortly. I shift in the cramped space, careful of broken glass, trying to test my limbs as much as I'm able. "I think so," I whisper. "I mean—I think I can get out."

An inch at a time, Ivan helps me crawl out of the wreckage. I see him wince when I hiss with pain, tears leaking out of the corner of my eyes. My palm scrapes over broken glass, and I cry out. The instant he hears the sound, his muscled arms go around me, pulling me free the rest of the way as he helps me to my feet in the bloodied grass.

The world tilts alarmingly around me, and I sway in place, grabbing at the front of his shirt. I feel him tense at my touch, sucking in a breath, but I'm too aware of what I'm looking at, at this moment to think too much about what that means.

"Easy," Ivan murmurs, his arm around my waist. His gaze sweeps over me, looking for anything broken, anything that—I assume—might mean I can't run. "We need to go, Charlotte. Right now."

I swallow hard as I look at Niki's unmoving body, facedown in the grass. At Lev, on his back, staring up at the sky, or—

I think I see him move, shifting, and I swear I hear him groan.

Maybe I'm imagining things. But it's enough for me to twist away, starting to hobble past the car. I see another body, Ivan's other brother, and I can't tell if he's alive or dead. I don't think I *want* to know.

"There's a gas station just up the road," Ivan says grimly, his arm still around my waist as he urges me to go faster. "We need to get there. I saw a sign—"

"But what about the people—" I start to ask, but he cuts me off.

"People have cars," he says shortly. "And we need a car."

I'm too breathless already from the pain to ask any more questions, or think too hard about what he means. I think I *know* what he means, anyway, and it feels like one thing too many right now.

We're going to have to steal another car. And we're going to do it like this.

We stumble away from the car, my legs feeling as if they've been dipped in lead, every step sending more of those white-hot jolts of pain through my body, piercing the fog. Ivan is supporting most of my weight as we half run, half stumble towards the road, staying slightly off the shoulder as Ivan leads me towards the gas station in the distance. I can see the lights flickering on, like a beacon in the darkness gathering around us.

"We're almost there," Ivan murmurs, his voice sounding strained. He's tense, every muscle in his body wound tight, and I can feel it radiating off of him. He's looking around constantly, glancing back every few feet as if he expects Lev to materialize behind us, chasing us down.

Except at this point, I don't think Lev would chase. I think he would just shoot us. Maybe even me. I think I might have become more of a problem than whatever value I have allows. And anyway, Ivan once said that they wanted me to get back at him. To hurt him by hurting me. If he's dead, that doesn't matter.

The thought feels so boldly foreign that it makes me almost laugh, the sound bitterly choking in my throat. It catches, and I see Ivan glance at me worriedly out of the corner of his eye.

He probably thinks I'm losing it. Maybe I am *losing it.* What I've been through in the last several days would test anyone. Especially when it's so far out of the realm of anything I ever imagined my life turning out to be.

I can barely even think about what's ahead of us. All I can think about is what's behind—the wrecked car, the bodies, the smeared blood turning the grass red. It feels wholly surreal, like a nightmare I can't wake up from, like a story in someone else's life. I keep seeing the wash of red as Niki's head opened up, the look on Lev's face as he pointed the gun at Ivan, the fact that it didn't seem to matter to Lev at all that one of his brothers was dead in front of him. That all three of them might have been about to be.

But then again, to hear Ivan describe it, he never cared about any of them. Their deaths would just mean that their father couldn't hang his possible replacements over his head any longer. He would be the only heir, his place unchallenged.

My head swims, trying to make sense of it all—a world that makes absolutely *no* sense to me.

There are three cars at the gas pumps when the station comes fully into view. Two are turned off, empty, their owners clearly inside paying. The third, a black Subaru, is also off, but the driver is standing next to it, about to hit the button on the pump to start filling the tank.

"Ivan—" I start to speak, but he shakes his head sharply.

"We need a car, Charlotte." The finality in his voice feels like a slap. He sounds cold, harsh. But he's right.

We won't get far without a vehicle. And much like the difference between knowing Ivan has killed and seeing it today, I'm only really more upset about this because I'm seeing the reality of it up close. I can admit that, at least.

I swallow hard, feeling as if I might throw up as we move closer, around the back of the unsuspecting man at the pump. The fact that it's a man makes me feel only slightly better—it might be wrong, but it would feel worse to see Ivan threaten a woman.

The man, an older fellow with a round, florid face and thinning hair, dressed in jeans and a Trans-Am t-shirt, turns at the sound of our footsteps. His face creases instantly as he takes in our battered appearance, caution and worry warring for primacy on his face.

He sets the nozzle back in the pump, hesitation evident in his movements. But his better nature seems to win out, which only makes me feel worse.

"You two alright?" he asks, his gaze sweeping over us, and Ivan's hand slips to the edge of his shirt, where I know his gun is tucked. My heart trips in my chest. *Please don't shoot this man.*

The man's gaze follows, too, and I see the fear that flickers in his eyes. "Hey now, I don't want any trouble—"

"And there won't be any," Ivan says easily. "Just so long as you hand over the keys to your car. Now," he adds, his fingers twitching against his side, and the man's eyes widen as his face pales. "No sudden movements or calling for help. And then we'll leave you be."

I see the man swallow hard, his gaze darting between me and Ivan. I can see him weighing his options, considering what the best choice is. If he should acquiesce, or if trying to call for help or running is an option. If Ivan will really do what he says he will.

My stomach twists, and I stare at the man, willing him to just hand over the keys. I don't think Ivan would hurt this man. I think he would just move on to another option. But I don't want to find out.

The man lets out a heavy breath. "Alright," he says, his voice taut with fear, the whites of his eyes rolling like a startled horse. "Just— don't hurt me. Please."

"Throw the keys over here, and it'll be fine." Ivan's fingers stay at the edge of his shirt, a warning. "And don't call the cops. You call anyone on us, put anyone on our tail, you'll regret it."

That can't possibly be true. We're leaving the state, and Ivan's family isn't answering favors from him. But the man is too frightened to question if Ivan is telling the truth or not. He just nods rapidly, throwing the keys across the pavement.

"Grab them and hand them to me." Ivan's voice is still sharp, unnaturally cold for how he usually speaks to me. "And then get in the car when I unlock it."

He doesn't use my name, and I can guess why. I *hate* that I can guess why, because that means I'm getting used to all of this. That it's all starting to make sense to me.

I scoop the keys up, handing them to Ivan. Almost immediately, he hits the button to unlock the car, and I go without thinking, half-hobbling, half-running to the passenger's side. I fling myself into the car, not daring to look and see if anyone else is noticing us, and stare down at my scratched, bruised hands, forcing myself not to listen. Not to try to hear what else Ivan might be saying.

A second later, he's in the car next to me. He presses a button on the dash, the car revving to life, and slams his foot against the gas, pulling out of the station a little too quickly.

"He's going to call someone," I whisper. My throat feels scratchy and dry, and I desperately want water. "He's going to report the car—"

"No, he won't," Ivan says grimly.

"How do you know—"

"He's too scared to do anything but follow instructions. And by the time he figures it out, or his wife or grandkids or someone calls the police for him, we will have dumped this car and gotten a new one. But in the meantime—" Ivan's jaw is set as he pulls out onto the highway, his eyes straight ahead on the road. "Now we're a step ahead. For a little while longer."

I sag back against the seat, not wanting to think about what happens when Bradley catches up. If Lev is still alive. About the fact that there's still plenty of miles between us and Vegas, and once we're there, we still have to finish what we're going there to do.

There's plenty of time left for it to all go wrong.

"I'm an accomplice now," I whisper. "Murder. Grand theft auto. Probably some other stuff I can't think of right now—"

"That's the least of your worries at this point," Ivan says grimly. He doesn't look away from the road, and I stare at him blankly, wondering if I hit my head harder than I thought.

"*Murder* is the least of my worries?" My voice rises to a higher pitch, and Ivan lets out a long breath, pinching the bridge of his nose.

"I'm sorry," he says finally. "I'm not trying to diminish it. And I suppose I'm a little numb to all of this, after so long. But before too long, we'll be in Vegas, and we'll scrub everything well enough that the law won't be able to catch us. And Bradley, local police—those I'm not afraid of. But—"

He trails off, and something in my stomach clenches painfully at the thought that he *is* afraid of something. Ivan, to me, seems almost invincible. I've never known anyone who lives the way he does, unapologetically and, until today, seemingly fearlessly. But I can see the pinched white at the corners of his mouth, the look in his eyes that tells me that's not entirely the case.

"I'm afraid of them getting you," he says finally. "My father. Lev, if he's not dead. Hell, even Ani, if he's survived. He's stupid, but he's still a useful enough tool. That scares me. And it should scare you, too, more than any crimes we've committed. Those I can wipe away. But if they catch us before we get to safety—"

Ivan lets out a heavy breath. "It'll be fine," he murmurs, and I half wonder if he's saying it to me, or to himself. "It'll be okay."

He glances over at me after a moment, the car slowing to only a little over the speed limit. "Can you make it for a while? Until I can find somewhere safe for us to stop?"

My eyes feel heavy. "Can I sleep?"

"You probably shouldn't. If you hit your head—"

Ivan is still speaking. But the rest of his voice drones away into nothingness, as the heavy fog slides over me, claiming me in the heaviest sleep I've had since Ivan stole me from my apartment.

24

IVAN

I debate, as I watch Charlotte fall asleep, if I should wake her up.

I know it's not wise for her to sleep. The wreck was violent—there's every chance that she could have a concussion. I should be waking her up—but she looks so peaceful that I feel an almost physical revulsion at the thought of disturbing her.

Today has been far beyond what I ever wanted her to experience while she was with me. Full of pain and violence and things that I know she'll never be able to unsee. And it's my fault.

I should never have left her alone in the car while I went into that gas station.

Logically, I know it doesn't all stem from that. Even if I could have avoided Bradley that way—which isn't a certainty by any means—Niki and Ani were an entirely different situation. They were hot on our heels, clearly, and a little more time and space between us wouldn't have made enough of a difference.

And Lev.

I grit my teeth, thinking of what just happened. Ani isn't dead, I don't think. I knocked him out, hard enough that I might have done serious damage, but I can't be sure. Ani is the weakest, the most stupid, and the most easily controlled of the three. I felt guilty at the thought of killing him in cold blood, like shooting a loyal dog that should have bitten its master a long time ago. But Niki—

The sight of him trying to cut Charlotte out of the car and take her with him had made me so blind with rage that I'd wanted to do horrible, brutal things to him. I've rarely ever *wanted* to cause pain, wanted to see how long I could prolong a man's suffering—but I wanted to hurt him. If I'd had time, I would have.

I hope Charlotte never knows that about me.

Niki is dead. There's no doubt about that. The part of his head that blew away with the shot was clear enough, and if he somehow had still been breathing, the bullet that Lev accidentally put in his back would have finished him off. But Lev—

I'm not sure that Lev is dead. And that means that for now, he's still a danger.

I need to put as many miles between what just happened, and us, as I can. I have an idea, as we pass into Idaho, of what we can do for a place to sleep. But we need food, and we need to clean up. And we need fresh clothes. Everything that we had was in the Corolla, now flung around in a mess in the wreckage.

Charlotte doesn't wake up until I stop at a 24-hour Walmart, far off the beaten path. She doesn't even wake up when the car stops—I have to reach over and gently shake her, acutely aware of the pain in my own shoulder as I touch hers.

"Charlotte," I say her name softly, thinking with a sudden, stabbing pain of the soft way she said my name just this morning. That already feels as if it was days ago. And I want to go back there, with a sudden desperation that startles me. I want her, sitting up in the thin, cold daylight, whispering my name behind my back.

I can't imagine she'll actually ever say it that way again.

"Mm?" She stirs, opening her eyes as if they're sticky. They probably are.

"We need clothes. Food." I look up at the brightly lettered sign. "I think—"

"Someone is going to call the cops as soon as they see us."

I run a hand through my hair, wincing as I feel my fingers catch on the dried blood. "You're probably right. But—"

"I'll go in," she suggests. "I'm banged up, but it's not too bad. I'll say I had an accident if anyone asks. Wrecked my bike or something. That I just need a change of clothes."

"I'm not letting you go anywhere alone."

"If Bradley or—" she swallows hard. "Or Lev shows up, you're better equipped to deal with them than I am. If it's just me out here, it'll just be a repeat of what happened all over again."

I don't ask why she thinks Lev is alive. I don't think I want to know. "And if they see you and follow you inside?"

"Then I'll scream. Cause a fuss. Claim that he's the one who hurt me, why I'm all bloody. While there's a commotion, I'll take off running." She gives me a bright look that I'm sure she's faking. "It'll be fine."

I hesitate. Every instinct that I have screams at me not to let her out of my sight again, reminding me of what happened earlier when I left her for just a few minutes. But she's right. We need food, first aid, and clothes, and in my condition, I'm more likely to raise alarm.

"Okay," I say finally. "But just take this." I slip a switchblade out of my pocket, the smaller of the two knives I carry on me—easier to conceal and easier for Charlotte to handle. "I don't expect you to have to use it. But I'd rather you have something on you just in case."

Charlotte's eyes widen, her teeth sinking into her lower lip, but she nods. Her fingers brush against mine as she takes the knife, and I feel my heart trip in my chest, the urge to tighten my hand around hers and pull her in almost overwhelming. But I lean back, watching as she slips the knife into her pocket. "I'll be quick," she says, looking nervously towards the store. "In and out."

I hand her a fold of cash, still fighting the urge to call her back as she slips out of the car and starts to hurry towards the store, her gait still slightly off from how sore she must be. She's not too badly injured, I think—more banged up than anything else, but I'm still worried about what might not have made itself known yet.

Waiting for her to come back is a million times worse than having gone myself. I try to distract myself while I wait, thinking of what comes next. We need to stay off the main roads and find somewhere to crash for the night. We both need rest, to sleep off our injuries as much as we're able. I'm worried about going to a motel, after the last few close calls we've had, and the best thing I can think of is to go off the beaten path into one of the parks, and find a safety cabin.

It won't be the most comfortable place to sleep, but we'll manage. And it'll be the best bet I can think of for staying off the radar of anyone who might be tailing us.

I watch the store entrance as I run through possible scenarios, thinking of what we'll do tomorrow, and the day after, until we get to Vegas. I'm constantly scanning the parking lot, looking for Bradley's car, for the ominous shape of my brother's muscled bulk, for any sign of trouble at all. Every minute feels like an hour, although when I look down at my watch, I can see that only about fifteen minutes has passed.

When the doors open and I see her walk out, I feel a wave of relief, letting out a breath that I hadn't even realized I was holding. She's changed clothes, wearing a simple grey t-shirt and jeans now, a thin black hoodie tossed over it. She has two bulging plastic bags in her hands, and I can see that she's walking a little more steadily—pain medication, maybe. That feeling of relief only grows, but I can't fully relax until she slides back into the passenger's seat of the car, setting the bags down on the floorboard as she shuts the door firmly behind her.

I immediately lock them, not taking my eyes off her for even a second. "It went okay?"

Charlotte nods. "It's so late that there weren't many employees. I got a couple of weird looks, but only one of them asked if I was okay. And I just told them I took a spill on my bike and needed to clean up, that I didn't want to freak out my family when I got home. They bought it easily enough." She reaches down, opening up the bags for me to see inside. "I grabbed some clothes, a first aid kit, and some more food and bottled water. And these." She pulls out two prepaid phones. "I figured you needed new burners."

I can feel my eyes widen. I'm more than a little impressed by her foresight in that—she's clearly been paying attention.

"You're a natural," I tease her, smiling. At least—it's meant to be teasing, but from the shadow that crosses her face, I don't think she takes it that way. "I just mean—you did a good job, Charlotte. All of this is good."

She gives me a small smile, but it doesn't quite reach her eyes. I can see the exhaustion in every line of her face—made more evident now, actually, by the fact that the blood is washed away. There's fear there, too, still in her eyes as she leans back against the seat tiredly and looks over at me. "What now?" she asks quietly, and I let out a heavy sigh as I put the car in gear.

"We'll need to stop somewhere soon. We're both exhausted, hurt, and probably in some shock. We need to sleep." I scrub my hand through my hair, once again wincing at how it feels, matted with blood as it is. "We need a day to rest, honestly, but I don't think we can swing that. We *need* to get to Vegas sooner rather than later."

"Okay, so where?" Charlotte's frown is audible; I don't even need to look over at her to know it's on her face. "The last time we went to a motel, your brothers caught us. And if Ani and Niki figured it out—"

"I think Lev figured it out," I interrupt. "And sent them. When they dicked around for too long, he came to check up on things, and that resulted in what happened yesterday."

"That's just as bad." Charlotte lets out a small, huffing breath. "So he knows what we've been doing. And you've said before major hotels are off-limits, because there are too many people. Which begs the question, what the hell are we going to do in Vegas?"

"There, we'll get the nicest hotel available. One with security, keycards, the lot. There, we can get the kind of room where it'll be harder for Lev to get to us, and where I can pay people to keep their mouths shut." I glance over at her. "In a place like Vegas, where there's plenty of criminal activity like the kind my family involves themselves in, silence has a price. But in backwoods Idaho, or any of the places we've driven through so far, we'd just be putting people in danger."

Charlotte nods. "And tonight?"

"Tonight, I think we should head into one of the national forests. There are safety cabins out there, shelters for hikers and campers who need a place to crash in a storm or some other kind of emergency. I think this counts as an emergency," I add wryly as I spread the new road atlas that Charlotte grabbed out on my lap, flicking on an overhead light. "They're pretty off the grid. Hard to find, unless you're looking for them specifically."

"And you think Bradley won't look for that specifically? Or Lev?" There's uncertainty in Charlotte's voice, and it makes a tangle of mixed feelings surface in my gut. On the one hand, I'm proud of her for thinking this through, for questioning it all, and for taking an active part in this. But on the other, I wish she trusted me. I wish that all of this had brought us closer, instead of seemingly pushing us further apart. Right now, I can't help but feel that more than ever, she's only still with me because it's her best option.

That as soon as she has the opportunity to safely leave, she will.

I take a deep, slow breath, pushing those thoughts aside. They're not helpful right now, for either of us. There's nothing I can do about it at this moment, and what Charlotte needs most from me right now, I know, is for me to focus on our immediate crisis.

The need for a safe place to sleep, and shelter, so we can recover before the morning.

"It's possible," I admit. "It might occur to both, or either of them, that we might try to hide away somewhere like that. But we have to stop somewhere. We can't drive through the night, not in our current state."

"This is an automatic," Charlotte points out. "I can drive this."

"Yeah, you can. But you shouldn't." I shake my head. "You were in shock earlier, Charlotte. I only let you sleep because I couldn't bear to wake you up, but you probably hit your head. We're both banged up, and our bodies can only take so much. We won't make it if we collapse before we get to Vegas."

Charlotte is silent, and I take a deep breath. "Those cabins are scattered all over the parks. Bradley and Lev don't know whose car we stole, or what roads we took. They won't have had time to figure it out yet. Maybe, if that guy called the theft in, Bradley could get to us quicker, but honestly—" I shake my head. "There's plenty of stolen cars every day. Maybe less so out here, but he's still gotta decide which one he thinks is us. He has to figure out which cabin we chose. Our odds are just as good as a motel, maybe better."

She nods, her lips still pressed together, thin with worry. "Okay," she says finally, on a long exhale. "I trust you."

Those three small words, three of the six that I've never really expected to hear from her, hit me harder than I expected. I feel as if the air has been knocked out of my lungs for a moment, and I swallow hard, trying to keep my composure. I hadn't realized just how badly I *wanted* to hear that from her, until she said it. Now, I just want to hear her say it again.

I nod, feeling briefly incapable of speech as I stare at the road ahead, following it until I turn down a side road marked on the atlas, towards one of the parks. We're both silent as I drive, the night closing in around us, deepening the further we get from civilization. The only sounds are the hum of the engine and the soft brush of the wind through the trees outside, along with the occasional rustle of Charlotte's clothing as she shifts in the seat or brushes against the bags on the floorboard.

It takes about an hour before I see signs for a cabin. I turn onto a narrow, thin road, grateful that I stole a car with all-wheel drive as I drive us further into the forest. The trees loom over us, creating a dark canopy that sends a shiver down my spine, blocking out the night sky above us and the shimmer of the stars.

There's something a bit spooky about it, especially this time of year. But I push the crawling feeling that creeps over my skin aside, focusing on the task at hand. The forest might be silent and dark, but there are far, far more dangerous things out there. And this, hopefully, will keep us shielded from them for the night.

As I expected, when we reach the cabin, it isn't much. I've stayed in places like this once or twice before, when I've gone off on long hikes to get away from my family and clear my head. It's primitive, without electricity or running water, but from what I know of these kinds of places, there will be a lantern, basic bedding, some bottled water, and a fireplace with some cut wood left from the park rangers who keep these cabins stocked. Enough to get us through the night, and after the day we've had, it looks as good as any five-star hotel to me.

I park the Subaru around the back, where it won't be immediately seen if Bradley, or maybe a park ranger, comes by and happens to look at the license plate. We won't be able to keep this car long, just in case the man that I stole it from does decide to call in the theft. But right now, I'm pushing that further down the list of things to worry about.

"Let's grab our stuff and get inside," I murmur to Charlotte, glancing around. There's no one to be seen, and no reason to think we've been followed, but I feel anxious all the same. "We shouldn't hang out in the open, just in case."

She nods, grabbing the bags from the floorboard and sliding out into the chilly night air. I hear her draw in a deep breath, and I can't help but smile, despite the hellish day we've had. It *is* nice, out here. Clean and fresh, the air cold and crisp, and I want to linger for a moment. But I see Charlotte shiver as she walks around the back of the car, and I hurry to grab the bags out of her hand as we walk to the cabin.

The door is unlocked, as I figured it would be, since these cabins are meant for campers and hikers in need of shelter during emergencies. It's dark inside, and I stomp my boots as we walk in, wanting to make sure to scare off any creatures. This time of year, stacks of firewood and any cracks in walls or under doors are prime places for snakes to hide.

When I don't hear the dry whisper of scales across wood or the chittering of any raccoons or other small furry creatures that might not like being disturbed, I fumble for the lantern that I know should be near the door, batteries already inside. My hand brushes against cold metal, and I find the switch, flicking it on and bathing the room in a warm, soft glow.

Inside, the cabin isn't much, either. It's sparse—small, with two beds made up with quilts, a rustic table and chairs, and a wood stove next to a fireplace. I glance over at Charlotte, a wry smile on my face.

"Home sweet home?" I shrug, and she manages a small smile back.

"I kind of like it," she admits.

"Better than our tent out at that campsite?" The question comes out before I can stop it, before I can remind myself that this isn't a conversation that I want answers to. I had told myself I'd leave this alone, that I'd push aside any further thoughts of how I feel about her. She gave me her answer, when she couldn't give me one.

But clearly, while I'm done torturing others, I haven't tortured myself nearly enough yet.

"Maybe a little better," she says softly, her gaze still scanning the room. "I think this will be nice and cozy, with a fire going. Warm."

"I'll get right on that, then," I promise her. "Look and see if there's any blankets in that closet while I work on a fire?"

Charlotte nods, setting down the bags and walking over to investigate while I kneel down by the fireplace. I can feel every inch of my body protesting as I arrange kindling and logs; my shoulder is starting to throb again. Whatever adrenaline was carrying me through has long since worn off, and I feel painfully aware of every bruise and scrape.

The fire catches, just in time for me to hear Charlotte's soft footsteps behind me. "I found more blankets," she says quietly, and I shift, turning to look at her. In the glow of the firelight, she looks even more beautiful than usual, and my chest aches.

Her gaze sweeps over me, and I see the concern in it as she tugs the corner of her lip between her teeth. "You need to clean up," she says softly. "That gash on your forehead—and your shoulder." She looks at me again, assessing. "Come sit on the bed, and I'll help."

Something in my chest squeezes tight at the thought of her touching me like that. *Caring* for me. Sexual touch is nothing new to me, but affection, caring—those are things I'm not familiar with.

Things I've never let myself want or have. The desire for affection is dangerous. Addictive.

Much like Charlotte herself.

"I can do it myself," I tell her, as I push myself up painfully from the floor. But the words come out weak, uncertain. It's easy to hear that what I really want is for her to touch me. To feel her hands on me again, just for a few minutes.

Charlotte looks at me for a long moment, and shakes her head. "Let me help," she insists gently, motioning to the bed again. "You're hurt. You shouldn't have to take care of it yourself, not when...when I want to."

Something about those last three words hit me like a punch, like hearing her say she trusted me earlier. I swallow hard, giving her a slight nod as I make my way to the bed, sitting gingerly down on the edge. Charlotte rummages around in one of the large plastic bags, pulling out a first-aid kit and setting it down next to me.

She hesitates as she opens it, glancing over at me again. "Can you take off your shirt?" she asks slowly, pressing her lips together. "So I can see how bad it really all is."

A beat passes. I can feel how tense she is next to me, as I debate whether or not I should do that. But I'm going to have to change clothes eventually, I reason, even though I know that's very different from sitting here shirtless in the glow of the fire, while Charlotte helps clean up my wounds.

I look over at her, searching for an excuse to say no. To tell her that this is a bad idea. I see the scratches on her arm, cleaned now but still red and angry, and gesture towards them. "You need to patch yourself up," I start to say, and she purses her lips, looking at me narrowly.

"I'm fine for now. Just—take off your shirt, Ivan."

I hesitate for a second longer, but I reach down, slowly peeling off my shirt.

25

IVAN

The movement tugs at my injured shoulder, and I wince, trying not to think of how the long hours of driving still ahead of me will feel. Charlotte's eyes widen as I toss the shirt aside, and as much as I'd like to think it's on account of my muscled chest and long-acquired tattoos, she's seen those before. I know it's because of what else she's seeing.

"Shit," she breathes, and I glance down, following her gaze. There are bruises blooming across my chest and ribs from where Ani and I scuffled, and I can feel the gash on my forehead starting to trickle blood again, breaking through the dried blood there.

Somehow, seeing the bruises makes it all feel worse. I suck in a breath as Charlotte silently reaches for an antiseptic wipe, ripping it open and starting to swipe it over the scrapes and scratches on my skin. She goes for the one on my forehead last, wincing as she begins to lean in.

"This is going to hurt more," she apologizes, ripping open a fresh wipe. "But I need to clean it."

"I know," I mutter grimly, trying to focus on anything other than the raw alcohol she's about to press against my open wound. Unfortunately, the closest thing to focus on is Charlotte's breasts, round and soft-looking under the thin cotton of her t-shirt, and very close to my face as she leans in to dab the antiseptic against my forehead.

I can recall with perfect precision how good they feel in my hands —how perfectly they mold to my palms, hard nipples rubbing against my skin, the sounds she made when I leaned down and ran my tongue across—

My cock twitches, stiffening at the same moment that Charlotte wipes the pad firmly across the bloodied gash, and for a moment, the abrupt clash of arousal and pain makes my brain stutter fully to a stop, my body unsure of how to process it. I've never liked to have pain inflicted on me in the bedroom, and the white-hot burn of the alcohol on my raw flesh isn't arousing in the slightest. But for a brief second, my cock throbs, still stuck on how close Charlotte's breasts are, before the pain takes complete focus, and my arousal fades instantly.

That, I think grimly as Charlotte continues to clean away hours' worth of crusted blood, *will go down as one of the more confusing moments of my life*.

"This might need stitches," Charlotte says with a frown, as she pulls back and looks at my forehead. "But we'll have to make do with butterfly bandages. Hang on—"

She turns, digging around in the first-aid kit, and I feel briefly dizzy as the shift of her body brings a wave of her scent, warm and sweet, directly to my nose. She's not wearing any perfume—it's just her own skin and sweat, but it triggers something primal in my brain, and it takes everything in me not to reach out and grab her hips, pulling her down into my lap.

Charlotte straightens, and I grit my teeth, willing my erection not to make a comeback. She leans in once more, her breasts shifting under her shirt distractingly, and I grip the edge of the bed as she spreads antibiotic ointment over the gash with her thumb, stretching the butterfly bandages over the skin a moment later.

"There." She steps back, surveying her work. "That'll do." She bites her lip, as if she wants to say more, but she turns away a second later and starts putting the first-aid kit back together, her back to me.

I move my shoulder experimentally. It's not dislocated, which is good, because as quick of a learner as Charlotte is, I don't think she could put my shoulder back into its socket if need be. "Thanks," I say quietly, looking at her back as she seems to take longer than strictly necessary putting the first-aid kit back together. The air between us feels thick with tension, and I know she can feel it, too. I know that's why she's not looking at me.

Charlotte goes still for a moment. "Of course," she says softly. "You needed help."

It feels like there's so much more to that statement. More than I can begin to try to unpack, exhausted and in as much pain as I am. I swallow hard, wanting to ask her what she's thinking right now, what she's feeling, and if anything has changed since last night.

But that question is only going to hurt when I get the answer that I know is coming.

"We should get some rest," I say finally. "We've got another long day ahead of us tomorrow, and another after that, before we get to Vegas."

Saying it out loud sends a jolt of pain through me that has nothing to do with my injuries. *Two days.* Two more days with her in a car, driving across the country, pretending that ticking clock isn't growing louder with every passing hour. Two more days before we get to Vegas, and then it's no longer a ticking clock, but a countdown until the moment she leaves me.

Charlotte closes the first-aid kit, crossing the room as she unpacks the bags onto the small table, laying out our supplies—folded clothes, granola bars, beef jerky, a bunch of bananas, and several bottles of water. She doesn't say anything else as she retreats to the back of the cabin, a pair of folded sweatpants in her hands, and I instinctively look away as she starts to unbutton her jeans.

That jolt of desire prickles along my skin again, my cock twitching as I lie back on the bed, reaching for one of the blankets with my good hand and shaking it out over myself. The fire has made the cabin toasty, and I can feel my eyelids getting heavy, sleep claiming me before I even see Charlotte cross the room to the other bed.

I'm not sure, exactly, what it is that wakes me several hours later. It might have been Charlotte's soft footsteps on the wooden floor, because when my eyes flicker open, I see her standing at one window of the cabin, her arms wrapped around herself as she looks out. It's dark, the fire burned down to embers, the moonlight the main source illuminating her as she stands with her back to me.

"Charlotte?" I push myself up to a sitting position, ignoring the throb in my shoulder. "Are you alright?"

She nods, and I see her shoulders draw up and drop again with a heavy sigh.

"You should get some rest," I tell her quietly. "Tomorrow is a long day. You'll have more long days, before this is all over. You need as much sleep as you can get."

Charlotte is quiet for a moment longer. "I can't sleep," she murmurs. "I tried. I think I drifted off for a little while. But I keep dreaming about—" She breaks off, her voice cracking slightly, and I think I can guess what she was dreaming about.

I should tell her again to go back to sleep. *I* should be sleeping, gearing up for what is doubtless going to be a painful and tiring day tomorrow, but instead, I find myself sliding out of bed, walking silently across the cabin to join her at the window.

When I reach out, touching my fingertips to the small of her back, she doesn't pull away.

"I miss them," she whispers, still not looking at me. "Jaz, Sarah, Zoe. I miss my apartment. I miss my *life*. Hell, my job was boring a lot of the time, but I even miss that. At least I wasn't—" She swallows hard. "I wasn't afraid all of the time. I didn't feel as if I'd been beaten within an inch of my life because of a car wreck. I didn't feel—"

She shakes her head, her arms tightening around herself. "I even miss you," she whispers. "*Us*. Back when I thought there would *be* an us. Isn't that crazy?" She twists around, finally looking at me, and I think I see the shimmer of tears in her eyes. "You stalked me. Lied to me. Hurt me. Kidnapped me. And I was still laying there, wishing—wishing that you were next to me. That I wasn't sleeping alone."

The vulnerability in her voice threatens to break me. To undo all the walls I've tried to build up since last night. My hand is still resting on the small of her back, and the urge to wrap my arms around her, to pull her close despite my injuries, and not let go of her until the morning, is almost overwhelming.

But what point is there in that? It will change nothing. It will only prolong the hurt for us both. And I've spent my whole life avoiding this exact feeling, only to be swept under by it for a woman who wants to have nothing to do with me once my temporary protection has served its purpose.

"You said you were sorry," she whispers. "In the car, when you were getting me out. You said you were sorry for all of it. Did you mean that?"

I know what she's asking. And I know I can't give her exactly the answer that she wants.

I guess, at this point, that neither of us can do that for the other.

"I'm sorry that it turned out like this," I say softly, my hand brushing up her spine despite myself. I feel her shiver, and desire prickles through me. "I'm sorry that we're on the run. That it's my fault you've had everything you care about snatched away."

"But you're not sorry for finding me. For meeting me. For dragging me into your web—" Charlotte breaks off, looking away sharply, and I close my eyes briefly, that pain, wedging itself into my heart.

"I can't be sorry for meeting you. For all the time I had with you. For—" *For falling in love with you.* The words are on the tip of my tongue, but I can't bring myself to say them. I can't bear to see them brushed away, ignored because Charlotte can't let herself believe that anything I say about how I feel for her is the truth, any longer.

"What are you going to do after all of this is over? After we have our new identification, and we—"

And we go our separate ways. She doesn't want to say it out loud, but that's the truth.

I think about it for a moment. I've been thinking about the answer to this for years, really, and it's always felt a bit like a mirage, shimmering just out of reach. I've never been entirely sure *what* I would do when I finally got there, when I had my freedom from my family, only that eventually I *would* have it.

And recently, I haven't been able to think very much at all, beyond Charlotte. Being with her. Wanting her. And now, getting her safely to Vegas, so I can undo what I've done wrong. Make it right, as best as I can. All of my focus has been on keeping us both alive, on outrunning the dangers pursuing us, on getting to my contact. Everything beyond that has been hazy.

"I don't need money." I shrug, thinking of what I have tucked away in my many bank accounts. "So I always thought I'd do something for fun. Make friends with some tattoo artists and talk them into giving me an apprenticeship. Learn to surf. Take up woodcarving. Open my own mechanic shop, just because I like to work on cars. Have a small place of my own, somewhere near water, where I can smell the salt." I let out a long breath, running a hand through my hair. "All that's really mattered to me all along was that I had the money and contacts to get free of my family. After that, I figured I'd stay on the move for a while. Stay off the radar until I decided where I wanted to settle, once the heat died down."

Charlotte swallows, her throat moving as she nods, still staring out into the dark forest through the window. Her gaze is distant, far-off, as if she's looking for something and not finding it. "I keep thinking about what I might do. Where I'd want to go. But none of it feels real. I can't *want* any of it. It feels like—like I'm planning someone else's life."

I wince, the knowledge once again that this is my fault settling heavily on my shoulders. I want to tell her that it doesn't have to be like that, for either of us. That if we're going to be lost about what our future entails, we could be lost together. We could find a way to make it work. Before all of this, before she knew the truth, we were happy in all the moments that we spent together.

But I lost her trust. She might trust me when it comes to our mutual safety, but she doesn't trust me with her heart. And I don't know what I can do to win it back again.

"I know the plan," Charlotte says slowly, still staring out at the trees beyond the window. "I know that we're going to Vegas, and that some man is going to give me a new social security card, and driver's license, and anything else I might need to start over fresh. Unfindable by anyone—even the people who I would want to find me." Her voice trembles a little, and I suppress the urge to pull her close once again.

"I'm supposed to move forward from all of this, but I don't know *how*," she whispers. "Everything feels...tainted. I feel like I can't trust my own judgment." She twists around finally, fully, looking at me as she leans back against the window sill, her arms wrapped around herself. "You lied to me, Ivan, but I let myself believe all of it because I wanted to. And now I find myself second-guessing everything I think."

That stabbing pain slices through my chest again, guilt welling up in me, hot and thick and suffocating. "I'm sorry," I whisper. "I never meant to make you feel like this."

Charlotte swallows hard, a bitter smile curving the edges of her mouth. "What is it they say about good intentions? And yours weren't even all that good to begin with."

There's nothing I can say to that. The silence hangs between us, as thick as the guilt weighing me down, and I want to tell her that it will be okay. That everything will be fine in the end. But I have no way of knowing that—and I'm long past being able to make those kinds of promises to her.

"We should go back to sleep," I say finally, shoving my hands into my pockets and stepping back. I don't know how much longer I can resist her pull. It's like gravity, begging me to hold her, to touch her, to pour everything I feel for her into her—and that is exactly what I shouldn't do. "We have a couple more long driving days ahead of us. And I'm sure you feel as bad as I do."

My shoulder is aching. I know from previous injuries that the second day is always worse than the first. Tomorrow will suck, but I'd endure any pain to make sure she's safe. I just don't want her to be hurting, as well.

Charlotte nods. "I can't ever remember having been this sore," she admits, and my heart twists in my chest. "I'll try to get some sleep."

She brushes past me, and it takes everything in me not to reach for her, to hook my hand in her elbow and pull her into me, to slide my fingers into her hair and draw her lips down to mine. Every part of me is aching to kiss her, but I let her go, standing there as she retreats to her bed.

I watch her slide under the blankets, rolling over to face the wall. I look at her face in the dim moonlight, and my chest hurts, my body crying out for a hit of the drug that I finally got hooked on.

Withdrawal is going to be a bitch. And I don't think I'll ever really get over her.

26

CHARLOTTE

The next morning, the sunlight streaming into the cabin is what wakes us. It's chilly when I throw back the blankets, cutting through my thin t-shirt, and I wrap my arms over my chest, feeling suddenly exposed. Ivan is sitting up, too, running his hands through his still-bloodied hair as he blinks away sleep, and something about the way his face is still soft and vulnerable in this in-between moment makes me want to get up and go to him.

It reminds me of Ivan before all of this. The man I thought I knew. The one I was falling for.

Aren't you falling for this one, too?

I shove the thought away, getting up to go and get a granola bar and bottle of water from the pile of our supplies on the table. The moment my feet hit the floor, and I straighten up fully, I let out a moan of pain, clenching my teeth against the bone-deep soreness.

Ivan is up in an instant, so quickly that I don't even see him coming towards me at first. I'm too focused on how fucking bad I feel.

"Charlotte?" His voice is strained, panicked. "Are you alright?"

"Yes," I bite out the word, swallowing hard as I try to force myself to move. "I'm just really, really fucking sore. I've done Pilates classes with Sarah, and I've still never been this sore."

Ivan lets out a sharp, startled bark of laughter at that, but all I feel is a sudden hollowness in my chest, a new kind of pain to add to the physical one. Because there won't *be* any more Pilates classes with Sarah, or sitting in the sauna afterward, or groaning over the pain together as we use the foam rollers to work out the leftover kinks. There's only an unknown, empty future in front of me.

Will I find another Sarah? Another friend to work out with? Someone else to share my days with that I'll be happy to know, who will make me glad that it all turned out like this? Another Jaz for happy hours? Another Zoe to shop with? The thought feels like a betrayal, and hot tears spring to my eyes out of seemingly nowhere, a weight crushing my chest.

"Hey." Concern laces Ivan's voice, and he reaches out to me, but I don't want any part of it right now. I brush past him, hobbling stiffly to the table as I snatch up a chocolate chip granola bar and angrily twist the top off of a bottle of water.

I would give anything for a hot shower right now. My muscles feel as if my body is one big cramp, and my head hurts. Ivan doesn't look much better—his forehead is bruised around the gash, and I'm sure the bruises scattered across his torso are livid. I can see the ones on my forearms, the scratches on my right arm still angry.

I took care of him last night. But right now, I don't even want to talk to him. I never used to be this moody, this mercurial. But I suppose, under the circumstances, it can be excused.

Ivan swallows hard, looking at me for a long moment before he swipes a couple of the bottles off of the table. "I'm going to go wash up outside," he says finally. "We need to leave in thirty minutes or so, tops."

The forest looks different this morning as we drive through it, back out to the road. Last night, it was dark and frightening, closing in around us as we exhaustedly made our way to the safety cabin. Now, in the light, it looks beautiful. Open. Free.

Maybe I'll go somewhere like this, after, I think. *The mountains. Colorado. Somewhere completely different from where I've lived my whole life*. After all, I'll be starting from a blank slate. I might as well do it all completely fresh.

It's worth considering, but it doesn't bring me any joy. My heart feels heavy as Ivan pulls back out onto the highway, and I sink back into the passenger's seat, trying not to think about how much pain I'm in.

"We're going to have to dump this car soon," Ivan says, watching the road. "Tonight, probably. I'll do what I did before—find some shitty small car lot and swap out a pair of license plates. Tomorrow we'll be in Vegas, and we'll get rid of that car. Then we'll be home free not long after."

I nod. I don't trust myself to speak right now. I shuffle through one of the bags that I repacked earlier for more pain medication, chasing it with water. I'm exhausted still, and the reality of stealing yet another car, of the fact that we're still being hunted by the FBI and the Bratva—all of it makes me feel an onslaught of emotions that I don't feel prepared to handle right now.

The Bratva want Ivan dead, and me dead or used to turn a profit for them. The FBI want to throw Ivan in the darkest hole available, and at this point, I'm pretty sure they would put me in prison too, if I didn't give them everything they want to know about Ivan. And while I *should* be willing to roll over on Ivan after everything he's put me through—I don't know if I would be.

For better or worse, I care about him. And that kind of betrayal feels wrong.

The miles pass by silently. I watch the forested landscape give way to open fields, the warmth of the car finally lulling me back to sleep for a little while. I'm dragged out of my half-nap by Ivan's voice, telling me that we should stop soon.

"We need fuel, and we should get something to eat," he says. "Probably should stretch our legs, too. After what happened, sitting for so long without moving isn't great."

I nod, not wanting to think about how it's going to feel when I finally get up and move. I can feel that everything has started to tighten up as I've been sitting and napping, and I'm sure it's not going to be good.

I wander through the gas station as Ivan gets something to drink and pays for gas, looking for snacks I might want. I feel stiff and sore, and walking around is both painful and helping all at once. Glancing at a calendar on one wall near the window, I realize it's only a few days until Halloween.

My chest tightens. Jaz, Zoe, and Sarah will have decided on costumes for this year by now. Decided which bar's party would be the best one to go to, or if they want to bar-hop downtown, seeing how many costume contests they can enter and how many free drinks they can get. I'm going to miss it this year.

And every other year, forever.

I grab a small bag of Cheetos and a bottle of Snapple tea, not really paying attention to what flavor. My interest in snacks has fled, at this point. As I approach the counter to set my purchases down next to Ivan's, I see a rack of postcards next to the register, and something about them makes the melancholy feeling settling over me feel even heavier.

They're all cheesy: overblown photos of landscapes and big slogans, announcing our departure from the Great Plains and our impending entrance into the Pacific Northwest—technically. But, of course, rather than continuing on to the coast, we're taking a sharp turn and heading down to Vegas. A lump rises in my throat as I look at them, realizing that there's no one for me to send one to now. If I did—if I reach out to any of my friends or the family I haven't really spoken to all that much in the last several years—I'd be putting them in danger.

Ivan pays for the food, and gas for the car. I can tell that he's being careful not to look as if he's scanning the parking lot, but I can see him watching out of the corner of his eye, see the tension in his shoulders as he waits for something to happen. For there to be another incident, now that it's a new day.

But this time, at least, it's fine. We make it back to the car without anyone cropping up that we don't want to see. Ivan fills the tank and gets back in, glancing over at me as I lean back against my seat with a groan. The pain meds that I took are starting to kick in, but it was just a combination of ibuprofen and naproxen, so it doesn't do much more than take the edge off. My body is still protesting every movement.

Ivan glances over at me as he begins to pull out of the gas station, his face etched with concern.

"Do you need to take a longer break?" he asks softly. "We can, if you need to. I'll find somewhere safe for us to stop—"

"No." I shake my head. "Let's just keep going. The sooner we get to Vegas, the better."

I know I'm not imagining the hurt in his face when I say that. He keeps his gaze fixed on the road ahead, and the silence between us feels heavier than ever, full of unspoken things that I don't know if we're ever going to actually say to each other.

What's the point, when whatever this is comes to an end in just a couple of days?

We drive for hours, only stopping a couple more times for brief bathroom breaks. The silence goes on for nearly as long, broken only by the low hum of the radio and the occasional rustle of a snack wrapper or crackle of a plastic water bottle. At this point, I don't know which of us should be the one to try to bridge the chasm between us. Ivan hurt me in ways that should be unforgivable, that should have broken the trust between us forever, but I know I've hurt him, too. He's been making himself vulnerable to me, trying to make up for what he's done, and I won't let it be enough.

I don't know if I can.

As the sunset starts to streak the sky, lighting it up in a painter's palette's worth of oranges and yellows and pinks, I try to focus on that, instead of the ache in my muscles and in my heart. All too soon, Ivan's voice, flat and toneless, cuts through my distraction. "I'm going to stop and swap the car out soon," he says, shifting lanes as he glances down at the atlas in his lap. "It'll be the last time before we get to Vegas."

He says it almost reassuringly, as if to make it up to me that we have to steal another car. *Just one more.* But honestly, at this point, after watching one of Ivan's brothers die in front of me, stealing a car seems less horrible than it did at first.

I nod, still not trusting myself to speak, still too tired to think of what to say. As the sunset fades and the sky starts to darken, Ivan pulls off of the highway, following a side road towards another small town.

He stops at a used car lot, much like the one we stole that first car from, dimly lit and deserted at the late hour. I feel a tightness in my chest as Ivan pulls the Subaru around back, out of sight of the road, his gaze quickly surveying the line of cars parked in the back of the lot.

The first time he did this, I was scared, and shocked. Now I just feel numb as I watch him expertly swap out plates on a Ford Bronco and a Honda Civic, moving at an abrupt pace as he glances over his shoulder, watching for anyone else.

I know the routine now, too. I get into the driver's seat of the car we've been driving as Ivan hotwires the Bronco, thinking of the list of crimes that Bradley will gleefully list off to me if we get caught. *Grand theft auto. Accomplice to murder. Accomplice to carjacking. Grand theft auto again.* The threats, the things he'll make me do in order to avoid a prison sentence. Things that I have no idea how I'll respond to, because until very recently, it never occurred to me in my wildest dreams that I would have to worry about any of this.

I follow Ivan out of the town, until we've passed the last of the stoplights, and the road darkens again. He takes me down a few side roads, out to an area where there's nothing but empty property, and turns off of the road, driving through a field all the way to a copse of trees.

When I stop just behind him, every muscle protesting the bouncing of the car the whole way, he gets out of the Bronco and walks over to the driver's side of the car I'm driving. He opens the door, gesturing for me to slip out.

"I'm going to wipe it down," he says. "Get rid of any fingerprints. Then we'll get on the road again."

I nod tiredly, jumping down out of the car and walking stiffly to the Bronco. I close my eyes while I'm waiting for Ivan to come back, and before I know it, I'm fast asleep.

27

CHARLOTTE

We get into Vegas around eleven in the morning, three days before Halloween. We spent one more night in the most out-of-the-way motel we could find, with Ivan sleeping near the door in case of trouble. But for once, there was no trouble. The night passed without incident, and even though I didn't sleep well, I did get *some* sleep.

I fell asleep again after breakfast, nodding off as Ivan turned onto the highway that would lead us into Vegas. My hoodie was tossed in the backseat, the day warm enough that I no longer needed it. A quick glance at the dashboard of the Bronco told me that the temperature outside had climbed to seventy degrees—downright balmy after the days and nights spent driving through the northern part of the country.

The bright sunlight wakes me up after a little while, just outside of the city. I look out of the window, and my eyes widen as I see the landscape around us.

Red dirt—desert and cliffs, stretch out on either side of the road. I lean my forehead against the glass window, staring at it, and I hear Ivan chuckle next to me.

"Gorgeous, isn't it?" There's something soft in Ivan's voice that makes me think he's not entirely talking about the landscape.

"I've never seen anything like it before." I've never seen the desert outside of movies. I'd always imagined it to be dusty and flat, but while there is a decent bit of flat space, the reddish cliff formations and the view spreading out to the horizon is remarkably beautiful. "It's so much better than I thought it would be." I turn to look at him. "You've been out here before, right?"

"To Vegas? Plenty of times." Ivan rotates his hands on the steering wheel, cracking his neck. "Business, pleasure, you name it. I'm familiar with the city. Which is a good thing."

I try not to think about the spark of jealousy that the way he says *pleasure* lights in me. I shouldn't care who else he's been with, what kind of pleasures he sought out on other trips. That shouldn't matter to me at all. But I feel the hot stab of it, all the same.

I turn back to the window, trying to shift my focus back to the view to quell the churning emotions. The desert stretches out for miles all around us, endless and more mesmerizing than I could have imagined, but my mind keeps drifting back to what kind of *pleasures* Ivan might have sought out in Vegas before.

Which also makes me wonder what he'll seek out after I'm gone. Regardless of how obsessed he became with me, regardless of all the things he's said to me, Ivan is no saint. He'll find another woman. He'll forget about me. And the thought of him in bed with someone else, his hands and mouth trailing over someone else's skin, makes me feel nauseous.

I clear my throat, forcing my mind away from that and to a different, more pertinent subject.

"So, what's the plan once we get there?" My voice sounds strained, even to my own ears, but I hope that Ivan doesn't notice.

Ivan glances over at me. "We'll check into a hotel. The Wynn has top-tier security, floors where the billionaires stay, accessible with only a keycard. Bradley will have to have a warrant to get any camera footage, and Lev will have to invoke some serious favors if he wants to get to us. And even if Bradley does have a warrant, and even if Lev does throw his weight around, I will have paid someone to keep an eye out for us. We'll be warned, if someone is coming. Money talks in Vegas, and I have plenty of it."

The cool confidence in his voice does something to me. I feel a flip in my stomach, a rush of adrenaline, and I swallow hard, trying not to think about the possibility of being alone with Ivan in a luxury room. A room meant for sin and excess, meant for all the *pleasures* that he hinted at earlier.

"And after that?"

"Once we're checked in, I'll contact my associate. Then we can get cleaned up, get a good meal, and I'll find out how long before we can get the new IDs and such." Ivan glances over at me. "We're in the homestretch now. It's going to be fine."

There's something strained about the way he says those last words, and it makes me uneasy. "You're sure this person can help us?" He must be, I think, or we wouldn't have come all this way. But now that the moment is all but here, I feel that fearful sense of overwhelm that's threatened to swallow me up before. This sounds dangerous, like something out of a movie. Not the kind of thing I ever thought I'd be involved in. "You trust them?"

Ivan smirks. "Trust is a strong word in my world. But I know them well. I've done business with them before. And they make it their job to do exactly what we need. What I pay them will make it worth their while to ensure that we get that without too much trouble."

I nod, turning it all over in my head. The past days of fast food, twenty-four-hour grocery stores, and shitty motels made me forget that Ivan is insanely wealthy. I don't know *how* wealthy, but someone who owns an Aston Martin *plus* the other cars he has must have plenty. And the way he talks about money makes me think that we could stay in Vegas for a long time, and not need to worry about it.

My heart is racing as the city looms ahead of us, a glittering mirage at the edge of the desert. Even in the bright daylight, it's overwhelming, almost shocking, after days of long, open roads and small backwoods towns. It feels like being thrust abruptly back into civilization, and it's strange.

"Look at that," Ivan says with a grin. "Sin City in all its glory."

The noise is a shock, too, as we merge onto the crowded freeway, cars speeding past us. The road ahead is suddenly filled with sleek sports cars and luxury sedans, and I bite my lip as I look out of the window, a part of me wishing that we had more time to explore.

"We won't be able to do much, will we?" I ask wistfully, and Ivan frowns.

"We'll see. Depending on how long it takes for us to actually meet with my contact, we might have a day or two in the city. And as far as what we can do—" Ivan drums his fingers against the steering wheel. "It's a big place. Loud and bright and full of people. It's a place to hide, but it's also a place where we could be surprised. So we'll just have to play it by ear."

Even in the bright daylight, the Las Vegas Strip is a carnival of light and sound. I'm no stranger to skyscrapers and cityscapes—I've lived a good part of my life in downtown Chicago—but everything about this place is so much *more*. Everything here seems meant to stand out—a recreation of the Eiffel Tower, a pyramid, a huge fountain, a rollercoaster twisting around one of the resorts. Much like the desert surrounding it, Vegas is something I've seen in movies before, but nothing can quite compare to seeing it in reality.

"I really want to explore." I bite my lip, looking around and trying to drink in as much as I can, as Ivan turns off the main road. "Surely, if we're careful—"

"We'll see," Ivan repeats, firmly. "We haven't come all this way to put ourselves in unnecessary danger now, Charlotte. This is the final step before we're free. But—" He pauses, and I can tell that he wants to say yes. That he wants to make me happy. "I'll do my best to make it possible."

I nod, shoving down the disappointment I feel at the possibility that I might have to just stay holed up in our room. I know I'm being a little childish—the room is no doubt going to be nicer than anything I've ever stayed in before. Probably nicer than my apartment. But I desperately want to explore every glittering attraction and colorful casino that Vegas has to offer, and I can't help but feel a pang of frustration that I might end up with it just within arm's length, but unable to explore.

A new experience is right here, and I want to enjoy it. But Ivan is right. We haven't spent all of this time covering our tracks and committing crimes just to get pinched in Vegas at the last moment.

We pass by several of the resorts, including a half-moon-shaped one with *Wynn* written at the top in curving script, and I frown. "Isn't that where we're going?"

"It is. But I can hardly hand a stolen, hotwired car over to the valet." Ivan looks over at me, smirking. "We're going to drop this somewhere less populated, over in the older part of Vegas. And then we'll get a taxi back here."

"Oh." *That makes sense.* I feel a little stupid for not thinking of that, but Ivan doesn't say anything more about it. He just keeps driving, as the scenery gets less polished and glittering and more weathered. We drive past a casino called the *Golden Nugget*, past some less glamorous shops, as Ivan turns into a neighborhood that looks much more ordinary than anything we've driven past so far since getting to Vegas.

"We'll leave it here," Ivan says, getting out of the car to unhook the battery. "I'll wipe it down, and then we'll catch a cab back to the Strip. Grab anything you want."

I make a face at the plastic Walmart bags still holding our single change of clothes, the leftover pain medication, and the one burner phone that Ivan hasn't used yet. He follows my gaze, and grins at me.

"We'll go shopping," he says, and even though I never thought of myself as a clotheshorse like Zoe, the thought of *new*, stylish clothes makes my heart jump in my chest. "I have plenty of cash, and we can at least do that. You'll have clothes that you actually like to wear."

"That sounds amazing," I tell him honestly, and his grin instantly spreads into a smile that looks as if making me happy has made his entire day. It makes me pause, because it startles me that my happiness could have that much of an effect on him. "Let's go."

It doesn't take Ivan long to quickly clean the interior, erasing all traces of our presence. I grab the bags, glancing back at the car once more before we walk away quickly, Ivan keeping an eye out for anyone who might have seen us with the Bronco.

I don't like to think about what he might do if someone *did* see us, so I force that thought from my mind before it can entirely take shape. That's the last thing I want to think about.

The day is warm, pleasantly so after the chill of the last several. The air is much dryer than what I'm accustomed to, and I swear I can *feel* the static, feel my hair frizzing as I follow Ivan back to the main road, where we can hail a cab.

"Stay close," he says, raising a hand as a yellow taxi comes around the corner.

I can't help but look around, anxiety churning in my gut, half-expecting Bradley or Lev to pop out of a corner at any moment. But they don't, and a second later, we're safely ensconced in the taxi, with Ivan giving the driver directions to take us to the Wynn.

I know I should play it cool, but I can't stop looking at the scenery. Even here, in what Ivan called the 'older' part of Vegas, it's eye-catching in a different kind of way. There's an old, retro sort of vibe to this part of town, with buskers and street performers hanging out under neon signs that haven't been lit up yet, the casinos and restaurants weathered in a way that still somehow feels exotic.

And then, when we make it back to the Strip, I suck in a breath as I take it all in again.

The cab driver glances in his rear-view mirror, clearly amused. He catches my eye, and I force myself not to wince. The last thing we need to do is draw attention to ourselves, and here I am, already doing that.

"First time in Vegas?" he asks, and I start to answer automatically, but Ivan cuts in.

"The first for her," he says with a companionable grin. "It's our anniversary. I wanted to surprise her with it."

The lie is so smooth that I would almost believe it, if I didn't know better. I force a smile to my lips, playing along. "It was *such* a surprise, too. I'm so happy."

I suppose the first part isn't entirely a lie. I *was* surprised to wake up in that first hotel room, and find out that I was going to Vegas with Ivan.

The driver pulls up in front of the Wynn, and Ivan hands him a thick wad of cash. Far more than I think the trip warranted, but it's definitely enough that I bet the driver will forget that he saw us.

I grab the plastic bags, staring up at the huge, curving facade of the casino. I feel a flush of embarrassment at the idea of walking into this ritzy place carrying two Walmart bags, but I forget all about it the moment we step inside.

It's like no hotel I've ever been to. The entrance almost reminds me of a wedding aisle, slick white marble fringed with arches of trees wrapped in ropes of lights, huge, brightly colored balls the size of beach balls hanging from the top branches, also webbed with lights. There's potted greenery and flowers everywhere, filling the lobby with a thick floral scent as Ivan leads me up to the marble-topped check-in, where I hang back slightly as he gets us a room. I see a bar over to one side, all red with black chairs and glass-topped tables, and I wonder if we could walk over there for a drink with a kind of longing that I know is me yearning for the life I had before this.

A life I'm never going to get back, at least not the way it was.

Two arched staircases lead up to the second floor. Ivan motions towards them, glancing at me, and I follow as he takes the keycards from the receptionist.

"Elevators can be dangerous," he says quietly, under his breath, as we walk towards the stairs. "Someone can catch us at a stop, get on, and we're trapped in there with them. This is more open. A little safer."

My leg muscles, still sore from the wreck, aren't thrilled at the idea of climbing stairs, but I don't argue. I distract myself instead by looking around as we walk up, taking in the luxurious, opulent surroundings. We walk past shops and through the main casino floor, the chime of slot machines filling the air. There's a haze of smoke, too, which surprises me—I've never been anywhere that it was possible to smoke inside before.

Ivan guides me through the casino floor to a set of elevators.

"These require a keycard to access," he explains, as he swipes ours. "Safer. They'll take us to one of the high-roller suites, which are the most secure in the casino. We'll be safer there than anywhere else."

Based on the fact that there's armed security on the floor that we get off on, waiting for Ivan to show his keycard, I believe him. He flashes it, leading me down the hall to a door, where he holds the card up again, and a light flashes green. When he opens the door, we're in a room that's like nothing I've ever been in before.

"Welcome to one of the high-roller suites in Vegas," Ivan says with a grin as he steps inside. "Back in the lap of luxury."

28

CHARLOTTE

It takes me a minute to fully absorb just how beautiful the room that we're in is. My feet squish into the thick carpet, and I take a few steps forward, looking around. The suite is the size of my apartment back in Chicago, complete with a separate 'living room' sort of area, with leather couches and a glass-topped table, lined with gold edging. There's a mahogany wet bar, a huge television sunken into one wall, and three of the walls in the living area are glass, overlooking the city. It's breathtaking now, and I can only imagine how beautiful it must look at night.

I try not to look at the king-sized bed that takes up most of the adjoining space, set in the center of that room against one wall. It looks huge and comfortable and soft, and all I can think about is the fact that Ivan will likely be sleeping in it next to me. It's big enough that we could probably pass an entire night without ever accidentally touching each other, but that doesn't matter. It'll be torment for both of us, all the same.

"Why don't you take a shower?" Ivan suggests. "I'll go down to one of the stores and get us something to change into. We can shop for more later. But for now, it'll feel good to clean up."

I'm tempted to argue, if only because I want to explore. But the thought of a hot, luxurious shower is tempting, and I nod, glancing at the bathroom.

"Okay."

Ivan smiles. "I'll be back before too long. If anyone knocks on the door," he adds, his expression turning serious once again, "don't open it. I have a keycard. I'll let myself in. Don't open up for anyone, no matter what they say."

"I won't," I promise.

After days and days of shitty motels, the bathroom is so luxurious that it makes me want to cry. I kick my shoes off before I walk in, curling my toes against the cold marble floor as I look around. There's a huge soaking tub, a separate shower that takes up all of one wall, and a long dual-sink counter that has a gilded tray with a number of different toiletries on it. I unscrew the top of the shower gel, and let out a sigh as I smell apple blossoms and honey.

I don't know whether to take a shower or a bath first. I figure I should start with the shower, so I turn the taps on as hot as I can stand, stepping under the multiple showerheads and letting out a moan as soon as the hot spray hits me. Sex with Ivan is the best thing I've ever felt—my emotions about what he's done aside, but this shower is coming in a very close second.

I stand under the shower until I lose track of time, just soaking in the heat. The water washes away days of grime and tension, and I can feel my muscles slowly unknotting, the stress melting away. I reach for the shampoo bottle, some kind of luxury brand that I bet Jaz would recognize, and lather it up in my hands, breathing in the sweet scent as I massage it into my scalp. I let out another moan, the sensation so pleasurable that I lean into the wall for a moment, soaking up the exhilaration of being clean and scrubbed.

It's almost intoxicating, how good it feels. I'm starting to feel like a person again, and the luxury of all of this is in stark contrast to the danger we've been running from for days on end. A not insignificant part of me wishes we could just stay here, that this luxurious space could be our sanctuary, and we could hide away forever.

And how would that go? I think as I rinse off. None of this changes what Ivan did. None of it changes the fact that he hurt me, that he lied, that my life has been upended because of him. All of the things he's done to try to make it up to me—they *can't*, because there's no making up for something like that.

Right?

I shut off the water with some regret, stepping out and wrapping a plush towel around myself, sighing at yet another simple pleasure that I'd forgotten. The mirror has fogged over, and I step up to the counter, wiping my hand in a small circle over the glass. My reflection stares back at me—thinner than the last time I looked, tired, with dark circles under my eyes. I look like I need to sleep for a week.

I hear the door open and jump a little, pressing my hand against my mouth to stifle the yelp that slips out. "It's just me," I hear Ivan call from the room just outside, and I bite my lip, embarrassed that I'm so jumpy.

I wrap the towel more tightly around myself, suddenly very aware of how exposed I feel, even with the towel covering me. My heart races as I hear Ivan's footsteps in the other room, along with the rustling sound of bags. I take a deep breath, trying to calm myself down.

It's just Ivan. It's not as if we've never seen each other naked before. But somehow, in the luxury of this room, with the privacy and the sudden time that we have available to us, it feels different.

"I got us some clothes," Ivan calls through the door. "I'll leave them on the bed. Take your time, there's no rush."

No rush. I exhale as I hear those words, a relief that I didn't expect washing over me. I hear him walk away, and I let out a breath, swallowing hard as I think of going out into that room, where he is. My reflection in the mirror looks flushed, and I have a feeling that it's from more than just the hot shower. I finish drying off quickly, wrapping my wet hair in a second, smaller towel before slipping out into the main room.

There's a bag on the bed waiting for me, a sleek pink bag with ribbon strings. It feels like Ivan got me a gift, and my heart turns over oddly in my chest. I walk over and open it, seeing a pair of soft-looking jeans and a black t-shirt inside. When I take them out, I see a new pair of black cotton underwear and a matching bra inside, and my cheeks flush hot, thinking of Ivan picking out underwear for me. I'm suddenly glad that he's not in the room with me to see my reaction.

The clothes all fit perfectly. The way the jeans mold to my body makes me think of Ivan gripping my hips, and I flush deeper, trying to ignore the racing of my heart as I tug the t-shirt on over my head. I can smell a hint of Ivan's scent on the fabric, and my stomach flutters, my traitorous emotions a tangle of confusion once again.

Ivan is in the adjoining living room, standing by the window with his back to me. He glances over at me, and I see the flash of heat in his eyes before he looks towards the bathroom. "My turn," he says, and his words sound oddly tight as he strides past me, straight into the bathroom, carrying his fresh clothes with him.

He shuts the door behind him, and a few minutes later, I hear the sound of the water turning on. I sink down onto the edge of the bed, trying not to think about him stripping down, his naked body under the hot water, the way it would look running over all of that taut, muscled flesh.

The temptation to go in and join him is strong. But he's made it clear that he only wants that if I'm willing to tell him that I believe him. That I believe what he feels for me is real. That I believe there's more to this than just his lies and deceit.

And if I admit that, everything changes.

When Ivan comes back out a little while later, he's wearing a pair of slim-cut black jeans and a fitted grey henley that accentuates his broad chest and muscled shoulders. I feel my mouth go a little dry as I see him, and I swallow hard, trying to ignore all the dirty thoughts swirling around in my head.

"Let's go shopping," he says, motioning to the door with one hand as he runs the other through his damp, dark blond hair. "Get some things you can actually pick out for yourself."

I can feel that Ivan is on edge as we head down to the shops. His head is on a swivel, constantly scanning our surroundings without being obvious as we walk through the lavish resort. His hand hovers near me, never quite touching the small of my back or taking my hand, but I can feel the heat radiating off of his palm, somehow even more than if he'd been actually touching me. He's tense, and it makes me tense too.

I catch sight of us, walking side by side, in one of the shop windows. We look like we could be any couple, on a shopping trip together in Vegas—on a vacation for our anniversary, even, like Ivan had told the cab driver. But I know better.

"Did you talk to your contact yet?" I ask quietly as we walk into the first store.

"Not yet." Ivan's voice is equally low. "When we get back to the room." He speaks louder, looking around the store. "Pick whatever you want. Make sure to get a bathing suit, too, there's a gorgeous pool here. And something nice to wear, in case we go out. Don't worry about the price."

I've done pretty well for myself in my life, but *don't worry about the price* isn't something I've ever gotten to do before. I feel a small thrill of excitement, momentarily forgetting about the situation that we're in. The store is full of designer clothes, shoes, and accessories that would make Zoe and Jaz both salivate just looking at them, and I know Ivan meant it when he said that I could pick out whatever I want.

A part of me feels guilty for taking him up on it. I'm planning on leaving him, and I know his generosity is about more than just keeping me safe here. He doesn't have to buy me fancy clothes to do that. It's about trying to make up for everything he's done. I don't have any intention of forgiving him, so I shouldn't take advantage of what he's offering.

But the temptation is there, and just now, it's one that I'm too weak to ignore.

I grab a few items as Ivan hangs out near one of the racks, half-watching me and half keeping an eye out for anyone suspicious. I slip into one of the dressing rooms, viscerally aware of the fact that Ivan is just outside. That he's undoubtedly thinking about me undressing in here, trying on the items I brought with me, just as I was thinking about him in the shower earlier. A hot jolt of tension prickles down my spine, and I yank an emerald green cocktail dress off of its hanger, trying not to wonder *exactly* what he's picturing right now.

I can't help but think of what his reaction would be if he saw me walk out in this right now, though. I can picture his eyes darkening with desire, the way his fingers would curl into his palms with the effort not to touch me. The moments we've shared together are an intimacy that means I've learned little things about him that I can't forget, and I realize that I've noticed more than I ever meant to.

And if I wore it out on a real date with him? Like the ones we went on before? The fantasy is too tempting. With so much unknown in front of me, Ivan is a familiarity that I want to reach out and cling to. I have to remind myself, constantly, of what he's done.

I step out of the dressing room a few minutes later, clutching the green dress and a few other items. Ivan's gaze immediately flicks to me, like a magnet, his eyes sliding over me intensely, as if he's imagining everything I just tried on. He sees the slip of green fabric, and I see his throat contract.

"Find anything you like?" he asks, his voice low and husky.

I nod, not trusting myself to speak. Ivan takes the clothes from my arms, his fingers brushing mine. A jolt of electricity shoots through me at the brief contact.

"I'll take these to the register," he says. "Why don't you pick out some shoes to go with that dress?" A small smile curves the corners of his lips, and my heart flutters despite myself.

As I browse the shoe section, trying to focus on stilettos instead of Ivan, I can't shake the feeling of being watched. I glance around nervously, but don't see anyone suspicious. Still, the hairs on the back of my neck stand up. I pick up a pair of nude heels, as well as a pair of black boots to go with the jeans I picked out, and look around again. I don't see any sign of anyone who resembles Bradley or Lev, but I still feel uneasy. Earlier I wanted to go out, but now I'm starting to feel as if I want to retreat back to the room.

I hurry over to Ivan, who's just finishing up at the register. His eyes narrow as he sees my expression.

"What's wrong?" he asks in a low voice, glancing around.

"I'm not sure," I whisper back, feeling that cold sensation prickle along the back of my neck again. "I just... I feel like someone's watching us."

Ivan's jaw tightens. He nods once, then casually drapes his arm around my shoulders, pulling me close. His lips brush against the side of my head, sending a different kind of shiver down my spine. To anyone else, we probably look like a couple sharing an intimate moment. But I can feel the tension in his muscles.

"Stay close," he murmurs in my ear. "We're going to walk out of here very casually. Don't look around. Just act natural. We're just out doing some shopping, going back up to our room before dinner."

My heart pounds as we make our way out of the store. Ivan's arm remains firmly around me, and as much as I don't want to let him touch me, as much as it rouses a storm of emotion in me that I'm not prepared to deal with, I don't pull away. Right now, he's the only safe thing I have.

I don't relax until we get back up to the room. Ivan closes the door firmly behind us, glancing over at me. "I'm going to make the call," he says, stepping into the bathroom and closing that door, too, cutting me off from hearing what he says.

I sink onto the edge of the bed, suddenly feeling exhausted all over again. I can hear the low murmur of Ivan's voice from the bathroom, but I can't make out any of the words, and I tap my feet nervously against the carpet, trying not to think about what's being said. That contact is who we've been trying to get to, the difference between starting over and getting caught, and my chest tightens. I don't want to leave my old life behind, but I also don't want to end up in Bradley's hands or Lev's. That contact is the only person who can ensure that doesn't happen.

I try to distract myself by unpacking the clothes I just bought, but my thoughts are racing wildly. What if the contact can't help us? What if Bradley or Lev have already found us? What if they're just biding their time, waiting to strike? The room, which felt so huge just a little while ago, suddenly feels small and claustrophobic, and I can feel myself wanting to pace, wanting to look out of the window to see if anyone is watching us from outside.

It feels like an eternity before Ivan finally emerges from the bathroom. His expression is unreadable, and my stomach twists with anxiety.

"What did they say?" I bite my lip, trying to keep my voice from trembling.

Ivan must see how anxious I am, because his face softens. He crosses the room quickly, coming to stand in front of me, one hand resting on the dresser where I just put my clothes, as if I'm moving in. "We have a meeting set," he says reassuringly. "But they can't meet us for a few days."

I let out a sharp breath. "A few days? What are we supposed to do until then?"

A small smile tugs at the corners of Ivan's mouth. "Well, I think we should stay in tonight. But I think, at the very least, we can explore this resort. I don't know if we should go out on the town, but there's plenty to do just in this one hotel. And if I do see someone suspicious, we can get up to our room quickly."

"Are you sure this isn't the diner all over again?" I raise an eyebrow. "We try to do something 'normal' again, and it ends up almost getting us caught?"

Ivan huffs out a breath. "I don't think so. I hope not." He runs a hand through his hair. "Do you really want to stay cooped up in here until the meeting?"

I shake my head. "No. I'm just—" *Scared*, I almost say, but I don't want to admit it.

I feel like I'm close to losing it, honestly. And truthfully, I think a few days staying in this room and not going out might just drive me over the edge. Luxurious as it is, it's going to give me way too much time to think.

"We'll order room service tonight," Ivan says. "Tomorrow, we'll get out and explore a little. And pretty soon, we'll get what we need, and get out of here."

Except *we* won't be getting out of here. He knows that as well as I do. We'll be going our separate ways.

Ivan picks up the room service menu and hands it to me, and I see his mouth tighten, his eyes suddenly shadowed as if he realized what he said, too. And the heaviness in my chest makes me wonder, once again, if I've made this decision because it's what I really want.

Or if it's just because it's what I think I'm supposed to do.

29

CHARLOTTE

When I wake up the next morning, despite the danger still hanging over us, I feel like I've had the first real night's sleep that I've gotten in weeks.

Ivan insisted on sleeping on the couch in the other room, so I had the king-sized bed all to myself. After we ordered room service—mushroom truffle burgers and the crispiest fries I've ever eaten—I couldn't stay awake much longer. I passed out in the middle of the bed, and when I wake, I smell waffles.

There's a breakfast tray next to the bed, waiting for me. When I sit up, blinking sleepily and pushing my hair out of my face, I see Ivan in the living room, a plate in his lap as he eats his own breakfast. I lean back for just a moment, stretching luxuriously as I savor the feeling of waking up on soft sheets and a plush mattress. For one brief second, I let myself pretend that I actually am on vacation, and not in a strange limbo between lives, wondering if the people who want me dead will show up any minute.

Ivan looks up as he hears me stirring, and I see the small smile at the corners of his mouth. "Sleep well?" he asks from across the room, and I nod.

"What about you?"

He shrugs. "Better than anywhere I've slept recently. This couch is more comfortable than my bed at home, I think." He says it casually, but I catch the slight twitch in his jaw when he says *home*. He hides it well, probably because he doesn't want me to realize it, but it hurt him to leave his home behind, too. That house meant a lot to him; I know that after what he told me the night we camped out.

What does it matter if it hurt him to leave it? It's his fault.

I push the thought away. After everything he's done to keep me safe, it feels unnecessarily mean and cruel. But at the same time, isn't it true?

I squeeze my eyes shut for a moment before reopening them and reaching for the tray of food. I'm too overwhelmed to sort through that right now. And I'm also starving, smelling the food.

The breakfast that Ivan ordered is poached eggs with Hollandaise, a waffle that's perfectly soft and crunchy in all the right spots, crisp bacon, and a glass of what is definitely fresh-squeezed orange juice. I let out a small sigh as I take a sip, letting the deliciousness of the food take a little of my tension away. It's been a long several days, and even if I can't relax all the way, I deserve a little bit.

"I was thinking we could go down to the pool this afternoon," Ivan says casually. "There's an outdoor one, but also one inside that's absolutely gorgeous. The outdoor pool isn't anything *that* different from ones you've probably seen before, just bigger, but the indoor is something special."

I immediately debate the wisdom of letting him see me in the bikini I purchased. I don't know if it's wise for *me* to see *him* in just swim trunks. The sexual tension between us has been simmering ever since that night in the tent, and Ivan is the one who stopped us last time. *Will he stop me again, if it goes that far? And should he?*

But if I tell him no, he's going to know exactly why. And my cheeks heat just at the thought of Ivan knowing that I'm so skittish of the tension between us that I can't even put on a swimsuit.

"Sure," I say bravely. "I think I'm going to take another shower after breakfast. And then I'll change, and we can go down."

Ivan chuckles. "It's brunch, really. Look at the time."

Glancing over at the clock, I realize I slept just past noon. I'd known I was exhausted, but I hadn't realized just how much.

I shovel down the rest of my food, before slipping out of the bed and going to the dresser to get my clothes. I'd bought a long, loose shirt to sleep in yesterday, and I see Ivan pause with his fork halfway to his mouth out of the corner of my eye, his gaze flicking to my bare legs.

If he's that distracted by my legs, I'm reconsidering the wisdom of wearing the bathing suit. But I grab it anyway, retreating quickly to the bathroom.

When I've changed, I look at myself in the mirror, biting my lip. It's been a while since I've had a reason to wear a swimsuit. I've lost weight since the last time, and not entirely in a good way, but there's still a curve to my chest and my hips. The royal blue bikini that I picked out, with a faint turquoise sparkle to the fabric, still clings to me more enticingly than is probably wise.

I grab the turquoise coverup that goes with it, throw it on, and wrap the tie around my waist. At the very least, it's better if Ivan doesn't see this until we're out in public.

I feel jittery as we head out into the casino. Even at this early afternoon hour, there are still people on the casino floor, pulling slot machines, throwing dice, and playing cards. They call New York City the *city that never sleeps*, but from what I've seen, I think that could be applied to Vegas as well. I follow Ivan down the stairs and to another section of the hotel, the scent of the chlorine hitting my nose before I see the pool area. And when I do, I stop in my tracks for a moment, staring at it.

It's incredible. A huge, shimmering circular pool filled with dark blue water is the centerpiece of the room, with a seashell-topped gazebo at one end, large golden lights hanging from the ceiling, and gold velvet curtains pulled back on either side at the center. The tile under my feet is a slick midnight blue, and surrounding the pool are gold and dark blue velvet couches. There's a bar at one end, and the entire thing is a picture of such exotic opulence that all I can do is stare for a moment.

"Isn't it gorgeous?" Ivan asks, and I nod, still taking it all in.

Especially after the time we've spent on the road, this feels like the most luxurious thing that I've done in a long time. Ivan orders us two fruity drinks from the bar, and I dip my feet in the cool water before untying my coverup and slipping it off.

The moment I do, I catch Ivan's eye. His mouth opens for a brief second before he shuts it again, dropping down to sit on one of the couches near the pool's edge. He seems momentarily speechless, and I slip into the water, letting it cover me up to mid-chest in an effort to ward off any awkwardness.

But it isn't awkward. Not really. That's not the feeling that's crackling in the air between us as Ivan looks away, seemingly trying to regain his composure.

I swim away from the pool's edge, letting the cool water wash over me, trying to slow my racing heart. The tension between Ivan and me is palpable, and I can feel his eyes on me even when I'm not looking at him. I take a deep breath, inhaling the scent of chlorine and tropical flowers from the nearby potted plants.

"The pool is great," I call out to him from where I'm standing, a more comfortable distance between us now. "Are you going to come in?"

Ivan hesitates for a moment, then seems to realize that's what we're here to do. "I suppose I should," he says, and there's a rasp to his voice as he says it, standing up as he reaches for the edge of his shirt. I look away instinctively, but I can't keep my eyes off of him forever, and I catch a glimpse of his muscled chest and abs, the black ink swirling over his skin, as he slips into the water. The bruises on his torso have started to fade a bit, yellowish-green in the golden light from the chandeliers.

"Won't anyone think it's odd, if they see the bruises?" I ask, glancing around to see if anyone is staring at us. Some other guests are starting to filter in to the pool area, and I feel a flicker of tension. We've been trying to stay out of sight for so long that it feels odd to have that restriction loosened now. But I don't see anyone who looks suspicious, or either of the men we're trying to actively avoid.

"Nah." Ivan leans back against the pool's edge, and I have to once again try to tear my gaze from his chest. "They'll just think I'm an MMA fighter or something. Plenty of fights are hosted here."

"Oh. That makes sense." I trail my fingers through the water, lingering for a moment longer before I push myself up out of the pool, trying not to think about how clearly I can feel Ivan's eyes on me as I walk over to where our drinks are waiting.

Screw it, I think, as I take a long sip of the fruity, vodka-laced cocktail. If we're going to be here for a few days, I want to enjoy it if I can. And I can't do that constantly worrying if I'm stoking the embers of the attraction that Ivan and I have for each other.

I take another sip of the drink, and stretch out on the velvet couch. The fabric rubs pleasantly against the backs of my legs, and I close my eyes, letting out a long, slow breath. I feel some of the tightness seep out of my shoulders, and I think I might drift off into a doze, because the next thing I know, I feel a damp palm against my shoulder.

I jolt back to consciousness, on the verge of scrambling back when my eyes open, and I see Ivan sitting on the edge of the couch next to me. It takes me a moment to see the worry in his eyes, and I go very still, watching him warily.

"What's going on?"

"There's someone who's been inching closer to where you're sitting." Ivan's voice is low, barely audible. "I've been watching him. I need you to get up, and we'll go together up to the hotel room. Slowly, as if nothing's wrong." His voice tightens, and I see him glancing over to one side, presumably where the man who's been trying to get closer to me is.

Slowly sounds like an impossibility in this situation. But I've learned to do a lot of things lately that have felt impossible.

I try to look normal, as I sit up. My heart is racing, but I force myself to move casually, wondering the whole time if that's somehow making it even more obvious that I'm trying to *make* myself behave naturally. I slip my coverup back on with shaking hands, standing up as Ivan stands with me.

We start to walk towards the exit, and I feel the heat of Ivan's hand against my back, his fingers tense against my spine. I resist the urge to look over my shoulder, to see if someone is following us.

As we reach the hallway to the stairs, I hear footsteps behind us, quicker now. Ivan's hand presses flat against my back, as if to push me forward, and we both walk faster. The elevators are to our right, and I can hear the footsteps getting closer.

"Elevators instead," Ivan says sharply. "Run!"

We bolt for the elevators. Ivan has his keycard out, and he flashes it at the car, the doors mercifully opening immediately. As I dart inside, I see a man behind us reflected in the mirror—a large, muscled man with black hair and a firm set to his mouth. He doesn't look angry or vengeful, just—focused. Like he was hired for this.

Ivan is already on his burner phone. "Yes," he says as the car shoots up, his voice taut and clipped. "One man. No idea. Okay. We'll do that. Meeting time is the same. Yes. More money, I understand. It's no problem."

He shoves the phone back into his pocket, and I look at him confusedly. "More money?"

Ivan shrugs, as if that's the least of his concerns. Maybe it is. "If there's active heat on us, that's more danger for my contact. Puts heat on everything he's doing, too. So the price goes up."

"And you're just...fine with that?"

Ivan shrugs again. "That's how this world works. Mine, anyway. I'm not worried about it." The elevator reaches our floor, and he walks out first, keycard in one hand and the other resting near the pocket of his swim trunks, where I feel sure there's a knife. Probably the switchblade he gave me when I went into the grocery store alone. "Come on."

We hurry down the hall to our room. The minute we're inside, Ivan goes straight to the dresser and yanks out clothes, tossing them on the bed.

"What are you doing?" I frown at him, confused, and he glances back at me.

"We have to go. I got instructions from my contact on what we should do. Change into something and grab the rest of your stuff. Five minutes, Charlotte. We've got to get out of here."

His voice has taken on the tone that he gets when he's focused. He starts to strip out of his clothes without another word, and for once, there's no tension to the moment. Just the absolute need for us to get out of here, moving with a quickness that tells me he's not thinking about anything else. I throw on my jeans and t-shirt, panic rising rapidly in my throat.

Is this how it's going to be forever? Days and days of running, of being safe for just a few brief hours and then panicking again, are compounding to the point that I'm not sure how much longer I can take it. This is all supposed to end when I have a new identity, but with every close call, I'm having a harder and harder time believing that day is going to come.

Ivan grabs a backpack that he must have bought when he got the first set of clothes, shoving what's on the bed into it. "Let's go," he says, giving me a sympathetic look. "I'll flag us down a cab."

Well, at least we don't have to steal another car. It's a weird thing to cling to, but it's really all I have as Ivan grabs the backpack and leads me to the door, glancing out into the hallway before stepping out. "Follow me," he says tersely. "Don't slow down, don't look around. We're going straight out the front. Stick to the crowds if you can, it will be harder for him to grab you."

My heart is in my throat as we head for the stairs. When we walk out onto the casino floor, moving at a quick clip, I think I see a glimpse of the black-haired man. But it could be anyone. I can't be sure it's him.

I follow Ivan, my heart pounding in my ears as we walk quickly downstairs, into the marble lobby, the brightness of the trees over the archway swirling in my vision as I try to stay calm. I can feel my breath hitching in my chest, and I press one hand against it, willing myself to remain calm. To not panic.

The warmth of the afternoon outside, hitting me in sharp contrast to the chill of the indoors, clears the fog from my head a little bit. Ivan links his arm through mine, tugging me forward towards one of the cabs waiting at the curb, and he yanks the door open, nudging me inside as he hands the driver cash, giving him the name of somewhere I'm not familiar with.

I don't ask Ivan where we're going. I'll find out soon enough, and I don't trust myself to speak right now. I feel like if I open my mouth, I might scream.

The cab pulls away from the curb, and I sink back into the seat, my heart still racing, my throat tight with nausea. Ivan's hand finds mine, and he squeezes it gently, a gesture that's meant to be comforting, but I yank my hand away, my panic suddenly transmuting into anger. I'd let myself stop thinking about his part in all of this, but now it comes back into sharp relief, and I press my lips together tightly. I look over at him, seeing the tension in his jaw, the way his eyes keep darting to the rearview mirror.

"Are we being followed?" I follow his gaze, even though I'm not sure what I would be looking for.

Ivan shakes his head. "I don't think so. But that doesn't mean they aren't still working on tracking us."

"Who?"

"Bradley. Lev. Lev might have hired others to help him. There's no way to know for sure."

The city blurs past, the huge signs and towering casinos somehow dimmed. Yesterday, it looked thrilling. Today, it feels looming, like the city is closing in around me. I try to focus on breathing, inhaling and exhaling slowly, as the cab speeds out onto the freeway. The panic recedes a little, but I remember the wreck all too well, and every time a car seems to come a little too close to us I jolt again.

"Where are we going?" I finally ask tiredly, leaning back in the seat.

"Another hotel." Ivan looks out of the window. "A smaller town, outside of Vegas. A place to hide out for a couple of days. My contact has some guys there, they'll help keep an eye out for us."

"More money?"

Ivan chuckles. "Yeah. But it doesn't matter to me." He glances over, his jaw tightening for a moment, as if he's considering whether he should say what's on his mind. "I'd pay any amount to make sure you're safe, Charlotte," he says finally.

And then he turns his gaze back out to the window next to him, going silent once more.

30

CHARLOTTE

As Vegas fades into the distance behind us, the view turning to desert stretching out on either side, the cab winds its way through increasingly narrowing roads. A smaller town comes into view, and when I glance off to my left as we approach, I see what looks like a county fair at the edge of the town.

I lean forward, almost pressing my nose to the glass, taking it in as the cab gets closer. The fairgrounds look mostly deserted for now—it's probably not open for a few more hours, but I can see the rides covered in unlit orange bulbs, a huge haunted house, and stands being set up for games and food. I swear I can smell the scent of caramel apples, even though I know it's just my imagination.

"Look." I nudge Ivan, momentarily forgetting how upset I am with him. "It's a fair. For Halloween." I feel a flicker of excitement, that craving for normalcy following close on the heels of it. "Could we go to that, tonight, do you think? They wouldn't look for us somewhere like that."

"I wouldn't risk it." Ivan's jaw is tight, his face blank. "We'll just need to stay in the hotel until our meeting. No more risks. I was wrong to take the one today."

The finality in his voice stings. And with the panic of our flight still bubbling in my chest, the thought of being cooped up in an even smaller hotel room with him makes me feel like I want to fling myself from the cab. I feel like I need air, space, like I need to be outside, instead of locked up somewhere waiting for the people chasing us to catch up.

But the look on Ivan's face says that he's not going to hear any argument. I bite my lip, still watching the fair out of my window as we drive past it and into town, the cab finally stopping in front of a small motel not much different from the ones we stayed in on the way here.

Ivan passes more cash over to the driver, and gets out, grabbing the backpack. "Let's get settled in," he says, his voice tired and drained, and I think I can hear disappointment in it. It hadn't occurred to me that he might have been looking forward to the luxury of Vegas proper for a few days, but it's clear that he's missing the chance to enjoy some comfort.

The room is very much like the ones we stayed in the last several days. Simple, a bit dingy, devoid of personality or much in the way of comforts. I sit down on the edge of the bed, feeling the craving to go out to the fair sweep over me again, frustration at being once again confined in a room only adding to it.

In a matter of days, my whole life has been turned upside down. *Is it so bad to want one normal thing?*

I know I'm being a little unreasonable. But the reality is becoming too much, and I want to hide from it. Just for a little while.

Ivan goes outside to make a call to his contact. I pace the room, take another shower, change into fresh clothes. The minutes seem to tick by too slowly. And as it starts to get dark and Ivan disappears into the bathroom to shower, I remember seeing a payphone outside of the hotel. I can't actually recall ever having seen one before, but I have a basic idea of how they work, and Ivan left a handful of cash and change on the desk.

He's going to be pissed at me if I do this. I know it. But I'm so desperate for some small part of my old life. I miss my friends. I miss everything that I've lost, and right now, when I feel like I'm clinging to my sanity with my fingertips, there's only one person that I really want to talk to.

I sweep the change into my palm, stuffing it in the pocket of my jeans, and hurry outside.

I've always been good with numbers—phone numbers, license plates, that kind of thing. I know Jaz's number by heart, and I drop a couple of quarters into the payphone, dialing her number as my breath catches in my chest.

"Hello?" She sounds confused when she answers, and I don't blame her.

"Jaz." All of the air rushes out of me. "Jaz, it's Charlotte."

"*Charlotte*? What the—where the fuck are you? We've been so worried. What happened? We called the police, but they said they were dealing with it, and they seemed to know *something*, but they wouldn't give us any answers, and—"

"I'm okay," I interrupt her stream of consciousness, my chest aching. I can only imagine how worried she's been, and I hate that it's because of me. I hate that I've caused this.

Ivan caused this. The small voice that won't let me forget that he orchestrated the beginning of all of it echoes in my head, and I close my eyes briefly, shoving back the tangle of confused emotions that always arise whenever I think of it. "I'm okay," I repeat. "I can't tell you where I am. I can't really tell you much of anything, and I'm so sorry. I don't—I don't think I'll be coming back home. But I'm going to be okay. I know that doesn't make sense, but—"

"It doesn't make sense!" Jaz cries. "That doesn't make sense at all, Charlotte. I saw Nate, by the way. Out at our brunch spot. He wouldn't talk to us. Just grinned like he knew something. You're not with—"

"I'm not with him," I promise her.

"Is it that guy? The one who came up to us at lunch? Did you like —run off with him or something?"

"Not exactly." I blow out a sharp breath. I want desperately to tell her everything, to ease her worries as much as I can, and tell her why

I probably won't ever talk to her again after this. But I don't know how. "I just—I can't tell you more, Jaz. I really can't. Just know that—"

The receiver is abruptly yanked out of my hand, and slammed down on the hook before I even fully realize what's happening. I jump back, my heart racing all over again, and I see Ivan standing next to me, his face thunderous.

"What the fuck were you thinking?" he growls, his voice a low, angry rumble. It's clear that he's doing everything in his power to stay quiet, so that no one hears us arguing. Because I can tell that's what this is about to be—an argument.

"I just—I needed—" The words break off. I know I don't really have any excuse for this. It was a stupid decision. And it might have put Jaz in danger, if there's any way to track the call I just made. I don't think there is—but I don't really know. And I did it anyway.

"You *need* to stay safe!" Ivan snaps. "All of this is to protect *you*, Charlotte! I could have disappeared so much faster than this alone. I could be long gone by now, but I've been keeping you safe, and now—"

"If you wanted to protect me, you should have fucking stayed away from me from the start!"

The words hang between us, heavy and accusing. Ivan's face pales, and he swallows hard. "I know that," he says tightly. "Fuck, I know that, Charlotte. But I didn't. I can't take that back now—"

"—and you wouldn't even if you could. I know the story, you've been telling me this whole fucking time." I glare at him, anger burning in my throat. "But that doesn't change what I've lost!"

"And you've been getting your revenge this entire time," Ivan snaps. "Teasing me. Using me for your protection and to get off when you want to, enjoying making me suffer to get back at me for what I did. And I haven't said shit, because I fucking deserve it. I know I do. But don't pretend that I haven't done anything to try to make up for—"

"It doesn't matter!" I whirl away from him, bolting back towards the room, and he grabs my elbow, dragging me back. The push and pull yanks me off balance, up against his chest, and for one brief second Ivan's arms go around me, his warmth and scent surrounding me as I feel his hard chest pressing against mine.

"I've tried," Ivan says quietly, his gaze resting on mine, flicking down to my mouth, and then back up again. "But you're right. Maybe it doesn't matter."

He lets go of me, and I bolt for the room again. I hear him follow behind me, but I don't turn to look at him as he walks in, gripping the edge of the desk as I try to regain my composure. He stalks past me, into the bathroom, the only way to put any space between us.

Except I have a different solution.

It's going to piss him off. More than the phone call, probably. But right now, I care even less. I'm angry and exhausted and scared, and I'm past caring what happens. I can't stay in this room a second longer.

I grab the cash on the desk, shove it into my pocket, and bolt out of the room before Ivan can emerge from the bathroom, closing it as quietly as I can behind me. There are no cabs anywhere to be seen, so I start walking instead, towards the music of the fair in the distance.

The road is dusty, and the night is chilly, but I couldn't care less. I suck in big lungful's of the cold, dry air, feeling the open space around me with a relief that makes me almost want to cry. It feels good to be outside, to be walking, to be *alone* for the first time in days. My head starts to feel a bit less foggy, and I pick up the pace, heading to the bright lights and jingling music of the carnival.

The fairgrounds are alive with laughter and color as I walk in, an oasis in the quiet desert night surrounding it. It's as full now as it was empty earlier, crowds of families, teenagers, and couples of all ages milling through the space. I can smell fried food and sugar and the grease and oil from the rides, and I draw in a deep breath, feeling momentarily better.

I shouldn't be out here. I know that. But the thought of going back to the motel room, to the tension between Ivan and I, feels almost unbearable. I need space, and to clear my head, and this is the best way I can think of to get it right now—doing something that I want to do.

The noise of the carnival envelops me as I wander past games and food stands, the tension draining out of me bit by bit as I surround myself with sights and smells that make me smile. I watch as a couple of kids run past me, their harried mother just behind them, mouths sticky with cotton candy. A couple is laughing by the Ferris wheel, the girl leaning in as the man slides his arm around her waist and presses his lips to hers, and I feel an odd pang in my chest.

Feeling for the cash in my pocket, I lose myself to the fun of the carnival. I buy an Italian sausage and a lemonade, eating it as I browse through the games, finally settling on one that has me throwing darts at a series of balloons. I toss balls into a hoop, try to dunk a clown, and eat a funnel cake. I go to the haunted house, laughing as 'ghosts' and 'killers' jump out at me, the manufactured scares seeming trivial compared to what I've been dealing with for the last several days. It's kind of nice, actually, in comparison. Fun.

I let myself lose track of time, wandering through the attractions until I realize that the crowds are starting to thin out. I decide to take one last loop through the haunted house before it closes, and by the time I come out, the fairgrounds are all but empty.

I pause, feeling a bit of unease for the first time since I walked in. With the noise and color fading, I'm reminded that this was actually a bad idea. That I'm alone here, and I'm going to have to walk back to the motel in the dark.

It's fine, I tell myself as I start to walk towards the entrance, careful not to walk too quickly. The fairgrounds are basically deserted now, and some of the overhead lights begin to go out, casting it heavily in shadow. *No one would think to look for me here, of all places. It'll be fine.* But my heart beats a little faster, picking up until my pulse is fluttering in my throat, my mouth dry.

And then, out of the corner of my eye, I think I see the figure of a man.

A prickling feeling runs down the back of my neck, and I spin sharply, my breath catching in my chest. I press a hand to my mouth as I take a step back, caught between fear and the memory of a fantasy that left me aching with arousal, fluttering through my veins along with the terror.

A man dressed in black jeans, a black t-shirt, and a hoodie is standing several feet from me, a skeleton mask that I recognize on his face.

I recognize it because it's the same one that Venom was wearing, when he sent me the photos of himself.

My pulse is racing for an entirely different reason, now. I step back a few more paces, and the man moves forward, closing in on me as I hear a dark chuckle that I swear echoes around me.

I know I'm imagining things. But I'm not imagining Ivan's voice when I hear it, clear as a bell in the cold night air.

"*Run,* little dove."

31

CHARLOTTE

I do as he says.
    I run.
    I'm not sure where I'm running to, exactly. I take off across the fairgrounds, my boots slapping against the dirt, but Ivan is keeping pace with me. I quickly realize that he's not just keeping pace—he's purposefully staying just behind me. Angling himself to send me in a particular direction, and I realize a moment later that it's toward the connected houses at the back of the carnival. The haunted house. The maze. The house of mirrors.

Fear beats in my veins out of sheer instinct, but underneath it, there's something else. Something darker. Ivan won't hurt me. I know that, deep down—that he never would. Not physically, even if the emotional wounds that he left are still raw. And if he wouldn't actually hurt me, then this is about something else.

Something we've both wanted for a long time.

I remember Venom, telling me he wanted to chase me through an apple orchard. This is a far cry from that, but it's somehow better, the close, shadowy darkness of the now-abandoned carnival, on the eve of Halloween, adding a layer of fear and ambiance to it that makes my pulse race faster, the heat in my blood singing through me until it's spread all throughout my body, a different kind of heat that has me panting by the time I duck into the first of the houses.

Ivan's footsteps are heavy behind me. "Run, little dove," he growls, his voice bouncing around the space until I swear I hear it from every direction, unsure of where he's going to come at me from.

I want to run. And I want to be caught.

The house is empty now, none of the killers or ghosts or skeletons left in the rooms, only the decorations. I almost trip over a fake gravestone as I run through one of the rooms, and I hear Ivan close, so close that as I dart around a medical table soaked in fake blood, I think he's going to grab me.

I think the only reason that he doesn't is because he's not ready for the chase to be over yet, either.

I bolt through the haunted house, down the hall that connects it to the next one, into the maze. My heart is beating so hard that it almost hurts, and the confinement of the maze, the twists and turns, only adds to the adrenaline. But this is a different kind of adrenaline than what I've been feeling for the last several days. This is an adrenaline that leads to something I want. An anticipation of something that I need—and I think Ivan needs it, too.

I hear his footsteps and swing left, darting down the next hall—and come out into a room of mirrors, my panting, breathless, figure visible from every angle.

Ivan appears in the mirror, a dark shadow behind me, that mask still firmly on his face. I hear a door slam behind me, hear the click of something, and he moves closer, that skeleton mask smiling at me in a tight grimace.

"Little dove," he murmurs, and when his hands touch my waist, I yelp. "Looks like I caught you."

I can't breathe. His hands slide up my waist, up to my breasts through my thin t-shirt, molding them in his hands as he pulls me back against him. My back is flush to his chest, my ass pressed to his groin, and I can feel how hard he is.

"I've been hard since the moment I started chasing you, dove," Ivan growls in my ear, his hands dropping to them hem of my shirt.

"I'm fucking *throbbing*, thinking about what I'm going to do now that I've caught you. My little bird, out of her cage."

He yanks my shirt up, over my head, leaving me in my bra and jeans. I hadn't even realized there was a chair in the room, but he reaches over and grabs one that I didn't see in the darkness, yanking it between us and shoving me down into it. I gasp, letting out a terrified squeak as I feel the sudden rough rasp of rope around my wrists, and Ivan grabs them, pulling my arms behind me and tying my hands together behind the chair.

"My pretty little captive. You want to be so angry at me for 'kidnapping' you, right? For chasing you down and trying to make you mine. I've tried to be patient, dove. I've tried to show you that I know I went about it all wrong. But you're angry at me anyway. I'm damned if I do, damned if I don't. So—" Ivan chuckles behind the mask, and I see the glint of a knife, reflected in what seems like a hundred mirrors. "I've decided to *do*."

He won't hurt me. This is a game. He won't hurt me. I know it, logically. But my instincts tell me that there's a man with a knife, a muscled, dangerous man who could *absolutely* hurt me if he wanted to. That I'm tied, and helpless, and that I'm in danger.

I kick out at him, twisting and opening my mouth to scream, and Ivan lunges forward, bending over me as he claps one gloved hand to my mouth.

The feeling of the leather against my lips brings back a flood of memories, and I gasp, arousal soaking between my thighs as I let out an involuntary, helpless moan.

"That's my good girl," Ivan murmurs. "I paid the carnies to ignore any sounds they heard. Paid them well, too. So I don't think we'll need to worry about that." I feel the cold slide of the blade against my back, and then the sudden looseness of my bra as he cuts through it, slicing away the straps until the garment falls to the floor.

My nipples instantly harden in the cold air, and Ivan sinks down, kneeling between my legs. He reaches up with the hand not holding the knife, cupping the curve of my breast, his gloved thumb rolling over my nipple.

The second he touches me, I let out a whimper, my hips arching up. Ivan chuckles darkly, tilting his head, that white mask staring up at me. My cheeks flush hot at my reaction to him, but it's been too long. The tension has been simmering for days, building since the last time he bent me over that sink, refusing to fuck me. We've come so close, teased right up to the edge of it, and now I'm desperate for him. Desperate for more, desperate for him to make me come.

"Little dove." Ivan reaches up, pressing the point of the knife tip into my breast as he circles it around my nipple. Not hard enough to draw blood, or even really enough to hurt, but enough for me to feel the sting. He traces the tip around, between my breasts to the other one, pricking my nipple with the knife as he leans in and captures the other hard, stinging point between his gloved fingers.

The sharp point of the knife and the pressure of his fingers against my nipples is almost too much to bear. My hips arch up again, and I moan, my head tipping back as my legs splay open. The knife presses deeper, and I feel Ivan pinch my nipple hard between his fingertips, hard enough to make me yelp.

"Keep your eyes open, Charlotte," he commands. "I want you to watch all of this. I want you to watch what I do to you. Watch how badly you need it. Watch yourself squirm and beg while I strip you down. And every time you close your eyes—" He twists the knife around my nipple again, rolling the opposite one, sending a shudder down my spine. "I'll make it hurt. But you like that too, don't you, filthy girl?"

I glare down at him, refusing stubbornly to answer. But Ivan just chuckles, tweaking my nipple as he digs the knife tip directly into the center of the other one, pushing me further.

The sensation jolts straight down to my clit, a flood of mingled pain and pleasure making me cry out. "Please," I gasp, and Ivan pulls back, looking at his handiwork. I don't have to look down to know my nipples are red and swollen, hard as diamonds from his attention.

"Please, what, little dove?"

I don't even know what to beg for. I want to come, but I'm not far gone enough to beg for that yet. Ivan laughs darkly, dropping the knife onto his lap as he leans in to reach for the button of my jeans.

"That's what I thought. But we'll get there. Now tell me, dove, if you don't want to be punished again. How wet are you for me? Have you soaked through those panties yet?"

I press my lips tightly together, still glaring at him. Some small part of my mind, in the back of my head, knows that I'm doing this on purpose. That I *want* the pain. That this is the filthy, perverse thing I was chasing when I logged onto that site in the first place, when I talked to Venom, when all of this began.

I wanted this. I wanted all of it. And Ivan is going to make me face it. I've been punishing him for it, so he's going to punish me in return.

He reaches up with both hands, twisting my nipples hard. I cry out, the sound ending in a moan as I feel myself clench, my hips arching up as if I can get any friction that way. My hands twist uselessly in the ropes behind me, and I want desperately to get them free, to get the pleasure that I so desperately need. But Ivan is the only one who can give it to me.

"You'll answer before I'm done with you." He reaches down, yanking my zipper and curling his fingers into the waist of my jeans, dragging them down my hips all the way to my boots. He pushes my legs open, leaning in as he tugs off one glove, his bare fingers dragging up my center between my legs, pressed against the wet cotton of my panties.

"So fucking wet," he groans. "My good little dove. All nice and wet for my cock. But you won't get that yet. Not until you tell me what I need to hear."

He reaches for the knife again, and I shudder as I feel the cold metal slide under the edge of my panties, tracing the taut flesh of my abdomen as he cuts the fabric away. I let out a small, helpless moan as he tosses it aside, pushing my thighs wider as he traces the knife tip over the swollen folds of my pussy.

"You need to come so badly, don't you, dove?" Ivan murmurs, his voice thick with lust. I shudder as I look down at him, kneeling between my legs, the mask still on as he tugs his glove back on and switches the knife to his left hand. Those gloved fingers stroke over my folds, a soft touch following the stinging caress of the knife, and I let out another whimper, my legs opening of their own accord now.

I can feel how wet I am. I'm drenched, throbbing, aching for him. I need to come desperately, and I can tell that he's going to draw it out. That he's going to make me beg.

His gloved fingertips brush over my clit, and I gasp, a sobbing sound tearing from my throat.

"You'd come right now for me if I let you. But I want to hear it, Charlotte." Ivan's voice is sharp, rough beneath the mask. "I want to hear you beg. I want to hear everything I've been asking for, and then I'll let you come. Then I'll give you what you need."

Somehow, I find my voice. "What do I *need*?" I snap sarcastically, trying to find my anger, my hurt. I try to drag it up through the desire, but I want him too badly, and it's hard to find. "If you knew what I *needed*, you would never have chased me down. Not then, and not tonight—"

I gasp as two of Ivan's gloved fingers push inside of me, spearing me firmly as he curls them, hooking me on his hand as his thumb starts to rub over my clit. "I knew what you needed that first night," he growls, rocking his hand against me so that I feel the thickness of his fingers inside of me, the leather adding to the sensation. "I knew what no one else had given you. I made you come all over my face, harder than any other man ever made you come. And I gave you other things you needed, too. I've done a lot that was wrong, Charlotte—" He thrusts his fingers, hard, and I cry out. "But I've always known what you needed. And tonight, you're going to give me what *I* need. And then I'll make you come on my cock, just like you've been begging. I'll make you come until you can't walk, and then I'll take you home."

Home. "That filthy motel isn't home," I spit, the words coming out weaker than I'd like as Ivan keeps fingering me, rolling his thumb over my clit. "You can't take me home."

"Fine." His voice is laced with anger now, too. "I'll take you back with me. But first, Charlotte—" His gloved thumb presses against my clit, and then slides away. I feel the sharp prick of the knife against it, and I cry out, fear and arousal mingling in the echoing sound of pleasure as Ivan holds the knife to my clit with one hand, his fingers thrusting hard with the other. "Beg me to make you come."

"I'm—I can't—I'm going to—" Every muscle is wound tight, and I'm on the verge of tipping over, the pleasure rushing through me to its apex. I open my mouth, crying out as I feel the tide swell up—and then Ivan suddenly jerks his fingers out of me, leaving me empty and hollow, only the knifepoint still pressed to me.

"No! Please, please—" I feel actual tears welling in my eyes, my body writhing at the loss of the orgasm. "Ivan!"

"That's how I feel," he growls. "Every time you refuse to tell me that you believe me. Every time you rip my fucking heart out, Charlotte, again and again. You're the only woman I've ever really given a shit about. The only woman I've ever opened up to. I fucked up getting you, and I fucking know it, but I can't be sorry. I can't fucking be sorry, because if I hadn't done it, I wouldn't have ever gotten to know the only woman I've ever loved."

His fingers thrust into me again, hard and relentless. "Fucking beg for it, dove."

My mind is a fog, the need shoving out everything else, even the fact that I could swear I just heard him say he loved me. I want to ask —but all that comes out is a sobbing moan as I give in, and I beg.

"Just make me come. Please, Ivan. Please make me come. I need it, please—"

He leans in, the slick, cold mask brushing against my face as he rotates the knife point delicately against my clit, his fingers curling in a rough counterpoint inside of me. "Then come for me, dove."

The orgasm explodes through me. Somehow, I manage to keep my eyes open, the visual of Ivan leaning over me, pinning me to the chair as he makes me come between the knife and his fingers only intensifying the sensation. My legs splay open, my hips bucking upwards, pain and pleasure jolting through me together as I scream his name, crying out with the force of it.

I've never come like that in my life. I'm still gasping, my pussy clenching as he yanks his fingers out of me and jerks me up off of the chair, my hands still tied behind my back as Ivan shoves me forward towards the mirrors. His hand on my shoulder, he pushes me up against one, the glass cold against my cheek as I hear the sound of his zipper coming down.

His thick, swollen cockhead presses between my slick folds, and he groans. He leans in, his tip pressed to my entrance, and I see the hovering shape of the mask over his face reflected in all the mirrors as he looks at me.

"You want this, too, little dove," he murmurs. "You want me to fuck you like this. You want me filling you up. You want to watch me fuck you, reflected like this, so you can see yourself come all over my cock."

"Yes," I whimper, too far gone to deny it any longer. "Yes, please—"

"Then tell me." He rocks against me, his cock so close to slipping inside. Only his other hand on my hip, holding me firmly in place, keeps me from rocking back and taking him inside of me. "Tell me you believe it's real. Tell me that you know I didn't mean to hurt you. Tell me you know that I've tried—" His voice cracks, and I don't think it's with anger this time. "I fucking love you, Charlotte," he whispers. "Tell me you know."

I close my eyes for one brief second, and then I open them again. And I finally, finally tell him the truth, too.

"I know."

Ivan's hips snap forward, his cock sinking into me to the hilt in one hard thrust. I cry out from the stretch of it, thick and long and rock-hard, and Ivan moans, shuddering as he sinks in as far as he can go and holds himself there for a moment. "Hang on, little dove," he whispers, and he yanks at the rope, untying my hands. "Brace yourself. Because I'm going to fuck you hard."

I only have a second to brace my hands against the mirror in front of me before Ivan makes good on his promise. He yanks me back with one hand on my hip, bending me over further as he starts to thrust, slamming into me. I cry out as he picks up his pace, fucking me harder than he ever has before, one hand on my shoulder and the other on my hip as he slams into me again and again. A stream of moans spills from my lips, the feeling of his thick cock pummeling me pushing me close to another orgasm, and the fact that I can see it all, reflected all around me, only adds to the pleasure.

Ivan slides his hand down, his fingers stroking over my clit. "I'm not going to last long," he growls. "Come all over my fucking cock, dove. Let me feel you fucking squeeze it before I fill you up."

That's all it takes. My back bows as I scream his name, the sound echoing for a second time as I clench around him, rippling along the straining length as Ivan's groan fills the air, his hips snapping hard against my ass. "Fuck, fuck—" he moans, and then he thrusts forward hard, his hands squeezing me almost painfully as he shudders, and I feel a hot, spurting warmth filling me. "Fuck, I have to come in you, I have to—"

I'm not even thinking about what a terrible fucking idea that is. I'm not thinking about anything other than how it feels, how the throbbing of his orgasm tips me over into a third, smaller climax, how I can feel him spurting as I clench around him, how he's filling me so full that I can already feel his cum dripping down my legs. I feel his fingers roll over my clit again, sliding down as if to catch the cum dripping out of me, and then as his cock slides free I feel his two gloved fingers push inside, holding his cum there as he reaches down to tug my panties up.

He pulls them up around my hips, only sliding his fingers free when they're fully on. And then his other hand reaches up, wrapping around my throat as he pulls me up and back against him, so I can see myself reflected in the mirror.

I look fucking wrecked. Ivan is fully clothed, except for his softening cock pressed against my spine. His face is still covered by the mask, but I'm flushed and reddened, naked except for my panties, my jeans tangled around my ankles. My breasts are swollen and pink, my mouth parted, my hair a mess.

"My pretty little slut," Ivan murmurs, and a jolt of pleasure ripples through me. "Be a good slut, and clean this up."

He presses his two gloved fingers, covered in his cum and mine, against my lips, pushing them into my mouth. And without a second thought, drugged with lust and multiple climaxes, I suck them between my lips, licking our mingled flavor off of them.

"Oh, *fuck*," Ivan moans, and I instantly feel him start to harden against my bare back. "Oh god, Charlotte—*fuck*—"

He thrusts his fingers into my mouth again, and before I can do more than let out a helpless moan around them, he spins me around to face him, shoving me down to my knees in front of him.

His cock is rock-hard again, the tip brushing against my lips, and Ivan fists my hair in one gloved hand.

"Suck it, dove," he orders, staring down at me, and the sight of him ordering me from behind the mask makes my swollen clit throb. "I want to watch you suck me with all of these mirrors around us. Make me come in your pretty mouth."

This time, I obey without question. I don't *want* to disobey. I want him, and I've given up pretending otherwise. I want all of this, and I open my mouth, leaning forward and wrapping one hand around the base of his cock as I suck the head between my lips, bracing my other hand on his hip.

"Oh, fucking *hell*—" Ivan moans as I start to suck, and I feel a flush of pleasure at the sound.

I don't tease him. I go all in, sliding my lips down his thick shaft, taking as much of him as I can. I let my saliva coat his shaft, making it fast and messy, licking and sucking ravenously as I push his cock into the back of his throat, moaning around it as I feel my own arousal rising to meet his. Ivan's hand tightens in my hair, and even with the mask on, I can see him watching us in the mirrors.

It just turns me on even more.

"Reach down and rub your clit," he rasps. "Use my cum to get it wet. I want to hear how sloppy it is. Fuck yourself with my cum."

I don't need to be told twice. I slip my hand into my soaked panties, my pussy already wet with his cum that's dripped out of me. I rub it over my clit, slick and hot, and the wet, mingled sounds of me sucking his cock and fingering myself fill the air as Ivan groans.

"I'm going to come in your mouth, dove. Come with me. Fucking come—"

His cock stiffens between my lips, and I feel my clit throb under my fingertips, my whole body tightening as another orgasm hits. I moan around him, his sounds of pleasure mingling with mine, and Ivan gasps, his hand closing around his cock as the first hot spurts of his cum coat my tongue, and he pulls back.

"Open up," he commands. "Open your—fucking—mouth—"

I part my lips, opening my mouth, and out of the corner of my eye, in the mirror, I can see him shooting onto my tongue. The sight is so filthy, so erotic, that I feel another jolt of pleasure rock me, my fingers still frantically stroking my clit as Ivan spurts onto my tongue again and again.

"Keep it there—" He moans, stroking himself hard, the last drops spilling out before he twists me around with his hand in my hair, so that I'm facing the mirror. "*Fuck*, look at you, dove. Such a good fucking slut, with your hand in your panties and your mouth full of my cum."

I look *filthy*. My hand is between my legs, my mouth full of his sticky white cum. It's coating my tongue and my lips, to the point that it's beginning to drip from the corner of my mouth. "Swallow," Ivan orders, and I obey, licking my lips clean as I swallow every last drop.

And then, as he reaches with his other hand to tuck himself away, it's as if his entire demeanor shifts in a second.

He rips the mask off, tossing it to the chair as he reaches down to get my shirt. Carefully, he helps me to my feet, tugging my jeans up and slipping my shirt over my head as I stare at him, feeling a bit in shock. "Are you okay?" he asks, the expression on his now-visible face one of concern. He yanks off his gloves, too, wiping at the corner of my mouth tenderly as he pushes my hair back. "You're alright?"

I nod, feeling confused. "You—love me?" It's the only thing I can think of, the thing that stuck in my mind, caught in the web of lust Ivan wrapped me in. "You—"

"You said you believed me." His tone is guarded, his face briefly shuttering, as if he thinks I might have lied.

"I do. I—" I really do. In that moment, what I said was the unfettered truth. But it's harder to face it now, in the aftermath.

Ivan looks uncertain, but he slides his arm around my waist. "Come on," he says quietly. "Let's go back to the motel."

I feel almost shaky, as we start to walk back. I do believe him. What he said—the way he said it—was too sincere not to. But I don't know what to do with it.

No matter how he feels, he lied to me, and he kidnapped me.

But he also risked his life for me, over and over. He's tried to prove to me that he wants things to be different. That he wants it to change.

And the truth is—I think that I might want that, too.

32

IVAN

In the aftermath, I can't help but wonder if I made it all worse.

When I came out to find Charlotte gone, I lost my mind a little. I followed her, determined to get her back for running off, determined to make her stop running from *everything*. And I got what I needed.

I think we both did. But I can tell that she's still struggling to accept it.

She's quiet when we get back to the motel. For the first time, we shower together, squeezing into the small space, and I want to joke about how much more space there would have been for this back at the Wynn. But I don't, because I'm not sure if that kind of joke is a good idea right now.

Instead, I help her clean up, trying to show her by the way I touch her, the way I look at her, how I feel. That I meant everything I said. I don't make up a bed on the floor—instead, I slide in next to her, resting my hand gently on her hip over the blankets. Charlotte doesn't push it away—but she also doesn't say anything.

She's overwhelmed. I can empathize with that. But when we get in the cab the next morning to head to the meeting with my contact, she's still only said a handful of words to me. And my chest feels tight, wondering if, by the end of the day, she'll be gone.

Loving her doesn't entitle me to have her. I know that. But I'd hoped that confession would change something. I'd hoped that what we did in the house of mirrors would be catharsis for the past, enough to open up the possibility of a future.

I'm not sure that's going to be the case.

We meet my contact in a residential house, on the far side of the older Vegas district. We're right on time, and I knock twice, sharply, Charlotte standing silently right behind me. I'm not sure what she expected, but I hear her quick intake of breath when the door opens, and a middle-aged man with thinning brown hair, dressed very much like an accountant, opens the door.

"I go by Dave," he says, as he steps back and lets us in. "At least right now. You can call me that."

"I'm—" Charlotte starts to say, and Dave shakes his head, holding up a hand.

"You're here to get new identities. Don't tell me your old one. I know Ivan here because I've known him for years. But you—don't tell me anything I don't need to know."

"Of course." Charlotte blushes, clearly embarrassed. "I'm sorry."

"No need to be sorry, either. Come on."

Dave leads us back into an office, near the back of the house. He sits down at a wooden desk, pulling out two folders. "Here." He slides them across the desk to us, one in front of each. Charlotte reaches for hers, her hands visibly trembling.

She opens it, and I see her lips press together. I glance at mine, making sure everything is in order, and then push the cash across the desk to Dave. Charlotte glances at the rolls of bills, and her eyes widen, but she doesn't say anything.

"It's all there," Dave says, before he takes the money. "New passports, social security, birth certificates, everything you could need to start a new life wherever. All as official as you please."

Charlotte swallows hard, and nods, clearly speechless. I stand up, taking the documents, and slip them into my pocket, handing him back the now-empty envelope. "Thanks." I give him a tight smile. "Probably the last you'll hear from me for a while. If not for good."

"Shame." Dave stands, too, and Charlotte slowly rises as well. "It was nice knowing you. Nice to meet you too," he adds to Charlotte. "Briefly."

She nods, stepping away from the desk. I start to walk towards the door, and halfway there, I hear her footsteps pause, and the sound of Dave speaking quietly.

"I dunno what you two have going on, or what's planned after this," he murmurs. "But he's a good guy. Or he tries to be, anyway."

"I don't know about that," Charlotte says quietly, and Dave chuckles.

"Girl, only a man who wants to be better than he is now works against the Bratva for the FBI. I don't think you know what they'd've done to him if they caught him, but it sure wouldn't have been good. There's a lot of ways to keep a man alive with very little skin on him, if you know what I mean."

"I don't—"

"Good. All I'm saying is—Ivan there has tried hard to make up for what they made him. If you wanna be a part of that, you shouldn't feel bad about it. That's all."

I hear the creak of him settling back in his chair, and Charlotte's footsteps quickly catching up to me. She doesn't say anything until we're outside and a good distance from the house, and then she glances over at me, blowing out a sharp breath between pursed lips.

"So—that's it." She looks uncertain, and I can tell that she has no idea what comes next.

"What name is on your new identification?" I look at her curiously, and Charlotte blinks, the uncertainty on her face growing.

"Should I tell you that? I mean—"

That sharp pain, one that I've become more accustomed to than I ever thought I would, jabs at my chest again. If she doesn't want to tell me, then that means that nothing has changed about her leaving.

She's still going to walk away from me. And there's nothing I can do about it.

"No. You probably shouldn't."

The words come out sharper than I mean for them to, and I see Charlotte flinch a little. I don't want to hurt her, but the thought that after everything, nothing has changed, cuts like a knife.

"Charlotte—"

My voice is lost in the sudden, sharp crack of a gunshot, and a hot, searing pain lances through my shoulder. Charlotte screams, and I duck forward, grabbing her as I start to run despite the pain.

"What's happening—"

"I don't know! Just run!"

Charlotte clings to my arm, both of us bolting down the street. I hear another bullet ping against the sidewalk, another striking the side of a building far too close to us, but I don't dare stop. I don't dare look back to see if it's Lev, or the FBI, or someone else who my father has sent, even as I hear the sound of boots hitting the concrete behind us. They sound close, but there's no time to find out for sure Further off, I hear the sound of a car engine revving, and my gut clenches, wondering if there's shortly going to be even more on us.

Another hot slice rips across my side, and I cry out, feeling my arm and my side start to grow wet with blood. I'm not sure how badly I'm bleeding, or if a bullet has lodged in me, or how badly I'm injured. But I know we need to get out of here.

"Get a cab," I tell Charlotte, and my voice sounds hoarse and wheezy, alarmingly so. "Get—"

Another bullet pings nearby, and Charlotte screams, her arm still locked around me as she looks around wildly. A cab is coming around the corner, and she waves at it, both of us moving down the sidewalk to meet it. The driver's eyes widen as he sees us, and he starts to turn, but Charlotte bolts out in front of the taxi, forcing him to slam on the brakes.

"We'll pay you whatever you want," she gasps out. "Whatever. Just get us out of here."

"Five thousand," the driver spits out, looking wild-eyed at something behind us. "Cash."

He's putting out what he thinks is an impossible number, I know that. Expecting us to gape at him so he can veer off and drive away, leaving us to our fate. But I nod, gasping as I lean against the door. "Done," I rasp, and the driver's eyes widen even further.

"Fine. Get in."

The sound of footsteps are closer as Charlotte yanks open the door, jumping into the taxi. She twists around, helping me in as more bullets pepper the sidewalk, and the driver slams on the gas, jolting forward as Charlotte yanks me into the car. She reaches over, hauling the door closed, and I feel the world tilting around me as the driver speeds down the road.

"Where to?" he snaps. "Give me the money, now!"

"In my—pocket." Speaking seems to be harder. I know that's not good, but I push away the thought, trying to focus on the here and now. On keeping Charlotte safe.

That's all I've wanted, all this time.

Charlotte reaches into my pocket, pulling out a roll of cash. She flips through it, tossing it into the passenger's seat before pulling out another, and throwing it to join the first. "There," she snaps. "Five grand." Out of the corner of my eye, I can see that the money is bloody, but the driver doesn't seem to be complaining about that, at least.

Somewhere in the back of my slowly fading consciousness, I'm immeasurably proud of her. She's tougher than even I ever gave her credit for, and even in this terrifying moment, she's holding it together.

She didn't leave me, either. Even though she could have.

The driver shouts again, asking where we're going. I open my mouth, trying to give him a place, but I can't speak. The pain is overwhelming, and I can feel the blood soaking my clothes. Dizziness washes over me, and I look up at Charlotte, her face swimming in front of my eyes.

"I—love you," I manage hoarsely. "I'm—sorry. You made me—

happy. But I dragged you—into—this. You were never—meant for—it. I'm—sorry."

"Don't be sorry," she says softly, so dimly that I wonder if I actually heard it at all. There's a roaring in my ears, and I feel her hand on my face, but I'm going numb at the same time, and my vision narrows.

The cab lurches around a corner, and everything goes dark.

33

CHARLOTTE

Ivan passes out in my lap, and I stare down at him, terrified into silence. He's still breathing, I can see that—but for how long?

Thankfully, the backpack with our things in it was still on Ivan when we clambered into the taxi. It's fallen to the floorboard, bloodied on the outside, but the first-aid kit is in there. I just have to get somewhere, and I can try to patch Ivan up. I can try—

I have no idea how badly he's hurt. I know better than to go to a hospital. Even with our new identification, while we're still in Vegas, it's a bad idea. The driver is still yelling at me to pick a location, and I reach down, grabbing the road atlas out of the backpack. I flip it open, look for the first smallish-looking town name that's outside of Vegas proper, and tell him to go there.

And then I sink back against the seat, cradling Ivan in my lap as the taxi speeds on.

When we get into town, the driver glances back at me. "Where do you want to go?" he asks curtly, and I pinch the bridge of my nose, exhaustion sweeping over me.

"A motel. Any out-of-the-way motel."

He nods, driving on until we find a two-story roadside motel. He stops in front of it, and I reach into Ivan's pocket, finding another few bills that I pull out. "Another three hundred," I tell him, "if you'll wait while I get the room and help me get him into it."

"Sure." He starts to reach for the money, and I yank my hand back.

"You can have it once you get him into the room, and you walk out again, without hurting either of us. Understand?" My voice doesn't even sound like my own. A couple of weeks ago, I wouldn't have been able to imagine saying anything like that. But now, it just seems like common sense.

The driver narrows his eyes at me, then nods. "Fine. Get the room. Hurry up."

I slide out from under Ivan, trying not to jostle him. My legs are shaky as I hurry to the office, praying they have a vacant room. From what I can see of the empty parking lot, I'd be surprised if they didn't. The bored-looking clerk barely glances at me as I request a ground floor room, paying in cash that sticks together a little with blood as I hand it over. The clerk doesn't seem to care, which doesn't bode all that well for this particular spot, but there's no time for me to worry about that. I glance back repeatedly as I wait for the key, and every time I look, I'm terrified that the driver will have taken off anyway, despite the fact that I took all of the cash out of Ivan's pockets to avoid any incentive for him to do exactly that.

The clerk hands me a key on a rusted white tag, and I grab it, muttering a quick "thank you," as I rush back to the taxi.

The driver helps me half-carry, half-drag Ivan to the room, only a few yards from where he parked. It's like every other motel room that Ivan and I stayed at on the way here, except a little worse—dingy, and this one smells of cigarettes. But it's the best I can do right now. Ivan is breathing shallowly, and I'm terrified that at any moment it's going to stop.

"Money?" The driver shoves his hand out and I point at the door. "Outside."

The moment he steps out, I shove three hundred dollars at him. He takes it, and I slam the door so quickly that it almost catches his hand, locking and latching it, my heart pounding.

I'm alone. Not physically, but Ivan isn't going to be able to help me right now if something happens. I don't even know if I can help him.

I have to. I have to figure it out.

One thing at a time, I reason. I grab the first-aid kit out of the backpack, and start to strip Ivan out of his clothes. The long-sleeved henley he was wearing goes first, and I drag the blood-soaked fabric over his head, stifling a cry as I see the damage that the bullets did.

One of them tore through his shoulder. From what I can see, it left a clean exit wound, although I don't really know enough about this kind of thing to be sure. Blood is congealing around it, and Ivan is pale, his skin waxy.

The other ripped across his side, leaving torn flesh dangling from an open wound. Tears fill my eyes as I look at it, and I know this is beyond me. It's beyond the cheap first-aid kit sitting on the bed. It's beyond any skill or supplies I have, but I have to do my best.

I'm all Ivan has right now.

And he's all you have.

It's the truth, now. I have new identification, everything I need for my new life. A passport, a birth certificate, a license, all saying *Anna Blackwood*, a name that doesn't feel real and that I certainly wouldn't have picked for myself. But it's a plain name. A simple name, one that thousands of other people have, one that can let me disappear.

I had thought that I was still going to leave Ivan behind. When "Dave" gave me my new identification earlier, I thought that I would walk away. But if I learned anything from what just happened, it's that I have to face a single, impossible truth that I've known for a while, and just haven't wanted to admit.

I love Ivan, too. And I can't walk away from him.

I open up the first-aid kit, getting out what I have that I can use to patch him up. Antiseptic wipes, antibiotic cream, gauze pads, bandages. I spread it across the bed, picking up each individual item as I need it, and as I get to work, I talk to him.

I hope he'll hear it, somehow, and it will keep him from slipping away.

"I'm sorry I didn't tell you this before," I say softly, as I start to clean away the blood. "I should have told you that as soon as you said it to me in the house of mirrors. But I was scared. I've been scared for a while, I guess. Scared of how I feel about you, scared of what that means, and scared to admit how long I really think I've known."

I start to wipe the alcohol over the wounds, wincing at the thought of it against the raw flesh. But Ivan is passed out so deeply that he doesn't stir—doesn't even flinch. Still, I keep speaking, hoping that some part of it will get through to him.

"All of this happened the wrong way. We both know it. The things you did were wrong. But you were right when you told me I was seeking out danger. That I was seeking out something different, something that I knew I shouldn't have. And even though I'm devastated over everything I've lost—I realized today, maybe too late, that I would be devastated if I lost you, too."

I uncap the antibiotic ointment, starting to spread it across the wounds. "My life was meaningless and grey before you. I had people who meant something to me—who meant a lot to me, like Jaz and Sarah and Zoe. I had others who gave my life meaning, but I hadn't given it any meaning for myself. I was too afraid to give myself anything that I wanted. And then I met you—and you didn't just give it meaning. You made me feel like I could do it for myself. Like I could reach out, and take the things I wanted, without being ashamed about it. Like I could live my life without having to apologize for who I was, adventurous or not. Brave or not. And in the process of that, I've found out I'm actually a lot braver than I thought I was."

I unwrap a gauze pad, pressing it over the wound on his shoulder, taping it down with medical tape. "I feel alive, now. Scared, and a little bit lost, but alive. I don't know how we move forward from this, but I want to. I don't want to go our separate ways, and I don't want to leave you behind. And even if everything was wrong from the beginning—I do believe you, Ivan. I believe you love me. I believe you care about me. I believe you want me...and I want you, too."

I finish bandaging his side, sitting back as I look at him. He's very still, breathing shallowly, and his skin still has that waxy grey cast. But there's nothing else I can do but wait.

I pack up everything left in the first-aid kit, setting it aside. I wash my hands, stripping off my blood-stained clothes, and I shower quickly, not wanting to leave Ivan alone for too long.

When I come out, he's still passed out, but still breathing. I crawl into bed next to him, once again careful not to jostle him. I'm exhausted, but I don't want to fall asleep. I'm terrified that when I wake up, he will have stopped breathing.

There's nothing more I can do, except stay with him, but I lay there fighting sleep for a long time anyway. Sleep comes all the same, the exhaustion of the past weeks and the day we just went through catching up, and it drags me under eventually.

It's fully dark when I wake up again. The clock next to the bed says it's after one in the morning. My stomach is hollow, grumbling from how hungry I am, but there's no food in the room and I don't dare go out for anything. I push myself up on one elbow, brushing my hair out of my face, and my heart leaps when I see Ivan blink his eyes.

"You're awake!" I gasp it aloud, and Ivan lets out a low groan, opening his eyes a little wider.

"I am. I think." He swallows, and it sounds sticky. "Water?"

"Oh! Hold on." I jump up, fumbling through the backpack for a bottle. "Do you want ibuprofen?"

"Anything." He coughs, and lets out a moan of pain. "Oh, god. Being shot sucks so fucking much."

I stare at him for a moment. "You're about to tell me this isn't your first time, aren't you?"

"It's definitely not. But I don't think it's ever been this bad before. Or maybe I just blocked it out." He takes the water and ibuprofen from me. "Thank you."

"I tried to patch you up. I don't know—" I frown, looking at the bandages, which have turned a bit pink from the blood trickle. "I think it helped."

"I feel like death warmed over, but I'm alive, so I'd say it definitely helped." Ivan manages a crooked smile. "And you said you love me, so that helped, too. And that you'd be—what was it? *Devastated* if you lost me."

My eyes widen. "You heard all of that? I thought you were passed out?"

"Maybe my next career will be acting." Ivan's smile spreads, though it's still weaker than usual. "Staying quiet while you put straight alcohol on raw gunshot wounds was definitely a challenge. But worth it, to keep you talking."

"You—" I lunge for him, stopping myself just in time before I accidentally hurt him. "I'm going to get you back for that later. When you're better."

"Just as long as you're still with me, I don't care." Ivan's gaze sweeps over me, and I see a hungry look flicker into his eyes, one that I hadn't expected in his current state. He's still shirtless, and as I let myself briefly look him over—telling myself that I'm just making sure he's otherwise uninjured—I see the ridge of his cock thickening against the front of his jeans.

"*Ivan.*" I stare at him. "You lost way too much blood for that to actually be happening."

"You would think." Ivan shifts, wincing. He starts to raise his hand, as if to reach down and adjust his rapidly hardening cock, but that seems to hurt too much, and he drops it again. "Fuck. God, just looking at you makes me hard."

I look down at myself. "I'm wearing a t-shirt and sweatpants."

"It doesn't matter," he assures me. "Just you being in the same room is enough to turn me on. Every last ounce of blood that was still in my body is in my cock right now. God, I'm so hard it fucking hurts." He winces, and then looks over at me, a hint of mischief in his eyes. "You wouldn't want me to be in pain, would you? You went to a lot of trouble to patch me up."

I narrow my eyes at him. "What do you want me to do about it?"

I meant it to be teasing, but Ivan looks at me with utter, desperate sincerity in his face and voice. "Your mouth," he manages, his voice breathless. "Please, little dove. Give me your mouth."

The way he says it sends a jolt of hot arousal flooding through me.

I nod, suddenly speechless, and shift over between his legs, sliding down as I reach for the button of his jeans. "You'll tell me to stop if this hurts you, right?" I ask cautiously, and Ivan nods.

"I will, but—*fuck*, please, Charlotte."

He moans as I undo the button of his jeans, his hips arching upwards, his cock a hard line threatening to burst out of his zipper. "Hearing you tell me you want me," he pants, "made me so fucking needy. I need you to make me come. Knowing you want to stay with me—god, I fucking need you right now. If I could, I'd pin you down to the bed and fuck you until you screamed my name. But I can't, so—" He groans again as I drag his zipper down, his cock pushing free of his boxers before I can even reach in and slip it out. "Make me come. Please. Make yourself come while you suck me. *Please—*"

The sound he makes when I wrap my lips around his swollen cockhead is enough to send a flood of arousal soaking between my legs. His hips buck weakly upwards, begging for more as I slide my mouth down his length, his tip already wet with pre-cum. I lift my hips enough to push my other hand beneath myself, slipping my fingers into my panties as I start to lick and suck my way up and down Ivan's hard shaft. I'm drenched, coating my own fingers the second I slide them over my slippery clit and I gasp as I slide my mouth up, sucking hard at his cockhead before I go down again, letting him push into my throat.

I'm close already. I grind against my hand, rubbing my clit faster as I run my tongue up and down, fluttering it just under his tip. Ivan moans, his eyes closing, his head tipping back as I work his cock, wrapping my hand around the base of it as I suck hard.

"Fuck, yes—" He gasps, and I moan as I feel my own orgasm approaching. "Get on top of me. I want to feel you come around my cock. I want to fill you up."

"Ivan—"

"Just do it. Please, dove. I need to feel you come on me."

His voice is so desperate, so full of desire for me, that I can't tell him no. I sit up, letting go of his cock, and he moans, looking at me with lust-darkened eyes.

"Take my jeans off," he orders, and the command in his voice sends a shiver down my spine.

"I don't have to do anything," I tease him, stripping my t-shirt over my head. "You can't make me right now."

"I could try," he says in a warning voice. "But I'll say please this once, dove. And then I'll punish you later, when I'm better."

"I'll look forward to it." I make him wait until I've stripped off every last bit of clothing, and then I reach up, dragging his jeans and boxers off as his cock juts up, dripping pre-cum and glistening with my saliva. "You want me to sit on your cock, Ivan? You want me to fuck you?"

His eyes widen a little at that. I've never said anything like that to him before, and that hunger deepens in his gaze, the muscle in his jaw twitching.

"Fuck me, little dove," he groans. "Please."

Carefully, not wanting to bump the bandage on his side, I straddle his hips. I arch up, wrapping my hand around him, and guide him between my thighs, gasping as I feel his swollen tip between my folds.

He feels so good. Better than anything I would have ever imagined, before him. And as I slide down on him, inch by inch, I can see from the tormented lust on his face that it feels the same way for him. That this is the best he's ever had, too.

It's a heady feeling.

I start to ride him, slowly, dragging myself up and down his cock, parting my folds with my fingers so he can watch as I rub my clit. Ivan groans, his hips arching up to meet me with every rocking motion that I make, until we're both breathless and on the edge.

"I'm going to come," he moans. "I'm going to—"

I start to move off of him, and he shakes his head. "I need to come in you. Let me fill you up, dove. Let me—"

"We shouldn't." Somehow that makes it sound even better, my orgasm rushing up to meet his as I frantically rub my clit. "I shouldn't let you come in me."

"No, you shouldn't." He moans aloud, hips thrusting up, all of his pain forgotten by this point. "I'll get you a pill tomorrow. It'll be fine. Just let me—*fuck*, dove, let me fucking come in you. I want to—"

"I want it, too," I whisper. And even though I know it's reckless, I sink down onto him, clenching around him as my orgasm overtakes me and I throw my head back, grinding on his cock as I come hard.

"Fuck, *Charlotte!*" Ivan cries out my name as his cock throbs inside of me, hot spurts of cum filling me as he throws his head back, moaning my name again. "Fuck, *fuck*—" His fingers claw into the bed, moans spilling from his lips as I rock against him, and he gasps for breath as I finally go still, his cum hot inside of me.

I sit like that for a long moment, trying to catch my breath, before I slide off of him. "Let me see," he gasps, and I obey without thinking, rocking back and spreading my legs so that he can see his cum dripping out of me, pearling along my wet folds.

"*Fuck*," Ivan moans. "As soon as I'm better, I'm never going to let you out of bed. I'm going to fuck you all day. I'm going to make you come so many fucking times."

"I'm going to hold you to that." I close my legs, sliding up to lie next to him, both of us naked atop the bed. "But right now, I need you to get well. And we need to figure out what we're doing next."

A soft snore escapes Ivan, and I laugh, realizing that he's already fallen asleep, before I even finished speaking. I put a pillow between us, wanting to make sure that I don't accidentally jostle him in his sleep, and I close my eyes.

We will have to figure out what to do in the morning. But for now, this is enough.

For now, I just want to sleep next to him.

—

IN THE MORNING, Ivan is stiff and sore and in pain, but he's alive. Despite his objections, I walk down to a nearby diner and get food for us, since neither of us has eaten in nearly twenty-four hours. He manages some eggs and toast, and I scarf down the rest, before throwing away the trash and settling back down onto the bed next to him.

"What now?" I ask quietly, and Ivan rubs his hand through his hair with his good arm, wincing as it tugs at the bandage on his side.

"We're going to have to get a ride to Mexico. It's going to take most of the cash I have left on me, but I can access more once we're out of the country. And then—" He frowns. "Then, I have some other calls to make."

"About what?" I look at him curiously, and Ivan hesitates.

"If we're really going to do this together, you have to trust me," I insist. "What is it?"

Ivan gives me a guarded look. "We'll find a place to hide out. It will take me a couple of days to sort it all out. But I think I can get you back home."

"What?" I blink at him. "But you said—"

"I know." He lets out a sharp breath. "I don't know. But I have something I can try—"

"Ivan, you don't have to do anything." I lean forward, catching his gaze with mine. "I've already resigned myself to not going back. And if I have you—"

"That's the thing." He shakes his head. "I have to fix this, Charlotte. And I will."

"Ivan—"

"I'm not going to let you lose your whole life for me." He looks at me, and I can tell that whatever he's thinking, he's not going to be dissuaded from it.

"Not when you've become my whole life."

34

IVAN

Charlotte doesn't know what I'm planning. If she did, she'd never let me go through with it. But I'm not going to tell her the details.

Just that I'm going to do my best to fix what I've broken.

We get a ride across the border to Mexico—an expensive one, given who I have to contact in order to get it, another associate of "Dave's" who doesn't come cheap. But we make it, and although I can see the fear in Charlotte's eyes when we hand over our forged passports, they go through without issue.

We're home free. She doesn't say anything else about my promise to get her back home, and oddly, I feel like she's hoping I've forgotten about it. Like she wants me to, because she's afraid of what I'll do to make that happen.

Truthfully, I'm afraid of what will happen, too. But I refuse to force her into exile with me. She's given up everything to be mine, and as much as I want to ride off into the sunset with her, I have to play this one last card. I didn't want to—but I can't in good conscience hold onto it.

Not when I know how deeply I love her, now. Not when I know there's a chance I can *really* make it right.

If I can give her her old life back, then I need to be willing to sacrifice my new one. And I'll do that, for her.

I've realized that there's nothing I wouldn't do for her.

"This is beautiful," Charlotte breathes, when we walk into the beachside villa that I rented for us. It faces the water, a sandy private beach stretching out in front of the porch, and inside is big and airy, all light wooden floors and huge windows. The outside is a pretty white stone, with a terracotta roof and flowers blooming all around it, and my chest aches for reasons that have nothing to do with the gunshot wounds in my shoulder and side.

I want to stay here with her. I want to throw out all the plans I've just made, wrap her in my arms, and tell her this is our new home until she decides she wants to move on to somewhere else. I want to tell her that I'll give her anything else she wants, so long as I don't have to lose her.

But she's made it clear from the beginning that what she really wants is to go home. That she wants her friends. The life I stole away. And I need to give that back to her, even if she thinks she's willing to give it up now for me.

For the rest of the evening, though, I pretend that's not what's going to happen. We shower in the huge outdoor shower in the back. Charlotte slides down to her knees, taking me in her mouth as I run my hands through her wet hair, until I can't stand it any longer. I sink down onto the wooden bench next to the wall, sitting back as she climbs into my lap and rides me until we both come. She keeps letting me come inside of her, and even though I grabbed some contraceptives from the last pharmacy we were able to stop at, I know we need to quit.

I don't want to, though. I want to fill her up, every time I fuck her. And neither of us seems willing to think too hard about the potential consequences.

When we're done, we dry off and get dressed, and we walk down to the store that's a few blocks away. I buy us a bottle of tequila, limes, and all of the things I need to make Charlotte a steak dinner—*not* over a campfire this time. She sits at the small island in the airy kitchen, sipping at the tequila soda and lime while I cook a steak with mushrooms and onions, street corn, and a salad. We eat at the island, with the salty breeze from the water coming in, and we go to sleep in the comfortable king-sized bed in the master bedroom, more of the salt breeze blowing in around us. I had thought I'd want to be inside Charlotte as many times as I could before I do what I need to in order to fix all of this, but I find that tonight, at least, I want to hold her instead. There will still be a little time, at least, and tonight, I just want her in my arms.

I give myself that one day, from the time we get to Mexico until the following morning, to just be happy with her. To have a taste of what it would be like if I could live this dream forever. I fall asleep knowing she loves me, and I wake up with her hair spilling over my shoulder, her sweet scent in my nose, and her soft skin against mine.

And I finally know—*really* know—what it means to be happy.

I get up, slowly, before she wakes up, and I go out to the back porch to make a call. I figure out what time it will be back in Chicago, and dial the number.

Dariev, one of my father's men, answers on the second ring.

"Dari," I speak quickly, glancing back into the house to make sure that Charlotte isn't up yet. "It's Ivan. I need you to do something for me."

He sounds gruff, a little sleepy. "What is it, Ivan? Anything?"

"I need you to find out which of the next shipments of women my father will personally be at. Me, Niki, Ani, Lev, we're all out. They're trying to catch me, I'm on the run. You know that, right?"

There's a sound like him scratching the stubble on his chin. "*Da.* I know that. I'm only speaking with you now because we were such close friends."

"And you hate what my father has been doing as much as I do, right? You told me before that you think this is bullshit."

"*Da,*" he agrees. "Drugs, guns, those are one thing. Women are another. It's not right."

"Exactly. If you can get the exact date and time of the next shipment that my father will personally oversee, and if you can *make sure* that he's there, whatever it takes, I'll pay you ten million. Wired to an account as soon as I'm sure he'll be there."

"Ten—Ivan, what's going on?"

I take a deep breath. At this point, I reason, telling Dari the truth about what I've been doing doesn't afford any risk. He doesn't know where I am, and I'm using a burner. More than likely, my father has already figured out that I was informing for the FBI. "I was working to take him down," I admit. "I had to cut out before I could finish the job. But if you can get that for me, and if you can make *sure* he's there, the FBI will get him. And if I can give Dima Kariyev to them, directly, I'll be able to ask for whatever I want."

"Shit." Dari sounds uncertain. "The fucking FBI, *brat*? What happens to me, if I get him there? They take me in, too? I've got no desire to go to prison."

"No. Amnesty for us both, for working with them. For getting Dima into their hands. I'll make sure of it for you, too. And with my father done, and Lev as well, we can pick up the pieces." I take a slow breath, considering. "I'll be the only Kariyev left. The other *pakhans* will want to challenge me, if I take it. They'd want to challenge anyone other than one of my brothers who did. But I don't want it. If you do, my father's empire, it's yours. I'll sign everything over to you, so long as I get to keep my own money I've accumulated. You can run it all, so long as you want the headaches that go along with it."

"You don't want to be *pakhan*?" There's still that doubt in Dari's voice.

"No," I tell him firmly. "Absolutely not. I want out. It's what I've always wanted. But I'll give you whatever *you* want, if you help me with this."

Dari takes a slow breath. For a moment, I think he's going to tell me no. And if he does, the only card I have left is the one I really, really don't want to follow through on.

But I will if I have to. For Charlotte.

"Aright," he says, finally. "For your father, I want the ten million. Amnesty. And you sign over his businesses when they're in your name. I get the title of *pakhan*. Full authority. You have no more input."

"Done." I agree without hesitation. "Call me back with the information. Just as soon as you have it. I'm counting on you. How long?"

"End of the day," Dari says. "Tomorrow morning at the latest."

"Good. Thank you, *brat*. This means more than you know."

When I hang up, Charlotte still isn't awake. I glance around to make sure, and then make the second call.

This one is to Bradley.

"Hello?" He sounds pissed off when he answers. I don't bother beating around the bush with him, or with pleasantries.

"It's Ivan Kariyev. I have a deal for you."

There's a long pause, one that stretches out far enough that I almost think he might have hung up. "Go on," he says finally, and it's clear from his tone that he's placating me.

"I'll turn myself in," I say flatly. "If you keep Charlotte safe. You can do whatever you want with me. I'll accept full responsibility for all of it. But nothing happens to her. No charges, no plea deals, no consequences whatsoever. And you get her a restraining order against Nate. He doesn't get to go near her." I pause for a moment, letting it sink in. "You know as well as I do that he'll take his anger out on her as soon as he can get his hands on her again."

Bradley is quiet again for a long moment. "That's a big ask," he says finally.

"No, it's not. Bring your boss along. I bet you get a raise for bringing me in. It'll be a big one for you. I'll go along with whatever you wanna slap on me. Just keep her out of it."

I have to force myself not to hold my breath. Bradley's boss being there is a big part of it. I need that, or the plan doesn't work. I can't really be sure that he *will* be there, but I have a feeling Bradley is susceptible to leading suggestions.

"Fine," Bradley says. "Deal. But no funny business, alright?"

"No funny business," I agree. "Meet me in the Tijuana River Valley, tomorrow at noon. I'll bring Charlotte to you, and you can take me in. We both get what we want."

Bradley is quiet again, and I can tell he's mulling it over, looking for a hole in the plan. Looking for a reason to distrust me. "I'll be there," he says finally, and the line goes dead.

I drop the burner phone into my lap, letting out a heavy breath. If Dari doesn't screw me over, this plan just might work.

If he does, then I'm looking at a life behind bars, or worse. But if there's one man from my former life that I trust, it's him.

And if it all falls apart, I've decided that doesn't matter. I look up, hearing footsteps, and see Charlotte through the window, messy-haired and sleepy-eyed, walking in one of my t-shirts into the kitchen. I know all over again, as I see her, that I'd do anything to keep her safe.

I've always feared prison over death. The end is preferable to a life in a cage. But all that matters now is that she gets to go home.

I've taken enough from her. And now, I'll do whatever I need to in order to give it back.

35

CHARLOTTE

I get two blissful days with Ivan before he tells me that we're taking a trip. He's rented a car with cash this time, he says—not stolen—and we're going to take a drive up to California.

"Is that such a good idea?" I bite my lip as I look at him, slipping into a pair of shorts and a long-sleeved T-shirt. "We just left the States to lay low. Should we be going back?"

He looks at me, hesitant, and I know I'm not going to like what he has to say. "Just tell me," I say finally, and Ivan lets out a heavy breath, sinking onto the edge of the bed.

"I called Bradley," he says slowly. "I made a deal."

"What? You did *what*?" For a minute, I think I'm not hearing him correctly. "What do you mean—"

"Just listen." Ivan stands up, grabbing my hands and holding them in his. "I need you to trust me. You want your life back, right? Your home, your friends—you want to be free to see them again, right? I took all that away from you."

I narrow my eyes at him. "I forgave you for that," I say slowly. "We've talked about it. I understand. And yes, I want those things—but I want *you*, too, Ivan. And those things—"

"Might not be mutually exclusive." He rubs his thumbs over my knuckles, his expression pleading with me to listen to him. "Trust me, Charlotte, just like you have up to this point. I made a deal with Bradley, but if all goes well, then it'll turn out in my favor, not his. And we'll both be free to do as we please."

I look at him suspiciously. "And if it doesn't?"

"Then I'll go to prison. But you'll still be free. You'll get your life back. It's a gamble, but—" Ivan grins, that mischievous look in his eyes. "We went all the way to Vegas, right? We've gotta place at least one bet."

I shake my head, chewing on my lip. "I don't like it."

"I knew you wouldn't," Ivan says softly. "But please. Trust me."

He's right that I have. And it's gotten us this far. I nod slowly, even though I still feel uncertain. But Ivan has been playing this game much longer than I have. I have to trust that he can see it through to the end.

"Okay," I whisper, and he pulls me in for a kiss.

I lean into it, savoring the feeling of his lips on mine, knowing that this could be the last day we spend together. The thought feels like it claws at something in my chest, and I want to change my mind, to tell Ivan no. To tell him that it's too dangerous, that we should stay here, in Mexico, in this little sunny bubble that we created for ourselves over the last couple of days.

It's been like a dream. Like heaven. With the anger and resentment gone, there's just been the two of us, in our own little haven.

But I know what Ivan's afraid of. That eventually, the shine will wear off. That I'll start to miss my friends again. My life. That I'll resent him.

I don't think I will. But I can understand why he would fear that. And while I would never ask him to risk his freedom to give me back my life—if he *could* get us all of that back…I can admit that it's tempting.

Ivan's fingers stay laced through mine for the entirety of the drive to the Tijuana River Valley. I try to soak it all in: the sunlight, the hours with him, the fact that whatever happens now, everything between us has been figured out. He loves me and I love him. And if for some reason this plan goes awry, I tell myself, I won't let Bradley win. I'll get a lawyer, a good one. I'll find a way to get him out.

We meet Bradley in a parking lot just as we get into the Valley, just over the border. It's an empty lot across from an old, closed-down furniture store, across from an In-and-Out. Bradley is standing just outside of his car, sunglasses on, seemingly alone. I feel Ivan tense as we pull into the lot, and he lets out a slow breath.

"If this goes wrong," he says softly, "I love you, Charlotte."

"I love you, too," I whisper.

And then, as Ivan starts to open the door, I see a second man get out of Bradley's car—this one taller, older, with a bearing that suggests he might be Bradley's superior. I feel a little of the tension drain out of Ivan, and I take a breath, hoping against hope that this goes according to plan.

We walk towards where Bradley and the other man are standing. Bradley straightens, sliding off his glasses. "Well," he says with a grin. "Here to turn yourself in, Kariyev?"

"Not exactly." Ivan turns his attention to the other man. "Special Agent Shelby, right? Bradley's boss?"

Bradley has frozen, a look of confusion on his face. "You talk to me," he snaps. "This is my—"

"It's your nothing," Ivan interrupts. "Special Agent Shelby, I have proof here that my father, Dima Kariyev, will be at this address in Chicago tonight, to move a shipment of women that are being sold to various buyers in numerous countries. My brother, Lev, will likely not be there, as he was engaged with tracking me down, and my other surviving brother, Ani—if he's alive—will also be busy trying to find me. But they'll be easy enough to track down, once you have my father. You can take him, and this business down, in one swoop tonight."

Shelby looks at the texts from Dari on Ivan's phone, his expression skeptical. "And why didn't you get this information for Bradley, when you were reporting to him?"

"Because I didn't trust him," Ivan says flatly. "My plan was always to find a way to get this information to you, once I had it. Bradley has disliked me and my work for you from the start. He resents that I can exchange my freedom for information. He resents it to the point that he tried to manipulate Ms. Williams here, to pin fake kidnapping charges on me, and use Ms. Williams' former boyfriend to threaten her and provide incorrect information."

I step forward, before Ivan can stop me. "I have texts from Nathaniel Taylor that prove that he was threatening me. Bradley should never have engaged his help in anything involving me. But Agent Bradley didn't seem to care much for my welfare, at least not past the point where it could help him."

"I planned to get this information sooner rather than later," Ivan continues. "But everything went all to shit a couple of weeks ago, as I'm sure you're aware. Bradley seemed to have gone rogue, so my goal was to stay ahead of him and my brothers, until I could get Charlotte to safety."

Shelby is still looking at Ivan through narrowed eyes. "And your reason for fabricating this handover today?"

"I wouldn't have gotten this meeting otherwise." Ivan shrugs. "I needed you to be here, or else Bradley would have thrown me in the deepest pit he could, and fabricated enough to make sure no one found out how he'd behaved."

"This is—" Bradley starts to splutter, but Shelby holds up a hand.

"It's not the first time Bradley has been censured for his conduct," he says slowly. "What is it you want, Kariyev?"

"I want all possible charges against Charlotte thrown out. I want her to be able to return to her former life once my father and his associates are arrested, without fear and with protection, if need be. I want a restraining order filed against Nate, so he can't threaten her. And I want amnesty for myself and the man who provided this information. I'll give his name when I have guarantees." Ivan holds his ground, unflinching as he lists it off.

Shelby draws in a slow breath, considering as he looks down at the phone. "I'll have you and Ms. Williams taken to a hotel," he says slowly. "And when we've made the arrests, if all of this pans out, I'll have an agent bring the agreement to you to sign. If not—if this proves useless—" He shrugs. "You'll be taken in and charged, and Ms. Williams will be questioned. Is that fair?"

Ivan hesitates, and I look at him. "It's good, right?" I whisper. "The information?"

He nods, swallowing hard. "So long as nothing goes wrong. As long as Dari comes through."

"Is it worth that chance? To get everything back?" I'm tempted to tell Ivan to jump into the car with me, and we'll run again. But he still seems determined to see this through.

He nods. "I think it is. You'll be safe no matter what. I'm sure of it."

"Okay." I bite my lip. "I trust you."

"That's acceptable," Ivan says, turning back to Shelby. "We'll take that offer."

Next to him, Bradley is spluttering, trying to get a word in. But Shelby raises his hand again, looking sharply at him.

"We're done here," he says curtly. "We'll talk about your future back at the office."

And, for once, as Shelby gets back into the car and motions for Bradley to follow him—Bradley has nothing to say.

—

THE HOTEL that we're taken to is comfortable and clean, with a huge bed made up with white sheets and a gorgeous view. I give the authorities my former phone number to pull the texts from Nate, and Ivan and I wait in the room to hear about our future.

It's impossible to sit still. We order room service and pick at it. Ivan turns the television on, but neither of us watches it. And then, just when we both feel like we're going to go mad as the nighttime hours tick past, Ivan gets a message on the phone that he was left with.

"It worked." He stares down at the screen, his face slack with disbelief. "I can't believe this is actually happening. It worked. We're going to be fine." He repeats it again, astonishment coloring his tone, and I jump up, looking over his shoulder to read the message.

Arrests made. Dima Kariyev and others in custody. Will come to hotel to sign amnesty agreement.
-**Agent Caldwell**

I SINK DOWN on the edge of the bed, the realization that it's almost over hitting me. That we're going to be safe. Ivan's father is arrested, and if his brothers weren't already—the ones that are still alive—they will be soon. The agent who comes to talk to us will tell me about keeping Nate away from me. And Ivan and I—we'll be free to live our lives. Not on the run, not as different people, but *our* lives.

"You fixed it," I whisper softly, half-amazed by it still. "You fixed it all."

Ivan smiles at me, setting the phone down. "I told you I would."

"So what happens after the agreement?"

Ivan breathes in slowly. "We go home. I'll be given amnesty so long as I stick to whatever probation they give me—I'll have to avoid some criminal activities, I'm sure. But I think I can manage that."

"Are you sure?" I can't help but grin, getting up from the bed as I walk over to him, wrapping my arms around his neck. "You'd have to stop stalking me. That's probably on the list."

"I don't need to any longer. You're right here." Ivan grins back, his hands on my waist. "And if you run, little dove, I'll catch you."

I suck in a sharp breath, as he leans in to kiss me, soft and slow. When he breaks the kiss after a long moment, he looks down at me, his hands still gripping me gently.

"What do you want to do after this?" Ivan asks curiously. "You probably just want to go home, right?"

I smile, feeling lighter than I have in a long time. "To see everyone and let them know I'm safe, sure. But not to stay."

Ivan tilts his head. "No?"

"No." I lean up, kissing him again. "Not yet, anyway. There are so many adventures that I haven't gotten to go on yet."

I lean in, pressing my forehead to his, my arms still wrapped around him as I breathe him in. "And I want to go on all of them with you."

EPILOGUE
CHARLOTTE

Outside, the Caribbean sky is a bright blue that almost matches the dazzling blue of the water. A sugary beach stretches out below the balcony of our beachside suite, the salty breeze tangling my hair as I look out, enjoying the sound of the lapping waves and the scent of the sea air and tropical flowers.

Behind me, I hear the pop of a cork as Ivan opens a bottle of champagne, the sound of him pouring it into glasses following shortly after. He walks up behind me, handing me a mimosa as he leans on the railing next to me, looking out at the beach below.

Zoe and Jasmine are already out on the beach, laying out on towels, enjoying the attention of the men who walk by and gawk. Sarah, I'm sure, is sleeping in—as she always has on every vacation we've ever gone on.

"To new beginnings," Ivan says softly, tapping his mimosa glass against mine. Our fingers brush as he does, and I feel a spark tingle over my skin, lighting me on fire even though we only got dressed an hour or so ago. We enjoyed a lazy evening in bed last night after dinner, and he woke me up the same way this morning, sliding under the sheets to tease me to a slow, sleepy orgasm.

"And all the adventures we can imagine." I sip my mimosa,

looking out at the sand. "We should go join them soon. We invited them on this trip—we can't stay in the room the *whole* time."

"I know." Ivan chuckles. "Maybe I should have waited. I still want you all to myself. But I also wanted your friends to get to know me. We got off on the wrong foot, after all."

"You mean the whole kidnapping thing? Yeah, Zoe is going to take a while to get over that. And Sarah. Jaz is—" I laugh. "Jaz is the adventurous type, herself. She thought it was exciting. And she trusts my judgment."

"The others don't?" Ivan asks curiously, and I shake my head.

"It's not that. It's just—Jaz and I were always the closest. I'm not super close with my family, and she's estranged from hers. It's different. Sarah and Zoe are just more protective. But after last night, they like you a lot more," I promise.

Last night, we had a beachside dinner with plenty of wine flowing, private for just the five of us. Ivan paid for all of it, and it was the most fun I've had in a long time. We laughed and drank and talked, and by the end of it, I could tell that my friends had warmed up to him much more. They'd been skeptical, when he'd proposed us all going on a vacation. But none of my friends are the type to turn down a free exotic trip, and Ivan can be convincing.

I know that firsthand.

"I love you," I say softly, leaning my hip against the railing and smiling at him. "That's what matters. The rest will come in time."

"I hope so," Ivan agrees. "Because I wouldn't want anything less than for all of your best friends to agree to be in your bridal party."

"What?" I blink at him, confused. "My—"

I gasp as he drops down to one knee on the balcony, slipping his hand into his pocket and pulling out a small black box. When he opens it, I see the most stunning engagement ring that I've ever laid eyes on.

It's a kite-shaped salt-and-pepper diamond, with a black diamond on either side, on a platinum band studded with smaller white diamonds. My mouth drops open, and for a moment, I can't speak.

"I love you, Charlotte," Ivan says softly. "And maybe this is too soon—I'll understand if it is. But you know I've been obsessed with you since the day I saw you. I knew since that first moment that I couldn't live without you. And if you feel the same way, I want to be yours for the rest of our lives—just as much as I want you to be mine."

Tears well up in my eyes, and I nod before I have the ability to speak again. "*Yes*," I whisper finally. "Yes. It's crazy, but—yes. I'll marry you. I love you, too, Ivan, I—"

His eyes are misty, too, as he slides the ring onto my finger, the diamond glittering in the bright sun. He stands up, pulling me in for a kiss as his mouth seals over mine, and then he picks me up, my legs wrapping around his waist as he carries me back to the bed. He spills me back onto it, dragging me to the edge where he's standing and tugging my leggings down as I feel him grind against me, already rock-hard.

"Once more," Ivan murmurs, his mouth already descending on mine as he strips us both naked. "One more time, and then we'll go down and find the others."

My answer is a kiss, as I wrap my arms around his neck and drag him down to me, hooking my legs around his hips as I feel him slide inside of me that first inch, teasing me with what we both need so badly.

"One more time, for now," I whisper, as he slides into me, groaning as his lips find my neck and he starts to thrust. "And after that—for the rest of our lives."

Ivan's thrusts are slow and deep, each one sending waves of pleasure through my body, pushing me closer to the brink. I arch my back, pressing myself closer to him, wanting to feel every inch of his skin against mine. Nothing has ever felt as good with anyone as it feels when I'm with Ivan. It was easy to say yes to this forever. I never want anything else.

"I'm yours," he breathes against my skin, his voice thick with desire. "And you're mine."

I moan, arching into him as his teeth graze the side of my neck, so close to the edge. And then, just as I can feel my orgasm on the verge of tipping over, there's a knock at the door.

"Hey, lovebirds!" Sarah's voice calls out from the other side. "Are you coming down to the beach?"

Ivan freezes, and I bite my lip, trying not to laugh. "We'll be right out!" I call, trying to keep my voice from sounding strained.

"Don't wait on us," Ivan adds, his hips rocking against mine, and I press my hand to my mouth to stifle a moan.

I hear Sarah laugh, and her footsteps fade away. Ivan picks up his pace again, pushing me further up the bed as he climbs onto it with me, his thrusts leisurely now, building the pleasure again.

I wrap my legs tighter around Ivan's waist, urging him on, pulling him deeper inside me. The interruption only heightened my arousal, and now I'm desperate to come. Ivan thrusts harder, his hands pinning my wrists above me as he grinds his hips against mine.

"Look in the mirror," he murmurs, nudging my head towards the huge mirror atop the dresser next to the bed. "Remember that night?"

"How could I forget?" I pant. "It wasn't all that long ago."

"I made you mine that night," he growls. "And now you'll be mine forever. My little dove. My obsession. My *wife*."

Every word pushes me closer to the brink. Ivan groans as I tighten around him, and I arch upwards, panting. "Please—" I rock against him, desperate for a little more friction, for a little more of *him*. He feels so good, and the feeling of his fingers around my wrists, the sight of him, muscled and gorgeous, stretched over me as he fills me again and again, is intoxicating.

"Come for me, little dove," he whispers, and I can feel him starting to shudder, on the edge along with me. "Come on my cock, and I'll come for you, too."

The tide of pleasure washes over me, pulling me under as I moan his name, and I hear him cry out mine. His fingers interlace with mine at the last moment, locking us together, my ring brushing against his skin.

I feel every thrust, every hot rush of his cum inside of me, and Ivan presses his mouth hard to mine, the sounds swallowed up in our kiss until we both finally go still, lying intertwined on the white sheets.

"I'm glad you found me," I whisper softly, as the sunlight streams over us both, still connected as I look down at the diamond sparkling on my finger. "For better or worse, I'm glad."

"Good," Ivan whispers, and he leans in to kiss me again. "Because, little dove—I'm never letting you go."

THANKS FOR READING! **I hope you loved the Endless series!**

I'm super excited about my subscription plan where you can gain access to the bonus scenes you've come to know and love. But readers are really loving the ability to read along as I write new stories. Plus, depending on the plan you choose you'll have access to exclusive short stories! Take a look here!

If subscriptions aren't for you, I totally get it—**Join my exclusive FB group!**

READY TO SWOON over another anti-hero? You can click here to read along as I finish writing my next Bratva romance, *Deadly Oath*, keep reading for a sneak peek, or preorder it now on Amazon!

Chapter One

Sabrina

I stare down at the clothes on my bed, a despondent feeling settling somewhere in the pit of my stomach, as I tug my bathrobe a little closer around me.

It's been a little over a month, and I haven't even started to get used to this new set of circumstances.

Reaching down, I pick up the pair of black denim jeans, one of the pieces of clothing I was taken to buy the first day I arrived here. I need to do laundry, so I'm down to just this pair and a couple of plain long-sleeved shirts.

Laundry. Less than six weeks ago, someone did that for me. Less than six weeks ago, my favorite pair of jeans was a dark-wash, boyfriend-cut pair that felt like butter against my skin from Dior. It paired perfectly with my favorite Chanel silk blouse and nude Louboutin pumps, and a pair of diamond stud earrings my father gave me for my eighteenth birthday. It was one of my favorite outfits, before.

Now—I don't have a favorite outfit. I don't have a favorite restaurant, or coffee shop, or part of town to shop in. I don't even have friends.

"Sabrina?"

Speaking of friends. The chirpy, happy-go-lucky voice of my neighbor two houses down, Marie Woodson, comes through the speaker of my phone and reminds me that I got lost in thought for a minute there. She, and a few other women that I've met here, are the closest thing that I have to friends these days.

But friends know personal things about each other. They know secrets and important moments, fears and hopes and dreams. I can't tell these women any of those things, so I can't really call them *friends.*

Not that I have hopes and dreams either, any longer. The ones I had before—such as they were—are all gone.

"I'm here," I say distractedly, pulling on the Target-brand jeans and long-sleeved shirt. I grab a hair tie from my nightstand with one hand, scraping my blonde hair up into a loose, messy bun. My hair is my one holdout from my old life still—I had it done right before the night when everything went upside down. The expensive balayage and perfect cut looks out of place next to the dressed-down outfit, and every time I leave the house, I can feel people looking at me. Noticing that while my clothing might have changed, the polish that's leftover from my old life, the way I've been taught to carry myself since I was small, the way I speak—it all sets me apart from everyone else in this small town.

"Daphne texted the group this morning with the new title for our book club. Did you see it? Cozy mystery is the theme this month. I was thinking we could go get coffee, and then swing by the bookstore to grab our copies. Unless you can't get away from work today?"

"No, that's fine. I make my own hours. I've been working more at night lately, anyway."

"Night owl." Marie laughs, clicking her tongue. "I'd be the same if it wasn't for the kids. I used to pull all-nighters all the time in college. Now I'm lucky if I make it to ten before I'm in bed."

"Yeah, me too." I can hear how hollow it all sounds. How detached my voice is. Marie must notice it, too, but she's not the kind of person to point it out. She brought me cookies the first day I moved in. Homemade, with those big chocolate chunks in them. I remember staring at them and crying because I couldn't make myself eat one.

I can't remember the last time I ate a cookie. My looks have always been my currency. My hair and my skin and my figure have always been immaculate. But here, no one cares about that.

They seem to care about kindness. Friendship. Goodwill. Neighborly affection. The people I grew up around didn't value those things. And what was elegant, sophisticated distance in the life I remember comes across as cold haughtiness here.

"You sound tired." There's a hint of worry in Marie's voice, now. "Maybe you shouldn't be pulling so many late nights. Sleep is important, you know. I keep telling my son that, every time he wants to stay up late playing video games."

"I've just had trouble sleeping lately, is all." I sink down on the edge of the bed, reaching for the black ankle boots that I bought last week. They look like a knock-off of a favorite pair I used to own, and I thought that buying them would make me feel better. But actually, it just makes my chest ache, every time I look at them. "I've always had trouble with insomnia. I thought being out here in the country would help. That it would be more—quiet, I guess. But it's been persisting." That's my cover story, flimsy as it is—that I moved away from the city because it was getting to be too much. That I needed a break, like a hysterical Victorian woman going to the seaside for her "nerves."

"Well, if you ever want to see a doctor, and you need a ride, just let me know. Dr. Thompson at the clinic here is good, but he's older, so he's skeptical of prescribing things like sleeping pills. I went to a doctor in Louisville when I needed anxiety medication. Fixed me right up." Marie's chirpy voice brightens. "Dr. Thompson wasn't happy when I had to tell him at my next check-up, but at that point, what could he do about it? I already had the prescription." There's a conspiratorial note to her voice now, like we're sharing secrets. "Anyway, if you need a little help getting better sleep, there's no shame in it. I'd be happy to give you a ride."

"Thanks." Not for the first time, I wish I had a car. I wish I knew how to *drive*. If I want to go anywhere further than the few stores that are within walking distance of my house, I have to get a ride from someone. I can't imagine actually explaining to anyone here how, at twenty-two years old, I don't know how to drive. I could pass it off as having lived in Chicago my whole life, I suppose, but it would still lead to more questions.

And questions are something I've tried very hard to avoid. Not easy in a small town, I'm finding, where everyone gossips about everyone else, and everyone knows everyone else's business.

"That's what friends are for!" Marie exclaims, and I can hear her indrawn breath as she gears up to run off on another tangent. She's like a small, excitable dog. A Pomeranian, maybe. Sweet and full of energy, and always ready to talk. I interrupt her, quickly, because I need a little time with my own thoughts before I spend the rest of the afternoon with her.

"I need to finish getting ready. But I'm fine with a coffee and book run. Can you pick me up in, say—an hour and a half?" I reason that should give me enough time for coffee and my breakfast, quietly, before the day starts.

"Sure thing! I'll see you then."

The phone clicks off, and I release a breath that I hadn't known I was holding. I reach up, rubbing my temples, fending off a growing headache. Everyone here is just so—much. All of the time.

I grew up with distance. Private school, where everyone was as stiff and formal as my father and his associates at home. A staff at the mansion I grew up in, who always kept a careful space between me and them. Friends from the same school, the same social circles, who also grew up believing that that kind of distance was the only acceptable way to behave. Even my closest friends and I gave each other air kisses instead of hugs. I can't actually remember the last time anyone hugged me.

The first day I met Marie, she gave me that plate of cookies. The second day I met her was at the book club I hesitantly attended, where she grabbed me in a full-body hug and told me how excited she was that I'd taken her invitation. I'd gone stiff, unsure of what to do. Marie hadn't seemed to notice, too caught up in her own excitement, but everyone else certainly did.

It set me apart, from the very beginning. But that was always going to happen.

I exhale another long breath, pinching the bridge of my nose before standing up. I feel strange, without my jewelry and makeup. But I haven't had the funds to get the kind of makeup I used to buy, and all of my jewelry is back home. The best I've been able to afford is the something close to the kind of skincare I used to use. Prioritizing purchases—another thing I've had to get used to.

Some of my expenses are covered by the FBI, like the rent on the small one-bedroom house I'm living in, and a stipend for food and basic clothing. The rest—discretionary spending for things like books, or skincare, or anything else that goes above and beyond the pitifully small amount deposited into my checking account each month, is up to me. Which is why I took on another new experience a couple of weeks ago—working for the first time in my life.

Just freelance editing work, but it pays something. Enough to cover the expensive moisturizer that I swipe over my skin, and the jug of flavored coffee that I pour myself a cup of as soon as I head into the kitchen. I didn't think it was all that pricey, but Marie looked round-eyed at the extravagance, when I could have just gotten grounds and inexpensive creamer.

There's a coffeepot on my counter, one of the things that the house came furnished with, but I haven't figured out how to use it yet. The first time, I burned myself. The second time, I ended up with grounds in the coffee. The third, it was too watery.

At that point, I just got overwhelmed, and bought a bottle of pre-mixed coffee on my next grocery run.

At least it's pumpkin-flavored, which is a nice touch this time of year.

I sink down at the table with a bowl of cereal and my coffee, nudging the mini-wheats around the bowl with my spoon. At this hour, the sun is spilling through the large windows above the sink and stove and through the window at the top of the backdoor, lighting up the kitchen with a soft glow. There are a number of trees in my backyard, and the leaves are rust-red, orange, and yellow, adding to the autumn morning ambiance.

It should be peaceful. Relaxing. Marie oohed and aahed over the view from my kitchen windows the first time she was in here. But there's nothing peaceful about why I'm here. And there's nothing peaceful about how little direction I have in my life now.

I take a bite of the cold cereal, still staring out of the window at the trees, and wince. There's nothing wrong with it, but I miss the breakfasts I'm used to. I miss poached eggs with hollandaise and crispy bacon. Toasted bagels with fresh tomato, cream cheese, and lox. Crepes filled with fresh fruit and honey. Quiche. I don't know how to cook any of those things, and I'm terrified to try. I already feel lost enough as it is, and all of the ways that I'm sure I'll fail will only make me feel worse.

If I told Marie, or anyone else, about all of the things I miss, the things I long for that are making me sad, she'd think I was spoiled. She'd be shocked at the kind of excess that used to be normal to me. And maybe I *am* spoiled—but it wasn't my fault that all of it was taken from me. I didn't ask for any of this to happen. And right now, it all still feels monumentally unfair.

I finish my cereal reluctantly and nudge the bowl aside, sipping at my coffee. Outside, a bird perches in the tree next to my window, chirping with a cheerfulness that reminds me of Marie. A wave of exhaustion washes over me, and I consider texting her and canceling our plans. Staying in, getting my editing done, and watching a movie alone or something. Reading a book that I picked out, instead of the book club pick of the month. I'm dreading that, too. Hours sitting in a strange living room that's not like any house I've ever been in before moving here, surrounded by people that I feel certain are all judging me. I want to cancel that, too.

But I can hear Agent Caldwell's voice in my head—the FBI agent assigned to me after I was put in witness protection. He checked up on me every couple of days, for the first few weeks. Now it's a monthly visit. But those first visits, he saw that I was staying in, avoiding everyone, not making friends. *You need hobbies,* he said. *This is for your protection, Sabrina, but you need to do your best to fit in. Just because we've hidden you doesn't mean that people might not still be looking. And if folks come nosing around, asking questions, looking—the more you stand out, the more you make yourself a target.*

He'd patted my hand reassuringly after that, a sympathetic expression on his face. I remember thinking that he looked like someone's father—short beard and mustache, a bit of a beer gut, a friendly look on his face. Not *my* father, but someone's. He looked like he was reassuring me that getting a C in geometry wasn't the end of the world, not cautioning me to not put a target on my back for people who want to kill me.

So I joined book club. I've gotten coffee with Marie. Joined her and a few of her other friends on grocery-shopping runs. Asked her to give me a ride to Sephora to get my skin-care items, which also horrified her when she saw the cost.

But none of it has made me feel like I belong here. None of it has made me feel like there's anything to look forward to any longer, anything to be hopeful for. My life has crashed and burned, and I'm sitting here in the ashes, trying to figure out who I'm supposed to be now.

Maybe I should see a doctor. Get something for depression. That's what this is, right?

But is it? Or is it just a natural reaction to having everything I've ever known upended in one night that left me reeling? How long is it supposed to take for someone to recover from something like that?

There's a knock at the door, just as I lift my coffee mug to my lips again. I jump, startled, setting the mug down with a *thud* as my heart starts to race.

It's just Marie, I tell myself, pushing my chair back. But Marie isn't the type to knock. We've known each other a little over a month now, and in her world, that's plenty of time to just "let yourself on in," as she would say. I can hear it in her voice, in my head as I think it.

But *someone* is at my door. And that painful adrenaline starts to race through me, reminding me of a night that I want so badly to forget.

Swallowing hard, I stand up, forcing myself to walk slowly to the door, as another knock sounds on the other side. Forcing myself to try to breathe normally. *It's just a neighbor. A door-to-door salesman.* No one has found me. Not so soon. Agent Caldwell promised me that anyone would be hard-pressed to find me at all.

I have a new last name here. A new life. I'm *safe*.

I'm supposed to be safe.

Taking a deep, shaky breath, I swing open the door, pasting the sort of down-home, friendly smile on my face that I know the neighbors here expect. But it falters, a little, when I see who's standing on my doorstep.

It's a man. A man wearing the uniform of a cop, specifically, with reddish-brown hair that glints the same color of the leaves outside in the sunlight, and green eyes that are fixed directly on me. He is, I think as I stand there stunned, possibly the most handsome man I've ever seen in my life.

And then, he says my name.

"Sabrina Miller?"

Chapter Two
Kian

The woman standing framed in the doorway is stunning. And

entirely out of place.

It's my first time laying eyes on Sabrina Miller, and it was worth the wait. But five seconds is all it takes to see that she doesn't belong here.

She stands there uncomfortably, like she feels not at home in her own skin—or more likely, the clothes she's wearing. Jeans that are too big, a plain, navy-blue shirt with long sleeves that she keeps plucking at. Definitely not her choice, not when the rest of her is so perfectly polished. She has a body to die for, the kind of body that's never been poisoned by a box of Kraft mac-and-cheese or a drive-through burger. Her hair looks expensive, as does her poreless, perfectly smooth skin. *She* looks expensive.

She should, considering what she's cost me.

"What do you want?" Her voice is all wrong too, clipped, cold, and cultured, with the hint of a city-born-and-bred Chicagoan accent. Nothing like the Kentucky drawl that I've been inundated with since coming here a few weeks ago. I meant to come and see her sooner, but there was a surprising amount of paperwork and responsibility that came with taking over a small-town police station. Especially when the former sheriff was an aging man who could barely use a flip phone, let alone a computer.

Standing there in the doorway, flaking paint and a rusty hinge framing her, a loose step under my foot, she looks like a mirage. Like she can't possibly be real. But she is.

"Well, ma'am, is that any way to greet a man who came all the way over here to check on you?" I smile at her, shoving my hands in my pockets, striving to look relaxed. "Kian Brady. I'm the sheriff here, if you weren't aware. And since you're new in town, living here alone, I figured I'd come and make sure there wasn't anything you needed. I know the man who you're renting this place from, and he's a bit of a scummy landlord. Doesn't do much for maintenance, overcharges on the rent. Wanted to make sure you were getting by alright."

By now, anyone else here would have relaxed, too. Given me a big smile, invited me in for a beer or a cup of coffee or offered a fresh-baked cookie. But Sabrina is still looking at me suspiciously, her gorgeous blue eyes going from wide to narrowed.

"The sheriff is a man named Wayne Smith," Sabrina says, her voice chillier than before. "I met him the day after I moved here. He showed up a lot like this, actually. On my doorstep, letting me know that if I needed anything, all I had to do was call." She purses her lips, a clear expression on her face that says she doesn't believe anything I'm saying now.

I don't let it rattle me. She's cold, sure, and suspicious, but I can work with that. "I know Wayne," I assure her, my voice easy. "I replaced him when he retired, a few weeks ago. Some health issues, I think. Normal stuff, for a guy that age. They decided to bring in someone younger. Bit more spring in my step, for chasing down the bad guys." I smile at her, letting it reach the corners of my eyes.

"And have you gone and checked on all the residents like this, *Sheriff* Brady?" She raises one perfectly groomed eyebrow. Too well-groomed, for anyone living here. If I wasn't already aware that she was a new arrival, I'd know just from that. "Or just me?"

"Oh, I've been making the rounds. Marie a few houses down makes a mean pumpkin peanut-butter cookie. If you haven't had the chance to try one yet, you should."

Something about the mention of Marie's name seems to relax her the smallest fraction. I see her shift, the tension in her face loosening just a bit. She smiles, but it still seems a bit forced.

"I'm sorry, Sheriff Brady," she says easily, although her voice is still cool. "I'm being terribly rude. Do you want to come in? I'm afraid I can't offer cookies, but I've got cold coffee."

"I can't say I'm a fan of cold coffee, but I'll accept the hospitality anyway." My smile doesn't falter as Sabrina steps back, giving me space to step into the house. "Although even in a place like this, you should be cautious of inviting strangers in. Woman living alone, and all of that."

"You've noted that I live alone once already." Some of that stiffness returns to her tone as she strides towards the back of the house, where I glimpse a table and kitchen appliances through an open doorway. The walls of the kitchen are a pale yellow, the table and chairs a worn wood, scratches of use indented into it. A flowered valance hangs over the sink, framing the large window. "And you're the sheriff, right? That's what you said? So I shouldn't be worried about letting you into my house."

She glances back, that eyebrow arched again, and I chuckle. "Well, I suppose you've got me there, ma'am."

"Sabrina. I've never been called *ma'am* before, and I think it makes me feel uncomfortable." She steps into the kitchen, yanking open the fridge with a bit more force than strictly necessary. "And I'm sorry, but I haven't quite mastered the coffeepot yet. So cold is the best I can do." She pulls out a jug of cold pumpkin-flavored coffee, and I resist the urge to wrinkle my nose. What I want is an opportunity to talk to Sabrina Miller a bit longer, and if drinking overly sugary, cold coffee is the way to do it, I'm willing to suffer.

"Then call me Kian." I sit down at the table, watching her as she moves around the kitchen, her shoulders and posture tense. "If we're going by first names."

She ignores the offer, pouring a generous amount of the coffee into a black mug and setting it down on the table in front of me, before reaching for a half-full mug that she must have abandoned when I knocked on the door. "So. Is there anything else I can do for you?" She leans back against the counter with her cup as she says it, instead of sitting down at the table with me. There's clear distrust still in her eyes.

"I'm just curious, is all. I'd like to get to know everyone I'm responsible for keeping safe, here. One of the benefits of small-town living, isn't it? You can get to know everyone you live near."

Sabrina snorts, then catches herself. "I'm still getting used to it," she says quickly. "I haven't been here long. But I suppose you knew that already. *How* did you know that already?" She pauses, and when I don't reply instantly, she answers her own question. "The neighbors, of course. Marie." She lets out a small sigh. "Another thing I'm not entirely used to. Everyone else knowing my business."

"It can be an acquired taste."

That eyebrow arches again. I feel an odd, itching urge to close the distance between us, reach up, and smooth my thumb over the curve of it. Close on the heels of that thought is the image of pressing my palm to her cheek, my thumb on that small dip in the center of her chin, pulling that full, frowning mouth into mine.

She wouldn't be frowning any longer by the time I finished kissing her. Her mouth would be soft, swollen, slack. Warm from mine. Her eyes luminous and wide instead of narrowed and suspicious.

My cock twitches at the thought, a pulse of arousal prickling over my skin as I feel it swell, pushing at the front of my zipper. I'm pretty sure the dark brown slacks aren't going to do all that good of a job of hiding my burgeoning erection, and I will it to calm down.

That's not what I'm here for. Not right now.

I clear my throat, shifting in my seat in a way that I hope isn't overly obvious. "What convinced you to move here? Since you seem so uncomfortable."

"Like you said, I'm sure it's an acquired taste." Sabrina takes a sip of her coffee. "I just haven't acquired it yet. I was starting to feel overwhelmed where I lived. I needed some peace and quiet. So I came here." She shrugs, but there's a stiffness to it that I notice. A practiced way that she speaks, as if she's reciting something she's memorized. "But it's been more of an adjustment than I expected. I'll get there, I'm sure."

"Well, if you need someone to show you around, I'd be happy to help." I set down the mug of coffee, unable to manage another sip, and lean one elbow on the table. "I could take you out for dinner one night. Give you a little taste of what the town has to offer."

That eyebrow somehow arches even higher. "Are you asking me out on a *date*, Sheriff Brady? And aren't you new here, too? I should be asking someone else to give me a *taste* of the town, don't you think?"

An abrupt, hot jolt of anger ripples through me at the thought of any other man taking the coldly gorgeous woman in front of me out *anywhere*, let alone on an actual date. Irritation at her refusal to call me by my name follows it, adding to the prickling running across my skin like ants.

"I am new here," I agree, keeping that anger out of my tone with some effort. "And what if I am asking you out on a date?" I smirk at her, and I see her eyes narrow.

"Then I'd have to say no," she says, her voice returning to that chilly calm. "I don't think I'm really in a place to go out with anyone right now. But thank you, *Sheriff* Brady. I'm sure you were just looking out for me, by asking."

There's no room for argument in the way she says it, so I drop it for now, standing up smoothly as I carry my mug to the sink. I pass by her as I do, and I get a whiff of her scent—sweet vanilla sugar with a hint of spice to it. My cock twitches again, that tingling arousal prickling up my spine, and I force myself to keep walking past her. I have the urge to turn and pin her against the counter, put my hand on those perfectly curved hips and show her exactly how little she's actually managed to put me off. How aroused I am by her, despite her coolness towards me.

But I ignore it. I was once a man of great self-control, and even if I've felt that control fraying as of late, I'm not that far gone yet.

Even when it comes to her.

"Thanks for the coffee," I tell her smoothly, picking up my sheriff's hat from the table and plopping it back atop my head. "Let me know if you need anything, Sabrina."

"I will. But I have a friend coming by soon, so—"

"Don't worry, I'm getting out of your hair." I smile at her. "I won't keep you any longer."

I stride back towards the front door, taking note of the house as I go. It's all simply furnished in a way that implies it came this way. I doubt Sabrina has had any hand in the decorating. The living room is wood-paneled, with a soft floral-print couch and what looks like a handmade quilt over the back, a slightly out-of-date television hanging on one wall. There are no personal touches that I can see that fit the person I met today—it seems like Sabrina is just existing here, without trying to make it her own. I imagine if I went into her bedroom, it would be much the same.

That prickle of desire runs over my skin again at the thought of her bedroom, but I push it away, opening the door. It squeaks on the hinges, and I glance back at Sabrina once before stepping out. She's half-visible through the kitchen doorway, still leaning back against the counter, clutching her mug as if it's a shield. I see a part of her face, thin-lipped and slightly pale, and I file that image away to consider later before I slip outside.

Outside, it's a chilly November day, and I tug on my jacket against the cold, heading out to where my truck is parked. Another concession to this place's small-town sensibilities. There's a police cruiser I could drive, but I like that even less than the truck I purchased shortly after moving here. I think, with brief yearning, of the car I left behind—and then unlock the door, hopping up into the warm, mint-scented interior.

I have every intention of coming back to check on Sabrina later on tonight.

Click here to read along as I write, or here to download the full ebook from Amazon!